NO MAN'S LAND

No Man's Land

MICHAEL CALIFRA

Hadrian † Books

NEW YORK

First Hadrian printing: 2015

ISBN-13: 978-0692342541
ISBN-10: 0692342540

Library of Congress Control Number: 2014922359

Cover photo: The Berlin Wall at Potsdamer Platz, 1988
Photo credit: Michael Califra

10 9 8 7 6 5 4 3 2

Preface

I LIVED IN GERMANY from 1986 to 1998, most of that time in Berlin. When I first considered writing about the city it was still divided, providing a backdrop more absurd than any fiction I could have invented. By the time I actually wrote this book in the early 1990s, the world had abruptly and permanently changed. The exhilarating events that ended the Cold War were still fresh back then and the reunited city was coming to terms with its regained role as the capital of a reunified Germany. A new iteration of Berlin was being birthed—the fourth in seventy-five years. Construction cranes were everywhere; empty swaths of land, once valueless because of their close proximity to the Berlin Wall, were being built upon in a frenzy, as if the history that had rendered them empty was a mark of national shame that needed to be expunged. Even as resentment between Ossis and Wessis set in, Berlin became a magnet attracting creative people from all over Europe—Russians, Poles, Romanians, Britons and many others. The eastern half of the city—still as dreary and war-ruined as depicted in this novel—was teeming with the creative energies of young people unfettered by a western bureaucracy that had not yet managed to completely fill the void left by the collapsed East German state. Artists of every stripe squatted in vacant buildings while new cafes and restaurants sprang up seemingly out of nowhere from one day to the next. Walk down a dark back street in Prenzlauer Berg or Mitte and you might stumble across a mysterious line of lit candles on the sidewalk leading into a previously empty cellar transformed into a smoke-filled, bustling nightclub complete with liquor for sale, loud music and dancing, all of which would disappear without a trace a couple of nights later. Simultaneously, there was a reckoning with the East German dictatorship; the Stasi files were made available to the public and former communist leaders were being prosecuted in courts of law. I once witnessed a confrontation outside a courthouse between a young man in a wheelchair, the result of being shot while attempting to flee to the West, and a former Politburo member standing trial for complicity in the deaths of people trying to escape to freedom. The man in the wheelchair doggedly followed the former government official asking only for a simple admission of responsibility—which he didn't get. Shades of Nuremberg fifty years later. People of high and low rank, once untouchable, were now vulnerable and alone. The mind-boggling scale of the East German State Security apparatus had been unmasked with many lives destroyed as a result. The old order had been upended. *The people* made it happen.

In the twenty-five years since, a world thought redeemed has been plagued by problems that ring hauntingly familiar: fanatical extremism and refugee crises; a near global financial collapse sparked by greedy speculation; profound inequalities of income. Are people better off than they were before the peaceful revolutions of 1989? Millions undoubtedly are. But the events of that time, no matter how extraordinarily promising they may have seemed, quickly devolved into the disillusionment and cynicism which now hallmark our age. Kati Weber could certainly see it all as a validation of her own negative worldview, but would Traudi Franzke regain her belief that something potentially better had been thrown away? And how would she rationalize her own small role in its unraveling? No one knows. They, along with the other characters of *No Man's Land,* belong to a place that has faded into history. Today, the people and neighborhoods of a new Berlin are no doubt providing fodder for stories from yet another young foreigner who has become fascinated by that city. I'm looking forward to reading what he or she has to say.

Michael Califra
New York, N.Y.
November, 2015

No Man's Land

The Real World

MY FIRST SIGHT, lying on my back and looking through one squinting eye, was of bright sunlight bursting through venetian blinds. It sent me reeling. The image lingered like a photo negative in my head long after I'd willed myself back into darkness. As it faded I suddenly became aware of the window being in the wrong place: at my feet instead of at my side. That realization shocked me into consciousness. I heard an unfamiliar sound: a child calling my name, the muffled young voice accompanied by a small hand banging softly against a door, *"Aufstehen! Aufstehen!"* Bewildered, I wasn't making the distinction between German and English. The child's voice was scolded by the stern, irritated whisper of a woman, *"Shhh! Komm hierher. Lass ihn schlafen!"*

I wasn't in my own bed; that was clear. Lying there with one arm across my face, I spent a seemingly long, hazy time trying to decide where I was. I could hear the child's voice singing happily to itself in another room. An uneasiness was setting in, yet an obscure fear of the unknown kept me from simply opening my eyes.

A telephone rang. A familiar, male voice mumbled something as he walked to the phone, picking it up on the third ring. "Wolfgang Beck." Always precise, Germans never answer the telephone anonymously. "Ah, hallo Christoph. Schon wach?"

I could relax. I knew where I was. What I was doing there really didn't matter. Wolf stuck his familiar, bearded face through the door. "Hey, my friend. You awake?" His tone was soft, apologetic, as if he had entered a sickroom. "It's Christoph on the phone."

I looked over at my watch on the coffee table next to the sofa where I lay: 9:35 a.m. The movement of my head made me feel sick to my stomach. I sat up and slid into my pants. They reeked of the cigarette smoke from the night before. I walked cautiously out of the living room, past Wolf and over to the telephone in the hall. Ina, Wolf's wife, glanced over at me from the kitchen table with an expression of pity. Standing next to her, little Katrin seemed nervous, as if the person walking out of the living room was a stranger just risen from the dead. Still disoriented, I put the phone to my ear. "Hello?"

"Yeah, it's me!" Christoph's irritated voice assaulted my eardrum. "Let's leave now, okay?"

"Now? You want to leave now? Where are you?"

"At a telephone cell. I spent the night with that woman with the eyes. Let's leave now, okay?"

Suddenly, everything came gushing back into my alcohol-soaked brain. Our weekend trip to Münster; Anke's big birthday party; the woman with the strange piercing eyes staring at Christoph from across the smoke-filled room; the two of them dancing together and, finally, their disappearance.

"Well, can't you wait a while? I'd like to drink some coffee and maybe take a shower—"

"I told her I had to catch an early train!" Christoph shot back. "I've been walking around this place since six this morning! You've slept at least! Where does Beck live? . . . Maximilianstrasse, what?"

"No, not the Maximilianstrasse." He was clearly agitated. I gave him the address yet again.

"Hurry up with your shower," he demanded. "I'll be there in twenty minutes." He hung up.

I moved slowly into the small kitchen, packed with new appliances, a sign of the recent affluence that still seemed out of place, and explained the situation to Wolf. After a quick cup of coffee, I went into the bathroom. While under the shower I heard the doorbell ring, then the friendly murmur of two male voices. When I emerged fifteen minutes later, Christoph Blessing was hunched over the kitchen table, his hands cupped around a mug of coffee. He was unshaven, looked pale, and his big body generally haggard. He threw a sharp glance my way, its meaning immediately clear: don't ask about last night. I complied. I didn't want to know about it, anyway. I tried talking him into waiting until early evening before starting back. I was still nauseous and my head was pounding with a dull ache that started at the back of my skull and worked its way forward around both sides of my cranium to somewhere right behind my eyeballs where it sat and wouldn't go away. Wolf suggested we stay for lunch and leave in the late afternoon when the traffic might be lighter. Ina tried to influence our decision by reciting the menu. But it was no use. Christoph politely kept insisting that he had to get back to West Berlin as soon as possible. He radiated an affability that stretched to the edge of intimidation around people he didn't know very well.

The coffee and shower were all the sobering up I was allowed. Little Katrin had just given me my *auf Wiedersehen* hug from the arms of her mother. We said goodbye with the usual bear hugs and I made my usual promises to visit again soon, next time for more than just a weekend. And maybe even to call first. I'd gotten into the habit of just showing up at their door when I needed a place to sleep.

A short time later, after we'd stopped to pick up Christoph's overnight bag from one of his friends, we were driving north on the Autobahn. Christoph moaned about the mathematics thesis he was writing. I knew the story too well and hated listening to it. Christoph despised his studies. History was his passion, and learning from it was the noblest thing a person could do, he would say. But his father, who considered history a "breadless art," insisted on mathematics. He also insisted his son finish his studies in West Berlin because he knew members of the university faculty there and could monitor his progress. Luckily, traffic was unusually light and, despite my hangover, I was able to ignore him by keeping up the velocity, shifting up and down and weaving in and out of traffic like a crazed teenager playing one of those car racing games in a video arcade.

Three hours later we reached the inner-German border, which was visible on each side of the highway as a wide break in the forest. All the trees along the line dividing the two Germanies had been cut down. We rolled over that immutable line on the map and into East German territory. Out of the first world and into the second. Here, the "West" ended and the "East" began. From this point, the Soviet Kremlin exerted its power and will over Eastern Europe and across the Eurasian landmass to the Bering Strait just a few miles from Alaska. The tiny, walled enclave of West Berlin was the only exception in this entire sphere of control.

Immediately after crossing that line, white concrete walls about ten feet high appeared along both sides of the Autobahn. The smooth asphalt road surface ended and the car thumped a measured rhythm as we drove over worn, uneven cement plates. A guard tower appeared on our right, then two large pillars on the center divide displaying the communist emblem of the German Democratic Republic: a draftsman's compass over a hammer encircled by stalks of wheat.

The white walls seemed to press in on the Autobahn as we drove, finally cutting across the roadway and funneling us into the large plaza customs area. Light towers capable of turning night into day were already burning white, even though the sun was still shining brightly.

On the plaza there were a dozen long lines of cars, each inching their way slowly towards booths where transit visas would be issued for the drive across East Germany to West Berlin. I pulled up behind one of them. Nearly everyone had their motors off and sat in their cars with doors open, ready to jump out every few minutes to push their vehicles forward a few feet at a time. The weather on this Sunday afternoon in January was unusually mild, creating a relaxed atmosphere. It was good to get out of the car and stretch my legs.

Twenty minutes later we were next in line. The border guard in his gray uniform sat in his booth looking down at his desk as he stuck out his hand and motioned us forward. The customs booth was on the passenger side. I handed my car registration and passport to Christoph as we rolled alongside and stopped. I immediately sensed the insolently casual air that all border officials display. But here, at this particular border, it was made sinister by the communist ideology they served. The guard in the booth held out his hand while still looking down at his desk. Christoph handed him our passports.

The officer took our documents impassively, not looking at us until he opened them and studied the photographs inside. He stared first at Christoph; cold, suspicious eyes darting back and forth several times between Christoph's face and the photograph in his passport. Then it was my turn. The guard flipped through the pages looking for my resident visa. "Page twenty-three," I said in English, not wanting to make things too easy for him. He didn't acknowledge. They never did. When he found it he studied it thoroughly before flipping back to my photograph. It was from 1983—six years old. In it I still wore the mustache and scrawny beard from my college days. The guard leaned back in his seat to get a better view of me, holding up my passport so the photo would be on the same plane as my face. I once heard that someone traveling to West Berlin who had grown a beard that wasn't in his passport photo was forced to shave there on the spot before being allowed to pass. I wondered if anyone in my position had ever been forced to wait until his beard had grown back before being permitted to proceed.

Finally, the border guard was satisfied. He took a last, well-considered look at both of us then asked, as they always did, "Kinder?" No, we had no children. He half stood up and took a look in the back seat of the car, just to be sure. Next, he put all the documents in a vinyl pouch and sent them via conveyor belt to another booth just a few feet behind his. We rolled to that station. When the pouch arrived at the second booth, another border guard with that same air of contemptuous indifference took the documents out and looked at the photos to make sure they were ours. He then stamped the passports with an official bang, inserted paper transit visas in them and handed everything back to Christoph. I could never figure out the reason for this duplication in the system, but guessed it had something to do with the official suspicion that was inherent everywhere behind the Iron Curtain.

We drove away from the customs area, past a large sign announcing the blood alcohol limit for drivers in the German Democratic Republic, and on to the transit highway, which we were not permitted to exit before reaching West Berlin. I accelerated to 100 kilometers per hour, the legal speed limit, and stayed there, careful not to exceed it by more than a hair on my speedometer. The moderate speed limit came as a relief after the continual aggressive coercion of the West German Autobahn. That was a world where speed and power alone determined one's societal rank; where a glance in the rearview mirror often revealed a light on the horizon, which suddenly inflated into a Mercedes or Porsche, relentlessly pressing down on you inches from your bumper, pushing you to yield. But my caution also resulted from knowing that fining western cars in transit for the slightest traffic infringement was a gimmick the East Germans often used to fill their hard currency coffers. And since I was certainly still well over the legal blood alcohol limit from the party last night, I wasn't about to do anything that might increase the risk of being stopped.

The transit highway to West Berlin cut through the very heart of East Germany, yet for the most part you saw nothing but fields and trees. Exit signs carried the names of cities and towns not visible from the highway, making it seem as if the entire country was conspiring to hide itself from the prying eyes of westerners. It was also one of the few places in the world where one could drive a six-year-old Ford *Escort* and feel like a big shot, accelerating smoothly past one wheezing and sputtering East German *Trabant* automobile after another, their drivers looking at us with expressions of unconcealed envy and contempt as we sailed by. The East Germans seemed to hate their squat little cars with their ridiculous stubby tail fins. The vehicle's design had changed little in thirty years, marking its occupants as belonging to that other, poorer, second-rate

Germany while an arrogant parade of big, wind tunnel-sleek West German cars racing toward West Berlin maneuvered effortlessly around them as if they were just one more of life's inevitable nuisances.

With nearly 150 kilometers to go, I decided to pull in at the next rest stop. We bought coffee and stood drinking it at a round, chest-high table. The sensation for me was one of non-being; afloat in a space that wasn't real. The room, which abounded with evidence of a split world, meant nothing. I heard Christoph droning on about his thesis, only occasionally hearing the keywords that defined a monologue I'd heard a thousand times already. The nausea I'd felt earlier that morning was gone but my head was still pounding. I stood there leaning on the table, looking through the window at the mystery in the parking lot. A woman sitting on the fender of my car. Alone. Waiting. For the next fifteen minutes I expected to look over and find her gone. But she was always there. How could that be? What on earth did she think she was doing? It made no sense.

I took a sip of coffee, relieved that the white noise coming from across the table had at last ceased, and looked around the room. The westerners were well-fed and tanned, dressed in loudly-colored or plaid sport jackets; the Easterners were smaller, generally pale, ruddy-faced and seemingly unhealthy. It was all not unlike people visiting incarcerated relatives in a prison canteen.

Across the table, Christoph was holding a pathetic pose, resting on his elbows, hands cupped over his mouth and nose. It was a pose I'd long ago become accustomed to seeing. It reminded me of the place we had just come from; where we both used to live, he for five years and I for nearly three. In fact, the night I first met Christoph he was leaning over a bar looking just that way. Münster was the second largest university town in West Germany. The German university system was extremely humane; there were virtually no time constraints on the length of study. The result was university towns like Münster that were filled with populations of aging "students" who were officially enrolled but no longer able to remember what they were supposed to be studying. Most seemed content living on a combination of odd jobs and various kinds of government assistance. The label "student" gave them a place in society as members of some kind of shadow academic elite, which was, in any case, better for the ego than the label "unemployed." The elite slept away a good part of their days and drank away their evenings in crowded bars, looking for love or discussing current events, routinely talking about the news in a manner suggesting that when their chance came, everything would finally be put right. They lived their lives in a sort of strange capsule, unaware of the passage of time. As a matter of fact, the friend Christoph had stayed with over the weekend seemed to be going for some kind of record; he was forty-seven years old and in his fifty-second semester.

A microcosm of West Germany in 1989, Münster was a safe, clean nest where even the poorest of the poor seemed to live no less than a middle-class existence. If so inclined, one could live off the wealthy state until retirement without the least bit of guilt because, well, everyone knew there weren't enough *good* jobs to go around, anyway. It was a place that most of the immense, teeming humanity alive in the world today would describe as the Promised Land.

Yet, every evening, the hour inevitably came when the inhabitants of that Land would cram themselves into clammy bars and drink themselves into a stupor. An activity from which all but the last of the church-going faithful were still recovering on this Sunday afternoon.

My response to Christoph's pathetic display across the table was automatic. "I don't know why you do this to yourself," I said. "If you don't like mathematics, then study something else. You've been a downer since you got me out of bed this morning. Do you think this is fun for me?"

"I can't study something else," he said. "My parents won't finance me."

I didn't pursue it, turning my attention instead to the woman sitting on my car. Why was she still there?

My indifference seemed to unsettle Christoph. "You know, I can't believe what I'm going to be doing with the rest of my life . . . crunching numbers in some big anonymous firm until I'm sixty-five years old. And I know what's gonna happen. As the new guy I'm going to get every meaningless, soulless task heaped on me that no one else wants to do . . . Stuck in some office with a bunch of other people who hate being there . . . Probably until nine o'clock every night! You know what my life is going to be? Working and sleeping, working and sleeping, that's what. I wish I had a job like yours—working two hours a day from my apartment and getting tons of money stuffed up my ass."

The "Goddamned Job." I never referred to it any other way. Others liked to call it the "Real World." I found it one Sunday at the end of 1984 when a cash squeeze brought on by a year of political campaigning for yet another losing candidate who promised to change everything had me halfheartedly looking through the Help Wanted section of the *New York Times* where I saw a small ad:

"*Sell computer software. No experience necessary.
Must be money motivated. Call Bob.*"

It caught my interest since I certainly had no experience, not at anything tangible, anyway. And I was money motivated, at least on the day I read the ad. But my feelings about sales jobs kept me from calling for a couple of days. As far as I was concerned, salesmen were endowed with a living by a primordial economic law: that anything created, no matter how brilliant, is useless if it can't be sold. That was more reality than I cared to confront.

Two days later, when my rent became due, I overcame my apprehensions and called Bob. To my surprise the position was still open.

The next day, I put on my gray pinstriped suit and took the subway down to 28th St. where the offices of the Software Company were located. When I got to room 604, the door was locked. I knocked once, then again. Finally, a young man answered. He had shoulder-length, wavy brown hair and was dressed in a worn *Grateful Dead* T-shirt, old jeans and sneakers. "Yeah?" he asked, the back of his hand wiping a runny nose.

"I have an appointment with Bob about a sales position."

"Wait here," he said, shutting the door in my face. A minute later he returned and let me in before pushing the heavy door firmly closed behind me.

I was in a large, dusty room where ten or twelve men, all in their early to mid-twenties, sat at desks in little cubicles. They all wore black T-shirts printed with the names of various rock bands, jeans and sneakers. The air was rife with the smell of marijuana.

I was led to an office separated from the rest of the room by large, frosted glass windows. It was cramped, with just enough space for two desks and a couple of filing cabinets. At one desk a slender man with thick, black hair, horn-rimmed eyeglasses, white shirt and yellow tie sat ramrod straight talking on the telephone. At the other desk sat Bob in a white V-neck undershirt and worn blue jeans. I guessed both men to be in their early thirties. Bob gave me a brief history of the firm, always speaking in a soft, monotonous voice.

The company sold software for large mainframe computers; the kind used only by the biggest corporations and the government. The software was developed by Len, the man on the phone, and telemarketed. Bob handled the business aspects of the firm. No experience was necessary for the sales position because each new salesman was given a list of data centers and contact names along with a short script. The script contained only the information necessary to get the contacts interested enough to accept a trial tape and test the software for themselves. Answers to the contacts' five most likely questions were printed on the back of the script.

"It's purely a numbers game," chimed in Len who was now off the phone. "The more tapes you have out, the more trial installations you'll have and the more . . . *deals* you'll make. It's just a numbers game." He spoke with an Australian accent and had to spit out the word "deal" as if it were a sour grape.

"Yeah," agreed Bob, speaking more rapidly but in the same monotonous voice. "And the longer you sell, the more knowledge you'll pick up, just by finding out answers to the questions you'll get on the phone. It's sort of a self-teaching process. We have guys here who never had any computer experience and can carry on a respectable conversation with technical managers of some of the biggest data centers in the country."

To prove the success of the method he pointed to a map of the United States that was hanging on the wall next to his desk. It was covered with the logos of big companies that had bought their software. After only two years in existence, the firm was doing more than three-million dollars a year in sales.

Bob then laid out the remuneration for the job: there would be just two-hundred dollars a week in salary but a ten-percent commission on all sales. He said average yearly income of a salesman in the office was around seventy-five thousand dollars, a sum I found mind-boggling having never really had a job that paid more than a "thank you." I became enthusiastic and wanted to sign on. I told Bob that working the phones was a major part of all the political organizing I had done. "Yeah, that's what I was thinking," he said. "I think I'd like to give you a try. Call me tomorrow afternoon and I'll let you know for sure."

The very next day I had the Goddamned Job. A temporary situation, I told myself. A year later I had earned just over seventy-thousand dollars. Others who had been there longer were earning much more. We were part of that tiny minority who were defining a decade by earning more money than we could possibly justify. It was, after all, 1985—*Morning in America* in the ruling political vernacular of the time.

During my first year with the company I developed a good relationship with both Bob and Len. But the decorum of the Real World was not what it had once been. There were often sudden, loud arguments over sales turf that sometimes came to blows while other salesmen were on the phone with potential customers. Bob would run out of his office and pull the guys apart, gagging them with his hands while everyone else tried explaining away the ruckus.

The Real World of the Software Company included salesmen Joe Jones who thought he would "stand out" if he took the professional name "Hardwick Johnson." You could always tell when Jones had a female contact on the line; he would speak in a soft, seductive voice while introducing himself as "Hard." A stunt that eventually got him fired. Steve Metropolis lived in the Real World, too. Metropolis, who had an accent like Marlon Brando's in *On the Waterfront,* would shout the most amazing gaffes into his telephone: "Yeah-ah, hello? Can you hear me? . . . Am I legible?" He was eventually fired for stealing jugs of water meant for the office water cooler. Then there was Jerry Epstein, the Real World's highest-grossing salesman who bought five-hundred dollars' worth of hashish from a contact in California and had it shipped to the office via overnight delivery service. When it didn't arrive on time Jerry frantically called the delivery service, demanding they track down the missing package. They eventually did, and Jerry was told to go down and claim it— *personally.* Over the next few months he spent more time in court than at work, a situation that got him fired, too. "Every day that fat fool isn't sitting in his cube costs me money," Bob told me. Others would get cocky; they'd stop coming in on time, not show up for days, or worse, do something stupid like take liberties with the office supply closet; just the kind of thing Bob couldn't stand. They came, made the company a little fatter, then for one dumb reason or another were fired. But it didn't matter all that much to the company since anyone working in the Real World could be replaced as easily as an office light bulb.

Yet Bob was always interested in ideas for expanding the business, so when I approached him with a proposal for marketing the firm's software in Germany, he was immediately open to it. Which is how I came to be standing here, at an East German transit highway rest stop, where wealthy West Germans filled their cars with cheap *Intertank* gas and ate in the restaurant while East Germans, stuck in a country they weren't allowed to leave, and dressed in clothing that seemed to have come from the most notorious American Dirt-Cheap-Mart, looked grudgingly on. I stood, staring out the window at a woman doing the most innocuous of things: sitting on the fender of my car in the parking lot, and wondered how that could be possible.

I noticed Christoph across the table, still holding the same pitiful expression on his face. "Let's leave," I said in disgust. "It's getting boring here."

As we approached my car, the woman on the fender smiled and asked if we were driving to West Berlin. She had enough long, thick, auburn hair for two heads and the lines etched in her face were those of a good-looking older woman. I was surprised to find out later that she was just twenty-eight years old.

"Ja, natürlich," I answered. It seemed she wanted a ride.

"Kann ich mitfahren?"

I was right. But what to do? This wasn't a place where something as simple as giving a ride to a stranger could be done without thinking. There would be consequences of some kind.

I looked at Christoph standing on the other side of the car. I'd already put up with him for an entire weekend; cringing at his mind-numbing rants about the "stinking thesis" he was writing; listening to him whine for the last three hours about the one-night stand he'd had while bemoaning that Linda, his American girlfriend whom he'd seen very little of over the last year, didn't deserve to be treated that way. In West Germany, where the ability to propel one's vehicle over the Autobahn at dangerously high speeds was considered a basic human right, I could drive fast enough so that the rapid movement of the car had a soothing effect on him. But the transit highway had a strictly-enforced speed limit, and you never knew how long the wait would be at the other end, at the border to West Berlin. So I took my chances and invited the woman sitting on the fender of my car to join us, consequences be damned.

"Steig ein," I said.

She picked up her overnight bag and hurried over to the passenger side. I got in and unlocked the door. "Let her sit up front," I told Christoph as he stuck his head into the car.

"Oh, no please. I can go behind," the woman said in English. Christoph didn't reply as he stuffed himself into the cramped back seat.

As we drove back onto the Autobahn she introduced herself as Katarina. "I'm Richard," I said. "That's Christoph," I added, pointing to the rear with my thumb.

"You come England?" She asked.

"No, I'm American."

"And you? You are American also?" She asked Christoph.

"No, I'm German," he answered, adding as he always did, "but I grew up in Ireland."

"Ah, that's why you speak so good English."

"How did you know he spoke English?" I asked, suspiciously.

"I heard both of you in inside. I saw you drive up and walk in. You looked to be okay so I thought I would ask you for the ride."

"How did you get here?" I asked. "You're in the middle of East Germany."

"Oh, I have been at a party in Hannover this weekend and got the ride together with the friend of a friend. But he got to be too much. I had to make him stop here so I could get out of the car. He was very angry. Latin types can be very pushy, you know what I mean? They don't know when it is enough sometimes. I thought you were one, too," she said, smiling at me. "Not like him I mean, but you look southern. I thought when I saw you that maybe you came from Italien or so."

"Only genetically," I answered. "My grandparents were Italian."

"That's America," she said with a laugh, "everyone from somewhere else. I must visit there sometime. It is a scandal that I have not been there yet."

I noticed a tiny gold stickpin in the side of her nose. She saw it drawing my eyes like a magnet whenever I spoke to her. Katarina grinned and said the pin was a gift from a friend in Nepal.

"Have you been there?" I asked.

"Oh, yes," she said. "I have been two times in Katmandu. It is wonderful there."

It was a relief having Katarina in the car. Unlike Christoph, who soon became tired of leaning forward in an effort to hear the conversation and mercifully fell asleep, she didn't seem to have a care in the world. Just looking at the electric excitement in her face when she spoke made me feel like a human being again. She was full of stories about places she had been and people she had met. I was amazed at how much she had traveled. A reference to almost any region of the world brought on a new tale, usually ending with the problems she'd had with men she met along the way. Katarina had been relentlessly pursued by a wealthy French champagne exporter in Rangoon, and by a Chinese yak-cheese salesman in Singapore. In Delhi she'd been tormented by a foul-smelling Turk, and bored in Sri Lanka by an Afghan carpet mogul. She had received marriage proposals from an English earl in Hong Kong, a nephew of Fidel Castro in the Dominican Republic, and in New Zealand from the wealthy, aged inventor of a hemorrhoid ointment made from ground ox penises.

"But you know I have never been to London, or to Paris, or even Rome. I have never been to anywhere in Europe outside of Germany. A real scandal, I suppose. Oh, wait . . . that's not right. There was one weekend in Amsterdam a few years ago. But all I did there was eat space cake. I can hardly remember it. Someday I shall have to see these other places, too."

"You obviously like traveling."

"I want to experience life. That's the only reason to be alive. You can't experience life if you don't experience the world. See the world and have babies! That's how you know what it is to be living! That's what gives these," she said, rubbing the lines under her eyes. "But so what? *Wooooooh,* they tell you that life is not passing you by!"

I took a glance at Christoph in the rearview mirror. He was sleeping with his head bent at an angle so acute that it hurt to look at him.

"So, you have children, eh?"

"Oh yes, a daughter. Anja is her name. She's three. I guess she must be wondering where Mutti is by now."

We came to the end of the transit highway and were funneled into another large customs plaza; the last obstacle before West Berlin.

I woke Christoph from a deep sleep. It was dusk and the area was lit up like Yankee Stadium during a night game. There wasn't as much traffic on this end; we waited just ten minutes before we were at a customs booth. A border guard took our documents. After glancing at our papers, the characteristic air of contempt I'd grown accustomed to turned severe. Permanent suspicions of westerners vindicated, the guard immediately wanted to know why there were now three people in the car when only two had come through at the other end of the border. Katarina took it upon herself to explain that we were traveling in two cars and that she simply changed cars at a rest stop.

"You should have known that is *verboten,*" the guard said sternly. He took a pen from the breast pocket of his gray shirt, circled a paragraph on the front of the transit visa and handed it back to Katarina. She read it and passed it to me:

"*A change of means of transport during transit is permitted only with the official authorization of the responsible organs of the GDR.*"

"No one changed the *means* of transport," Katarina told the guard. "I entered in a car and I'm exiting in a car."

Not impressed by her argument, the guard picked up his telephone and dialed. I passed the transit visa back to a sleepy, somewhat incoherent Christoph who barely had it in his hands when the guard demanded it back.

Katarina again pleaded her case, this time with growing irritation. "There was no *change* of means of transport," she said angrily. The guard ignored her. Another border guard appeared on my side of the car with a list of questions on a clipboard. The first few I answered: *At which rest stop did the passenger transfer take place? What was the reason for the transfer? At what time did it occur?* Then came questions for which only Katarina knew the answers. She answered none of them with certainty, sometimes giving three or four different answers to the same question.

What was the license number of the other vehicle? "I don't know. It was a Hannover number plate . . . or Hamburg. Something with H in front."

What was the make, model and year of the other vehicle? "It was an Opel or Mercedes or something. Maybe five, ten years old."

Who was the driver? "He was a friend of mine. His name was Aldo, or . . . yeah, Aldo . . . I think."

He is a friend but you do not know is name? "I have a lot of friends; I can't remember everybody!"

When he asked why it took so long for us to reach this end of the transit highway, stating the time down to the minute, she shot back "If you want people to get here faster you should raise the speed limit!"

The guard patiently wrote it all down, then held a conference with his counterpart in the booth. Another telephone call was made. The guard with the clipboard used it to wave off a line of cars that had formed behind us. He instructed me to get out and open the trunk. I did, noticing that Christoph had again fallen asleep.

The telephone in the booth rang. There was another conference between the two guards. The one with the clipboard disappeared, then came back a few minutes later.

Through it all I thought it wise to say as little as possible, knowing full well that the East Germans could bar any of us from using the transit highway again in the future. But Katarina made no effort to hide her frustration, periodically telling the guard in the booth what a lot of nonsense she thought it all was. She looked at me for support a couple times, but I didn't oblige. It took a good forty minutes before it was all over and we were allowed to continue. We were sent on our way with a stern, official warning that such a careless infringement of the law on the sovereign territory of the German Democratic Republic would not be tolerated again.

Back on the Autobahn, we drove past the WWII-era Soviet tank heroically perched on its pedestal at the East German side of the entrance to West Berlin. The road surface, which consisted of bumpy concrete plates since the start of the transit highway, again became flawless asphalt when we drove through the Berlin Wall and past the deserted Allied Checkpoint Bravo.

As always, it was good to be back in Berlin. Before I moved here from Münster, people told me I'd regret it. There was an old joke about West Berlin being the place where two million free people lived in the same cage. I was told that the Wall made it impossible for anyone but native Berliners to stay here for long. But for me, any such claustrophobic feelings came not in the city but on the transit highway where there was always the possibility of problems with the East German authorities. Once inside the city, it was easy to lose myself in it. I always knew the Wall was there; I caught a glimpse of it just about every day. In the back of my mind I knew that if I went far enough in any direction I would hit it, and that leaving town meant a 110-mile drive to the West German border, often with long delays at the checkpoints on each end of the transit highway. Nevertheless, the more I saw of the Wall the less I thought or cared about it. Berlin was Berlin. The mere word concocted images in my mind. They happened to be of spiked helmets, dueling scars, prosthetic limbs and Brown Shirts, but so what? Unlike Münster, it was somewhere. And I never had to tolerate dumb comments about cheese when people at home in New York asked where I lived.

I noticed Katarina watching the street lights flashing by on the Avus with a grin on her face. "Glad to be back in town?" I asked, wondering if my lack of support at the border had caused any ill feelings.

"Me? I'm always glad to be back," she said with a big smile, making it clear the incident had already been forgotten. "If it wasn't for this place I would have left Germany a long time ago."

"Where can I let you off?"

"I live in Charlottenburg, but you can leave me anywhere. I can go with the U-Bahn or bus. It is not a problem."

I insisted on driving her home. Before getting out of the car she suggested exchanging telephone numbers. "It was very nice driving with you," she said, staring intently into my eyes. "I hope I see you again sometime. Really."

She gave me a kiss on the cheek and got out, throwing a quick "*Tschüs!*" at Christoph when she noticed him still sitting in the back seat. He moved to the front, rubbing the back of his neck and somewhat dazed from his long nap. "Wow, I don't believe I slept the whole way. I feel a lot better. Was there a problem at the border?"

I didn't feel like explaining. "No, it was nothing."

"What's the story with her? You gonna see her again? I have the feeling she likes you."

"I don't know. We exchanged phone numbers. She has a kid."

"So what? Is she married?"

"I don't know, she didn't say."

I dropped Christoph off at his room and went home, having to drive around for nearly twenty minutes before finding a parking space. The Kreuzberg district, like most of West Berlin, was thick with cars parked in every conceivable position. They were squeezed into any free space on the street, over the curb and on the sidewalk. While traffic in the city was never particularly bad, every square inch of possible parking space was taken. Many vehicles had not been moved in weeks and were covered with that grimy film that fell from the sky in the form of rain. They were there only as a means of quick escape; for use on those occasions when life in the great walled city became too oppressive.

I took the small elevator up the three flights to my apartment. The ascent was painfully slow and when I reached my floor I swore to myself, as I always did, that I'd take the stairs next time. Inside my apartment I tore off my coat, turned on the TV and fell into my wicker rocking chair. It had been a long end to a long weekend. Now that it was over my body became heavy. Within minutes I was asleep in front of the television.

The Harsh Edge of Non-Existence

IT WAS WEDNESDAY MORNING before I could bring myself to try to get some work done. I had taken Monday and Tuesday off for no reason other than the sight of the telephone making me sick. I could have easily taken Wednesday day off, too. After all, what difference would one more day really make? But then I thought about Wolf in Münster.

Wolfgang Beck was not only my closest friend but now also my business partner. It was in 1976, when I was eighteen-years old and took a trip to Spain that I met him in a Dutch bar in Torremolinos. We spent that night talking about politics and changing the world in a loud, smoke-filled room.

From the first I liked Wolf. I instantly identified him as a member of that enduring class of people who felt an obligation to do all they could to make even a slightly better world. He was part of that generation of Germans who had to deal with the legacy of concentration-camp genocide their parents had left behind—as powerful a motivation for political activism as was the famous bursting head accidentally captured on Abraham Zapruder's home movie film I'd seen in my childhood, accompanied by platitudes mourning all that might have been, but now would never be.

It was three years ago, early in 1986, that Bob had let me come to Germany. I remembered the very beginning, sitting in Wolf's apartment in Münster talking about the job. I showed him a list of my targets, which were the cream of German industry.

"You are going to try selling software to *these* companies? . . . From your apartment? Do you think that's possible?"

"Sure it is."

He wasn't convinced. Telemarketing was unheard of in Germany in 1986, and the idea of someone trying to sell something he knew nothing about to the biggest and most arrogant of German corporations was too much to believe, especially in a country where a formal education was required to be a wallpaper hanger.

Nevertheless, my first year was very successful. So when Wolf finished studying law, I let him in on the numbers game, too, just so he could earn some extra cash for a while. By early 1988, we had moved the whole operation out of my apartment and into a real office with four full-time salesmen, a secretary, a back office guy, and more than $1 million in sales.

That's when the anxiety began to set in that sometimes kept me awake at night. Behind it all was a deep-rooted fear that the more successful we were, the more likely it was that I would wind up telemarketing software for the rest of my life. For Wolf on the other hand, the opposite was true. While I could never drag myself into the office before eleven each morning, he was always there by nine o'clock, robust and ready for action. When I asked him how he did it every day, he said, "Because I finally found what it is I want to do."

That was it. The Goddamned Job had ceased being a vehicle to be exploited for short-term financial gain. It had become the source of income on which all long-term hopes and plans would depend. I suppose it was inevitable; Wolf did have a family to support. And he was now making much more money with the Goddamned Job than he would have as a new lawyer. The pressures and duties of making a living in the Real World had taken precedence.

It was just past 10 a.m. when I dragged myself from my bed to my desk. I flipped through the folder containing my accounts, reading the notes I'd written over one of them. It was an enormous conglomerate instantly known to every conscious soul on the planet by virtue of a simple emblem. I'd recently managed to discover that they had gotten a new technical support manager. The old one was a stiff whom I had spoken with a half-dozen times with no success. This was a promising new development that could finally open the way to a test installation and to vast sums of money. But my leaden lethargy at having to sit at my desk and call these people returned when I actually picked up the phone. Normally, it would have won out. I'd have walked away from my desk and found something else to do. Then I thought about last Sunday in Münster. How, just before I left Wolf's place, he had given me two back issues of the *Computerwoche.* "I've been wanting to send you these," he said. "It would be good if you read them, eh? . . . Okay, Richard?" Wolf was always nudging, trying to get me to do what was good for business. I guaranteed him that I would. But on the way to my car, I looked at the front page of one of them and saw a colored graph detailing net savings in CPU seconds next to the delighted, smiling face of a middle-aged data center manager with a bad toupee, all of which made my hung-over head pound even more than it was already pounding. I stuffed the newspapers into someone's mailbox just before Christoph and I hit the road.

I felt genuinely guilty about that. I should have forced myself to take them home and read them. I should do more to pull my weight in the business. I should do it for my good friend Wolf. After all, I would never have been able to set up shop Germany if he hadn't selflessly taken so much time away from his studies to deal with all the bureaucratic red tape that was constantly being thrown at me in the beginning. Nor did he complain when I suddenly quit Münster for Berlin just because I was bored. I owed it to Wolf to help keep the business a success so that Bob wouldn't shut us down. And this firm, the one with the ubiquitous symbol, could go a long way toward that. Just one contract from this company could set a good sales record for the rest of the year.

I dialed the new manager's telephone number. Waited. Nothing. Blank. It wasn't unusual. The German telephone system was surprisingly inadequate. First you had to wait six weeks just to get a phone installed, and then there were always problems like the one I'd just encountered. I tried again, dialing each number with care. Waited. Still nothing! I put the receiver down, got up and paced across the room and back. Always the same shit, I thought, and always when I'm in the mood to work. And people here just put up with it. What a bunch of sheep! I sat down, picked up the receiver and redialed. To my relief, I heard the numbers slowly crank through. I couldn't believe my good luck when the manager himself answered the phone. I put my brain on autopilot, introduced myself, rattled off statistics about reduced elapse times and resource savings so wonderful they were hard to contemplate. As I spoke, I kept registering sounds, not words, just sounds that told me he was impressed. I had just recited the part about the ease of copying data sets from one device to another when he suddenly interrupted me. "Now, what would I want to do that for?" he asked.

I stumbled into inept silence. "Well?" he repeated. "What would I want to do that for?"

It was clear that he was having tremendous fun when he said, "What's it going to bring me?" I was stumped. No one had ever stopped me at this point in the pitch before. What could I do? He was an absolute stranger, yet he was thoroughly enjoying his chance to humiliate me. I ran through more of those statistics. Again he wanted to know, "And why is that good?"

"*Uhhh* . . . it's all well documented in the literature," I said, promising to send a copy right off to him and got off the phone.

"Fuck you!" I yelled at the telephone in disgust. "You lousy shit! Take one of your computer tapes and shove it up your ass until you choke!"

For the next couple of minutes, I hurled every vile and nasty insult I could squeeze out of my brain at the phone that I would have liked to have thrown personally at the man in the data center for being an asshole, at Bob for paying me so much money to do this job, and at myself for not knowing what else to do with my life. Finally, I calmed down and tried to think reasonably. There was still Herr Arp at the German Labor Federation. He was actually the reason I had been able to get myself to my desk this morning. You could be sure of doing business with his kind of large organization if you could just get them to install the software. My last conversation with him had given me high hopes for a quick deal. By now he should have installed the software and done enough testing to have conclusive results. Already, in my mind, I counted him as a closed deal.

I dialed the numbers, relieved to hear them crank through. I cleared my throat a couple of times. It was a bit hoarse from the technique I had developed for screaming at the telephone in my home, concentrating all my energy around the tonsil area. Not only did it allow me to vent my entire spleen without being overheard by the neighbors, but it took a lot of energy as well, returning me to a relatively calm state in a couple of minutes.

The phone rang. Once . . . Twice . . . "Arp."

Arp. From that one utterance I could detect in his voice the usual mixture that made up his state of mind: harried, but masked by sham firmness. Under control for now, but I always felt that the pressures of Arp's job could cause the voice at the other end of the line to crack at any moment. He was chief attendant to the two powerful machines that kept his large organization functioning by managing its swelling mountains of data. That's probably why he was also a nervous chain-smoker. Each sentence Arp spoke was punctuated by long drags on a cigarette.

(While I had never set foot inside a data center, I had once seen a picture of a mainframe computer in a book that Len showed me: a nondescript blue metal box about six feet high and four feet wide with nothing to distinguish it in any way from the office coat closet but a little silver tag on the upper right embossed with the IBM corporate logo. That image always came to mind when I spoke to Arp. I found it perverse that people would devote their lives, even ruin their health, servicing the needs of such an ordinary-looking object.)

Nevertheless, at that moment I was happy to hear his frazzled voice. But as I cheerfully introduced myself I heard him blow a long, tired exhale of cigarette smoke. I could actually *feel* him rolling his eyes in his head and knew, even before he spoke, that he didn't want to be bothered. But I kept going, telling him that I just wanted to check on the results of those tests.

"There have not been any tests. We have too much to do now and I don't see any time for tests in the foreseeable future. I have your telephone number and we will contact you if anything changes."

He was as blunt as he possibly could be. A total brush-off. I couldn't believe it. Three weeks ago he told me list generation (whatever that was) was a big problem for them. That they were looking for something like our product. "Send the tape," he said. "We'll have a look at it." Now he was trying to push me off for good. But I wasn't about to let him get away so easily. I couldn't. I pressed on, desperately reciting lines full of meaningless terms and statistics from a script learned years ago, hoping to hit the one number that would rekindle his interest. Then Arp detonated over the phone, *"Listen to me!"* He began speaking slowly in English with a heavy German accent that made him sound particularly evil as he took a long suck on his cigarette after every sentence. "Vee haff read your in-for-matzion. Vee haff no need of your Produkt. Vee are not buying *any*ting from you." As he spoke, I couldn't help but picture him standing over his desk in the computer center dressed in SS black leather with a long cigarette holder clenched between his teeth and a swastika armband on his sleeve.

I backed off in disgust, "Well, then . . . um, thanks for looking at the material. If anything changes, just let us know."

Arp hung up with no acknowledgment.

I slammed down the receiver and began yelling at the phone again. "You lousy, lying, chain-smoking fuck!" Arp! What the hell kind of a name was that? The guy was such a fucking Neanderthal that he had a noise for a name. *"Shithead!"* I picked up the receiver and feverishly dialed his number again, not knowing why. The numbers cranked through. It rang. He answered, "Arp . . . *Arp!*"

I slammed the receiver down on the phone, momentarily pleased with my revenge. At least I made that moron bark like a dog for my trouble. But then I thought about all the work I'd have to do to make up for the two deals I had just lost. For every new contract I would have to spend my time wrestling, pleading, with ten Arps. I felt a tremendous weight on my shoulders and wanted to vomit. My hatred of the Goddamned Job was all I could think of. I scanned the notes on the pages in front of me: *Left message . . . Has not received tape . . . Received material but misplaced it . . . Gave material to someone else, call there . . . Left message . . . Left message . . . Not interested.* They read like an indictment of an empty life; an ode to the pointlessness of existence.

I couldn't stomach another call. Since moving to Berlin the Goddamned Job seemed more remote than ever. I hadn't spoken with Bob in months; everything ran through Wolf and the office in Münster. I was convinced the numbers game would soon be over. But what would I do with myself when the end finally came?

Sitting there at my desk, I began to pick over the alternatives to my current existence. The possibilities in Germany were limited; my work permit applied only to the job I was doing. I could legally do no other. Even if I could, what would it be? All of the things that interested me either required qualifications I didn't have or were impossible to earn a living doing. Even if I could find that magical *something* that might bring some measure of fulfillment, there would be the inevitable battle with the authorities in order to get a full work permit. It would mean a headlong dive into the *garbage of the bureaucracy* as the Germans called it. I thought about packing up and going home, but that idea didn't provide any relief. What would I do there? I had already been away three years. That large block of time on my resume would only recommend me for more of the same. And since moving to Germany, I had earned an average of over $100,000 a year. My salary was the one thing about my existence that seemed to command any respect. Because I earned that magical six-figure number, I was shielded from accusations ranging from laziness to stupidity. Anyone who earned that kind of money was considered either smart or industrious and usually both. What would I be without it? If I gave it all up and went back to America I could easily picture myself stuck doing something I disliked just as much, getting paid one-third of my current salary and working six hundred percent more hours. And all that with ten lousy days of vacation per year! What barbarism! I felt absolutely desolate. Life was shrinking before my eyes. I could *feel* it slipping through my fingers. There would be no future. For me there was only the present. Anything to come would only bring more of the same with increasing age.

My thoughts were suffocating me. I quickly washed up and got dressed. Surrendering another business day without a fight, I told myself that tomorrow I would begin anew. Pulling my coat on, I slammed the apartment door behind me. Too restless to bother with the arthritic elevator, I ran down the stairs. My goal was the Café Einstein. There I could sit over a mélange, read the newspaper and observe the pretty new *Kellnerin* whose name I somehow knew as "Kerstin." The weather was still unseasonably mild and the "greenhouse effect" that everyone was talking about had people in a good mood. If I got there before the lunchtime rush, I might be able to engage her in fruitful conversation.

Just before reaching the ground floor landing, I heard the unmistakable sound of a woman rummaging through her handbag looking for keys. I froze in my tracks. Elderly women inhabited both ground floor apartments. One of them was my landlady. As a matter of fact, old women, either widows or spinsters, inhabited twelve of the fourteen apartments in the building. The only exceptions being myself and my next door neighbor, a nondescript, forty-one-year-old bureaucrat with the city traffic department named Bernd Schenk. Bernd annoyed me no end by habitually greeting me with the word, *"Na?"*—"Well?," his voice always rose with expectation, as if by announcing himself with that sound he would extract some juicy morsel of gossip from me. I suppose it worked with the other tenants. What little I knew about my neighbors in the building I heard from Bernd when we'd accidentally meet in the stairway or on the street, which were the only times I ever saw him. Unlike me, he was extremely outgoing and liked being the young-man-about-the-house, son-I-never-had, performing odd jobs for the old women from time to time and hanging around for a cup of coffee afterwards. He, in return, would get them to do things like make tubs of potato salad and coleslaw for his birthday party buffet, or keep his plants watered while he was on a six-week holiday in Thailand. It was from Bernd that I knew that Frau Mayer-Burkhardt (second floor center) was secretly relieved when her seventy-eight-year-old husband, who had lost both his legs and an eye in Stalingrad in 1942, was killed three years ago when a gasoline truck backed into his wheelchair. Evidently, a lifetime of pushing the cranky old man around town was enough. I also knew that Frau Eppert (fourth floor right) had a drinking problem brought on by agonizing over a nineteen-year-old granddaughter who worked as a prostitute in order to support an artist boyfriend she believed to be the reincarnation of Otto Dix. It also was from Bernd that I learned that our landlady's son, with whom I'd signed my lease, was a rich investment banker who flew in from Frankfurt religiously once a month to visit his mother. Luckily, I had never formally met the landlady or any of the other women in the house. Finding my occasional short, forced conversations with Bernd tedious enough, I had no intention of getting ensnared in a hairnet of prying old ladies.

The handbag sounds finally ceased. Some shuffling noises followed. Then the sound of a key pushed into the keyhole, the click of the lock and the slight creaking of a door opening. The sounds came from the left—the landlady's apartment. I waited till the door slammed shut before making my move. I descended the last flight of stairs, taking the four at the bottom in one leap and landing with a thump. To my astonishment I found myself standing over the person I was trying to avoid. The landlady was kneeling down to the floor, reaching for mail she'd dropped while holding on to the door handle. Startled, she looked up just as I landed in front of her.

She took the mail and slowly, painstakingly stood up, moving as though she'd been squatting in the same position for hours. The weight of her long wool coat seemed to make rising even more difficult. When finally erect, her slight frame was hunched forward. She looked up at me with a faint smile, waiting for me to say something. In that same eternal moment, I saw her up close and in minute detail for the first time. This person was old—alarmingly so. Her face was a mass of deeply wrinkled, age-spotted skin hanging from high cheekbones. Her yellow, watery eyes were set deep in dark sockets. One didn't need much of an imagination to see the skull underneath. Her short hair was more yellow than white, and the few teeth left in her mouth were discolored and stuck out at acute angles. As far as I could tell, there were no gums. She stood there silent, bony ankles sheathed in baggy nylon. I could hear short, hollow inhalations that whistled slightly as she breathed; air filling brittle, old lungs. Sounds from the edge of the grave. It was like standing in front of a 5,000-year-old mummified corpse suddenly come back to life. I finally managed to cough up a "guten Tag" and made for the door. Out on the street, my heart was pounding. I couldn't shake a feeling of dread.

I wandered up to the Landwehrkanal where the Mehringbrücke crossed it under an elevated section of the U-Bahn. The few mild days were already pulling the canal's foul smell out of hibernation. Leaning over the railing, that ancient face seemed to stare back at me from the glistening water while the clanging racket of trains passed periodically over the girders above me. Could she possibly have been somebody's baby once? Of course she was. People aren't born like that. She was once young. And there must have been friends; people of her age. Other faces from generations ago. Where were they all now? Probably dead—or, if they're lucky, in the same state as my landlady: alone with a head full of memories on the harsh edge of non-existence. Where would I be in another ten or twenty years? That was hard enough to imagine, let alone another fifty. Fifty years! A journey through a lifetime. I thought about all the mundane things I would need for this colossal voyage. All the food I would have to fight my way through supermarkets to buy and consume a meal at a time; all the toothpaste, toilet paper and deodorant I would need to keep myself respectable in the eyes of others; all the shoes and pants I would wear out along the way; the strange, lonely apartments in which I would find myself passing away the days and nights; all the money I would have to earn to pay for all those things; all the boring, unsatisfying jobs it would take to earn that money, and all the false good impressions I would be forced to make to get those jobs. Maybe I'd still be telemarketing software years from now, being rudely put off and scorned by Arps and other monsters not yet born. That was the future I felt was becoming a reality. The eternal salesman! I had found my damnation through an ad in the *New York Times* classifieds. A gaping, empty sensation opened up in the center of my chest. I suddenly felt as though I were the one standing on the harsh edge on non-existence. For the second time that morning I wanted to vomit.

I turned away from the canal and walked, rubbing my chest, trying to rid myself of the numb sensation that had planted itself there. Before I knew it, I had walked within easy reach of the Einstein. And while I no longer had any desire to go there, I forced myself, hoping that doing something routine like drinking coffee in a café would return me to a normal state of mind. I tried working up some enthusiasm by telling myself that Kerstin was waiting.

Entering the café, I took a newspaper off the rack near the door and sat down in a corner where I had a full view. Only a few tables were occupied. No one was behind the bar and Kerstin was nowhere to be seen. A moment later, the tall middle-aged bartender came out of the men's room drying his hands on the white apron tied around his waist. He had thick wavy black hair, a bushy mustache and wore his usual worried expression as he took up his position behind the bar. The giant bags under his eyes always gave me the impression that he had money problems that kept him awake at night. I got up quickly and left before anyone knew I had been there.

Back outside I started walking in one direction, then without knowing why, I turned around and went the other way. Suddenly, I realized that I had nowhere to go. I was thirty-one years old. It was a weekday. I was, for some reason, living in West Berlin, and I had absolutely nothing worth doing. No task in life other than annoying one poor slob after another with my telephone calls. And why? So I could continue in my current unsatisfying lifestyle. I thought I was going to jump out of my skin. Again, that nagging, indefinable emptiness began eating away at me from deep inside. Desperate for any kind of distraction, I decided to stop in on Christoph. At times like this, I thought, it's important to be around friends.

I made my way down to the side street where Christoph lived in a large apartment he shared with three other students. The bell on the street listed all four names. I rang and was buzzed in. By the time I reached the second floor landing, Cliadhna Sweeney was waiting at the apartment door with a book in her hand. She was a student from Ireland studying German in Berlin. The unexpected sight of a pretty female face immediately lifted my spirits. Unfortunately, she was involved in a never-ending feud with Christoph and any of his visitors were automatically subject to a cold shoulder. Upon seeing me her expression turned slightly but obviously sour.

"Hi, Cliadhna. Is Christoph in?"

"Yeah, he's here," she said in a dry brogue, turning away as I neared the door and sliding her way over the polished wood floor in her fluffy pink slippers, tights and sweatshirt toward her room. "He's in his cave screaming at his computer. I think your friend has finally lost his hat."

The door to Christoph's room was in the middle of the hall opposite the kitchen where the sink was piled high with unwashed dishes topped by a greasy frying pan filled with water. The residue of last night's dinner still hung in the air. I knocked on his door and pushed it open. The small room was, as always, strewn with newspapers. Christoph liked to keep files of interesting articles "to document the times in which I live." He was sitting at his desk in front of his new computer and swiveled around in his chair as I walked in. "Good, you're just the one I wanted to see." he said, not at all surprised that I was there. "You need to help me with this thing. I've been trying to get it to print for two hours now."

"I see Cliadhna is still angry with you."

"What?" He wasn't really listening, concentrating on the keyboard in front of him. It took a moment before he heard what I said. "Oh, it's always the same shit with her. She sits on the telephone for hours at a time talking to that ridiculous boyfriend of hers. Then, when you *finally* get her to put the phone down, five minutes later *he* shows up. Are you gonna help me with this thing or not?"

"What about the fella-in-the-cellar? He set the whole system up for you, didn't he?"

"He's not around. Besides," Christoph added bitterly, "I can't stand that creep anymore. First he makes me buy all this stuff, then when I need him he ups and disappears for days."

I picked up a copy of the yesterday's *BZ* off the floor. The loud headline paraphrased something the East German Communist Party leader said in a recent speech: "*Honecker: The Wall Will Stand Another 100 Years!*" I skimmed the article. Apparently, the Berlin Wall was needed to keep East Germany from being "looted" and it would remain until the reasons for its existence made it unnecessary. Whatever that meant.

"I wish they would write these instruction manuals in plain German!" Christoph shouted looking down at the thick book opened on his lap. "This is incomprehensible. A psychotic with a diseased brain must have written this stuff! And don't throw those newspapers around, they're in order!"

I picked up another from a wooden folding chair, looking over the pages without seeing any of the words. "Ah, fuck!" Christoph cried out, red-faced and clenching his fists on his lap. "Help me with this thing, will you please!"

"What's the matter?"

"It should be printing, but when I press the D for DRUCK all I get is the stupid message, '*Drucker ist nicht betriebsbereit!*'" I watched him try again, carefully pressing the appropriate keys—**ESC**, then *D*. The instant he touched that last button he jumped out of his seat, bouncing around the room like a chimpanzee in the monkey house at the zoo. It was as if the smug little machine with the one big eye was testing Christoph's intelligence, snidely punishing him with a nasty electroshock whenever he gave an incompetent answer. "You see that?!" he yelled through his teeth. "It happens every time! What could be the problem? I've done everything I'm supposed to and it still doesn't fucking work!"

"Here, let me try." I sat in his chair. "What was it? ESCAPE, then what? . . . D for DRUCK, right?" I pressed the keys on the keyboard. In a flash, the same message came up on the screen: *Drucker ist nicht betriebsbereit.* "It says your printer isn't ready."

"I know what it says! *Why* isn't the printer ready?!" He was looking down at me, his face on fire.

"Are you asking me?"

"Of course I'm asking you! You sell this stuff, don't you? You make your living selling software, right?!"

"Well, don't bother asking me. Why don't you try reading the manual?"

"I've *been* reading the manual! I just told you, I've done every step and it still doesn't work!"

"If it doesn't work, you didn't do every step."

"Get up!" he said, chasing me out of his chair.

I wasn't in the mood to spend the rest of the day in his little room fighting with a machine. Christoph was the only close friend I had in Berlin and I really just wanted to talk. I suggested we leave. "Why don't you get away from it for a while? Take a break. Let's go out for a coffee or a mélange or something. I'll buy."

"I have no time to waste sitting around drinking mélange and watching you chat up some waitress. You've got to help me fix this thing!"

"But I told you, I can't!"

"*What?!* I can't believe you. You're good for nothing but a fucking bad example, you know that?"

"Look, what do you want from me? Maybe learning how to use a computer in the middle of writing a thesis isn't such a smart idea. Come on, let's get out of here for a while. You're gonna give yourself a stroke with that thing."

Christoph wouldn't hear of it. He sat back in his chair concentrating on the user guide in front of him, pretending I wasn't there. I left, slamming the door behind me. Outside, Cliadhna was talking cheerfully on the telephone while washing the dishes in the kitchen sink, ignoring the shouting coming from Christoph's room. She turned away from me as I bent under the phone cord stretched across the kitchen from the telephone on the opposite wall. I got to the door leading to the stairway and heard a last muffled shout of frustration come from Christoph, "Oooh, fuck this fucking thing!"

Good riddance, I thought once I was out on the street. I was sick of his moods of late; listening to him complain on the telephone twice a day, or while eating dinner three times a week at that same bad pizzeria, choking down salty, burnt lasagna or salads smothered in a strange pink dressing. Then that numb sensation returned to my chest. What the hell was I doing here? Why was I wasting away in Berlin of all places? For the first time since moving here I felt alone in a foreign city. I began to hurt for the familiar sights, sounds and faces of home. Home sickness. The Germans called it *Heimweh*, a term implying pain. Now, really for the first time, I understood why.

I took the U-Bahn back to my apartment. Sitting there in the train, I felt myself getting tired. It was as if life itself was being sucked from my limbs. By the time I got home I could hardly keep my eyes open. Before I knew it I was asleep on my bed.

I woke up a couple of times during my nap, but couldn't muster the desire to pick myself up and fell easily back into a deep sleep. Finally, I awoke staring at the ceiling. The room was dark. Night had fallen and I had no idea what time it was. I might have slept the whole night and through the next day, it wouldn't have surprised me. The clock radio next to my bed told me that it was still Wednesday at 9:48 p.m. I must have slept away five or six hours. Standing up made me feel a bit lightheaded. I was experiencing the same dislocated sensations one has after spending days in bed convalescing from an illness; as though I might still be dreaming. Turning on the reading lamp near my bed added to that dream-like feeling by casting a soft, yellowish glow across the room. I walked into the kitchen and switched on the light, which came on like an atomic blast. I checked the refrigerator. Inside was the usual wide variety of condiments, a liter of milk gone sour, a container of *Rote Grütze* pudding and some very old Chinese food. I hadn't been to the supermarket since getting back from Münster on Sunday. If it hadn't been for the hunger churning in my stomach I could have easily gone back to bed and slept until morning. But I forced myself to go out to my usual *Kneipe* for a couple of beers and something to eat. There, at least, I was sure to see some familiar faces.

The Troika was a ten-minute walk from my apartment. The balmy day had turned into a cool night. It must have rained while I was unconscious in my bed; everything was wet and there was a cold dampness hanging in the air. When I arrived I saw the Troika's large windows were steamed over. Above the entrance a simple neon sign—**BAR**—threw off a purple glow as if to direct passersby through the heavy, floating mist. From across the street I could hear the muffled sounds of music and the tumult of people within.

I entered, pushing aside the thick draft curtain, and was hit with a hot blast of smoke-filled air. The place was teeming with activity, giving me the feeling that I had just returned from a lengthy hiatus from civilization. The Troika had a long bar that stood opposite large picture windows. At the end of the bar, it opened up to a large room where ten or twelve tables were squeezed tightly together. The regulars I knew normally sat there in the back.

As I made my way to the rear, squeezing myself between bodies, Rolf, one of the three owners who was tending bar that night, gave me a two-eyed wink and a big smile as he washed a couple of beer glasses. He greeted me that way every time I walked in, although I'm sure he didn't know my name. I was just another familiar object that regularly tossed more money into the till.

I noticed Geoffrey Biggs standing at the bar. Biggs was a thirty-four-year-old chain-smoking Scotsman. Tall and rail-thin, he had thinning curly brown hair and fine facial features, including a nose that looked as if it could break if he blew it too hard. Biggs was a man who thoroughly enjoyed being British and once told me that the best place to be British was anywhere outside Britain. Geoffrey loved playing the part, wearing a Sherlock Holmes hat and using mannerisms with just the right nuance of starchy deference to make himself stand out against a background of what he considered "wishy-washy" German men. Strangely enough he had an uncanny ability to pick up the most big-boned, full-figured women imaginable. Biggs came from a long line of career Royal Navy officers, the last of whom had managed to squander what remained of the family fortune. According to Geoffrey, his was the first Biggs' generation in at least 150 years that had had to work for a living. He managed that, barely, by selling tacky German landscape oil paintings to the large contingent of British and American army troops stationed in West Berlin.

When I say that Geoffrey barely managed to make a living, I don't mean he couldn't sell. I had seen him in action several times, accompanying him as he drove door-to-door in a big Volvo station wagon owned by his employer, its rear filled with paintings and frames. Geoffrey was a master at convincing people that, not only were they buying a beautiful work of art that would enrich their lives as well as their children's, but making a sound financial investment at the same time. And he took his craft seriously. I once inadvertently insulted him by asking if he'd like to earn a little extra money by screening some of my leads. "I'm not a canvasser," he said, looking down his nose at me. "I'm a salesman!" Geoffrey's major problem was that he was absolutely reckless with money. The moment he got his hands on any, he would insist on taking you out for a large dinner and a night of drinking until he'd run through everything he'd earned that day. I took this eccentric behavior as a sign that the tale about his lineage was a true one.

At the Troika that night, he was trying to engage an obviously disinterested woman in conversation. Geoffrey was leaning on the bar holding a cigarette to his lips, his other hand buried in the pocket of his dingy tweed jacket. He appeared deep in thought, as if trying to come up with that one line that could change her mind. This wasn't unusual. Geoffrey played his own never-ending numbers game: the more women he approached in an evening, the better his chances of landing in bed with one of them. I put my hand on his shoulder as I walked by. "Oh, hi," he said in a reserved voice, looking down at my shoes; a clear signal that I was interrupting his efforts. I kept moving.

At the end of the bar was the guy I'd seen sitting in that same spot every single time I'd been in the place since Christoph first brought me here more than six months ago. His chubby face had its customary two-day beard and alcoholic grin that sometimes broke into a full laugh. He always sat alone and never talked to anyone except himself, or occasionally to Rolf when he brought over refills of beer. As I walked by he was smiling, shaking his head and mumbling as if he'd been considering the result of a private prank he'd been planning to pull.

When I reached the back of the room I found Ulrich and his girlfriend, Anne, just back from their trip to America, sitting at the usual table. As always lately, Torsten was there, too. I pirated a vacant chair and joined them.

Ulrich Botz was a fast-talking business and economics student studying at the Freie Universität. His face was almost perfectly round and his lips thick and pink. Botz tried to conceal the fact that he'd prematurely lost much of his hair with a bad combover. Although he held a German passport, Ulrich had spent much of his life in the United States where his father was an engineer with a German firm in Connecticut. His girlfriend, Anne, was from some small town near Hamburg. She was also registered at the university but never seemed to be working toward any degree. Never having very much to say, she seemed content to sit and listen to others talk.

Torsten was a skinny musician in his early twenties with long, sandy blond hair parted in the middle and a long, thin aquiline nose that dominated his gaunt face. I was never clear about Torsten's relationship to the others. I think he had recently moved into the same student apartment that Ulrich was living in, but never cared enough to ask. I did know that he was in Berlin avoiding the fifteen-month West German military draft and its alternative eighteen-months of civilian service at low pay. His older brother had avoided both by claiming to be a homosexual bed-wetter; a wise-guy declaration that now always seemed one step ahead of him in life. Torsten had chosen to simply move to West Berlin where residents were exempt from conscription. The hitch was he had to stay for seven years before he could officially take up residence in West Germany again. Torsten had five years to go and survived by giving private violin lessons and taking various forms of government assistance.

The military exemption was one of the things that pulled people onto this island city. Others included generous subsidies and tax concessions provided by the West German government to keep the isolated enclave alive. I guess it worked. After six months of living in West Berlin, I couldn't remember meeting even one native Berliner. Everyone seemed to come from somewhere else.

I took my seat with Ulrich and Anne whom I had not seen since they got back from their trip.

"You look like you just woke up," Ulrich said.

"Are you kidding?" I answered in dead seriousness. "I've been working all day. I'm burned out."

He took that line at face value. Ulrich had only a vague idea of what I did for a living. He knew that I worked from home and earned good money with "high technology products," as I referred to them. I think he classified me in his mind as some kind of new generation computer entrepreneur, a notion I did nothing to discourage.

"By the way, I got some interesting quotes on car insurance," Ulrich said, pulling a business card out of his wallet. "This should be cheaper and better than what you have now. Here is the agent's name. Give him a call. Tell him I sent you."

That was typical. I had long since forgotten that, before their trip, we talked about car insurance. Ulrich was sure that I could get a better deal and promptly set off to find it for me. He never forgot anything and always liked to offer himself, at least to me, a foreigner, as a model of helpful efficiency in the fine German tradition. I think Ulrich saw me as a forerunner of a new world; one where people were high-tech, self-reliant and had as much leisure time as they could engineer into their busy but rewarding and productive schedules. Ulrich took great pride in being a "Euro-patriot." He believed fervently that the European Economic Community was about to bloom into a United States of Europe, a truly shining city on a hill; the most compassionate and civilized of all places on earth. It would become a great society that had learned all the bitter lessons history had to teach. It would be what America should have been: the last best hope.

For Ulrich, the Cold War was too stagnant to be exciting. Nuclear bombs kept armies from marching and communism had shown itself a miserable failure. He thought that the real competition for the hearts and minds of the world was between the "European way," which was providing everything from universal healthcare to free universities, subsidized opera and safe streets in inner cities that were still desirable places to live in, and what he considered to be the brutal and self-defeating ways of the Americans.

"You definitely had more than enough chances," he constantly reminded me. "Especially after the Second World War; you could have built any kind of society you wanted. You were really number one. But you screwed up in a big way."

He often told me the story of his move to the United States when he was ten years old. It was shortly before the first lunar landing.

"My father, the engineer, he was so excited. He went out and bought this big television set. We all sat in the living room that night and watched, and when one of the astronauts saluted the flag on the moon he kept saying over and over, 'See what a great country this is!'" Ulrich always ended his recollection with a condescending wave of his hand and his tone scornful. "And look at it now. Forget it, it's over."

I took the insurance agent's business card and promised Ulrich I would call him first thing in the morning. Then I ordered sausages, potato salad and an Alt beer from the waitress. "You should have ordered the steak, its excellent tonight," Ulrich said. He was also a self-anointed *Feinschmecker*. And despite the fact that he ate his dinner at the Troika almost every night, Botz took delight in ridiculing the Turkish cook, often to his face, calling him "pork chop," saying that salmonella was his favorite spice and routinely accusing him of "crimes against gastronomy."

"Good that you know to keep away from the Pilsner in this place," he said. "I've complained to Rolf about that a hundred times."

"So, how was your trip?" I asked.

"Good. The trip was good. I got to see the folks," he replied with his girlfriend nodding in agreement.

"His parents are great," she said.

"Ja, saw the folks, and we took a little trip down to Florida. Got a good deal on airfare."

"I thought you both looked tanned," I said. Actually, they were both white as bed sheets, but I felt I owed Ulrich a complement since he had troubled himself with the car insurance.

"Oh! I almost forgot," he said, pulling a sheet of paper out of his worn leather satchel. Whenever Ulrich pulled anything out of that satchel and gave it to me, I could count on it being a newspaper or magazine article containing some shocking statistic that I as an American should be appalled at and ashamed of. He often took pleasure in reading those excerpts out loud. This time it was a page torn from a German magazine lambasting the *New American Life Style*—a frenzied, overweight population spending their lives in their cars, inhaling exhaust fumes while choking on meals of loafy fast-food meat as they inched their way against the clock over jammed, crumbling highways, commuting between two and three low-paying jobs in a failing effort to make ends meet, usually just a paycheck away from homelessness.

"Is that why are you not living anymore in America?" Torsten asked Ulrich in his usual quiet, calm manner. Torsten never seemed capable of any emotion.

Ulrich laughed in his typically arrogant way, "That and more." He then began rattling off the usual litany of American failures: streets rotten with crime and littered with human debris; a society addicted to drugs, a perverted obsession with guns, and hopelessly overrun by both. From there it was only a short leap to a place so vile that visiting tourists were either to be found shot dead on vibrating beds in flea-bag highway motel rooms, or wrongly charged with murder by a nightmare of a criminal justice system, in which case they'd find themselves begging some redneck governor for clemency while the bloodthirsty mob outside chanted for them to fry.

My food arrived. Torsten wished me "good appetite" in English. Ulrich warned that he didn't want to see me eating sausages without mustard and pushed the jar on the table toward me with an assuring, "It's *mittlescharf*, it's good." Anne sat there and smiled.

"So why are your parents still living there?" Torsten asked, not ready to drop the subject just yet.

"Well, for them it's different. They have a house in Riverside, which is still an island of prosperity. My father has a good position in the firm . . . They've just been there too long now—nearly twenty years. At their age, they're just too invested in the illusion to uproot their lives now. It's just too difficult for them. For our generation it's something else. There are just too many problems and it's only going to get worse. Soon it's going to be impossible to live like a human being anywhere over there."

Torsten turned to me with skeptical grin and asked, "Is that true, Richard?"

Ulrich took it upon himself to answer. "Of course it's true!" he shouted. Then he assaulted me with, "And can you honestly imagine it ever getting anything but worse? Honestly?"

I avoided a response to that remark by concentrating on my food. But the truth was that my answer was no, I couldn't. Not any more than I could imagine it ever being what I'd been told it was in my childhood. Yet, until a year or so ago, I would still have offered stiff resistance to Ulrich's kind of talk. Nothing makes one more of a patriot than living abroad. I often found myself defending things American that I had spent most of my adult life railing against when I lived there. I would go out of my way, offering a different set of facts and figures; excuses based on cultural or historical differences; use the explanation that fate had charged the Americans with the weighty duty of defending the free world; therefore, some things had to be overlooked. But that all ended suddenly one day, and I don't even know why. Inexplicably, from one moment to the next, what was once holy became common and commonly corrupt. Now my defense consisted of answering in a patronizing tone. "I guess he knows what he's talking about," I said. Admitting any of my own hard disappointments, especially to a foreigner, was still not possible for me. That would somehow set them hopelessly forever in stone.

"Look, Torsten," Ulrich insisted. "Just take a trip there. Go to any big city, then come back any tell me it isn't true. Just be careful. Don't go thinking that you can walk the streets with the same freedom you have here."

"But you were just in Florida and you had a good time there," Torsten said.

"What really scared me were the milk cartons," said Anne.

"Oh, that's right." Ulrich squeezed her hand as if to thank her for not having to answer. "On all the milk cartons there are pictures and descriptions of children who disappear without a trace. Tell me that's not a sick place. Tell me that if you came to Earth from another planet today, forgetting all the history and all the propaganda, and were looking for somewhere to live, that you would choose America over anywhere in western Europe!"

Just then Geoffrey Biggs came to the table, beer glass in hand. "Tearing down the flag again, old man?" he said, patting Ulrich cheerfully on the shoulder. Pulling a just-vacated chair over from a neighboring table, Geoffrey squeezed in between Anne and me. Everyone readjusted their chairs to let him in. Only Ulrich didn't move.

"What's the matter, Biggs?" he asked bitterly after everyone had settled down. "Made enough women gag for one night?"

Geoffrey let out a good-natured laugh. He wore an armor that nothing Ulrich could ever say would penetrate. That was one of the reasons Ulrich disliked him so much. There was a long list of other reasons as well. First, Geoffrey was British and it was the British and their island mentality, Ulrich thought, who were trying to put the brakes to European integration. Second, being British, Geoffrey could never resist rubbing Ulrich's nose in German history; a history Ulrich didn't care to hear about. Sometimes a news report containing a negative remark by Prime Minister Thatcher about "those bureaucrats in Brussels" would launch Ulrich into a long, angry harangue about the backwardness of British society; a place, he said, where all people ever ate were meat pies or cucumber sandwiches and still suffered from diseases like rickets, scurvy and gout. Geoffrey would sit and listen to it all, smiling until the very end. Then he'd jump out of his seat and goose-step around the table, spastically shooting one arm up in the Hitler salute while other people in the room looked on, grinning uneasily. The message was simple, sharp and cutting: but *it* happened here, didn't it?

But for Ulrich, there was a long list of other offenses Geoffrey was guilty of. He never registered his address with the authorities, which everyone in Germany was required to do; he never paid taxes; he ate foods with obnoxiously high garlic content, the odor of which would exit through his pores and hang on him for days; he worked only when no one would lend him money; and when it came to a place to live, well, there always seemed to be a basic philosophical difference between Geoffrey and his landlords: they believed he should pay rent, and he believed that he shouldn't. At least not if it proved inconvenient. His possessions were limited to an old, stained mattress and a couple of trashy novels which lay about the floor of whatever room he happened to be inhabiting amid the dust, spent condoms, crumpled tissues, yellowed crescent toenail clippings and unopened letters from tax authorities and creditors. The sight of Biggs' room once moved a Berlin marshal, who had shown up to evict him, close to tears as the man shook his head and mumbled the word "pitiful" again and again. "How can a human being live like this?" he moaned.

In short, Geoffrey Biggs was not the kind of person Ulrich Botz thought should be living in his new world. Yet, when Geoffrey threw his money around buying drinks for everyone at the table, Ulrich would quietly accept. It was only when Geoffrey was absent that Botz would speak about him with brutal contempt, referring to him as "that island ape," often voicing the opinion that he and his kind should be condemned to a remote penal colony for the rest of their natural lives. In Geoffrey's case, a sentence Ulrich would gladly impose and carry out himself, if he only could.

Geoffrey put on his thick eyeglasses, rolled a cigarette and silently stared into space. He would often lapse deep into his own thoughts while sitting with us.

Ulrich resumed his orations about the U.S.A., concluding as he always did, that eighty percent of America's problems could be solved with a long, sustained effort in education and large investments in mental health. "It will take them a couple of generations to reach European standards," he'd say with a smugness that made me want to hit him over the head with an iron frying pan. "But that's the only chance they have if they don't want to wind up being just another banana republic."

That comment brought Geoffrey out of his trance. He laughed, almost to himself, then wildly waved his hand in front of him to get everyone's attention. "Last year, ja? Last year, I was listening to the BBC World Service. There was some kind of referendum to make English the one official language in California. They were interviewing people, asking what they thought. One chap said—and I'm not inventing this—he said, 'If English was good enough for Jesus Christ, then it's good enough for me!'"

Biggs' face turned red with laughter. He was rocking back and forth with his mouth wide open, not making a sound. Ulrich was howling and beating his fists on the table. Even a couple sitting behind us overheard and were laughing. "If was good enough for Jesus Christ, it's good enough for me!" Geoffrey repeated, now doubled over with one hand holding his side.

A few minutes later everyone had settled down. Ulrich seemed to think he owed Biggs a compliment, "The BBC is excellent, Geoffrey, excellent." Then he engaged him in conversation with a friendliness I had never seen before.

I finished my third beer, paid and left. The bar was now empty except for the drunkard sitting at the end. He lifted his head from his folded arms as I went by and gave a sleepy look around the room. Rolf was cleaning up and gave me that two-eyed wink as I went out the door.

Outside, I checked my watch: 1:15 a.m. I stuck my hands deep in my coat pockets and made my way back to my apartment, mad as hell. That was the first time I'd heard such laughter at the expense of the Americans; the first time I'd felt the humiliation of seeing yourself as others see you.

I began to feel the lubricating effect of the alcohol on my brain. Walking along the deserted, dimly lit back streets of Kreuzberg, I also experienced that liberating feeling I had become used to since moving to Germany: freedom from fear. I thought about my trips home; how it took a good three or four days before the uneasiness was gone. I thought of the stories my parents would tell about what a different place it was when they were young, and what it was like when I was a child. I thought about the present and wondered what had gone wrong. I became angry and bitter. How did it happen? Who was to blame? I thought about politicians and their perpetual fund raising; about televangelists selling their crocodile tears and owning theme parks, yet I couldn't understand how it had come to this. I felt as though I'd been cheated, swindled out of a future by some cheap crook. I thought about the usual American response to any criticism: if you don't like it, leave. Then it occurred to me that that's just what I had done. It was then that I understood the real reason I was still here in Berlin. But I still hadn't gone far enough. That feeling of having been swindled churned in my stomach and stuck in my throat and I was waiting for the day when I could cut the cord for good and just not care anymore.

A few yards from my apartment I was jolted by the nasal beep of a car horn. I turned and was confronted by two glowing headlights going dark in the mist. Then that familiar, irritating sound rose up into the night—"*Na?*" It was my neighbor, Bernd. He had just driven his Austin Mini up onto the sidewalk perpendicular to the curb, sandwiching himself in between two parked cars. I felt my heart pounding in my chest as I watched him struggling to hatch his tall, lanky frame from the tiny car.

"*Naaa?!*" I yelled back him. "What are you trying to do, give me a heart attack?" Bernd didn't take me seriously. He walked over with a stupid grin on his face, twirling his car keys around his finger, obviously happy with himself.

"Was macht die Frauen?" he asked jovially, patting me on the back.

"Not much, Bernd. I'm afraid the women aren't doing much for me these days."

He couldn't wait to tell me that he had just come from a birthday party where he'd met a woman with very large breasts. Bernd, recently divorced, was always on his way to or returning from one social engagement or another. As we walked toward our building I'd stopped listening as he recited all the boring details. Inside the entrance he fell silent. I wanted to say "goodnight" and run up the stairs to my apartment, but I didn't have the energy. Besides, he would have just followed me. In the elevator he whispered, "I hear you gave our landlady quite a scare today."

I had to think for a moment before I remembered. It seemed ages ago. "It was nothing compared to the scare she gave me. News travels fast around here."

Bernd laughed. The elevator finally reached our floor and its aluminum doors folded back slowly. "*Na*? When are we going to have breakfast together?" he asked as he unlocked his door. He was always asking me that. Evidently he was looking for a bachelor buddy. I wasn't interested.

"Whenever you like, Bernd. Just come over." That was my way of defusing the issue. I was gambling on the belief that, as a German bureaucrat, he would never take the initiative.

Inside my apartment I couldn't believe I could be so tired after sleeping all afternoon. Yet, once in bed, I tossed and turned under the sheets and blankets. My bitterness was making it impossible to fall asleep. I lay on my back, resigned to staying awake, listening to the sounds echoing up from the street: the occasional distant swish of automobile tires speeding along the drizzle-soaked pavement of the Gneisenaustrasse; a cat moaning in the night sounding more like an infant child; the hollow thud of a heavy wooden door somewhere on the street; grainy footsteps making their way along the wet sidewalk, growing louder then ever more faint as they receded into the night. Sleep, when finally it came, took me without my realizing it.

Everything Gets Better

I WOKE RELATIVELY EARLY the next morning, about nine-thirty, and lay listlessly staring out the window next to my bed. The sky above Berlin was uniformly gray. Cheerless winter had suddenly returned to the city; the pleasant spring-like weather of the last few days had disappeared overnight. I peered down into the somber street. A fine, persistent drizzle was soaking the terrain. Up at the intersection, dark hulking silhouettes made their way along the Gneisenaustrasse bundled up in long winter coats, their heads and umbrellas bowed against the wind. Down at the other corner, the elderly Turkish men had pulled in their folding chairs from the sidewalk in front of the fruit stand. What would follow now would be months of short, depressing days; skies so heavy with gray that they seemed to press down on you. I ran my finger across the white aluminum window frame next to my bed. It was cold to the touch, chilled by the cold air outside. It was also covered with a fine, dark powder accumulated over the past few days when, for a couple of hours each afternoon, I had left the window open. The famed *Berliner Luft* was severely polluted from the burning of brown coal that warmed the homes of the surrounding GDR. That biting odor, which filled the dead cold and stung the eyes until they watered, would now settle upon us once again.

My attention turned to the row of buildings across the street. The Kreuzberg district where I lived had survived World War II largely intact; a bit of old Berlin in sharp contrast to the ugly modern buildings grouped around the Memorial Church in the city center. Starting at the far corner of my street, the turn-of-the-century Beaux-Arts buildings stood massive and melodramatic, many complete with elaborate balconied facades. But in the middle of the block the architecture changed. Directly across the street from my apartment stood a flat concrete wall with windows punched through it. Some catastrophe had apparently occurred here during the war, destroying the apartment house that once stood there. A single bomb that fell from the sky, perhaps intended for another target? Artillery fire a degree or two off the mark? And what of the inhabitants? Were they taken from this life while having their breakfast? Or in their sleep? Or while reading a book during a rare lull in the unimaginable chaos of the time? Had they dutifully gone off to work, performing a task already made senseless by war and the disorder it wrought, desperately clinging to that last strand of normality in their lives, only to come home and find all they had valued or loved in this world suddenly obliterated? At the opposite end of block, across the Gneisenaustrasse, the large, white neon cross of the Free Evangelical Congregation glowed in the gray mist. It seemed to float in the air like a silent memorial to the nameless, faceless victims of the human tragedy that took place here. Sometimes Berlin is full of ghosts.

I was still in bed when, shortly before ten o'clock, the telephone rang. It was Wolf, and he was in a good mood.

"Hey, still asleep?"

"No, I was just looking through my files."

He knew I was lying.

"I have good news for you," he said.

The big German bank had just called with two big new computers that needed our software.

None of my customers knew I had moved to Berlin. When anyone called the Münster office asking for me, they were always told that I was not available and would get back to them. The big German bank was among my oldest European accounts.

"It's going to be a good deal," Wolf said. "I figure about fifty-thousand dollars. You should give him a call right away."

And so it went. Sales to customers who bought additional computers and contracted software for them were counted as new business. It seemed I was destined to stay in Berlin making money whether I worked at it or not.

A short telephone conversation confirmed Wolf's suspicions. The sale would be just over fifty-thousand dollars. Doing business with the big German bank was always a pleasure. Money was never an issue. They knew what they wanted, signed the contracts and paid promptly. The organization operated like a huge *Panzer* tank. It decided on a target and then rolled over anything in its way until it reached its goal. Combined with some other contracts I had been waiting for, this deal would keep me at a more than acceptable sales level for the next few months. I could relax. The numbers game would continue at least until the end of the year.

The morning's business had taken all of forty minutes. I finished it feeling as if I'd just put in a full and productive ten hours at the office and was pondering how to reward myself. I decided to take the rest of the day off. Over orange juice I scanned a magazine listing the vast cultural offerings in West Berlin, searching for a museum exhibit where I could spend the afternoon. Normally I would have asked Christoph to join me, but in his current mood that was pointless.

The telephone rang again. Great, I thought. Maybe it's Wolf with more good news. Reaching for the phone, I'd already made up my mind that any more business would have to wait until tomorrow.

"Ja? . . . Hallo?" A female voice was on the line. "Here is Kati Weber."

My mind went blank. There was an awkward silence before it came back to me. "Ah! . . . Ox-penis hemorrhoid cream!"

She laughed, "So you remember, good. For a moment I thought you maybe forgot about me."

"No, not at all. I just didn't expect to hear from you."

"Why not? You think I ask your telephone number for nothing? Do you perhaps have time for a lunch together today?"

I certainly did.

We arranged to meet at a restaurant near the old Anhalter Station. I arrived right on time and took a seat at one of the big windows through which I had a good view of the ruins of the old train station across the road. All that was left was a small jagged portion of the main entrance. The West Berliners liked to keep a couple of blatant war ruins around and floodlight them dramatically at night. In a city where the most obvious evidence of the Second World War had been wiped away by forty-five years of frenetic renovation and rebuilding, it seemed nobody wanted to lay themselves open to accusations of trying to forget an ugly history.

Directly in front the station was a taxi stand. Four or five taxis were lined up as if waiting for phantom trains to discharge passengers from another era. Nearby was one of the large war-era bunkers that you still saw at various places in Berlin. On this particular bunker beside the ruins of the old train station, someone had painted ominous graffiti in large letters: *Those who build bunkers throw bombs*.

I decided to order a mineral water. Time and again the young waitress walked directly past me without once looking in my direction. She cleaned ashtrays and picked up used glasses from empty tables, or stood with her back toward me. Behind the bar another waitress stood, dazed, while leisurely sucking on a cigarette. I managed to bring her out of her trance with a few waves of my hand. "Meine Kollegin," she replied, motioning to the other waitress. Then she checked her watch then went into the restroom.

It was always the same. Either one had to eat in an expensive restaurant where the personnel had spent years learning to wait tables, or in places that were staffed by students who made it a point of honor to show that the job was beneath them. I was starting to smolder.

Suddenly Kati burst through the thick curtain covering the door. Looking more attractive than I remembered, she took a quick glance around the room before seeing me and hurried over with a big smile.

"Sorry I'm a few minutes too late, Richard. I hope you're not waiting too long."

The frustration that had been boiling inside me evaporated. "Not at all. I just got here."

She took off her long coat and put it on the chair next to her, exposing black tights and a black turtleneck cashmere sweater that just barely covered her posterior. "So nice to see you again," she said. The smile never left her as she sat down and picked up a menu. "How have you been?"

"Fine." But my answer wasn't enough. She stared at me, expecting more. "Working hard . . . Working a lot, but otherwise I can't complain."

"Yes, you look like you have been working too much. I think you could use a drink. I know I could." She opened the menu and scanned it briefly. "Ummm . . . perhaps a Campari-orange. That sounds good in the afternoon, doesn't it?"

"That does sound good. I'll take the same."

Katarina thrust her arm into the air, snapping her fingers at the waitress, "Hallo?! Zwei Campari-orange, bitte."

As if under a spell, the waitress made a beeline for the bar and prepared the drinks.

"How did you do that? She's been ignoring me since I got here."

"Don't you know? Make them feel low. To get anything done in Germany, put people in their place. That's what they like . . . Why are you laughing? It's true! Germans like being put in their place," she said loudly, not caring about being overheard, "Especially by big institutions like the banks and the telephone company. It makes them feel secure. You have a lot to learn. Don't worry, I will teach you."

When she mentioned the phone company I thought maybe she was onto something.

"I want to thank you again for the ride back last Sunday. It was very nice of you, especially with the trouble I caused at the border. That added another hour to your trip and you looked so very tired."

"Don't mention it. It was nothing."

"How is your friend? What is his name?"

"Christoph."

"Oh yes, Christoph. He does not seem to be a very happy person, I think."

"Well, he's all right. He's just under a lot of pressure at the moment. Or rather, he's letting other people put him under a lot of pressure."

"Oh, I hate that," she said with mild agitation, as though it was a problem she knew too well.

The drinks arrived. Kati lifted her glass in a toast and took a sip.

"I really don't understand why people do that to themselves," she said. "Life is too short for that kind of thing. Your friend really needs to enjoy himself more, that's what I think. Walk down the street here in Germany and all you see are people with long faces, you know what I mean?"

Unwilling to discuss anything that had to do with Christoph, I announced that I was going to have the ratatouille and closed the menu with the resolve of someone who had just come to a monumental decision.

"Ratatouille, eh?" she said, glancing at the menu before deciding on a salad. Kati snapped her fingers in the air again and ordered for the both of us.

"Sooo," I asked hesitantly. "How's your daughter?" I always felt as though I was asking about an embarrassing personal injury when forced to make conversation by asking women about their kids.

"Oh, she's very fine. I should have brought a picture with me to show. Next time I will. I'm lucky that my husband is not working today. He is taking care."

"You're married then?"

"Yes, for several years now. I can hardly believe it myself sometimes."

Kati's husband was a pilot for a regional airline. When he wasn't flying to London, Saarbrücken or Amsterdam, he liked nothing better than staying home with their daughter or reading a good book.

I knew little about Kati and nothing about her husband but they seemed an unlikely pair. She was so extravagant, even excessive. I couldn't see her married to someone with the emotional stability of an airline pilot. And although I hardly knew her, I couldn't picture her mothering a child, either. I could easily imagine her in the physical act of giving birth, lying on her back screaming in pain. The fine lines on her face revealed that she had experienced a lot in her life—physically, anyway. But the role of a loving mother just didn't suit her, somehow. Later, when we talked about the birth of her child, she reinforced my impressions by comparing the labor to a severe case of gastritis that had once almost killed her in Madagascar. She even went on to say that her only thought immediately following the birth was how wonderful it was to finally be alone again.

During lunch it soon became clear that, not only was Kati incredibly un-German, she was without a doubt the most impulsive person I'd ever met; often recklessly so. She had done one thing after another in her life on a whim, from traveling to Istanbul with a Greek rock band when she was sixteen, to marrying someone twenty years her senior, to having a baby. The only explanation for everything she did was that it was what Katarina Weber wanted at that moment. And she was utterly open; perfectly ready to answer any question without hesitation, no matter how personal, and never asking any questions in return—except when it seemed she had to force herself to ask, "And you are working for an American company here in Berlin, I suppose?"

I told her I was and that was the end of it. Mercifully, I never had to explain that my sole purpose in life consisted of sitting alone in my apartment tormenting strangers from the end of a telephone line. It seemed that Kati developed pictures of people within the few first minutes of meeting them and that was enough for her. Getting acquainted beyond that was a formality for which she had little patience and was desperate to get out of the way as soon as possible.

That afternoon I learned that Kati was an only child. She grew up in a small town near Hannover where her father owned and operated a funeral home. All through her childhood her family lived in an apartment above the home, which sometimes reeked powerfully of formaldehyde and other embalming agents. Having spent her entire young life there, Kati never noticed the odors until school friends began to visit and always wanted to know what that funny smell was. A man who made coffins lived next door. Kati recalled the sound of the man's electric saw "screaming" through planks of wood every morning starting promptly at seven o'clock. When she misbehaved her father locked her in the dark basement room where he stored the man's coffins, sometimes for hours at a time, telling her that the coffins were filled with evil spirits who ate bad girls. She said that even the threat of that punishment was enough to terrorize her, and when it came, no amount of pleading, begging or apologizing could save her from it.

Kati's parents were both *ordentliche Menchen,* meaning each day had a routine that could never be altered. Her mother insisted that Kati be at the corner bakery every morning at six o'clock to pick up *Brötchen* so that breakfast could be served promptly at six thirty. Every Saturday was spent cleaning the house, every Sunday sitting at home "resting" with her parents. Holidays were spent *schön gemütlich* with stiff, boring, childless relatives who couldn't stand one another. Kati's parents kept separate bedrooms and dreaded with a passion any occasion that might require them to travel more than twenty miles from home, preferring the orderly environment of their clean, familiar surroundings.

As her father's business prospered he became more important and well known in the community, often taking part in many of the town's social functions. About the time Kati entered secondary school, her father began advertising his business in the local newspapers, which was unfortunate, for the family's surname was much too close to the German word for mortuary. As a result, Kati suffered. Her home was referred to as "the morgue" or "the bone box," and she was called

"Frankenstein's daughter." Rumors floated around school that she helped her father embalm bodies, kept jars containing everything from shrunken heads to male sex organs preserved under her bed and slept in a casket.

At age fifteen, Kati saw her best friend get struck by lightning in a field near her home. She described that as a major turning point in her life. "What I am really remembering most is her face," she said. "She was on her back, you know? Her eyes were open and her face . . . *her face* just had no expression on it. I never saw a face so empty. Her eyes looked just like a doll's eyes. The life was sucked right out of her in one instant. Just in a flash. I mean, I saw bodies in the house all the time, but it never meant anything until then. That's when I understood what *dead* meant. That's what made me start thinking about what it takes to be alive. That's when I saw how dead my parent's eyes were. It was a shock for me to see that. Just dead, dead, dead, dead. I was never able to see it before. Then I looked at myself in the mirror and I just knew that I would become the same way. It scared the crap out of me. I want to be alive! My father prepared my friend's body afterwards. I wanted so much to see her once more after that, but my parents didn't allow it. They got it in their dumb heads that it wasn't proper or that I was too young or something like that. Can you imagine such a thing? I mean, this was the only real friend I had during my whole miserable youth. I just wanted to say goodbye. Anyway, I named my daughter Anja for her."

After that, Kati began living her life exactly the way she wanted, which convinced her parents that the experience of seeing her friend killed had made her go a little crazy. She suddenly became "hard to handle," as they put it. Kati was barely seventeen when she left home for good, running away to West Berlin in the middle of the night with the clothes on her back and a thirty-eight-year-old photographer whom she'd met at a bus stop three days earlier. That relationship lasted nearly six months. Throughout the years that followed, she broke off all contact with her family and, in order to break completely with her past, she traveled constantly. Kati did nothing else. She took the odd job to earn enough money for a plane ticket somewhere, the further away the better, often putting herself in a faraway place with no more than a few marks in her pocket. She slept on the streets and begged, or found menial jobs to earn money. Soon Kati was using her good looks to manipulate those who could help her, sometimes engaging in what amounted to rank prostitution. I was amazed by the nonchalant way in which she told me the details; things I would have difficulty revealing to a close friend, never mind someone I'd just met. When she cut herself off and casually asked, "You're not offended by any of this, are you?" I suddenly realized I was staring at her with my mouth hanging open.

"Uh . . . no . . . uh . . . of course not," I stammered. "I just find it sad that there . . . when there are times . . . when people . . . get exploited in a degrading way like that."

"Oh, don't ever feel sorry for them," she said. "I always made everyone happy!"

That was the life Kati led for nearly seven years—leaving Berlin for three or four months at a time before returning, staying with friends, working a few months, then leaving again. Her parents hired a private detective who finally found her, but she still refused to have anything to do with them. Yet, every month, for many years thereafter, no matter how often she moved, she received a check in the mail from her father. And no matter how much she might have needed the money, she never cashed any of them.

At one point, Kati began a relationship with an Australian aborigine who was studying medicine in Berlin and soon moved in with him. A couple of months later they took a trip to Australia. There, in midst of a prolonged argument about something Kati could no longer remember, she decided he was a big mistake and went off on her own. It was at a bar in Perth that she met her future husband, a fellow Berliner named Hanno. Kati spent the next couple of weeks traveling through Australia with Hanno before they returned together to West Berlin. She went home with him from the airport and they've been together ever since.

Soon after they got back, Kati realized that she was pregnant. Not absolutely sure who the father was, she secretly went to Amsterdam and had an abortion. "I couldn't very well take a chance on dropping a little brown aborigine into Hanno's lap, now could I? Not after he'd just asked me to marry him and all," she recalled as if being romanced off her feet.

"I think life is a very simple proposition for you," I said, and was disappointed when she didn't get the old pun.

"Why should life be complicated?" she replied. "Complications bring unhappiness and waste time. Life is too short for that. Just look at your friend, what's his name again? When I see him I must to think of my parents—*ugh!* My father forever tied up in that miserable business of his, working, working, always working, and always saving every pfennig. They never bought anything new except a big car every two years because it was important for them to be seen in a new Mercedes. Other than that, nothing in the house was ever changed. They never spent money unless they absolutely had to. Did you ever notice that Germans are scared to death of being poor? It's their biggest national nightmare. Then my father spent what little free time he had involved in his stupid clubs—the carnival society and that Schützenfest shit—all the stuff that only dead people think about. Everything has to have the proper appearance, and as long as the neighbors are talking about someone else and not you, the world is in order. Good old German stubborn stupidity. Then my father tries to comfort himself by sending me a check every month. It was a cheap way to convince himself that he's done all he can and if anything happens to me it will be my own fault. And you know what? I don't even care anymore. It all seems like six lifetimes ago. In the end we all get the life we deserve. All I know is that I left there telling myself that I'd never, ever, live like I watched them live for seventeen years and I have never regretted it."

"I doubt you've ever regretted anything," I said.

"You're right, I never have. Well . . . maybe once I did. I was young at the time, maybe eighteen or so. I was taking a holiday in Morocco and had just arrived at the train station in

Marrakech. I met this Belgian guy there, I don't remember how. He was some kind of a businessman or something. He said he knew a cheap pension and was willing to drive me. I was tired and it was hot, the station was one big confusion and I really didn't know where to go, so I said okay. He was a real jerk, you know? Thought he could impress me enough with his fancy linen suit and air-conditioned car to get me into his bed or something. Anyway, we are driving along and he's talking and talking about how important he is and how much money he's making and all this kind of things. Then we drove in front of this palace and I had to make him stop the car. It was really unbelievable, really beautiful. All these soft pastel colors with flowers and palms, like something out of a fairy tale. I couldn't take my eyes off it. Today I probably wouldn't even notice it, but back then it gave me this wonderful warm feeling inside. I remember feeling that, for the first time in my life, I was at home. The Belgian guy said it was once the sultan's palace or something like that, I don't remember anymore. But I was very impressed, so I picked up my camera to take a picture of it. In those days I liked to take a lot of pictures. Anyway, I put the camera to my face and through the lens I saw this guard who was standing out front. He spotted me with my camera and jumped headfirst behind some hedges. I could not believe it."

"He jumped behind the hedges?"

"Ja! Head first! I wish I could show you the picture, but there are so many things I lost by moving so often. You could see his army boots upside down on the other side of the bushes. It was like he was diving into a swimming pool. The Belgian guy laughed and told me that many of the people in Morocco believe that if someone takes their picture it steals part of their soul. This story really fascinated me. I started to think, what would it take for a man to sell his soul? You know what I did then? I started walking by the palace every afternoon and began talking with the guard. He was always standing out front at the entrance to the driveway. I guess he was about forty; a big guy in an army uniform with muscles everywhere and a thick black mustache. I went there every day for a week. It was a kind of experiment for me. He was really very friendly; seemed to like to talk more than he was supposed to. After ten minutes or so he would look over his shoulder to see if anyone was watching. But whenever I would even touch my camera he would get nervous and his eyes would be glued to my hands and he would back away, like I was fooling around with a grenade or something. And when I asked him straight out if I could take his picture that would be the end. His hands would fly around and he would shout 'Noo, noo, noo, noo, noo!' and disappear into this little guardhouse next to the driveway until I left. But every day I would show up at the palace, and every day I would dress myself in a little less and then a little less and the last day I was covered up in all the wrong places, you know? That's when I told him that I would be leaving the next day. He seemed to be very disappointed. Then I told him that I was very sorry because I really liked talking with him and asked if I could take his picture as an . . . *Andenken*. What is the English? . . . Souvenir? Yes, of course, a souvenir. He refused, "*Noo, noo, noo, noo, noo!*" But I wasn't convinced because this time his hands didn't fly around and he didn't go into his little house. Then I told him again how I really liked him and really wanted his picture to take back with me to Europe. All the time he was getting nervous, but it wasn't the same as usual, I could tell. Then I told him that I would do just *anything* if he would let me have his picture. That's when he started sweating, I mean, *really* sweating. It was pouring off his face, his shirt under his arms was all wet and so was his back. Then I went into that little house. It was very small; there was a small writing table, a chair and a telephone. I went in and sat down—in a certain way, you know?"

Kati struck an exaggeratedly seductive pose before returning to the proper position in her chair. She suddenly looked so prim.

"He stood outside for a minute like he was thinking it over, then he started walking toward me. I picked up my camera and put it to my face thinking that he would jump out of the way like before and then I would get up and leave. But he didn't. He just stood there with a strange pose and with a strange expression on his face—like he was proud or defiant or something. And he just waited until I took the picture. So I did."

"I guess he thought you were worth a bit of his soul," I said. "You should be flattered."

"Oh, I was. But then he kept walking toward me and I suddenly realized I got myself into trouble because I never really thought about having sex with this guy, you know? He was just about on top of me and I was thinking, well, he's not bad looking in an Oriental sort of way when someone outside shouted his name, 'Achmid!' and he said something I couldn't understand, but I think it was something like, 'Oh, shit!' and he ran outside pulling up his pants. That's when I got up and left."

"Ha!" I slapped my hand on the table, thoroughly enjoying her nonsense. "So what's to regret? I think it's a great story."

"Well, now it is. I mean, we all sell our souls every day of the week, right? It's part of what makes us all human. But I didn't know that at the time. And I think I was disappointed at how easy it was—to get a bit of his soul, I mean. Then something strange happened to me. I started to think maybe I really did steal some of it, you know? I mean, do people really believe in these things for no reason? What if it was true? What does that mean about me? I felt really awful. I took that film out of the camera and threw it away. I thought that would make me feel better, but it didn't. For a week after that, until I was back again in Germany, I felt . . . well, I don't know how to say it . . . like dirty or evil or something. Like I was the work of the devil. What? . . . Don't laugh, it was terrible! I wanted to go traveling around North Africa for one or two months, but after a week I was feeling so bad that I came back home. But the day after I got back I felt better—just like normal. The very next day! I thought the whole thing was just stupid and I was angry at myself for coming home so fast. But you know what? That's when I learned my most important lesson about the world."

"Really? And that is?"

"I learned that everything gets better," she said with searing resentment, "but nothing ever really gets good."

During lunch we drank quite a bit. First the long drinks, then we each drank three beers with our food, followed by Milchkaffee with amaretto, topped off with *Fernet-Branca* as a digestive. When we were done, Kati insisted on paying the bill in gratitude for my picking her up on the transit highway. "Really, Kati, you don't have to do that. Making your acquaintance is more than thanks enough. I would have made the trip ten times over for the pleasure."

It was a lot of nonsense driven by alcohol along with those full lips and figure of hers. But Kati seemed to take the words to heart, as if they were some kind of declaration of love. She clasped my hands together in hers on the table and looked at me as though she was going to cry, "Oh, Richard. Du bist aber *süss!*"

Outside the restaurant, Kati suggested we take a walk. We started down the Anhalter Strasse. I stuck my hands deep in my coat pockets while Kati took my arm and held it tight. The afternoon was dark and dismal. As we walked I wondered what kind of relationship she had with her husband. She seemed to lead a pretty free life while he was content to sit home with their daughter and read.

We continued, deep in our own thoughts down the Wilhelmstrasse until we were standing in front of the Wall.

"Dead end," I said.

"Scheiss Mauer," Kati grumbled.

"Which way, left or right?"

"Hmmm . . . Left," she answered. "All the way to the Reichstag."

I led the way as we walked holding hands over a narrow, muddy path between the Berlin Wall and an area overgrown with brush and weeds, occasionally standing aside for smiling, giggling tourists walking in the opposite direction. Their reaction was not unusual. This most frequently visited section of the Wall between the Brandenburg Gate and Checkpoint Charlie often seemed to have had that effect on visitors. For the border, as brutally cruel as everyone knew it was, had been visually sanitized over time. Gone were the barbed wire and tank traps seen in the early photos of three decades ago. The border guards still had their shoot-to-kill orders, but there were no roaming dogs and no sweeping searchlights at night. Just concrete slabs about five feet wide and twelve feet high, seemingly welded together with a slit pipe running along the top that would make it difficult for anyone trying to climb over to get a firm grip on. The Wall's western side was covered with colorful graffiti; everything from banal love declarations to wisecracks like *Do like the birds—shit on the Wall*, or *Last one out remember to turn off the lights.* There was even a time, not long ago, when someone attached a urinal to the Wall near Potsdamer Platz and painted big letters over it that read, *Piss here.* An act of defamation that apparently went too far for the East Germans for it wasn't long before a couple of border guards appeared on the western side of the Wall, clinging to the strip that was officially East German territory, and removed the fixture. Sometimes the Wall became the canvas for real works of art—a door half-open with East Berlin on the other side in perfect perspective, or the Wall unzipped from top to bottom. Seeing all this, people were struck more by the Wall's absurdity than the tragedy of forced division.

For me, in any case, the Berlin Wall had become just another city landmark. When anyone at home in America asked me about the Wall, however, I would describe it in stark terms: inhumane, barbaric, a crime against humanity. But that only served to enhance the recognition I received for living so fearlessly with the monstrosity in my backyard.

Kati and I reached Potsdamer Platz where a viewing platform had been erected that let people look over the Wall to East Berlin. At first glance there was little to see from here, but for me this was one of the most interesting places in the city. Since moving to Berlin, I had made use of my abundant free time by doing a lot of reading about its history. If you knew where to look you could find artifacts of societies long gone; of civilizations that now existed only in books, on aging pieces of celluloid, or in the memories of that dwindling population old enough to have lived in them. Worlds that had been violently wiped away in giant conflagrations leaving only traces behind in remote corners like fossils in an archaeological dig: curbstones in the middle of the No Man's Land; a cobblestone thoroughfare holding rusted streetcar rails running directly into the Wall; vast empty lots in the geographical center of the city. To really appreciate it all, one had to become familiar with Berlin's past; with World War I and the fall of the Kaiser; with the Weimar Republic, when Berlin was the most decadent city in Europe, and its economic collapse, which sent people fleeing to political extremes that battled for control on these very streets. And above all, with the great evil of the Nazis who, from this very spot, reached deep into the blackest corner of their dark souls, planning horrendous crimes for which millions of people were still paying a heavy price.

The intersection here at Potsdamer Platz was once the busiest in all Europe. But the urban excitement that spread over the streets and sidewalks of this place had been killed by the war and buried by the border that now split Berlin. The great buildings that once ringed this place when it was the epicenter for that wave of amusement which overtook Berlin in the *Golden Twenties* were long gone and the ground itself was slowly being reclaimed by the Prussian forest.

From the platform, Kati and I looked over the Wall at East Berlin. Everything was gray. It was impossible to tell whether East Berlin reflected the gray sky, or the gray sky the dullness of life behind the Iron Curtain. From here we had a view across the grassy, venomously-guarded field sandwiched between the inner and outer Walls, snaking their way through the heart of the city. The Germans, in the stark accuracy of their language, referred to it as the *Todesstreifen*—the "Death Strip." I always preferred the more nuanced phrase *No Man's Land* with its dark connotations. One succumbed to it with the past an uninhabitable wreckage and any hopes for the future vanquished by absolute despair and desperation.

Just over the Wall before us we could see the remnants of an old cobblestone street with its streetcar rails intact—the last vestiges of the Leipizger Platz, once an official entrance to imperial Berlin. One of the many guard towers along the border stood about fifty yards off to our right, and through the haze in the distance stood a structure that could be seen from almost everywhere—the Television Tower at Alexanderplatz. The tallest structure in either Berlin, it resembled a giant aluminum golf ball impaled on an enormous asparagus stem reaching high into the gray sky with its aircraft warning lights flashing in a defiant exhibition of prowess and permanence. Behind us in the West stood the golden facade of the Berlin Philharmonic, and further west, the office tower of the Europa Center with its big revolving Mercedes-Benz emblem on top. An architectural Cold War had taken root in Berlin on both sides of the Wall. In the East they built landmarks carefully calculated to portray the superiority of the socialist way of life while the West seemed content just flaunting its wealth.

I decided to give Kati a historical tour of the area. From the moment I started talking it was clear that she knew almost nothing about the city she had been living in for the past twelve years. I wasn't surprised. Kati lived her life in the present. For her, yesterday was as dead as the bodies that passed through her father's basement, and tomorrow was nothing more than a rumor.

I pointed out the empty lot behind us where the Potsdamer train station once stood. I had Kati picture Joseph Goebbels, the wretched, miserable little Nazi with his clubfoot and venomous tongue, limping away from the station in the mid-1920s and into the clamoring city, ready to take up the task of organizing rogue Berlin for Hitler, growling through his teeth when he saw that it was a cauldron bubbling with all the things he so virulently despised: the scantily-clad showgirls, the rowdy drinking halls, the Marxists, the Jews, the American Negros and their jazz, the "degenerate" art, the human race. I pointed to the barren plot of land where the Haus Vaterland once was, telling her that in the 1920s and 1930s it was known as the "amusement battleship." In it was a movie theater in a giant drum and at least a dozen restaurants including a Turkish *Mokkastube* where you would be waited on by someone wearing a fez; a bistro featuring a giant panorama of the Rhein where, on the hour, patrons watched a simulated thunderstorm that always ended with a rainbow; and a dance hall with a special padded floor so people could dance all night long without getting tired calf muscles. I pointed out plots where elegant hotels once stood, as well as the Pschorr Beer Palace, the Europa Tanz Pavilion and, finally, the Weinhaus Huth where Hitler's half-brother, Alois, worked as a waiter in the 1920s, often telling his employer, "Adolf's time is coming, just you wait." By a strange perversion of fate, it was the only building on the Potsdamer Platz to have survived the war intact.

Kati listened to it all, not saying a word. When I stopped talking she murmured, almost in disbelief, "Huh, all the things you know." I couldn't tell whether she was impressed by all that had once been here, or was wondering why anyone would bother reading about it in the first place, let alone commit it all to memory.

"Wait," I said, "there's more. You see that little grassy hill there in the No Man's Land? Hitler's bunker is under there. That's where he married Eva Braun in the closing days of the war. That's where they committed suicide together and that's where Hitler's last order to burn his remains until nothing was left was carried out. Right there."

I imagined the pandemonium that had taken place here: Berlin shattered; bombs raining down from the sky; the Russians closing in on the Potsdamer Platz, fighting their way from one building to the next as streams of Red Army soldiers emerged from the U-Bahn tunnels, and even from under manhole covers in that final push to capture Hitler. Then, that final moment when the dictator put a gun to his own head and blew his brains out onto the walls of his subterranean headquarters. It all happened less than forty-five years ago. My landlady's face entered my head. She had lived through it. She would have been around forty-five years old herself when it all happened here; already in middle-age.

The fate of her generation consumed me. I thought about the people who drank themselves silly in grand

Weinstube, stuffed themselves in restaurants while waiting to see the ersatz rain showers over an artificial Rhein, or danced all night on the floor that prevented sore calves. I saw their behavior as the ultimate expression of hopelessness. They must have sensed what was coming; a tempest of hate with winds of vindictiveness had been blowing all around them. Their world ending. An immense sense of powerlessness must have prevailed. They chose to evade the gathering storm, hell-bent on living every last moment before it annihilated all they knew. Suddenly, this wasn't just an interesting archaeological site. It was as human and eerie as a sodden old tomb in some far corner of a forgotten cemetery.

Kati pressed her chest against my back and wrapped her arms around my waist. For a moment I'd forgotten she was there. I quickly picked up the tour. "See the old curbstones there in the shape of an octagon? That's the Leipziger Platz, where East Berliners pelted Soviet tanks with stones during the insurrection in 1953."

"Oh, *really?*" Kati whispered seductively in my ear. "How *very* interesting."

Just then she noticed the East German border guard in the tower staring at us through binoculars. "Fucking asshole," Kati said, letting me go. She turned squarely toward him sticking her middle finger up in the air with contempt. The guard picked up a camera and started taking pictures of us. None of that was unusual. It happened all the time. But for some reason it made Kati angry. She stood there next to me mumbling one blistering obscenity after another at the guard.

"Hey, it's nothing to get upset about," I said. "The worst that can happen is the next time you leave Berlin they'll try selling you a souvenir picture of yourself." Kati didn't get it or wasn't listening. She was too worked up.

"Why are you so angry?"

"Hanno, my husband; he's from East Berlin," she said bitterly. "His mother still lives there."

"He's from East Berlin? Really? How did he get out?" Even before she had a chance to answer I'd conjured up a vision of a desperate young man sprinting across the No Man's Land while dodging a hail of bullets.

"Oh, he left before the Wall," she said. "But I don't remember the details. I refuse to think about such things."

"You mean he just decided to leave and walked away? What a bore. Do you ever go over to visit?"

"No, I don't go. I hate it there. You always have the feeling you're being watched by some piece of shit like him," she said, motioning toward the guard tower with her chin. "It's depressing, especially where Hanno's mother lives in the Marzahn district. It's all big concrete boxes and it's all falling apart. Besides, she doesn't like me very much. I see her once or twice a year when she comes over. She is allowed to come over because she is old. They don't care if the old ones leave and don't go back. Otherwise, Hanno will visit her with Anja.

Kati asked if I knew anyone "over there." It was odd to even hear the question. For me that was another planet. Even the way we referred to it—*over there*—made it seem as if East Berlin were separated from us by an impassible natural divide. Of course it wasn't really impassible. I could go through the formal procedure and visit for a day. But how on earth would I know anyone *over there?* That was a realm reserved for Germans like Kati who happened to have a relative there.

"No, I don't know anyone in East Berlin. I've been over a couple of times but never met anybody. It doesn't seem possible, somehow. I'd like to meet some East Berliners, though. I'd like to see what all the propaganda has done to them, especially people our age who were born into it all. I think it would be interesting to talk to them about things, like the Wall, to see what they have to say about it."

I told Kati about a trip I had taken to the Soviet Union a few years earlier. I'd gotten into a discussion with a young *Intourist* guide who had been assigned to show me around Yerevan. The entire time she did nothing but spit out proclamations about great socialist achievements. I tried debating her about the political system, but it was impossible; she kept answering with the official line. I finally gave up and pulled out the old standard, "And what about the Berlin Wall? How can you defend that? If this is such a paradise, why do you have to wall people in to keep them from leaving?" She looked at me and said, "Why are you so sure the Wall isn't there to keep people out?" I let out a laugh that left her lamenting that Lenin had died too soon. "If only he had lived another five years," she said, as if none of this would have been necessary if he had.

"What do you do with people like that?" I asked Kati.

"People like that?" She laughed loudly, almost viciously. "What do you mean *like that?* What makes her different from anyone else?"

Kati had a talent for mocking a good part of humanity in a single phrase that left no doubt that, as far as she was concerned, everything was corrupt everywhere. It always bothered me. "People need that stuff," she continued. "What I need is to be close to someone, physically and emotionally. That's the best thing any of us can ever hope for."

Kati pulled herself close to me. I was thinking about responding with a snide remark about her husband sitting home alone with only a book to keep him company when she again spotted the guard in the tower still observing us through binoculars. "Asshole," she grumbled, throwing him an Italian salute.

We left the Potsdamer Platz and walked along the Wall to the Brandenburg Gate. The grim weather had sent most people away. The Reichstag had a huge West German flag flying from one of its four towers, its horizontal black, red and gold bars stretched in the wind. It was a display obviously meant to be as irritating to the other side as the East German flag that claimed the top of the Brandenburg Gate was meant to be to ours.

The section of the Wall that looped around the front of the Brandenburg Gate was not as high as the rest and about ten feet wide at the top. Directly in front of the most fortified border in the world stood an absurd official sign on a pole:

ACHTUNG!
YOU ARE NOW LEAVING
WEST BERLIN

Someone armed with a magic marker had scribbled the obvious question underneath: "How, then?"

From the top of the platform here we could see that one had been erected on the other side of the Wall. It was filled with school kids in their early teens. A soldier in a long gray coat was giving a lecture, pointing to the West while making large sweeping motions with his hand. The students stood motionless as they listened.

"What do you think he's telling them?" Kati asked.

"I bet he's giving them a history lesson."

The lecture was soon over. The students stood facing us, and we them. Kati cut the air with a big wave. There was no response. We both tried. They stood motionless, staring at us in the cold. Then Kati stuck two fingers in her mouth and blew an ear-splitting whistle that could have hailed a cab from as far away as Smolensk. "Hey, come on over!" she shouted in a display of rebellious spite directed at the students but aimed at the guards. "Come on over!" she repeated. They just stood there staring. The soldier finally ushered the students off the platform. Back on the pavement, the border guard handed the group over to another man who walked them up the Pariser Platz.

Suddenly a booming voice came out of nowhere, "*Sie da!*" It stunned us both with its intensity. "Sie da! You think this is some kind of a game?" It came from a fat bald man wearing a black trench coat at the foot of the platform's steps. "By what right, Miss, do you encourage those children to break the law?!" he shouted, pointing at Kati from below. She was confused, thrown off balance by the accusation.

"What? What are you talking about?" She said.

The man's face reddened. Still pointing at Kati, he shouted, "I've been standing here watching as you deliberately encouraged those children to break the laws of their country! By what right do you do that? By what right, Miss, do you encourage those children to cross the border?"

Kati stood there numb, not knowing what to say.

"The border is a disgrace," I said. "Everyone should have the right to cross it."

At that he started up the stairs, climbing nearly to the top before stopping. "I'm talking to the lady, not to you!" he yelled. A silent, tense moment followed. Finally, with an expression of scorn, he retreated down the stairs. When he got to the bottom he turned around and shouted, "I hope to God you have no children. You're not fit to mother a child!" Then he waddled swiftly away toward the Reichstag where his car was parked at the curb. It was over as suddenly as it had started.

I looked at Kati. She was shivering; her face fallen like a young girl who had just been scolded by her teacher. She turned away. "Hey, what's wrong? You let that guy upset you?" I was surprised when I saw her cheeks wet with tears.

"How dare he say that! I'm *not* a bad mother. I love my baby. He had no right to say something like that. I'd like to have ten more children!"

Kati turned glum after that. We walked past the white crosses, hand-cut memorials to people who'd been killed while trying to flee to the West, then further along the Wall to the river Spree. A guard in the watchtower just beyond the Wall began observing us through binoculars. I took Kati by the arm and led her into the Reichstag. The old parliament building was now a German history museum. I tried cheering her up, treating her to coffee and cake in the cafeteria and telling her a joke about the East German leader I'd heard from Ulrich:

"Erich Honecker gets out of bed bright and early every morning and has his daily conversation with the sun before driving to the Politburo. 'Good morning, Comrade Sun,' he says. 'What can you tell me today?' Every day the sun reports that the crops are flourishing, the factories are humming like finely tuned machines, the five-year plan will be met and the people are happy.

'Good morning, Comrade Sun, what can you tell me today?'

"The sun reports that the people are content, socialism is working and the capitalists are faltering. Every morning it's the same; Comrade Sun glows with a more beautiful picture each day. Then one morning, Honecker oversleeps and has to rush out of his dacha without talking to the sun. Later that evening when he gets home from work, he stands out on his porch and asks the setting sun, 'Well? What can you tell me today, Comrade Sun?' The sun replies, 'Get lost, asshole. I'm in the West now!' "

Kati forced a smile, then said she had to go. She seemed fatally stricken by the obese stranger's attack on her motherhood. I put her in a taxi and she promised to call. At that moment I doubted that she would.

A Melody without Lyrics

NEVERTHELESS, A COUPLE OF DAYS later she did call, again her high-spirited self. The incident at the Brandenburg Gate was forgotten and never again mentioned. We got together for dinner and a movie. Kati was determined to see a film that was showing at a theater near the Südstern, not too far from where I lived. It was a French art film with unending bedroom discussions and lonesome walks on windswept Normandy cliffs that seemed to go on for hours, just as I feared it might. Through it all, Kati kept looking over at me with an expression that asked if I'd had enough. But since she was the one who insisted on seeing it, I was resolved to make her sit through every minute of it. Afterwards we took a walk. Before long we were standing in front of my apartment building. We stood there in the doorway next to the landlady's bedroom window as I whispered stories about my neighbors; about my horrifying experience with the landlady's ancient face; about Bernd the gossip and his *"Na!";* Frau Meyer-Burkhardt, the merry widow, and Frau Eppert's prostitute granddaughter and Otto Dix. Kati listened with her arms around my waist and her head against my chest, occasionally whispering, *"Oh, Mann," "Ach, meine Gute!"* or just suppressing a giggle. When I finished talking she looked up at me with those red roller-coaster lips shining in the dim light while her unblinking, open expression made it clear that she would accept any advance. And it was cold; Kati made no secret of the fact that she was shivering.

"Do you want to come upstairs?"

"I thought you were never going to ask," she said.

In my apartment I uncorked a bottle of wine. We sat on my sofa and drank, making conversation about the movie we had seen and about the food we had eaten. In the middle of a sentence Kati let out a sneeze that made the tiny gold pin launch itself like a rocket from the side of her nose. We spent a good ten minutes on our hands and knees combing the floor before finding it. "Happens every time," she said in between a couple of sniffles as she pushed the pin back into its tiny hole. "I should be more careful. I'd hate to lose this thing." Back on the sofa, Kati quickly finished her wine, reached over for the bottle on the coffee table and topped off my glass before refilling her own. She kicked off her shoes, curled up next to me with her head on my shoulder and said, as if to no one in particular, "I feel like doing something nice."

"You feel like doing something nice?" I repeated, looking into my glass, swirling my wine. "Nice like eating something that's bad for you? Or nice like something good for humanity?"

She looked at me smiling, "I feel like doing something . . . *nice.*"

Of course I knew what she was getting at. But until that point in my life I had always avoided sleeping with married women. There were certainly enough opportunities in Münster, which seemed to have an abundance of bored, married women. But I declined them. I couldn't even tell you why. It certainly wasn't for religious reasons; I had never been a religious person. And if there was indeed a Hell to burn in one day I could count a dozen other offenses that would send me there. (Make that a baker's dozen: I never paid *Kirchensteuer*. The German government, not content to leaving the financing of faith to the uncertainties of a collection plate, collected six percent of one's total income tax for the Church. Not paying meant excommunication and, I suppose, eternal damnation. Although I would have to check with my district tax office to see if that also applied to holders of foreign passports.) I guess I was really holding onto the last vestige of a middle-class upbringing that counted honesty and decency as virtues, not impediments to success. All the previous illusions from my childhood had long since been demolished. This single thread was my last link with the past. Cutting it might somehow banish me into the dark cavity of absolute alienation.

"You want dessert?" I said. "I have Rote Grütze."

Kati gave me a sly grin, as though she had just been offered a dare. She got up off the sofa and walked over to the bookcase against the opposite wall, looking over the spines on one of the shelves. All the books on it were about Berlin.

"Ach! Berlin, Berlin, Berlin," she said in a voice mixed with melancholy and exasperation. She pulled a couple of titles halfway out, looking at the covers before sliding them back in again. Then Kati pulled out a large photo book, *Berlin aus der Luft*, and started flipping through the pages. I put down my wine and walked over.

"That's a great one. You can see the way the city looked from the air in the 1920s and 30s, and the way the same areas look today. Some of the earlier pictures were taken from zeppelins." I took the book from her and turned to the appropriate photographs. "Look, you can see their shadows on the ground."

Kati walked leisurely out of the living room without responding. I followed, book in hand. She stood at the entrance to the kitchen and turned on the light. "You didn't give me the apartment tour."

"Oh, sorry. I didn't think . . . This is the kitchen . . . As you see."

"Yes, I see," she replied. Then she did what I hoped she wouldn't do—she took a look in the refrigerator. Its emptiness embarrassed me.

"I haven't had time to go shopping. Everything closes so early in Germany."

Kati pulled the aluminum foil off the Chinese food still fermenting within and winced. "Why don't you throw that away?" she said, switching off the light and going directly across the hall where she made a short inspection of the bathroom.

Then Kati walked over to the bedroom. She switched on the light and stood in the doorway.

"Is that your bedroom?"

"Yes."

"Is that your bed?"

"Yes."

"I would like to go there and do some nice things with you."

She took the book from my hand, tossed it on the floor and began kissing me. The loneliness I had for so long tried my best to avoid seeing was quickly dissolving. I had absolutely no desire to spend another night alone and could feel any misgivings separating from me, ripping like burlap, slowly at first then faster and faster until the weight of any uncertainty just fell away. "I think you have a zeppelin in your pants. Can that be?"

"The Hindenburg," I confessed.

Early the next morning I was woken by cold drops of water landing on my face. My eyes fluttered open to see Kati hovering over me, gently rubbing the back of her wet head with a towel. She had just taken a shower and was sitting on the side of the bed in my bathrobe, staring down at me with an inquisitive expression.

"Don't tell me you feel bad about this," she said. "You don't have to you know."

I didn't answer. A couple of minutes later she was dressed and out the door. Then I waited. I waited for pangs of guilt. They weren't there. I fell asleep for another hour or so and woke up again to just another day. My only feelings were of annoyed regret for the opportunities I had forsaken in the past. It was somewhat disappointing; in its way even more disturbing than the remorse I had feared. Two days later, Kati called and asked if I'd like to see her again. I said, "Sure I would."

After that we started seeing each other two or three times a week. Having Kati in bed was like sleeping with pure lust. She made certain that the other tenants in the building, lying alone in their beds at night, heard sensations of raw sex.

Libidinous friction so hot the apartment was in perpetual danger of erupting in a dazzling flash of spontaneous combustion that could incinerate the entire district. If this is the way *ordentliche Menschen* raise their daughter, I thought, then I've been seeing the wrong women.

Whenever she spent the night, Kati would somehow always, without the aid of an alarm clock, wake up by six o'clock so she could be home by six-thirty. Sometimes, on those nights when we didn't plan to meet, she would stop by my apartment at three o'clock in the morning, smelling of sweat and cigarette smoke after several hours of dancing at one or another discotheque. She would take a shower, throw on my bathrobe, rush into the bedroom, jump on top of me full of goose bumps, and make all kinds of physical demands. Then, like clockwork at six o'clock in the morning, no matter how little she had slept, Kati would be off home, wide-awake and in the best of moods. She was a bundle of kinetic energy; a lit fuse that never seemed to reach a destination.

At the very beginning of the affair I made a couple of simple resolutions to myself. One was not to become involved with her daughter. I had visions of meeting Kati and her husband on the street and hearing the little girl say, "Papa, that's the other man who sleeps with Mutti in the same bed." Then one day, a week or so after that first night, Kati paid me a surprise visit with Anja. Soon I was meeting them both for a day at the zoo or an afternoon at the movies. I was struck by their relationship. It seemed less a mother-daughter arrangement than that of a child and her nanny. Anja, for example, almost never referred to her mother as *Mutti*, but almost always as Kati. I once asked Kati if her daughter slept the whole night through. She told me Anja often woke up at two o'clock in the morning looking for her, and if she wasn't there it could often be a problem for her husband. "She used to go on crying for an hour, sometimes even two. Now, when she wakes up and sees that I'm not there, she just asks Hanno if you and I are having a beer together. All Hanno has to do is say, '*Ja*.' Then she rolls over and just goes back to sleep. As long as she thinks I'm having a beer together with you, it's all right that I'm not there."

"You mean your husband knows about me?"

"Of course. Hanno knows about all of my friends."

Hanno knew about all of her friends? Strange. But I didn't see any point in asking unpleasant questions just when I had become comfortable with the relationship. Her remark just reinforced my second resolution: that I would never allow myself to meet her husband.

Early one afternoon, I went to pick up Kati and Anja at their home for a fresh air excursion out to the Wannsee. She and her husband had a large apartment in a beautiful prewar building in one of the more exclusive tree-lined streets near the Savignyplatz. I had met them there two or three times before, each time her husband had been at work. I arrived and pressed the bell on the street. Kati's harried voice came over the intercom, "Ja? Hallo?"

"It's me." I was buzzed in, jogged up the three flights to her apartment and knocked on the door expecting the usual: a flustered Kati throwing open the door while a half-dressed Anja sat on the living room floor playing with toys. But this time a man came to the door. He was of medium height with short, graying blond hair combed straight forward, a gray goatee and was carrying a copy of *National Geographic* magazine in his hand. For a moment I thought I was at the wrong apartment. Then the obvious occurred to me—he was the husband. The only time I'd seen him until then was in photographs that Kati had shown me. He looked older in person, fatter around the middle. I stood there frozen, not knowing what to say or do. Hanno smiled. He actually seemed to be enjoying the situation.

"Hello, Richard. Good to meet you," he said cordially in English while shaking my hand as if we were old friends.

He closed the door behind me. Kati stuck her head out from Anja's bedroom, "Take a seat, we'll be right there." Anja herself jumped out into the hallway, topless, and sung out, "Haal-*loo*, Rik-*ard*," before Kati hurried her, giggling, back into the bedroom.

"I'm afraid Anja took an extra-long nap today," Hanno said before offering me a drink from a cabinet filled with bottles. I declined. "You're sure?" I said I was. There was no way for me to hide the fact that I was uncomfortable. On my other visits here, I had no qualms about taking a seat in front of the TV or raiding the kitchen as if it all belonged to me; an attitude encouraged by Kati constantly asking me to look for things for her in this closet or that cupboard. But now with Hanno here, just standing in the living room made me feel as if I were invading the most inner sanctum of his life; I didn't want to move from the spot unless given permission. He tried making conversation by talking about the weather, which didn't work too well. Then he asked where I came from in the U.S. I told him. When he saw that I was having trouble loosening up, he said, "I understand you're interested in Berlin history." He motioned for me to follow him. "I want to show you something you'll like."

Hanno led me into his study. This was the one room I'd never been in because the door was always locked. We walked over to his desk. Above it was a large, weathered placard in a frame—a picture of a finger-pointing Walter Ulbricht, the General Secretary of the East German Communist Party at the time the Berlin Wall was erected. On it was a quote from an infamous press conference he had given: "Nobody has the intention of building a wall!"

"Isn't that great?" Hanno asked. "Ulbricht said that in June, barely two months before they closed the border, and the West made sure nobody forgot it. They had these signs posted all over western territory at the same time workmen were building the Wall. An American friend gave it to me before he got shipped back stateside. He collected so many trinkets during his tour that he couldn't get them all home with him."

Hanno was going out of his way to make me feel comfortable. He seemed so sincerely concerned about my uneasiness that his efforts were soon having the desired effect. I complimented him on his placard and asked him questions about some small model airplanes he kept on his desk. Then Kati called from Anja's bedroom and Hanno excused himself.

I stood there looking at a sea of small, framed photographs that were hung on the wall; pictures of Kati and Hanno in different parts of the world. In all of them I could see in Kati's face a familiar momentary annoyance, presumably at having to stop and be photographed. I'd seen glimpses of that same split-second irritation many times. It was always there, just a scratch below the surface. Three or four other photographs, probably from the mid-1960s, showed a young Hanno together with airmen in American and British uniforms. When Hanno returned, we picked up the conversation about the model airplanes just where we had left off while I waited for Kati to finish piling layers of clothing on Anja.

Finally, Kati shouted from the living room, "Okay, we're ready to go!"

I was suddenly confronted with the unpleasant predicament of having to excuse myself from Hanno while I made off with his wife and daughter. In a pitifully desperate attempt to try and convince him that I had nothing to hide, I asked Hanno if he wanted to join us. I felt awkward immediately after suggesting it, but then Kati walked in from the living room carrying Anja and, without missing a beat, encouraged him to come along. "Oh, come on, you never get any fresh air," she said in English. Hanno thought it over, stroking his short beard as if pondering a chess move, then agreed, "Ja, gut. I could use some air."

We took Hanno's car. I sat up front while he drove; Kati sat in the rear next to Anja, buckled into her child safety seat. On the way we passed a road sign for the American Forces officers' golf course and yacht club. It gave Hanno a thrill. "You ever been to these places, Richard? . . . No? Wow, that's too bad. They're great facilities. You *Amis* really do good by your military."

It turned out that Hanno was a real America fan. It was the Americans who taught him to fly and, as I had seen from the pictures on his wall, he had spent long stretches at a U.S. air base in Texas. Hanno told me he still had many friends there although, to his disappointment, he hadn't been able to get back in nearly ten years. I found it somehow reassuring, given the history of Berlin since World War II, that the only native Berliner I could remember meeting turned out to be so pro-American. At least something of our past was indeed real and tucked securely away from present realities. But Hanno was apparently of that age. From what I knew from Kati, I figured that he had to be about forty-seven years old. That meant that he was about six years old during the time of the Berlin airlift. An impressionable age. But then Hanno did, after all, grow up in the Soviet sector. I couldn't imagine that he would have absorbed anything good about the airlift or the Americans.

Then he proudly told me that he saw JFK make his famous *"Ich bin ein Berliner"* speech here in 1963. "I still remember those words like it was yesterday, *'All free men, wherever they may live, are citizens of Berlin. And, therefore, as a free man, I take pride in the words: ich bin ein Berliner.'* God, there were thousands of people there listening to him, and I don't think more than a few understood English. But when he said that last line, 'I am a Berliner,' you could imagine the reaction. I remember very well the delirious cheering. Some people actually fell into each other's arms and cried. They were able to take all the solace they needed from those last four words. Not abandoned. Not alone. It's really astonishing when you think about it, isn't it? I mean, the effect a few words can have on so many people when they are desperate."

At the Havel I played the third wheel while Hanno carried Anja or walked with his arm around Kati as we strolled along the large lake. Hanno told me about his childhood in 1950s Berlin. What he described was almost unimaginable now: Berlin at a time when the border was still fluid; when the line separating two worlds was no more than a white stripe painted on the pavement. A time when thousands fled the eastern sector every week, filling refugee centers in West Berlin, while thousands more crossed the line between the East and West daily with no motive other than to go to work or to do a little shopping. Those going east referred to it as "going to Russia." Yet, it was also a city where people wanted for political reasons by the communists could be kidnapped off the street in the West Berlin, only to vanish forever into Soviet gulags or unmarked graves.

I looked over at the far bank of the lake where the Berlin Wall stood strung out before its accompanying square watchtowers. On the water, colored buoys marked an exclusion zone. As Hanno spoke, an East German military patrol boat cut through the water causing the buoys to rock violently in its wake. A cool, gray mist hung over the far bank, giving this section of the Wall a much more menacing appearance than that which cut through the city center, adorned with its colorful and harmless graffiti. Here it seemed real.

Hanno told me that on the day they built the Wall, he was a twenty-one-year-old university student on his way to Italy for a holiday. "I was studying engineering at the time. Even in those days, engineering students were not allowed to travel directly to the West Germany as tourists. We were considered too important to the economy to risk being lost to the West Germans. The simple solution was to walk to West Berlin and fly out to Frankfurt. That took most of my funds so I had to start hitchhiking toward Italy. I picked up a ride near Ulm and the first thing this guy asks me is if I knew about the Wall. I hadn't seen a newspaper in days. Wall? What Wall? He turned on his radio and suddenly the world was turned upside down."

"Must have been a shock."

"Sure it was. But you know what was most striking? That a lot of the West Germans I met at the time were actually pleased about the Wall. It meant the East German population was being kept in East Germany, and that after reunification— people still thought in those terms back then—the West Germans would inherit an East Zone still populated by Germans and not Poles, Bulgarians, Romanians or whatever other groups the communists would have been forced to bring in to run the factories and do the other things that need doing. Back then nobody would have ever dreamed that the Wall would still be here almost thirty years later."

"Well, maybe we'll see some changes sometime soon," I said, trying to sound upbeat.

"Changes? Well, everything changes sooner or later. That's the only certainty, as they say. Things finally are moving in the right direction, anyway. Something is bound to give one of these days. I won't be here to see it but my little angel here will," he said picking up his giggling daughter and giving her a big hug.

That was the common consensus. *Glasnost* and *Perestroika* let people see rays of hope in a world that had, for decades, been happy enough just to maintain a status quo and not blow itself to smithereens. I remembered seeing a leading West German politician give a campaign speech in Münster the previous year. He railed against the Green Party for caring more about potato chips than computer chips before launching into a harangue about how it was important to hold the course. "Things are moving in the right direction," he said. "I won't be around to see the day the Wall comes down, but I have children who will certainly see big changes someday."

Big changes someday. It was like a popular song title; a melody without lyrics that everyone could sing their own version of.

As the afternoon wore on I got to like Hanno. I imagined that in the future, it wouldn't be unusual for me to pick up Kati at their apartment, feeling as if I was picking up a date with Hanno assuming the role of a father figure in my mind rather than husband. A whole scenario unfolded in my head. I would arrive and try to linger as long as possible, sometimes even showing up early so that I would have time to talk with him. He would offer me drinks, we would talk about Berlin history, trade books and tidbits of information on the subject. We would become good friends.

At one point during our stroll, Anja said she had to use the *Klo* and Kati took her into a nearby public toilet. Hanno and I waited at a wooden picnic table. Suddenly, despite all the soothing thoughts about our future relationship that had been going through my mind just a few minutes earlier, I hated being alone with him. It was impossible for me to look Hanno in the eyes. I turned my attention to the Berlin Wall on the far bank of the lake. But then I began to feel a little guilty, so I finally looked at him and said, "It must be a lot of fun . . . being married to Kati."

I was in the presence of a stranger. Hanno wasn't the same calm, confident person with whom I had spent most of the afternoon. He stood there with one foot up on a picnic bench looking thoroughly fatigued as he rummaged through a soft pack of cigarettes with his finger before pulling out the last one, crumpling the empty pack and tossing it contemptuously at a nearby garbage can.

"Yeah," he answered as he took his first long drag. "A lot of fun. I'll tell you one thing for sure: she's gonna keep me young. That's why I married her." He was smiling now. Severe nicotine fit, I thought. He probably doesn't like smoking around his daughter. A few minutes later, when Kati and Anja returned, Hanno was able to pull himself together in an instant, stamping out his cigarette and hurrying over to take Anja from Kati's arms. As it turned out, that afternoon was the first and last time I ever saw Hanno.

The whole situation seemed a little strange, but I never once questioned Kati about their relationship. They obviously had some kind of understanding, the particulars of which I didn't want to hear about. It was the same sort of feeling I had about my job; learning too much about it would just get me more involved, sucking me in so that it would be impossible to get out. For me, it was entirely comfortable the way it was. Kati was usually fun to have around and unbelievable in bed. Our outings with Anja were pleasant enough. For the first time in my life, I could imagine what it would be like to have my own family, and without fear of forfeiting my youth. When I tired of playing family man, or on those fairly rare occasions when Anja would take a crying fit the way three-year-olds can, I could just walk away with some vague excuse, like I had a lot of work to do. Then, I'd sit myself in a café somewhere and peacefully read the newspaper, lighthearted and pleased to know that they weren't my burden twenty-four hours-a-day, every day. For Kati, though, it may have been different. Mornings before going home, she would cover me with kisses while I slept. I would brush her away with my hand and she'd look up at the ceiling and sigh, *"Oh, es muss die Liebe sein!"* But it was very clear to me that it all had nothing to do with love. Kati had a need for everything in her life to be extreme, including her relationships, her joy and her pain. Now threatened by the ordinariness of her marriage and the anchor of motherhood, she was desperate for any kind of diversion. So if exultation had to be invented now and then, well, so what? A little harmless illusion could never hurt anyone.

One night at the end of February, I decided to take Kati around to the Troika to meet the crowd. She had never been there before. She came by my apartment and rang the bell; I met her downstairs and we walked over. The place was full as usual. We made our way to the back and found Torsten, Ulrich and Anne sitting around at the usual table. We had to hunt for an extra chair, finally having one sent to us over the heads of seated patrons. I sat next to Ulrich. He leaned over with a smirk on his face and asked, "New girlfriend?" That was strange to hear. Even in my own mind I never thought of this married mother as a "girlfriend."

"No, just a friend," I said.

He wasn't convinced, leaning back in his chair with one raised eyebrow. "No wonder you haven't been around," he said, as if I'd just implicated myself in some shady dealings.

As was usually the case in Germany, nobody bothered introducing themselves. That was a practice reserved for more formal occasions. Kati commandeered the waitress and the table ordered a round of drinks. Then she peeled off her long coat, exposing every curve in a mini-dress that fit her like a piece of industrial-strength Saran Wrap. The roundness of her breasts, like two ripe cantaloupes that somehow defied gravity, immediately drew astonished double takes and stares.

"Geoffrey's not here tonight?" I asked with an overly unconcerned air. It even took a moment for the normally neutered Torsten to answer. "He's washing his hands," he said, his eyes fixed on Kati. (Geoffrey's code of conduct dictated that he could never speak the words "toilet' or "men's room." He would always excuse himself saying he needed to "wash his hands.") A quick shake of the head brought Torsten back to himself, "So, you have a new President," he said. "What do you think about him?"

Yes, a presidential inauguration had taken place. For me, what would once have seemed like a monumental event was now a minor drama.

"About George Bush? Not much . . . other than for a man without a spine he's got pretty good posture." Everyone laughed.

Geoffrey came back to the table and patted me on the shoulder. "Richard, good to see you," then added, "Have you been away?" Before I could answer, his eyes started darting around as if he had misplaced something. I had taken his seat.

"Oh, sorry," I said, offering him the chair back. He insisted I stay seated. There was a short commotion while we looked for another chair.

No sooner were we all settled when there came a shout from across the room, "Kati! . . . Kati Weber!"

An Indian-looking guy was standing, waving from his table in the corner.

"*Farooq!*" Kati jumped from her seat, hurried over and gave him a big kiss and a hug. She spoke with him for several minutes. Everyone at the table except Ulrich was watching her.

"It's so typical," Ulrich said, ignoring Kati's bolting from the table, as if she had somehow proven herself unworthy of his attention. "The Americans are gunning themselves down left and right, people are terrified to walk the streets, and they elect someone who brags about being a card-carrying member of the gun lobby. I think the entire population has gone nuts."

Geoffrey taunted Ulrich by saying he'd watched the inaugural on AFN. "He seems serious about the drug problem," he said. Then he leaned toward me and asked, "Who's the woman, Richard?"

"A friend of mine," I said. "I know her husband."

"She's married then, is she?" I nodded. "All *right*," he said under his breath, apparently crossing her off a list in his head.

That surprised me. I'd never suspected that Geoffrey's numbers game took moral questions into consideration. Then he leaned toward me again and asked, "You wouldn't mind if I gave her a go then, would you?"

"What?"

"Your friend. You wouldn't mind if I gave her a go."

I didn't answer, but in my mind I was busy cursing the skinny shit for wanting to hit on the woman I'd shown up with.

Kati gave Farooq another hug as if she were taking leave of him. Then he took both her hands, pulled her close and said something in her ear to which she responded by giving him yet another hug and a kiss on the cheek. She was on her way back when she was grabbed by the arm. "*Ach, Nasser! You, here?*" Again there was a big hug and more conversation.

"If you really believe any of that inaugural bullshit, Biggs, you're brain damaged," Ulrich said, annoyed by our preoccupation. "I guarantee you that in four years all the same problems, including the drug-addicted society, will still be there, only worse. You can't solve problems of that size by telling people to '*just say no.*' It only proves that nobody in the U.S. government, from the president down, is interested in problem solving. They're only interested in playing to the crowd. I guarantee you that it won't be long before Bush is here in Berlin, having is picture taken at the Wall saying, 'Oh look, what a terrible thing, vote for me.'"

As Ulrich spoke, I watched Kati leave Nasser. She was again on her way back when she was caught once more, this time by a big African man wearing a colorful dashiki and a knit skullcap. More kisses, hugs and conversation followed. I couldn't help wondering if she'd slept with all these men. For the first time since I'd known her, I experienced feelings of jealousy.

Until this point, I had always assumed that I was the one in firm control of the relationship. I was the one with the official stamp of approval from her husband. I wondered if these guys were the other "friends" that Hanno knew all about, and if maybe his shakes at the picnic table by the lake had been something other than a nicotine fit. I became instantly resentful of her; of the way she decided to dress herself, the way she bounced from one table to the next dishing out hugs and kisses to these people, as if they could possibly be unaware of her curves, or her cantaloupes, as she stood carelessly chatting away.

She was on her way back. I pretended not to notice, leaning into the table, listening to Ulrich deliver his lecture on the hopelessness of American society.

"It's an unfortunate fact," Ulrich declared, "that the only thing there's any real respect for in America is celebrity. You can be considered a respected authority on anything if you are a two-bit actor in some failed television series. Just watch the evening news over there; you'll see it in one commercial after another. Some guy you know you've seen before on TV but don't remember where will be telling you what kind of food to feed your dog. Two minutes later, the same guy is telling you what medication to take if you can't shit. How do you think Ronald Reagan became president?"

"I'm not sure it was by telling people what to do should they become clogged, old man," Geoffrey said, thoughtfully scratching his chin as if he were going to elaborate but saying nothing.

Kati pulled up a chair behind mine and put her arm around my neck. Everyone at the table was staring at her. "Oh, there you are," I said, as if I hadn't noticed where she'd gone.

Ignoring everyone else, she put her lips close to my ear. "I just met some friends here. You see that guy in the corner? That's Farooq. His father has the biggest toothpaste factory in all Pakistan. And the guy at the table there in the middle? That's Nasser, from Iran. He was an aide-de-camp to the Shah. And the black guy there? That's Mobou. He's a dessert chef. You really must to try his tarte tatain sometime."

"Can't you have any *Aryan* friends?" I said, trying to hide my bitterness.

"Well, well," Kati whispered, pleased with herself. "Are you perhaps a little jealous?" I removed her arm from my neck and was saved from coming up with an answer by Ulrich and his determination to dominate the conversation. Besides, it wasn't any of her business, anyway. She was married.

"Look," Ulrich droned on. "There are more people, especially young people, more . . . *damaged* in America now than at any time in its history. Just look at what's going on! Name one European society that has produced the kind of underclass monsters that the Americans have. It's the most savage form of capitalism you can imagine; it feeds off future generations for quick profits today. Forget it," he said with a disgusted wave of his hand. "It's over."

At that point when the table, tired of the subject, had lapsed into numbed silence, Kati cheerfully said, "I would like to visit America sometime."

"Oh, really?" asked Ulrich. "And why is that?"

"I would like to see it, that's all."

"But why? You'll go there, rent a car, drive for days from one end of the continent to the other, and in the end it's just another hamburger."

"Don't be such an asshole," she said with disgust. "I want to see it, and why I want to see it is none of your goddamned business. It's a scandal that I haven't been there yet."

Ulrich stared for a moment. "On second thought, I think you should," he said in a patronizing tone. "I think every European school child should be required to spend a month in the U.S.A. as a warning to each future generation."

Kati shot him a look that drove a stake through the monster's heart, yet he wouldn't die.

It was at that point that Geoffrey decided to make his move. "Pardon me. Uh . . . would you be fond of Thackeray?"

Kati looked at him in bland bewilderment, "Are you talking to me?"

Before Geoffrey could respond, there was another call, this time from the bar, "Kati Weber!"

"Hey, Klaus!" Again she bolted from the table leaving me and Geoffrey staring at each other.

"Biggs," Ulrich declared, sitting back in his chair and shaking his head with a satisfied grin on his face. "You're as appealing as gum disease."

This time the call came from the drunkard at the end of the bar of all people. As Kati rushed over to him, he tried to stand up and fell backwards against the wall. Recovering, he settled back onto his bar stool. They embraced. Kati stood there sympathetically stroking his cheek while he spoke to her.

A couple of minutes later, Kati called after me, "Richard, come here!" I joined her and her inebriated friend at the bar. "This is Klaus. You told me once that you wanted to meet East Germans, remember? Klaus is . . . I mean . . . *was* one." Klaus took his arm from around Kati's waist and shook my hand. He was wearing his alcoholic smile and his eyes were, as always, half-closed, lids heavy with beer.

"So, you come from the East?" I asked.

He stifled a belch with his hand. Kati moved over to me, putting her arm around my waist. I was still angry at the idea of her having slept with every third man in the Troika, so I freed myself by lifting myself onto a bar stool. "Actually," Klaus started, "I'm from Dresden. You know Dresden? But I had been living in East Berlin for a while before I . . . before . . . I . . . um . . . decided to leave."

"And how did you leave? Were you free to go?"

"Ah, free to go." he said. Kati let out a giggle at that. "No, I wasn't free to go." Klaus stared down into his half-empty beer glass. It seemed that he was trying to be unnecessarily mysterious. In my sour mood I was already losing patience with him. Then he looked up and said, "Perhaps you know the incident. It was reported in the press at the time. In July, 1986, there was a bomb attack on the Berlin Wall. Some crazy West German group. They blew a hole about a two square meters right through it. Really crazy," he said shaking his head.

I did remember it—a group called the *Berlin Kommando* claimed responsibility. The East German government labeled the attack "a grave provocation."

"Ja! That was it," Klaus said excitedly. "They must have been some bunch of really . . . just crazy guys. Well, the Wall of course had to be repaired. And of course, no one is allowed to do any work on the Wall unless they are accompanied by armed border guards. At that time, I was one of the *Grenztruppen*." He was again looking down into his beer, shaking his head with a smile on his face. "There were three guards watching over two work troops; one on the eastern side of the Wall, one on the western side, and one up on a ladder watching both sides. I was the one on the western side. Three of the concrete segments had to be replaced. Just as they lowered the last one, I ran. I don't even know why. I just threw down my gun, turned around and ran like hell. I ran about a half a block down the Charlottenstrasse and looked back from behind a parked car. I saw the workman and the guard on the ladder staring. They were dumbfounded. I myself was dumbfounded. I don't even know why I did it. It was just a chance, and in a flash it was done."

"Wasn't it something you had been thinking about doing?"

"No. No, it wasn't. I used to sometimes dream about defeating the system; about going over the Wall and looking around. I knew where some of the weak points were. But it was kind of a game or a dream. Until then I'd never really considered leaving. I mean, sooner or later I think everyone thinks about it, the way just about everyone thinks about suicide at one time or another. But I never seriously planned leaving the GDR. Why should I want to leave?"

"Why?" I was at a loss. It was the first time I'd actually met an East German, one who had gone over the Wall no less, and he was defending the GDR. Until then, the only people I had ever met with good things to say about East Germany were trendy leftists who enjoyed singing the praises of the socialist state, but of course preferred living in the West. I rattled off the usual, "Freedom, Klaus. Freedom to travel, to speak your mind. All the usual things people leave for. Maybe you wanted those things more than you thought."

"*Quatsch*," he said in disgust, again looking into his beer before downing the remainder and holding the glass up over his head so that Rolf could see it was empty. "It was just that I found myself outside the Wall for the first time . . ."

"Actually," I interrupted, "you were *inside* the Wall."

"What?" He was momentarily confused.

"You mean inside. The Wall surrounds West Berlin. East Germans are on the outside."

"You're right," Klaus conceded immediately. "In any case, once I was on *this side* of the Wall, all kinds of strange thoughts were going through my head. It occurred to me that it was an opportunity that a hell of a lot people wanted to have. And I probably would never have such an easy chance again in my life. I started thinking about all the precautions they constantly took with us, like switching our patrol partners every two days so we didn't get too friendly, and I just went. I don't know why. I just ran. Just a knee-jerk reaction. It was as if someone else was doing the running for me and I was just along for the ride. It never even occurred to me at that moment that I would never be able to go back again. I didn't realize that until I was standing there behind a parked car watching the workman hand the border guard my rifle and then climb back up the ladder. Only then did I know what I had done; when they all disappeared."

"You seem to regret it," I said as Rolf the bartender put another large half-liter beer in front of Klaus.

"I wouldn't do the same thing again."

"Do you really dislike it so much here?"

"*Scheiss* elbow society," he said with contempt dripping like sweat from his face. "All they care about here is money. That's all anyone thinks about. Money and being envied by their neighbors. At least in the East it is the personal relationships that are most important. So they can't drive a big Mercedes, or go to Ibiza on holiday twice a year. At least they don't have to work themselves sick just to pay for the rent and the other things they need just to live."

That seemed wildly overblown. In nearly four years of living in Germany, I hadn't yet met anyone who worked themselves particularly hard. Generating prosperity was the job of those anonymous souls flying frantically over the Autobahn in powerful cars, and maybe of Herr Arp, stressed out servicing his two big machines like one of those exhausted underground workers in *Metropolis*. Most of the people I knew were surviving by living off the generous West German state or doing odd jobs from time to time. And like every worker in the country, they all took their six-week vacations every year, without fail.

"I have to tell you, Klaus, I can't say I find it all that harsh here. Why don't you try another part of Germany? Move to another city?"

"It takes money, like everything else here. I don't have any."

"What money do you need? Just pick a city and go. Who's going to stop you?"

"First, I am a deserter from the National People's Army. At the border I would certainly be arrested. Do you really think a West German passport can save me once I cross over the line?"

He was looking at me, waiting for an answer. "No, I guess not."

"No, you guess not," he mimicked with sarcasm. "The only way I can get out of West Berlin is to fly out. That alone is more money than I can imagine. And then, where the hell would I go? You people think everything is so easy." Klaus excused himself and staggered away to the men's room.

In the mirror behind the bar I noticed Kati standing next to me, staring back with a sulking expression on her face. "Hey, what's going on?" I asked.

"What's going on with you?" she answered, upset at being ignored, immediately making me feel childish for my wounded ego.

"Your friend is an interesting case. How do you know him?"

"Through Hanno. In his spare time he used to volunteer for an organization that helps East German refugees adjust to the West. He brought Klaus home for dinner a couple of times."

"It doesn't look like they did a very good job with him—helping him adjust, I mean. He's a pretty bitter guy."

"He's no more bitter than anyone else here tonight. Besides, it's his own fault. Why doesn't the guy just get on with his life? He is enrolled in the university, but he doesn't attend classes. He has no money because all he does is drive a taxi just enough to pay his expenses. If he doesn't like it here, he should leave. All he does instead is drink himself stupid and complain, 'Oh, poor me!' So typical. I've got no time for people like that. All that crap about not knowing why he ran away? He did it because he was depressed and angry that his girlfriend left him for the local butcher."

"How do you know that?"

"I know it because he told me once. Now he acts like it's all a big mystery. Come on, let's go home."

"What about Klaus? You want to leave before he comes back?"

"So what? He's too drunk to remember we were here."

Klaus came slowly back to the bar and picked up his beer, ready to resume conversation. Kati told him that we had to leave.

"You have to go? . . . Now?" he asked, visibly disappointed. Klaus wrestled briefly with the cuff of his worn denim jacket and took hold of his watch, holding it up to the light. "But it's still early. Rolf will normally stay open until two o'clock."

"I have to get home. Anja wakes up early, you know." The excuse satisfied Klaus. He took Kati in his arms and smiled. "Be sure to say hello to Hanno for me."

"I will. And it was nice seeing you again." Kati broke free of his grip and grabbed me by the arm. She was determined not to spend another minute in the Troika. But I wasn't ready to go. And her self-centered behavior had begun to make me resentful again, especially after she'd just made me feel juvenile by provoking my jealousy.

"It's only eleven o'clock," I said. "We can stay a little longer." I thought I'd bring Klaus over to the table and introduce him to the others. He agreed without hesitation, immediately standing up, beer glass in hand, ready to move. I led him to the back. Kati followed reluctantly.

"Hey, we have a special guest tonight," I declared to a group of expressionless faces as I moved over a couple of chairs. "This is Klaus, an East German border guard who came over the Wall." The faces remained expressionless. The meaning of what I'd said hadn't sunk in. I had Klaus tell his story, which he did like a man forced to confess a crime to an attorney he hoped would defend him in court. After he'd finished, there was a moment of blank stares, then a general reaction of amused disbelief.

Klaus suddenly seemed relatively sober and was thoroughly enjoying the attention being heaped upon him. Ulrich summoned the waitress and briefly told her the tale. She in turn told Rolf who stood watching us with a surprised smile glued to his face. Evidently he hadn't known the history of the guy slouching over the end of his bar night after night. The waitress returned with a bottle of sekt, a gift from the house. Rolf even joined us at the table for a few minutes to get the story firsthand. We all saluted Klaus, the hero of the evening. Geoffrey unintentionally put a damper on our mood by asking Klaus if he might have known the border guard who, just a week before, had shot and killed a young East German man trying to flee over the Wall to the West. Klaus no longer read newspapers and didn't own a radio or television. At first he said he didn't believe it had happened, but confirmations from each of us forced him to accept the fact. He then became nervously defensive, saying that the death toll at the Wall and the inner-German border would be much higher if the border guards had been as ruthless as they were often portrayed in the West. He said that most border guards, faced with six months in prison for taking no action, shot, but not to kill, and that he himself, luckily, had never had occasion to act.

The table fell silent. Then Geoffrey spoke. "Well," he said merrily, raising his glass in a toast, "I suppose we shouldn't, all of us, be held responsible for the foul behavings of others, should we?" His comment returned everyone to their relaxed and festive mood.

Through it all, Kati was remote and quiet. I, on the other hand, was very pleased with myself for instigating this grand accommodation between East and West. Feeling like a great statesman who had just pulled off a major diplomatic coup and was looking forward to his next mission, I decided to take Kati home and please her as well. "You ready to go?" I asked. She nodded with relief.

Klaus immediately noticed as we stood up. The good cheer that had invaded his face was switched off. The blank stare that replaced it signaled an alarm that suddenly perceived the Troika and everyone in it as part of an elaborate East German plot to recapture him. "You are leaving now?" he asked nervously.

Ulrich put his arm around his shoulders. "Don't worry, Klaus," he said with exaggerated reassurance. "You're among friends." Then he added with a sly wink, "Those two have to be going."

I paid the waitress at the bar and we made our way forward. Just as we had reached the door, Christoph walked in, blue-cheeked from his long bicycle ride in the cold air. "Hey, where have you been? You're never home anymore. Is anybody here?" Then he noticed Kati, recognizing her at once. "Ah, hallo," he said with a smile. She forced a smile in return but didn't say anything. I don't think she remembered who he was. I had to remind her. She forced another smile and said that of course she remembered. But for Kati, Christoph was just another burden to bear there in the bar.

"They're all in the back," I told him. "Along with an East German you should meet."

"Call me tomorrow," he said as he made his way along the bar.

On the way back to my apartment, Kati gave me her assessment of my friends: Torsten was a bore; Christoph, whose name she could never remember for some reason, was dooming himself to unhappiness; Geoffrey was "invested in being oblivious," and Ulrich she described as an "arrogant bastard," as the German equivalent of "scumbag," and finally as a "dangerous clown."

"Yes, I know he can be hard to take, but at heart he's all right. I think he's the one person in Berlin I could really count on if I needed help."

"Don't be such a fool, Richard. He'll help you out all right, but only if he gets something in return, even if it is just the satisfaction of knowing that you need his help. People like that scare me. No matter what they say, they're always ready to jump into the first pot that starts boiling. He's slimy . . . One of those guys you'll read about in the newspaper someday standing trial for molesting children or something like that. He reminds me of my Uncle Horst."

Mundus Vult Decipi, Ergo Decipiatur

THE NEXT DAY, Christoph and I met for dinner at our usual Italian restaurant. I arrived to find him sitting at our usual table. It was my first visit here in more than a month, by far the longest stretch since I'd moved to Berlin. My relationship with Kati during that time made it seem far longer. Christoph and I started coming here in the first exciting days right after I'd found my apartment in the city. I looked around the place under a spell of nostalgia. The room, like the food, was an astounding exercise in bad taste. All the tables were decorated with black and red checkered cloths and dusty plastic flowers. The tacky Italian seascape paintings hung from walls laid thick with heavy swirls of dust-covered white stucco. On the wall near the kitchen, there was a childish oil painting of the owner carrying an oversized, steaming lobster on a platter with the name "Angelo" scripted flatly across his chest. From the ceiling hung two Mediaeval-looking chandeliers made of heavy wooden rings and twisting bands of black iron. As always, the air was filled with the smell of something burning. Angelo himself was in the kitchen yelling at the cook at the top of his lungs in Italian, perfectly audible to his guests even over the harsh rock-and-roll voice of Gianna Nannini made shrill by the two small loudspeakers hung at each end of the room. Such an indigestion-producing atmosphere, I thought to myself. What on earth could have possessed us to endure it three times a week? The reasons failed me. Yet the realization that our old routine was no longer routine gave me a good feeling. It was a sign that my life in Berlin was moving along independently of Christoph.

Just then, Angelo burst angrily through the swinging kitchen doors and stormed halfway past our table before noticing us. He grabbed a couple of menus and offered them to us with a false smile. *"Bittesehr,"* he declared in heavily accented German loaded with patronage. One glance at the menu reminded me why Christoph always insisted on coming here: it was cheap. As always, we looked at the menus for a respectable length of time before closing them. That was Angelo's cue to come and take our order. We ordered what we always ordered. Angelo made the facial contortions he always made, as if he personally approved our good taste. Then he grabbed the menus from us and made for the kitchen where another loud argument ensued.

Christoph was making progress on his thesis and was in better spirits than I'd seen him in for a long time. He kept his complaining to a bare minimum, holding back just as he'd get rolling. I got the feeling he was afraid of putting me off permanently after not seeing me for so long. Most of the time we discussed my relationship with Kati. While I slurped soggy pasta and he ground burned lasagna, we each thought up one theory after another to try and explain her relationship with her husband. But in the end it remained a mystery. The only conclusion we could arrive at was that I must be doing both of them a favor in some way.

After the meal, Christoph sat back in his chair and began chewing on a toothpick, deep in thought. He looked as if he might be mulling over his future, and that made me want to make a break for home. "What? You're not going to have dessert?" he asked. Then, as though embarrassed by the severity of the disappointment in his voice, added comically, "How can you do that to poor Angelo?" I stayed for a pile of chocolate ice cream served in a thick parfait glass.

It was then that Christoph told me he had gotten a call from Knut, a mutual friend in Cologne. We met Knut Heino in Münster where he was studying to become a Roman Catholic priest. Not to say Knut was a believer; quite the contrary. He was, in fact, fond of repeating a Latin phrase as a sort of theme song to show off his irreverence: *Mundus vult decipi, ergo decipiatur* — "The world wants to be deceived, so let it be deceived." According to Knut, marriage was an institution designed to entrap men and love was a common mental disorder that led people to develop an unhealthy addiction to one another. He believed only the most arrogant among us could think that there was a point to existence and lived by the credo "Don't do to others what you wouldn't want done to yourself—unless they deserve it." In Münster he sailed through his studies by ticking off his duties: an hour of singing, an hour of prayer, an hour of quiet contemplation, or whatever else was required of him. Then, in the evening, he would don a jacket and tie, leave the solemn halls of the Collegium Borromaeum, and discretely slip into the city's student population in hot, sticky, smoke-filled bars. Knut was heresy by divine inspiration. And what he expected for it was an existence free from the fears, pressures and uncertainties that most human beings are forced to live with. His final reward would be retirement behind a monastery wall at age fifty, where he could quietly enter his *Vita Contemplativa*, drink good wine and not be bothered by other people's problems. Work, he always said, was a consequence of original sin; therefore, he wanted nothing to do with it. His needs were modest: a decent room in which to live and enjoy his large collection of Wagnerian operas; enough alcohol to drink, of which he could drink a disgusting amount; and lastly, with the appropriate discreetness of course, the possibility of having an occasional woman to relieve the "pressures of his manliness," as he always called it. And he wanted to have all those things in Cologne, because Cologne was the wealthiest diocese in the world. By Knut's reasoning, not only could he live better there than anywhere else, but as the richest *Bistum*, it would be the last place in which the steady decline in church membership would make itself felt materially. Now, at last, he was within easy reach of his goals. He had gotten himself to Cologne as a

Diakon. The next step, full priesthood, was simply a matter of time.

Christoph was scraping the last of the ice cream from the side of his parfait glass when he told me that Knut had invited us over for the coming weekend. I really wasn't interested in taking the drive, especially with his bad mood during our trip to Münster still all too fresh in my mind. Christoph waited a few moments then asked hesitantly, "What's the matter? Don't you feel like going?"

"No, I don't think so," I said, sitting back in my seat.

"You don't? I don't believe it! You know Knut is always good fun, and we haven't seen him since he moved to Cologne."

"It's a long drive. I think I'd rather skip it this time around."

"We can drive on Saturday morning, early, say around nine o'clock . . ."

He wasn't getting it. "I'm really not in the mood. If you want to go so bad, take the train."

"I can't afford the train!" he shouted before pulling himself together. "Look, Richard, I'm sorry about the Münster trip. But that place always gives me a fit, you know that. Cologne is different. I promise I'll be civil this time. Everything's under control now, anyway. Besides, the weather is going to be shit here this weekend. You really want to hang around this town and have dirt raining down on you for two days?" It didn't sound like a pleasant prospect. I told him I'd think about it and let him know. But Christoph was convinced that I had caved and cheerfully changed the subject as he asked for separate checks. "By the way, the East German last night . . . Klaus . . . it's really an unbelievable story. How do you know him? I could swear I'd seen him before somewhere."

"Kati knew him. And you've seen him in the Troika every time you've been there. Haven't you ever noticed the guy on the end of the bar?"

Oh, that's right . . . the drunkard. He seems all right. A little confused, maybe. I think he and Ulrich really hit it off."

The next day I telephoned Kati. Hanno was going to be away all weekend and she had to stay at home with Anja, who was sick with the flu. I decided to go visit Knut with Christoph after all.

We arrived in Cologne as planned at about eight-thirty in the evening. Knut met us in the lobby of the Priesterseminar. His new life evidently agreed with him; his pale, round baby face and curly, golden locks of hair seemed to radiate out of the top of his black clothes. Brother Heino took us up to his room, which was three times the size of the one he'd had at the Borromaeum in Münster, then showed us around the building, walking slowly through the halls with his hands clasped in front of him and speaking in a hushed, reserved voice. Occasionally, we would meet other priests and Knut would introduce Christoph and me as friends from Münster. A minute or two of excessively polite small talk would follow about what a charming city Münster was, then we would all laugh exaggerated laughs at a bit of wholesome humor before moving on. The tour ended with a look at the sauna and the large swimming pool in the basement. We watched from the edge of the pool as a skinny old man dog-paddled to the ladder and lifted his frail body out of the water. Knut, standing there with clasped hands, turned to me and whispered, "I dream of that pool filled with vestal virgins frolicking with beach balls—*stark naked.*" I raised an eyebrow and slowly nodded my approval of his fantasy. Then Christoph suggested we go out for some food. Back in his room, Knut traded his collar for the customary jacket and tie.

We ate dinner in a Greek restaurant. It immediately became apparent that, apart from the new surroundings, nothing had changed. Christoph was always trying to provoke Knut into committing one blasphemous indiscretion after another, and Knut was always happy to oblige. When Knut asked me how I liked living in Berlin, Christoph blurted out,

"He's sleeping with a married woman! Can't you absolve him of his sin, Knut?"

The holy man leaned toward me from across the table with a look of grave concern and firmly clasped my hands in his. "Is that the truth, *mein Sohn*?"

I gave him a blank stare. Knut jumped to his feet, head bowed in reverence with the palms of his hands up at his shoulders as he began chanting loudly in Latin while other people in the restaurant looked on. The booming ancient maxims were toned down to a deep mumble when he picked up a spoon, stuck it in his beer and flicked it at me. He did this three times before giving me a long list of prayers to recite that evening. I thanked him. "Mundus vult decipi, ergo decipiatur," he replied. Christoph asked about the pressures of his manliness. Knut admitted that they hadn't been relieved as often as he would like since moving to Cologne, but said that he had recently received an invitation from a woman in Münster and was planning to squeeze in a visit early the next week between two baptisms and a burial.

After dinner, our host took us to some of his favorite bars; his "sanctuaries" as he called them. Places he'd often go and anonymously drink himself silly. They were all small neighborhood establishments; the kind of places where casual visitors were so few that you had to wonder how they managed to stay in business. All were populated by four or five middle-aged men lethargically smoking cigarette after cigarette as they stared into drink with expressions that begged for relief from nagging lives. All had big-breasted, big-haired barmaids in their mid-forties, showing their age and a lot of cleavage, besides. We hit four or five such places before staggering into the last at about 1:30 a.m. That night, as always, Christoph and I had made the awful mistake of trying to keep up with Knut's drinking, matching him glass for glass. It was impossible. By the time we found our way into the last bar, we'd had it, both falling into the first booth that came into view. Knut hung up his coat and was drawn like a magnet to the cleavage behind the bar directly opposite us where he ordered three beers. Although he seemed mentally sharp, Knut's true condition was revealed by his attire: his shirt was sticking out of an unzippered fly and his tie was crooked with the knot pushed up so tightly around his neck that it severely crimped the sweat-stained collar of his poly-blend shirt. I looked over at Christoph slouched under his coat on the seat next to me. He was pale, also perspiring heavily, and could barely keep his eyes open. At the back of the room, a lone drinker sat on a bar stool with a cigarette hanging from his lips while he dumped one coin after another into a *Spielautomat*, clearly hypnotized by the machine. Its wheels spun and its lights blinked; periodically it would spit back a little change and pipe a congratulatory electronic tune over the German carnival song coming from the tape deck: "*Alles hat ein Ende, nur die Wurst hat zwei.*" At the bar, the only guest besides Knut was about to take his leave. He must have been a regular. As he was putting on his hat and coat he asked the barmaid about the health of her grandmother. "Oh, she's fine now," she told him. "Back to her old self, *Danke.*"

"I'm glad to hear it," he said as he left.

The barmaid put three half-liter beers on the bar in front of Knut. The sight of yet more alcohol made me sick to my stomach. Our friend brought two of them over to Christoph and me, then went straight back to the bar and made conversation with the barmaid, "Your grandmother's been ill?"

"Just a little influenza. But at ninety-one years old you can't be too careful."

"And she is all right now, I hope?"

"Doctor said she has the body of a seventy-year-old woman."

"Oh, how nice."

The man at the Spielautomat appeared at the bar asking for change of a ten-mark bill. The barmaid changed it for him and he went back to his game.

"So . . . what do you do when you're not working here?" Knut asked.

"When I'm not working here? Taking care of my daughter."

"And how old is she?"

"She's just turned fourteen."

"Oh, how very nice for you." A slimy grin. "And your husband?"

"I'm divorced."

"*Ach!*" Knut acted as if the news pained him, "*O tempora! O mores!*" he pleaded at the ceiling. "All the divorces these days—just a sin."

"Believe me, it's better this way," the barmaid said as she bent slightly forward, vigorously washing a couple of glasses in the sink. Her face displayed that here-we-go-again annoyance when she looked up to see Knut staring at her quivering bosom. "And you?" she asked curtly, "What do you do?"

"Me? I'm a priest in the service of the Lord."

Knut's response seemed to annoy her even more. She began collecting ashtrays from around the room and emptying them into a trash bin behind the bar. "You don't believe me?" She didn't answer. "Shall I prove it to you? Just ask my friends here."

"If you are a priest then you shouldn't be here like that—in the state you're in," she said sternly. "It's not right."

"Oh, I don't *practice* morality; I just *preach* it."

"You and your friends drink your beer and go. *Ich hab' Feierabend.*"

"Gnädige Frau," Knut continued blandly before suppressing a belch. "I happen to work for an organization that offers services to its members. I provide them the services they need and I'm compensated for my efforts. So why shouldn't I be allowed to sit here after work with my friends and drink a few beers like any bricklayer?"

And as he sat there pleased with his argument, a long flabby belch took him by surprise, bubbling up his throat and flying out of his mouth before he could cover it with his fist.

"You're disgusting," snapped the barmaid, unwittingly giving Knut an opportunity to use another of his favorite phrases.

"I'm only being true to my own self," he answered with pride.

At that very point in the evening I had consumed just the right amount of alcohol to be transported outside myself. I sat back in the booth, listening to Knut and watching the scene at the bar unfold before me. The tape deck was playing "*Es gibt kein Bier auf Hawaii*"; a few coins clanged as they fell from the mouth of the Spielautomat at the back of the room, and the machine celebrated by tooting its electronic tune; Christoph woke himself from his half-sleep with a powerful hiccup and mumbled something about an "over-acid stomach"; and suddenly, I felt as if I were inside Kati's head, looking at the world the way she sees it—at a truth that sobriety suppressed in me. Misery, ignorance, atom bombs, the Berlin Wall—they were all perfectly normal. Things are the way they are because nothing else is possible. Yes, Kati, you are right. That's the soul of humankind sitting there at the bar right in front of me. Enjoy yourself, Knut! Let's just keep squirting our genes at the next generation and see what happens. It doesn't really matter. And now I don't care, either. I looked at Christoph and thought, "And what about you? Do you care?" I must have said it out loud. His head fell toward me, mouth hanging open and his eyes half closed. "*Whaa?*" he managed to say. Never mind, I thought. You don't care. I know. Drink your drink. I know.

Christoph and I spent most of Sunday in Knut's room recovering while he went about his business. Our hangovers were so severe that we decided to leave for Berlin on Monday. Because of heavy traffic on the Autobahn and at the inner-German border, the trip back took more than seven hours. That didn't seem to bother Christoph. As a matter of fact, we were both in an uncommonly good mood. At the same East German transit highway rest stop where we picked up Kati weeks before, we found ourselves laughing and joking loudly about the weekend. "Maybe we should visit Knut more often," I said, wiping tears of laughter from my eyes. "It does a lot of good."

"Of course it does. It's always gratifying to see that there are people worse off than we are."

"What do you mean?"

"The only person Knut is perfectly honest with is himself, right? 'True to my own self,' he always says. And look at what he is. Don't tell me you aren't glad you're not him!"

He was right. And as we drove back onto the transit highway we celebrated Knut by energetically singing the fanfare—a tribute composed long ago in a taxi at the end of another drunken evening by someone neither of us now remembered: *Hei-no Hei-no, Heineho Hei-no, Heine-heine-heine-ho!*

It was late Monday afternoon when we arrived back in West Berlin. I spent Monday evening on the phone talking with friends in New York. Telephone conversations were not itemized on phone bills in Germany. One received an invoice with just a lump sum to be paid. And since the money for the phone came from the Software Company, running up a bill by talking with America was one way that I could at least make it appear that I was hard at work. *Bob vult decipi, ergo decipiatur.*

It was after nine when I finished my calls and sat myself in front of the television. Flipping from one channel to another, I felt the effects of the Cologne excursion fast catching up with me. I stopped at the East German DDR 1 channel just as *Der schwarze Kanal* was coming on. The "Black Channel" was a pitiful, weekly attempt to counter-argue what East Germans saw on West German television news programs. I tuned in just in time to see the amateurish opening animation: the West German ARD and ZDF TV network logos spinning around East German rooftops while the national eagle of the Federal Republic rose up above them, only to come crashing down accompanied by corny atonal music meant to be humiliating. The show's host, Karl-Eduard von Schnitzler, appeared on screen and immediately began talking non-stop from behind his thick eyeglasses. Struggling to stay awake, I watched this old, gray embodiment of the East German media fling one obtuse socialist word salad after another at his audience: "Lawless provocateurs and their mean-spirited interference" . . . "Electronic and printed purveyors of filth." *Der schwarze Kanal* was one of those shows that I always meant, but somehow never managed, to stay home and watch. For westerners it was an amusing political cabaret, and for me, another one of the things that I would like to ask people behind the Wall about. But that night, as much as I wanted to watch, I was just not able to stay awake. Throughout the program I sat in my rocker, passing in and out of consciousness, catching only the very end when the man with the little eyes sarcastically asked his viewers if they would really prefer an economy of brutal competition to one that was rationally and centrally planned.

The next evening, I had planned on going to the Troika for dinner but then I got a call from Kati. She came over on the pretense of wanting to go to the movies, but in reality she wasn't interested in leaving my apartment. It was Wednesday before I got back there again. Klaus was sitting with Ulrich and Torsten while Geoffrey was talking to a woman at the bar. Klaus' appearance had changed. His eyes were wide open and alert and he was clean-shaven, which made him look younger. I had always assumed him to be in his early thirties, but now it was clear he was ten years younger than that; certainly no older than Torsten. And although it was nearly midnight, Klaus was also absolutely sober. That almost incomprehensible Saxon accent of his was the only remnant of the dipsomaniac I had known before. Both he and Ulrich had plates in front of them that bore the well-picked remains of a steak dinner. Klaus sat back in his chair, relaxed and satisfied while Ulrich lectured him on the Troika's menu. "Don't ever order any other cut of meat. The filet is too expensive; the entrecote is by far the best value here. The rest of the card is only mediocre."

Klaus laughed, "In the East we always thought mediocrity was good. It meant that everyone was equal."

It was immediately clear that Ulrich had taken Klaus under his wing. He helped him find shortcuts that would get the most out of the West German social bureaucracy; had had him to his home for a wine tasting evening; explained the fine points of the complicated German insurance maze. The next day they were even going to inquire at the university about changing Klaus' course of study from *Ethnologie* to BWL—business and economics; "Something solid on which you can build a future," as Ulrich put it. "This way you won't have to spend the rest of your life living in tiny little rooms like the one you have now. You should see this place, Richard. You can't even fit a real bed in there. Klaus can't even have an erection in that room without opening the window first!" Everyone had a good laugh at that line, and Klaus laughed hardest of all. I was amazed at the speed at which their relationship had developed. When Ulrich spoke, Klaus hung on every word as if it were Gospel being delivered personally to him; as if Ulrich held the key to success and happiness in this new world in which Klaus had suddenly found himself. He needed only to behave as he was instructed.

But even more amazing than the speed at which their relationship had grown was the speed at which it deteriorated. Within three weeks, Ulrich had managed to become so overbearing that Klaus would only sit at the table if I was there, too. On one occasion I arrived at the Troika to find that Geoffrey had managed to leave with a woman and Torsten was absent. Klaus had again taken up his old stool at the bar while Ulrich and Anne sat at the usual table and ate steaks. It wasn't until I took my seat with them that he wandered over. Not that I cared very much one way or another. For me, Klaus turned out to be more than a little disappointing. He was either unwilling or unable to tell me anything interesting about life behind the Wall, and as far as I was concerned, that was the whole point of having him. Getting the most rudimentary information out of him was a struggle. A simple question, like what his father did for a living, would be answered by a shrug of the shoulders. Continual prodding produced the reluctant confession that "he worked in a factory." Soon I just quit trying.

That night we sat and drank over forced conversation. Ulrich was in a particularly obnoxious mood. He said several times that East Germany was the world's biggest concentration camp and wondered how Klaus ever managed to "do the right thing" in leaving. He kept rubbing the fact that the area of the GDR that Klaus came from was referred to as the *Tal der Ahnungslosen*—"the valley of the unsuspecting"—because its topography made the reception of West German television impossible. "We all know why you left, Klaus," Ulrich said. "You were just too curious. Why don't you just admit it? And we all know why you're still here. You just don't want to give up the good life to become the New Socialist Man." At one point Ulrich told Klaus that if he was really as unhappy as he wanted everyone to believe, he should just walk back home. "Just walk over to Checkpoint Charlie and tell them that you came, you saw, and it was awful. They'll gladly use you for propaganda. You'll be a hero—the one who went the other way!" Ulrich ended a long diatribe by gesturing toward me, saying, "You're not alone, Klaus. Look at Richard. We not only gave him a civilized place to live and work, but *Kultur, Kultur!*"

That's when I decided to go home. Sitting between Ulrich and Klaus wasn't pleasant and Anne, as usual, had nothing to say. I called the waitress over and paid my bill. Klaus did the same, standing up and following me out of the Troika. Once outside, he began buttoning up his jacket, finding himself unsteady and suddenly aware that he was drunk.

"Are you okay, Klaus?"

He looked at me with an alcoholic grin. "You know, I like you," he said, struggling with the buttons on his jacket. "You're all right. Not like that asshole, Ulrich."

"Well thanks, Klaus. You're not an asshole like him, either. I'll see you around." I turned and walked down the street. It was cold, I was getting tired and looking forward to my bed. Klaus followed. "Don't you need to go the other way?" I asked.

"It is still early," he said. "I think I need some air."

I made my way home with Klaus staggering a step or two behind me. Whenever I turned and looked at him, he smiled pleasantly. I nodded and smiled back. But within a few minutes, he was so wobbly he almost fell down, saving himself by grabbing onto my shoulder. I steadied him. Under the harsh light of the street lamp I saw a strange expression on his face. He looked as though he was going to cry.

"Hey, Klaus . . . What's wrong with you?"

He pulled himself together. "Richard, I was wondering if maybe you could help me. Maybe do something for me?"

"What is it?"

Klaus wiped his teary eyes and took a slightly crumpled envelope from his jacket pocket.

"I was wondering if maybe you could mail this letter for me."

"Mail a letter? Don't you know how to use a mailbox? Just throw the letter in, Klaus. The rest takes care of itself."

"No, I mean go over to East Berlin and mail it for me there." Klaus put his arm around my shoulder, moving me along until we had past my street and were approaching the Mehringdamm. "It's a letter to my mother in Dresden," he whispered. "I've written a dozen letters since I've been here but I have never gotten an answer. I don't think they're letting my mail get delivered to her."

"What? Who isn't delivering the mail?"

"Tja!" A fit of exasperation at my ignorance. "The state security—*The Stasi!*" he yelled, then stole a glance behind us as though someone might be following. Klaus returned to a whisper. "I thought if it was sent from East Berlin it might slip by them. I even had someone else write the address on the envelope so they won't recognize my handwriting."

"You had someone else write the address? Do you really think they check the handwriting on every single piece of mail?" I asked skeptically, thinking maybe too much beer was beginning to damage his brain, making him paranoid.

"They can do anything," he said loudly with flat resignation. Evidently, there was no longer any danger that we might be overheard. At the Mehringdamm, we stood on the corner of the intersection. "I don't know what they've told her," he said. "She's old and living alone. Maybe they told her I'm dead or something. Or maybe something has happened to her that I don't know." Klaus sat down on the fender of a parked car holding the envelope in one hand and rubbing his red eyes with the other. He was a pathetic sight.

"All right, Klaus. Sure, I'll send it off for you. No problem."

His face brightened. "You know there is that twenty-five mark forced exchange at the border," he said, worried that it might cause me to change my mind. "But I'll give that back to you. I can even give you ten now." Klaus pulled a crumpled note from the pocket of his jacket and offered it to me.

"Don't worry about it. I've been thinking about going over, anyway. It's been awhile. You can buy me a beer at the Troika."

Klaus quickly wiped his eyes with the palm of his hand, "Vielen Dank, Richard." Then he caught sight of the Television Tower at Alexanderplatz, its strobe lights blinking defiantly in the distance. "You know, it's really not fair. One lousy mistake and you have to pay for it the rest of your life. I wish I hadn't done it," he said, sobbing. "I just want to go home. I wish I hadn't done it."

By that time, I was wishing the same. The wind was kicking up and the cold was getting at me through my coat. I took the letter from his hand and told him not to worry, that I'd take care of it. "When?" he wanted to know.

"Tomorrow. Friday at the latest," I said, just wanting to end the conversation.

Klaus stood up and felt the need to give me a big bear hug in gratitude. He had one last thing to say as I walked away, "Uhh . . . you won't tell Ulrich about any of this, will you?"

The next morning, Wolf woke me up around nine o'clock with a call. The big German bank contracts had arrived. He also had a short list of people who were waiting for return calls from me. One seemed certain to be a deal if I could negotiate a good price. That took care of that day. Friday also came and went, as did the weekend. Each night I was forced to avoid the Troika; over each day hung the annoyingly pathetic image of Klaus wiping tears from his eyes. His letter, lying undisturbed and gathering dust on my desk, was becoming more and more of a burden to look at.

It took a week and a half before it became unbearable. On a Tuesday at about noon I started thinking about my mission to East Berlin. I had no desire to go, but was finally determined to get it over and done with.

Before moving to Berlin I had counted the eastern city as one of the benefits of living here. That it was going to offer a constant source of interest was a notion that Christoph had pushed after he had moved from Münster and was taunting me daily by telephone for not being here. But when I got here it was forgotten. We had planned on going over once but something came up and we didn't. I had been there a couple of times and knew what it was like, anyway. There was just no real reason to go back. No one I knew besides Klaus had any connection to it. Kati had them by marriage, but she was happy enough to have it all kept on the other side of the Wall. For the people I knew, forking over twenty-five west marks in a forced exchange to a regime that showed no interest in following Gorbachev was an unconscionable if not downright vicious thing to do. I thought for a moment about giving Geoffrey a call. He was the only person I was sure would be happy to come along. But that meant I would probably have to pay for him, too, so I decided to let him go on sleeping. Resigned to going alone, I became angry with Klaus for getting himself into this mess in the first place.

Locking my door on the way out I realized that I had forgotten my passport and ran back into my apartment to retrieve it from my desk, leaving my door wide open and the keys hanging in the lock. On my way out the second time, Bernd was waiting at the elevator. Normally he'd never take the elevator down. But I was reckless, failing to cover my tracks when I left my door open. "*Na?*" he asked with a smug smirk on his face. By now the entire building had seen and heard Kati coming and going at all hours of the day and night, either through the peepholes in their doors or echoing through the tiled walls of the staircase. A fortunate byproduct of Kati's carnal wailing was that it caused my neighbors in the house to avoid me the way they avoided the drunk who sometimes urinated on the tree planted in the sidewalk near the entrance to our building, his demented, dirty face deformed by spite. Bernd was the only one I still had to avoid on my own.

"*Naa!*" I sneered back at him. "Don't you have to work today, Bernd?"

"Of course I do. I'm on my way there now."

He was on his way there? Bernd worked on the Puttkamerstrasse, just a couple of blocks from Checkpoint Charlie. I asked for a lift and he gladly obliged.

On the way down in the elevator he told me that he had taken the morning off to go visit with our landlady who was in the hospital with a case of pneumonia. When we got to his car, Bernd hesitated for a split second and sighed. I knew it hurt him to give up a great parking spot.

From the moment he put the key into the ignition, Bernd talked nonstop. I was astonished at how much information he could pack into the ten-minute ride to his office. I was informed of a whole history that I'd been totally unaware of, though I lived right next to him. The landlady had been in the hospital for nearly three weeks now; her son and daughter-in-law came in from Frankfurt fearing the worst; the first week was critical; Bernd took Frau Eppert and Frau Meyer-Burkhardt to visit last week; the landlady's husband was killed in the war, he must have been wealthy because she remained well propertied thereafter; Frau Eppert disliked the landlady and was secretly trying to convince her son to put her in a nursing home so that she could take over the ground floor apartment; Frau Meyer-Burkhardt disliked Frau Eppert because she flushed the toilet too often during the night, had too much money and a better view; "Oh, and everybody's always wondering what you do up in that apartment all day, and by the way, that's a cute girlfriend you've got. She wouldn't happen to be *married*, would she?" Within five minutes, my head was ringing. I couldn't wait to get out of the car.

Just as we turned the corner onto the Puttkamerstrasse, Bernd asked how long I'd been living in Germany, and actually waited for an answer. "About three and a half years now."

"And you are still driving with an American driver's license by any chance?"

"Well, yeah. Why do you ask?"

Bernd grimaced as if he'd just felt a shot of pain race up his spine. "Three years," he said. "That's too long. Within the first two years they would have just transferred your American license to a German one. But *three* years? I think they will make you learn to drive all over again in a driving school."

"What?! Who? I've been driving for fifteen years. I know how to drive."

"But now whenever you drive a car you are breaking the law. If you ever have an accident here you will be in serious trouble. It is as if you are driving without a valid license. I'm just telling you the law so you'll know," he said innocently.

I felt a surge of anger. The legal implications took a back seat to the idea that a quick escape from Berlin had been despotically ruled out because of a technicality of the traffic code. I knew all too well that no German bureaucrat would ever bend the rules and transfer my license, even if the two-year limit had expired by five minutes. The prospect of doing battle with beings whose sole object in life was to thwart you at every turn had me fuming. Bernd pulled over to the curb and I jumped out of the car. He rolled down his window and yelled after me, "Na? When are we going have breakfast together?"

I ran over to the Friedrichstrasse, rounded the corner and stood there feeling a surge of adrenaline over the injustice of it all. Across the street I noticed a building, probably a leftover from the Nazi regime, crowned by a huge sculpture of an eagle, wings spread, and head turned triumphantly to the north. It seemed to point the way to the border, reminding me why I had come here in the first place.

I made my way down the Friedrichstrasse to the Zimmerstrasse intersection—to Checkpoint Charlie—one of two entrances into East Berlin for non-Germans. (The other was the

Friedrichstrasse Station, which was accessible only by train.) Bernd had gotten me so wound up that I decided to stop in at the Café Adler for a drink before going across.

I sat at a table by a window, ordered a cognac and a cup of coffee and decided just to forget the whole thing; that in reality nothing had changed. If that idiot neighbor of mine had driven a little faster, or stopped talking two minutes earlier, or if he even once had given me the chance to respond to one of his questions about Kati, he would have never gotten around to asking about my driver's license. I could just go on living and driving as I always have. The thing to do was to forget about it all, and if the Germans wanted to throw me out of the country over a lousy technicality, then let them. At least it would give me a good story to tell. I ordered another cognac and did my best to put it all out of my mind.

Sitting there, I saw the small American control house planted in the middle of the Friedrichstrasse. Inside, a lone soldier sat at a desk with his hands clasped behind his head, looking bored. My current distress led me to feel an immediate affinity for him as a fellow American living in a foreign country. The soldier sat facing the large East German customs area with its dozens of guards. The Americans never seemed to do any checking at the checkpoint. They sat there because an agreement signed at the end of the Second World War, which had never quite ended in this city, gave them the right to sit there. And none of the Western Allies—American, British or French—ever gave up any of their legal rights in Berlin. Nobody dared do anything that might give the Soviets the impression that they were getting tired of maintaining the status quo.

On the other side of the border, I could see that a couple of cars heading into East Berlin were having their trunks thoroughly searched by border guards. Just behind them was a big sign that read: *Warm Welcome in the Capital of the GDR, Berlin.* The border crossing was thoroughly planned and effective with watch towers and heavy steel gates that could seal it off completely. But it also seemed a symbol of national pride, with a large hammer and compass emblem and, in the summer, a couple of patches of well-manicured lawn before it.

I drank up and paid, wanting to get my obligation to Klaus over and done with. I had the feeling he'd already caused me more trouble than he was worth.

Leaving the café, I saw my American compatriot taking a break from his monotony. He was standing outside the door at the rear of his long hut, stretching up and down on his toes with his arms behind his back, giving me the impression of a time-killing night watchman. I wanted to talk with him; to get his thoughts about the job of defending Western civilization with his bare hands. Actually, I wanted to start with that and steer the conversation to the problems of living in Germany, leading up to my driver's license dilemma. I was hoping that, after I'd casually told him the story, he would just laugh it off and agree that I should ignore it all. Hearing that from somebody in a uniform would somehow make it much easier to do. I quickly decided on a strategy to start us talking: ask a simple question about the procedure for going across the border, one U.S. citizen to another, and move on from there. He obviously had time on his hands.

I walked over and innocently asked the soldier what I, as an American, needed to do if I wanted to go over to East Berlin. He kept his arms behind his back, looking past me at the pedestrians on the sidewalk, and with the blunt severity of a drill sergeant asked, "You military?"

I told him I wasn't. The soldier proceeded to give me my orders. "Pay five marks visa fee and minimum twenty-five marks exchange," he said before inhaling a nose full of air.

"That's all?"

"That's all," he said, never once making eye contact with me. He then signaled the end of my audience by noisily heaving up phlegm from deep down in his throat and hurling a ball of mucus powerfully from his mouth before going back inside his hut. I watched through the window as he sat at his desk and busied himself with the sports pages of *USA Today*.

Beyond the Divide

I MADE MY WAY into East Berlin feeling as if itching powder was being pumped through my veins. I walked past the big wooden sign advising people in English, French, Russian and German that they were leaving the American Sector, through the Wall, past the watchtowers and along a curved sidewalk that led to the single-story customs building. Inside was a rectangular room with walls that were covered in cheap wood paneling. To the immediate right of the entrance was a photo machine, the kind that are common in train stations. At the far end of the room, a man with his back toward me was having his passport checked. He was wearing a brown corduroy overcoat, blue beret and had a brown travel bag made of worn, cracked vinyl slung over his shoulder. In front of him, an East German guard sat behind a thick slab of glass. The only other people in the room were three Scandinavian tourists; two women and a man in their early twenties. Huddled together, speaking in hushed tones, they smiled anxiously, uncertain either about the procedure for passage or whether going across was such a good idea after all. The wood paneling in the room must have just been cleaned; it was streaked with a faint white film and there was a slight antiseptic odor, which mixed with the nervousness in the air giving the place all the charm of an abortion clinic. I moved behind the man with the beret. A minute later the guard behind the glass slid the man's passport back to him and he was buzzed into the socialist worker's paradise through a steel door off to our right.

I moved up and brazenly shoved my U.S. passport through the slot at the guard. The anger I had been feeling instantly turned to defiance, for this room was special. Here it was easy to forget Ulrich's statistics about Third World infant mortality rates in America, the senseless slaughter on its streets, the teenage pregnancies and grinding poverty of its inner cities. Any previous feelings of being cheated out of a future by a nation in decline didn't exist here. It was pure magic. A vanishing act. Here, one felt instantly morally superior. After all, this entire security apparatus was the system's most damning indictment. And the conflict that produced it was so wonderfully simple; so perfectly black and white. One needed no understanding of history, politics or ideology to see it, or to make a career from it. Virtue was as easily identifiable as the symbol embossed on the front of your passport.

The guard was busy for a moment, looking down at the desk in front of him, working on a surface below my line of vision. To the right of his elbow was a boxy plastic telephone with a single call button and a blank disk where the dial should have been. Next to it were three small wooden file boxes. To the guard's right hung a blue curtain and up toward the ceiling a video camera stared at me incessantly through the glass.

Finally, the guard lifted his head and, without looking at me, took my passport from the slot. I heard him flipping through the pages. Although I couldn't see it, I got the impression he was checking my passport against some kind of list. Then he looked up and began alternating slowly back and forth between my face and the photograph in my passport. Again, I wondered if the old picture with the scrawny beard might cause problems. The guard behind the glass gave nothing away. He sat stone-faced, shifting his suspicious eyes between the passport photo and me as he was trained to do, carrying the full authority of his uniform, the paranoid East German state bureaucracy and centuries of goose-stepping Prussian military tradition with him. In the end he was the gatekeeper; the one with his finger on the buzzer. It was within his power to simply turn me away and give no reason. Finally, while again looking down at his desk, he passively muttered the words *"fünf mark."* He wanted the five West marks I had to pay for the *Tagesvisum.* I'd been approved. I slipped a five-mark coin through the slot. He took it, stamped my passport with an authoritative bang and inserted into it a slip of paper on which he had filled in my name, citizenship, the date and my passport number. It stated that I was permitted to remain within the boundaries of East Berlin until midnight. The guard buzzed me in through the steel door. I heard it latch-shut behind me as I made my way down a long, narrow corridor. The sound under foot was hollow, like that inside a mobile home, making the facility seem like something temporary. Although it was a far cry from the makeshift wooden structures you saw in early photographs from the 1960s. Constant improvement over the decades had caused it to slowly harden like cement into permanence.

The corridor led to a room where bags were searched. I saw the man with the blue beret slowly repacking the unlikely contents of his travel bag under the supervision of a border guard: five cans of tuna, three fat rolls of toilet paper and a package of *Mars* candy bars, all surely meant as a treat for some poor East German relative. Three other guards gave me a thorough look over as I walked slowly by. I made the required exchange of money; laying down twenty-five hard West marks for twenty-five East marks at the arbitrary one-to-one rate, getting back two small slips of paper that looked and felt like play money. I stuffed them into my wallet, feeling as if I'd just had money extorted from me. Again, I was angry with Klaus for getting himself into this situation.

Finally, I found myself on the *other side,* in East Berlin, feeling as though I'd just found my way out of a winding labyrinth. I couldn't resist a look back at Checkpoint Charlie and the Café Adler, now a block away, just to be sure they were still there.

I walked down the Friedrichstrasse to the Leipziger Strasse intersection. Here, a block away from the border, East Berlin began to come alive. A few Trabant automobiles sputtered their way along the Leipziger Strasse sounding like so many poorly-tuned lawnmowers trailing plumes of exhaust behind them. From here, looking West, I could barely notice the Berlin Wall cutting across the Liepziger Platz, although it was just a few blocks away. Klaus, in a fit of candor, once told me that its height had been carefully calculated so that anyone falling from the top in an escape attempt would be incapacitated by broken bones. But its height also made it almost unnoticeable, even from a distance of just three or four city blocks. The view to the West was dominated by the golden facade and pitched roof of the West Berlin Philharmonic, making it possible to imagine for a moment that this city had once been a connected whole. Up the Liepziger Strasse were the huge apartment blocks visible from Potsdamer Platz and so many other places in West Berlin. The hulking blue and white tiled facades, caked gray by the polluted air were less than inviting, but I continued in that direction thinking that there must be a post office in such a large, densely populated community.

As I walked, recollections began jarring themselves loose from my memory. That feel of walking through socialism returned. The smells of traffic exhaust, the clothes people wore, and even the way they carried themselves were different than they were just a few blocks away in West Berlin. I saw again that East Berlin, like all of the other East Bloc capitals I had visited, be they Moscow, Warsaw or Prague, was windswept by a fine layer of dust. Evidence, I was once told, of too many open wounds in the earth; too many construction projects that central planning never got finished. Unlike the filthy air, this was the one form of socialist *Dreck* that the Wall did keep out of West Berlin. I stood at the Leipziger Strasse /Charlottenstrasse intersection realizing that it was here, at the end of the street, that Klaus made his ill-considered escape. There on the corner, I also encountered one of those strange little figures on the traffic lights that signal "walk." Unlike the trim and confident silhouettes that marched across the streetlights in the West, here was a pudgy little man wearing a wide-brimmed hat. Strange as it was, the figure belonged here. It seemed to embody that East German national inferiority complex and was just the kind of silhouetted profile I would imagine driving a Trabant automobile.

I found a post office. Inside, I was immediately confronted by that smell: musty air tinged with the odor of a backed-up drain that one found in all public buildings in East Berlin. There was a counter with three windows, but only one was open. Six people were standing in line. The women were all carrying gaudy, floral-print nylon shopping bags at their sides. On the wall behind the counter hung an official portrait of a relatively young General Secretary Erich Honecker. He wore eyeglasses with thick black frames, a "mod" tie and a Communist Party stick pin in his wide lapel. His head was cocked awkwardly in three-quarter profile making him look like a fifty-year-old class nerd in a high school yearbook photo.

It was uncomfortably warm standing in line. I kept looking irritably at my watch—one minute passed like ten; ten minutes like forty-five. I was perspiring under my sweater and coat. The line didn't budge as the continual hiss of the radiator pumping even more heat into the room got on my nerves. When three more dour faces appeared behind me I left the place in disgust, swearing to myself that this would be the last time I did Klaus or anyone else any favors.

I continued toward Alexanderplatz, walking past block after block of monotonous buildings, some low-rise, some high-rise, all socialist prefab drab. Off the bleak main road, I came upon an old stone church. A bronze plaque out front said it had been restored after having been destroyed during World War II "by Anglo-American bombers." Isn't it great, I thought, that the Soviets were able to conquer this city in savage house-to-house fighting against fanatical Nazis without so much as breaking a window.

A bit further on, at the red-brick East Berlin city hall, an idealized sculpture of a shapely young woman worker, dressed in overalls with her hair tucked under a kerchief, is shouldering a shovel like a weapon. Her male counterpart is rolling up his sleeves, evidently ready to get down to business. Atop the city hall clock tower, the East Berlin city flag, with its black bear standing upright, flapped in the wind. It was identical to the West Berlin version, and probably the only thing besides the sewer system (which was sealed-off with steel bars under the border) that the two cities still had in common.

The city hall stood along a wide mall stretching from the Spree River to the Television Tower at Alexanderplatz. Much of it was lined on both sides by modern prefab housing; the gray concrete slabs that formed the facades were caked with brown soot in patterns resembling stalactites formed over the eons in ancient caves.

It was up near the Television Tower that I found the next post office. Inside was a long counter with eleven windows and the obligatory photo of Erich Honecker on the wall behind them. I stood in a short line with four women, all of whom were carrying those gaudy, floral-print nylon bags I had seen at the last post office. At the far end of the room, a kitschy socialist mural covered an entire wall: trim young men, happy children, scantily clad women setting white doves free into a blue sky while a young couple sat naked on a red blanket having a picnic in the middle of a lush landscape. The man was reading a copy of the Communist Party newspaper, *Neues Deutschland*. Apparently, no paradise was complete without it.

The courageous faces in the mural were in sharp contrast to the expressionless people standing in line with me. When my turn came, I slid Klaus' envelope across the counter to a woman with blue-tinted hair. She looked at the address and mumbled, "twenty pfennig" while tearing a postage stamp out of a large book and sticking it onto the envelope. I handed over my tiny five-mark bill and got back four marks and eighty pfennig in alu-chip coins. The task was finally accomplished; the burden of obligation finally lifted from my shoulders. I felt like a new man.

Back outside I walked past the Alexanderplatz station while an S-Bahn train began emitting a slowly rising electric hum as it pulled out of the train shed over my head. On the other side of the station was the famous Berlin Alexanderplatz of the Alfred Döblin novel. Its socialist custodians over the past forty years had erected a concrete desert in the middle of this once dense and seedy neighborhood, surrounding it with modern facades of glass and tarnished aluminum. On one of them was another ridiculous socialist mural. It featured two scientists in white lab coats with one of them holding a humongous atom out to his side, as if trying to avoid irradiating himself with it.

Government planners tried creating some urban glitz with staid-neon advertising for East Bloc companies with awkward names like *Intersigma, Balkancarpodem* and *Mashpriborintorg*. Other ads encouraged people to buy electronic equipment made in the Soviet Union and to travel in the sleeping cars of the Soviet railways. Then there was the "espresso bar." Any dreary corner was never very far from a café with big sign advertising "espresso." I imagined a *People's Committee for the Creation of International Flair* strategically placing "espresso" bars around the dull city. The results, nonetheless, were as faceless and gray as the aging bureaucrats that filled the Politburos across Eastern Europe. Architecture once meant to signal a new dynamic at work in the world had, in reality, created places that no one would want to be in if they didn't need to.

I walked as far as the Mollstrasse intersection where streetcars, long gone from West Berlin, rumbled along the center of the avenue. This was as far as I could push myself. I realized why I hadn't bothered visiting in so long—it was pointless being here. If there was any "interesting" aspect to it all, it was how uninteresting it was. Going through the border was always fun; there was always a little espionage thriller with you. The silly public art praising a system that no one wanted and showing a bounty that didn't exist was ironically amusing, but not worth the price of admission. The tired and unapproachable faces wandering around a mostly bleak landscape of run-down, prefab buildings were nothing more than depressing. I decided to head back to Checkpoint Charlie.

I made my way to the Marx-Engels-Forum, just beside the Spree River, where larger-than-life bronze statues of Karl Marx and Friedrich Engels looked toward the east. Nearby, the pompous Berlin cathedral was reflecting itself in the bronze-tinted windows of the modern marble and glass *Palast der Republik*, seat of the East German rubber-stamp parliament. It had been built where the Kaiser's palace once stood. In front of the Lustgarten across the street was a stone cube memorial bearing the inscription, "Tied Forever in Friendship with the Soviet Union." I recalled old newsreel footage I'd seen of Soviet troops celebrating here in the days right after the war: men and women in tattered uniforms joyously dancing to Russian folk music after years of savage fighting. I thought for a moment about going into the antiquities museum at the other end of the square but couldn't summon up the desire.

I walked down Unter den Linden toward the Brandenburg Gate; through the historic heart of old imperial Berlin. Restored after the war, these classical buildings had originally been arranged here to assert Berlin's dignity as a capital city worthy of a European power. Now they were just as important to the communists in providing *their* capital a certain measure of dignity and a credible link with the past that the prefabricated concrete slabs could not. A shield, in their eyes at least, from the most scathing of all attacks—that East Germany was nothing more than an artificial puppet state whose authority came solely from the barrel of a Soviet gun.

In the window of a bookshop, "deluxe" leather-bound editions of books by Erich Honecker were on display under a large, triumphant sign: "DDR 40," commemorating the fortieth anniversary of the founding of the East German state, which was coming up in October. Further down, in front of the Hotel Unter den Linden, was a kiosk with a neon sign advertising the Soviet press agency, *Novosti*. It offered a selection of East Bloc newspapers and magazines. An old man sat inside cutting into a small apple with a penknife. A few months earlier, the East Germans had taken the unprecedented step of actually banning a Soviet publication. The magazine, *Sputnik*, taking the new press freedoms unleashed by Mikhail Gorbachev seriously, printed a series of articles that not only detailed the monumental crimes committed during the Stalin era, but had actually compared Stalin to Hitler. That was an unforgivable act of heresy for the old men running East Germany who were doing everything possible to keep *Glasnost* at bay. I decided to ask the man in the kiosk for a copy of *Sputnik*, wondering what his reaction might be.

"Sputnik gibt's nicht mehr," he said before stuffing an apple slice into his mouth.

"Why not? Is it sold out?"

"Gibt's nicht mehr!" He said again, annoyed at having to repeat himself. That was it. "*Gibt's nicht mehr.*" There wasn't any more Sputnik. Here today, gone tomorrow, no questions asked. It might as well have never existed at all.

Eager to rid myself of some East German money, which I wasn't allowed to take back across the border, I bought a copy of *Neues Deutschland* and a *Berliner Zeitung* as souvenirs. That came to a grand total of just thirty pfennig. I spotted a tourist map of Berlin. It cost four marks, which made me feel a little better.

Down at the Brandenburg Gate, the platform on this side of the Wall that Kati and I had seen filled with school children was now empty. Standing there, I recalled an event from the previous year that was widely reported in the western media: This part of the Unter den Linden filled with thousands of young East Germans trying to eavesdrop on a rock concert taking place in front of the Reichstag on the other side of the Wall in West Berlin. The impatient East German crowd pushed closer and closer to the Brandenburg Gate as the police began pushing back. Defiant shouts of "*The Wall must go!*" and for Mikhail Gorbachev, "*Gorbi! Gorbi! Gorbi!*" could be heard. Fights broke out; riot police were seen on television lunging at the crowd with clubs.

I was getting hungry and thought food would be a good way to unload more East German money before walking over to

Checkpoint Charlie. I went up the Linden to a small restaurant named for someone called Egon Irwin Kisch.

Inside, a well-dressed elderly couple at one table were obviously from the West. Two women at another table were engaged in a conversation in Spanish. A man about my age sat alone at the counter. All eyed me suspiciously as I took a seat at the window. Near the entrance was a large oil portrait of Egon Erwin Kisch. One or more framed charcoal sketches of him hung on every wall. The guy sitting at the counter was reading a house newspaper about Kisch. The place could have been a cult hangout dedicated to those who couldn't get enough of Egon Erwin Kisch, whoever he was.

The restaurant was directly across the street from the large Soviet embassy building which stretched for a nearly city block along Unter den Linden. It was a pure example of 1930s Stalinist "sugar cake" architecture. A red hammer-and-sickle flag flapped from the top of a central tower guarded by heroic statues of workers and peasant farmers. A modern bust of Lenin was added to the front court, obviously much later, as if to remind passersby just who was responsible for it all. Although the old men running East Germany had already made it clear that they intended to go on living with Stalin. The memorial in the Lustgarten came to mind, *Tied Forever in Friendship with the Soviet Union*. The unbelievable reality was that Soviet big brother was becoming a thorn in the side of the East German leadership. Young East Germans had actually chanted the name of the Soviet leader in the streets of East Berlin and were beaten over the head for it. The East German government had, in fact, banned a Soviet publication for being subversive.

A lanky waiter eventually appeared at my table. Lost in thought, I hadn't looked at the menu. I flipped it open and ordered the first thing my eyes focused on: goulash.

"No goulash today," the waiter answered.

I moved my finger down the list. "Then I'll have the pork . . ."

"No pork, either."

"How about the steak sandwich and salad?" Even before the words were out of my mouth, the waiter turned and walked away. I shouted after him that I also wanted a cup of coffee.

"Kaffee *komplett*?" he asked. I'd never heard that term before. I stared at him. Then he explained dryly, "Milk and sugar?"

"Ja, komplett," I said.

I unfolded the newspapers I'd just bought, spreading them out on the table. As I held up the *Neues Deutschland* in front of me, I noticed the guy sitting at the counter look over at me before quickly turning away. I scanned the front page. Above the title banner was the call for the proletariat of all nations to unite. The lead story was about a speech Erich Honecker gave to a special session of the Central Committee the day before. Too many German words and too much small print for my current mood. I unfolded the Berlin tourist map instead. It was published by the *VEB Tourist Verlag*. The prefix "VEB" for *Volkseigene Betrieb*—"people's plant," was attached to nearly all company names in the East. I had the map spread out on the table in front of me, but something about it wasn't right. I couldn't get my bearings by it. Berlin was printed on the cover, but this wasn't Berlin. The boundaries of the city on the map didn't have their familiar shape. Then I realized that the map showed only East Berlin. West Berlin was missing. The Tiergarten district of West Berlin that surrounded the area west of the Brandenburg Gate was left blank with the words *Berlin (West)* printed in small letters over white space. It actually made perfect sense. Why sell a map of a city that people from the West didn't need and East Berliners would never get to visit?

Eventually, my food arrived. Pork. I guess they found some after all. Two long, thin strips of it on a slice of white toast along with two small pieces of cauliflower, some coleslaw, and of course, a cup of coffee—*komplett*. I folded up the Berlin map and put it and the newspapers on the empty chair next to me. The guy sitting at the counter was looking at me again. It seemed as if he wanted to tell me something. Again, he quickly turned away, staring down at his cup of coffee. He was wearing a cheap, light blue nylon anorak, somewhat dingy, and American blue jeans. His shoes, though, definitely struck me as East German: a half boot made of flimsy turquoise suede glued onto a thin rubber soul. He looked at me again, this time to catch me staring at him. He was beginning to make me uncomfortable. I kept my head down and ate quickly. When I was done, I pulled the coffee toward me, stirring it until I was ready to gulp it down. When I brought the cup to my lips I saw the stranger walking slowly toward my table with his eyes fixed on me. He paused and hesitantly asked me something in a low voice in what might have been bad French. I didn't even try to hide my annoyance at his intrusion, "*What?*"

He had a nondescript head with one of those trendy crew cuts where the hair was half an inch long but somehow still stood up on end. "You are coming from England and are here on holiday?" he guessed as he sat down opposite me.

"I'm American. I live in West Berlin," I said as I tried to get the waiter's attention.

"I once met an American here. He was very nervous. Thought that behind every corner there was a KGB agent waiting to shoot him."

I again tried summoning the waiter only to see that he had disappeared.

"You are interested in the East German press?" the nondescript head asked, pointing to the newspapers on the chair between us. "You should read the *Wochenpost*. It is the only interesting paper in the GDR. Problem is that it is immediately sold out. Unless you have a subscription it is almost impossible to get one. I could get one for you."

When he said that, I suddenly realized that this was my first encounter with a real East German; one who lived day-in and day-out, *over here*, on this side of the Wall.

"I'd be more interested in a copy of Sputnik," I said.

"They banned Sputnik," he said, bitterly.

It was clear that he was uneasy speaking with me. His eyes often darted around the room, as if he was nervous about being seen here.

His name was Kai. He asked if I'd like another cup of coffee. I said *"komplett."* While he was off trying to find the waiter I decided I was going to get something for the money I paid to get into this city and when Kai returned to the table, I pummeled him with questions about daily life in East Germany. He answered everything I threw at him as though my interrogation was the most natural thing in the world. In time, his apparent apprehension faded, although it never left him completely. His eyes still darted nervously around the place from time to time.

I went on to find out the cost of things, from mass transit to a loaf of bread, secretly entertained by quaint prices that probably hadn't risen in forty years. But while the basics were cheap, anything that could remotely be considered a luxury item was expensive and hard to get. A color television, for example, was out of reach of most people. One generally had to wait from ten to twelve years for one of those Trabant automobiles, and when you finally had one, its immediate availability made it worth three or four times what it originally cost. Selling a car, whatever its condition, was easy. Just park it somewhere with a "For Sale" sign on it, leave the window open a crack and wait a couple of hours for a hopeful public to pile their best offers onto the driver's seat.

No, it wasn't officially forbidden to watch West German television or listen to West German radio. Neither was having contact with foreigners. Perhaps both were until the early or mid-1960s, Kai wasn't sure. In any case, Kai liked the Café Kisch precisely because it was a good place to meet foreign tourists. About the Berlin Wall, he rejected out of hand and with a laugh the official East German explanation that it was an *anti-fascist protective wall.* "It is there to keep people from leaving," he said flatly. "Nothing more and nothing less." I found it interesting that he, like Klaus, often spent time daydreaming about defeating it. Kai gave an amused cringe at my mention of Karl-Eduard von Schnitzler and *Der schwarze Kanal.* At first he expressed surprise that I would know the broadcast, but then immediately caught himself with the realization that, of course,

East German television would be received in West Berlin. I had to laugh when he referred to von Schnitzler as "Doctor von Click," the sound that was made by the millions of East German televisions being switched off simultaneously when his face appeared on the screen. In the army, he said, his unit was forced to sit down together every Monday night and watch it. Kai also told me that, a couple of years ago, West German television had broadcast pictures of von Schnitzler doing his shopping in West Berlin, noting that the most privileged are always the biggest boosters of any system.

We left the café and walked up Unter den Linden. While answering my queries about one thing or another, Kai would occasionally interrupt himself to point out something he thought I'd find interesting. He was like a tour guide in a safari park when an elusive animal was suddenly to be seen. I soon learned that Kai had a keen eye for things that westerners would find amusing or absurd about life in the East, which led me to believe that I wasn't the first person he'd escorted on this kind of tour. Kai was in the middle of telling me how the East German leadership officially explained away the need for Perestroika and Glasnost when he cut himself off and pointed to an elderly man waiting at a bus stop. "Look," he said, "he's wearing East German blue jeans." According to Kai, the indigo pigment they used never washed out, making them "totally uncool." He recalled the time when he was sixteen years old and agonized over spending his entire savings on his first pair of *Levis*, which were worn, faded to the point of being white and were full of holes, before finally sealing the transaction with another pupil in the boy's bathroom at school.

I asked him why it was so important to own a pair of American jeans. "Because, they were a small part of a world they would love to keep us from seeing, but can't," he said before returning to his explanation about the official shunning of Glasnost.

Kai made his living as a bartender in a youth club, one of a series that had been established to counter the cultural influence of the West on young people and to give them a place to gather and let off steam. They were about the only nightlife there was in the East. The entertainment in them had to be approved by the communist youth organization, *FDJ*, which also used them about once a month for political meetings. The DJs in these places where all trained by the state in a two-year course, and were officially referred to as *Schallplattenunterhalter* in an effort to avoid the western term "disc jockey." They were taught that it was their duty to make sure everyone let their aggressions out on the dance floor and went home in a good mood. Kai was taking the course and knew the details: sixty percent of the music played had to originate from the "socialist brother countries," forty percent could come from the West. An easy way around the quota was to count music from the West that had been licensed by East Bloc record labels as music originating in the East. Unfortunately, Kai had played too much of the wrong thing on his final exam recently and was accused of "spreading American subculture" before failing. On his next try, he said, he'll be better prepared and ready to give them exactly what they wanted.

We decided to have yet another cup of coffee in the Linden Corso, an absolutely nondescript box of a building on, what was before the war, one of the most fashionable intersections in all Berlin. No wonder it carried the biggest "Espresso" sign I had seen so far. Inside, I decided to finally take them up on their offer and ordered an espresso. The waiter looked at me like he'd never heard the word before. Kai ordered its substitute for me—*mokka*—then explained that there wasn't any real espresso in East Germany. They simply didn't have the machines to make it. He said the term "Espresso Bar" was used to "give East Berlin a little international flair." I was pleased with myself for being so perceptive.

Kai told me more about his job. Although he was now just tending bar at the club, he had once been the "club leader," a position that was a mix between nightclub manager and social worker. His demotion had to do with a trip to Hamburg he took with the *FDJ* youth group. It required a long and bitter campaign with the authorities to get permission take part in.

But Kai was determined and succeeded, prompting him to comically utter the slogan, "Only the best can go to the West!" On his way back from Hamburg, the train stopped at the Zoo Station in West Berlin. Kai covertly got off the train and paid a surprise visit to a woman he'd also met at the Café Kisch. I asked why he didn't stay in West Berlin when he had the chance. Kai recalled standing on a platform overlooking the Wall, "I saw that it was true what people from the West always say about East Berlin: that it's gray, it's dirty and it stinks. But when I saw it from a distance I had the feeling that it belonged to me—that it was mine and I was, in a strange way, responsible for it. I couldn't say that about West Berlin, even if it was colorful and smelled like roses."

A week later, Kai boarded the S-Bahn and went back home to East Berlin. At the Friedrichstrasse checkpoint a border guard took his passport, entered information into a computer and wanted to know why he was "one week late."

"I told them that I had one whole week holiday, not just the three days we'd spent in Hamburg. But it was no big deal, he just let me back in. That was on a Saturday. On Monday, I got a letter from the police. The very next day I had to go straight to the Polizeipräsidium in the Keibelstrasse, behind the Alexanderplatz. A guy met me down at the reception and took me up to the sixth floor. Everyone knows that the sixth floor isn't the ordinary police—it's the Stasi. Upstairs we had to go through three or four doors, a couple of them had these code buttons," he said. The security mechanism obviously intrigued him; he mentioned them as if only the highest echelons of the state would possess such things. "They brought me into this room. There was another Stasi guy and a typist. They turned on a tape recorder and for three and a half hours asked me a lot questions about what I did in West Berlin; if I went there for political reasons, who I met there, if I had contact with the CIA or West German intelligence . . ."

"They asked you if you had contact with the CIA?"

"Of course," he said. "Why wouldn't they?" Then interrupted himself with some excitement, "Hey, you see that guy sitting there in the corner? You know what his shirt is made of? It's DeDeRon." Kai then explained that the East Germans, in an attempt to show off their engineering ability, had developed their own version of nylon. They proudly gave their invention the name "DeDeRon," a play on the letters DDR, the German initials for the East German state. According to Kai, the material was so dense it made one sweat profusely, even in cool weather.

Over the next couple of hours, we each drank three cups of mokka in that loud hall. I asked Kai if he thought he would ever get to travel to the West again given his history. "I think I'd feel hopelessly trapped in your situation," I said. For some reason, I wanted to hear him confess that he regretted not staying in West Berlin when he had the chance.

"*Faack dem!*" he said defiantly in some approximation of English before returning to German. "I can honestly tell you that I don't have that feeling. It just means that I will have to fight a little harder and longer next time. It is all part of a bureaucracy that you have to learn to overcome here. Like at the club; when we want to have concerts we normally have to let the authorities know six weeks ahead which bands will play there and what songs they will play. But if we go to them and say that we want to make a concert for world peace, or for solidarity with Nicaragua, they say, 'Oh, that's a great idea.' Then we give them a list of bands we know they will like. Their whole attitude changes and we get permission right away. That doesn't mean there will not be other people playing there who weren't on the list. It's all something everyone learns to live with and work around. It's no big deal. Anyway, changes are coming. The old men at the top, they can't live forever."

Maybe not. But I noticed that Kai only seemed really at ease since we'd been sitting in this room, which was big and loud and with no one else sitting in our immediate vicinity. At the Troika, Ulrich always enjoyed needling Klaus by referring to the East Germany as a "terror state." I asked Kai if he felt terrorized by the system. "They always use pressure to get you to do what they want," he said. "Like demoting me at work. Some people get it really bad if they do things that threaten the existence of the established order. But I can't say I feel terrorized by them." Kai even seemed a little offended when he said, "This isn't Nazi Germany here. People aren't being rounded up and sent to concentration camps."

"But people can't speak their mind, can they? Don't you have to be careful who's listening? What about the Stasi?"

"People set their own limits," he said. "They do what they feel comfortable doing. We are speaking now, aren't we? The Stasi? They come around to the club sometimes to ask if there is anything going on that they should know about. I never tell them anything."

"They come around to your club? What do they look like?"

"What do they look like?" Kai was amused by the question. He laughed, shrugged his shoulders and said, "They look like normal people."

At six o'clock Kai said he had to leave. Out on the street he invited me to his club. "Why not come by on Friday night about nine o'clock?" he said. *"Dare will be many womens dare."* Kai took a pen from his pocket and marked the club's location on my map of Berlin, circling the street a couple of times. "The Sophienstrasse has been completely restored," he said. "It is one the most attractive streets in East Berlin."

"Well, I'm looking forward to it," I told him, although I had no intention of going. All his details about life behind the Wall were fun, but at that point I'd already had my fill of East Germany and had no desire whatsoever to return.

Then Kai took me by the arm and said, "Listen, Richard. When you come could you bring some blank cassette tapes with you? Blank cassettes are difficult to get here and we need them at the club."

Knowing his true motive for entertaining me all afternoon made me pity him. I told him it would be no problem and, for some reason, felt the need to give him my address and phone number, writing them down on an old receipt I found in my coat pocket. I felt stupid while I was doing it—as if I'd gotten into an elevator and asked the guy in front of me to please press

"10" before realizing he's blind. But Kai reacted as though it was perfectly normal. He showed me on the map where his apartment was, also circling the street with a pen. "I would give you my telephone number but I don't have a telephone. I applied for one eight years ago and I'm still waiting."

Later that night I showed up at the Troika eager to tell Klaus that I had mailed his letter, only to find that there had been a rapprochement between him and Ulrich. Evidently, Klaus, in a state of depression, had run up a mysterious and possibly dangerous debt that he could never hope to repay. He made the mistake of asking Geoffrey for money. Geoffrey in turn told Ulrich, who bailed out Klaus with a generous loan.

I sat at the table while Ulrich solemnly went over the carefully typed monthly repayment schedule he'd drawn up, explaining the compounded interest rates he used. "That's why if you do nothing but work like a maniac in double shifts, seven-days-a-week for the next six to eight months, it's good for you. If you only work a few hours a day, it gets very expensive and it's good for me, understand?"

Klaus, relieved and grateful, listened attentively, agreeing but not quite comprehending. Ulrich turned to me and whispered, as though he couldn't believe what a sucker he'd found, "Do I know an opportunity when I see one or what?"

When I got the chance I told Klaus that I had mailed his letter from East Berlin. Not only did he react as though it was a minor detail that really didn't matter, but he seemed embarrassed to be reminded of it. "Oh," he said with a nervously dismissive laugh. "Thanks a lot."

A Halo in the Darkness

I'M NOT ENTIRELY SURE why I decided to go back to East Berlin on that Friday night. Maybe if Kati hadn't come by at three o'clock in the morning a couple of days before, smelling like a locker room on fire and breathless with the news that "Hanno is taking us to Turkey for three weeks," I wouldn't have bothered. But when she came out of the shower covered with goose bumps and jumped on top of me in bed repeating herself with a good deal of excitement, "Isn't that great? Hanno is taking us to Turkey for three weeks!" and I assumed I was going along, only to have that notion laughed at, I knew it was time for some kind of change.

Friday afternoon, I purchased a six-pack of blank cassettes at a department store on the Hermannplatz. I arrived at Checkpoint Charlie at about six forty-five. While visitors could stay in East Berlin until midnight, they were not permitted to enter after 7 p.m. My plan was to have some dinner, then take a stroll before going to visit Kai around nine o'clock.

Another gray day had already disappeared into darkness as I walked through the Berlin Wall and over the curved sidewalk to the customs building. I slid my passport under the thick slab of glass. As usual, the border guard took it, not looking at me until he had studied the photograph inside. Sporadically, visitors were coming back to the West through the door off to the right. I was the only person going in the other direction. Finally, the guard spoke to me from behind the glass, "What are you going to do in East Berlin?"

I was a caught off guard by his question. "I don't know . . . Look around, maybe see a museum."

"The museums are already closed," he said, staring at me, waiting for a better answer. I didn't know what to say. I didn't want to tell him what my plans were. First of all, they were none of his goddamned business; second, I wasn't sure if it would be good for Kai to be receiving visitors from West Berlin. Despite his invitation, I couldn't help but think of his nervousness the other day. "I just want to look around a little," I said.

"You want to look around but you don't know what you want to see."

His tone made me angry. To hell with the whole fucking bunch of you, I thought. "Look, if you don't want me to go across, just give me back my passport!"

I was ready to go straight back home. But then, from one moment to the next, the guard's attitude changed entirely. "Why don't you want to visit East Berlin?" he asked. "You are free to stay until midnight. You still have a good five hours." He even seemed vaguely insulted that I'd asked for my passport back.

I couldn't believe it. I slid five marks for the Tagesvisum under the glass and thought, you miserable shit. The only thing you're really worried about is the twenty-five West marks you'll lose if I decide to turn around and leave. It was an awesome feeling; as if the entire East German state had knelt before me, ready to kiss my ass for a lousy twenty-five marks! The border ceased being the least bit intimidating after that. The sinister air that surrounded the border guards rolled off them at once, like water off grease. It was now impossible for me to take any of them seriously.

He stamped my passport, inserted the paper visa and buzzed me in. In the room where bags were searched, one of the guards insisted on checking the bag I was carrying the cassettes in. "What are you going to do with these?" he asked in a voice that suggested I'd better have a pretty damned good answer.

"They're a gift for a friend," I said with a smug grin. "I'm told that such things are an extravagance around here."

"Or perhaps you are going to try and sell them?" he asked menacingly.

"Sell them for what? . . . *East marks*?"

He handed me back the bag. I made the required exchange of money and went back to the Café Kisch for another slice of ham on toast. I ordered from the same waiter who was there the other day and threw in a coffee, *komplett*. He gave a resolute nod that said, good, now you've caught on.

After dinner I wasted time by slowly walking toward the Alexanderplatz; to the landmark I had anchored in my mind: the pollution-stained facade of the apartment block carrying the big neon sign proudly announcing that East German chemical products were finding their way into markets around the world. From there it was just a short walk to the Sophienstrasse.

Kai was right. From what I could see of the area in the dim light of the old lamps it looked like a charming prewar European street. About half the way down the block I found the place; a storefront establishment. I walked through the door and was immediately confronted by another, padded one. Inside I paid the three marks and ten-pfennig cover charge to a woman who reluctantly lifted her eyes from a book just long enough to take my money. The club was a small, dark room with two big, throbbing loudspeakers hanging from the ceiling. Under them, three people were dancing, absolutely indifferent to each other and everything else in the world. The disc jockey stood on a platform in the corner off to the right, bobbing up and down to the rhythm while searching for his next selection in a wooden crate full of record albums. Empty benches ran along one wall with three or four small, round unoccupied tables in front of them. It didn't seem like a very popular place. At the back of the room was a wood and glass partition with the French doors removed from their hinges. In the room beyond it, Kai was standing behind the bar waiting on a lone customer.

I walked over to the bar, which was unusually high, reaching almost to my chest. Kai, busy pouring a couple of glasses of wine, didn't notice me. On the wall behind him, over racks of bottles, was a framed portrait of Mikhail Gorbachev.

I lifted myself onto a towering bar stool in the corner. With my back against the wall, I had a clear view of the whole club. Kai glanced up and smiled. "Good evening, Richard," he said, as though he'd been expecting me. "Wery glad to have you here dis night."

"Very nice to be here," I replied, holding up the bag of cassette tapes.

Kai's face lit up as if I had managed to smuggle gold across the border. "Tank you wery much, sir. Now, what can I get for you?"

I ordered a beer. As Kai was pouring it from the tap, I pointed to the portrait on the wall behind him and jokingly asked, "Hey, who's that?"

"Mikhail Sergeyevich," he said, adding with a fist clenched in supportive enthusiasm, *"Gorbi!"*

Kai put the glass of beer in front of me as a couple of people came to the bar. He was obviously in his element here; totally relaxed and exhibiting none of the nervousness he had shown the other day. He swayed slightly to the music while pouring drinks or wiping the bar clean. The Plattenaufleger introduced something from the band *Pink Floyd*. Kai smiled, motioning toward the DJ with his chin, *"Dark Side of the Moon.* That's my record. I had to change money on the black market at seven-to-one so I could buy it with West marks at an *Intershop*. It cost me over 100 marks, that's more than two months' rent. Two weeks later it was licensed on *Amiga*, the East German record label. Cost sixteen marks and ten pfennig."

"Bad investment," I said.

He laughed, "You can say that again."

I leaned into the bar and asked him to let me know if anyone from the Stasi showed up tonight. Kai gave an uneasy grin, wiping the bar between us with an old cloth. I could tell he was sorry for having brought it up the other day.

"I don't think they will come tonight," he said quietly. "Once, maybe two times in a year they come, not more." He perked up, "Oh, I almost forgot, I have something for you." Kai disappeared into a room behind a curtain at the far end of the bar and came back with a large manila envelope. "I thought you might like these."

Inside were old promotional brochures for Trabant automobiles; western-style ads complete with attractive women used as marketing tools for the awkward little car. One from 1969 made much of the fact that the Trabant offered a bigger engine: *"Now with more power—3 horsepower more!"* Another showed a Trabant turning a corner among the prefab boxes of the Alexanderplatz with the Television Tower in the background, noting that the squat little car was as *"modern and generous as the capital of the GDR itself."* I looked over the brochures, shaking my head with amusement. They were impossible to take seriously. Kai had again demonstrated that he knew what westerners liked.

While I was reading them, the DJ played *Born in the U.S.A.*, which caused Kai to come over. "It took them a long time before they licensed this one," he shouted. "They couldn't make up their minds whether it was pro-American propaganda or not." Then he went back to the middle of the bar where he had been serving a customer.

That the East Germans bothered licensing music from the West at all came as somewhat of a surprise. Here they were, reduced to pulling every humiliating trick imaginable, like randomly changing speed-limit signs on the transit routes in order to grab badly-needed hard currency from West German drivers, then they had to go and spend God-knows how much of it on Pink Floyd and Bruce Springsteen records. The riot at the Brandenburg Gate again came to mind. Pop culture was probably the most powerful weapon the West had in its arsenal. If the Cold War was one of attrition, an old Johnny Rotten tune suddenly making it back onto the charts could be a more harrowing prospect for the East German leadership than any number of American atomic cruise bombs.

I continued reading the brochures. Before I knew it, the place was absolutely packed with people and filled with cigarette smoke. Most were dressed in colors that ranged from black to charcoal gray. They were standing three or four deep at the bar and the dance floor beyond the partition was packed with a horde of bouncing and wildly gyrating heads. A small fan up in one of the windows opposite the bar was shooting a jet stream of exhaust into the alley outside. My eyes were watering and it had gotten so hot that I thought my beer might turn to steam. I took off my coat and draped it over my bar stool. Kai had been joined by a boney colleague wearing a pair of black "skinny" jeans. I had to wonder if it was possible for him to sit down in them. Kai took a moment to show him the bag of cassettes I'd brought. The colleague signaled his gratitude with a smile and a nod.

When I finished my beer, my new friend immediately placed another one in front of me. Although he was now too busy to talk, Kai seemed determined that I be well taken care of.

I sat back against the wall and watched the crowd, immensely enjoying the fact that I was certainly the only westerner here. The other day, Kai told me that the United States was one of the two most interesting places in the world for young East Germans. The other was West Germany, but only because showing interest in it was an easy way to stick-it to the establishment. For now, I would hold the secret of my national origin to myself and revel in the feeling that I'd been bold enough to covertly penetrate deep into the bowels of East Berlin nightlife while my friends stayed behind on our side of the Wall and safely drank their beer at the Troika.

From my high perch I watched the *Plattenaufleger* as he worked over a sea of bouncing heads crammed into the small, dark room. He's like a Top-40 AM-radio personality working a local high school dance. His persona seemed perfectly harmless and in sharp contrast to the streetwise look of everyone else in the place. At one point he pulled someone out of the crowd and introduced him as a member of an evidently well-known East German rock band. The dance floor roared its praise. Had the *Plattenaufleger* known the secret of where I came from he would surely have introduced me to the crowd, which would have celebrated its approval with applause. If they had known that I'd just made the entire East German state apparatus genuflect before me for a little hard currency change, they'd probably carry me triumphantly away on their shoulders as if I were *Gorbi* himself.

I had been indulging my vanity with that thought when I glanced down from my bar stool and first caught sight of her face. She was sitting at the small, round table directly beneath me in the overcrowded room opposite an apparently distraught woman. She had just extinguished a cigarette in an ashtray and was leaning into the table, occasionally nodding in sympathy while the other woman talked nonstop. Her face was full of quiet concern, yet her eyes were strangely expressionless. Her shoulder-length, luminous blonde hair shone almost like a halo in the surrounding darkness. Her face and perfect complexion were a combination of soft, gentle curves that could easily provoke stalking or other obsessive behavior in men. One of those faces that I, for some reason, always seemed incapable of meeting. Then I noticed that the style of her dress was out of place here: a pink T-shirt with very short sleeves and a pair of those baggy, pleated blue jeans with an elastic waist band and covered with that strange stonewashed pattern that marked the East Germans at the transit highway rest stop. A long, beige gabardine coat was folded over the back of her chair and there was a nearly empty sekt glass on the table in front of her. She nodded again in sympathy while arching her back, taking an automatic glance up in the process. Our eyes met for several blank seconds. Her expression was a combination of solace and listlessness. What a smile she must have. If only she would smile. I turned away for a moment, took a sip of beer and looked over at Kai. He was busy dealing out drinks like bread to a starving mob. I stole another glimpse down at her, again wishing she would smile. It wasn't long before I began asking myself who this person was. What kind of childhood did she have here behind the Wall? How did she earn her living here in this socialist paradise? Was she happy here, or would she give anything to get out? I knew then that this was a moment I would always remember. When I was old and gray and living somewhere that would, without a doubt, be far away from here, I would remember this girl's face with wonder and regret. But what could be done? What excuse could I possibly give for injecting myself into what was obviously a private moment between two friends? I asked myself what Geoffrey would do. He would casually force himself in next to troubled woman and, while slowly rolling a cigarette, cock his head toward her like a bird with a put-on, debonair expression simply say, "Hi." A minute or two after being scornfully ignored, he'd go back to the bar and stakeout his next victim, at peace with himself for at least having tried. I turned away again, admiring Geoffrey for his thick skin.

Kai gave me a look of resigned frustration; we weren't getting the chance to talk. He pointed to my almost empty glass. I motioned that I was okay for now and turned around, sitting with my back against the bar. A man had appeared at the table below me, squeezing himself in next to the distraught woman and comforting her with his arm around her shoulder. This gave the girl with the wonderful face time for a pause. She slid back in her chair, stuck her hands in the pockets of her pants and pursed her lips ever so slightly, as though considering all she had been listening to. There was now as definite emotional distance between her and the other two. It seemed a liberation of sorts. She stared at her lap while listening to her friends talk. But the more she listened, the more unsettled she became. She seemed to be the kind of person who couldn't hide her feelings from others. They would become known through her wonderfully expressive face whether she wanted them to or not. Little by little I could see what she was listening to become intolerable. She downed what was left in her glass and stood up, asking the others if they wanted anything from the bar. The woman's wine glass was still full; the guy next to her asked for a beer. I watched with a growing sense of excitement as she squeezed herself in right next to me at the bar. My mind raced, trying to think of a line that might start us in conversation, but drew nothing but blanks. She got Kai's attention by calling out

his name and ordered. He couldn't have heard her over the
noise in the place but by some telepathic power seemed to know
what she wanted. I was busy observing the slight forward bend
to the back of her neck and the soft, golden line of peach fuzz
that began at the top of her spine when Kai abruptly appeared
with the drinks. She pulled some aluminum coins out of her
purse, paid and was gone. Kai asked me again if I wanted
another beer. I did. When he brought it I asked if he knew her.
"Only by sight," he said. "Why do you ask?"

"She knew your name. I thought maybe she was a friend
of yours."

"A lot of people somehow know the bartender's name.
Sorry."

That was it. The perfect opportunity had come and gone
in a flash. I'd blown it. But it didn't matter. This was East Berlin.
For a moment I'd forgotten that. Nothing could have come of it,
anyway. I kept telling myself that because it was the simple
truth. I was only a visitor to this world and would soon be forced
to leave it. I checked my watch. It was twenty past ten. I'd wait
until eleven o'clock, then go with my envelope full of souvenirs,
giving myself plenty of time to get back to Checkpoint Charlie
before the midnight deadline. The Trabant brochures had made
the trip worthwhile enough.

I leaned back against the bar, trying to enjoy the loud
music and the East Berliners as they jumped around on the
dance floor but found my eyes constantly drawn to her. She was
again sitting back in her chair with her hands in her pockets,
staring at the ascending stream of tiny bubbles in her glass. The
other two were deep in conversation on the bank opposite her. I
got the impression that she would rather be somewhere else but
was being kept here by some sense of obligation. I felt
affectionately protective of her and found myself wishing I could
help her out of the situation, whatever it was. She glanced up at
me. Our eyes met again for a few moments. This time she
registered that I was staring at her. Looking down again at her
glass she smiled ever so slightly. Maybe what I'd exhibited was a
more a gawk than a stare. Her reaction made me feel silly. From

then on I was determined to keep my eyes locked on the dance floor and not look at her again. It was a resolution I was able to keep for about thirty seconds. Her faint smile had disappeared. I took another sip of beer and turned my attention back to the proletarian masses beyond the partition. There was a tightly packed throng four or five deep standing along the walls, watching the dancing crowd. Heads bobbing, long, sweaty locks of hair and clenched fists shooting up in the air to the rhythm of the music. The loudspeakers were pounding with an old song from *The Police* that was a favorite of mine during my college days. In the dim light of the club the scene was not unlike a strange, ancient rite being celebrated by a primitive lost tribe. Then I noticed something cutting its way through the crowd. People would stop or slow their gyrations momentarily while looking down at their feet, as if they were letting something pass by. Whatever it was, it was being escorted by one of the clientele. I thought it was probably a large dog. The Germans were always taking their dogs to places dogs didn't belong. But as the escort's head neared the partition, the bodies parted revealing not a dog but a little old blind man. He shuffled his way through the crowd of perspiring young people, holding his cane in one hand and trying to feel his way with the other. His thin, gray hair was combed straight back and his gaunt face unshaven; the deadened eyes were wide open, as was his mouth, making the man look as if he'd been traumatized by the bedlam going on around him. The person escorting him shouted something in his ear, then passed him off to others who, one by one, directed him with great care toward the bar.

The girl with the beautiful face motioned for him to be sent to her table. As he came closer, I heard the people helping him along shout in his ear over the music, "Hallo, Erich!" He responded by giving each new hand on his shoulder a pat in gratitude. The girl took possession of him, sat him down in her chair and knelt next to him for a few minutes, talking close to his ear. Even then it seemed that he was having difficulty hearing her. The old man, whose shell-shocked expression never left him, sat patting her hand on his shoulder as she spoke.

Strangely, his attire—the frayed, black knit polo shirt buttoned up to his neck and tattered dark gray suit—were more appropriate in this crowd than hers. As she knelt beside him I noticed for the first time that she was wearing white shoes.

A moment later she had again crammed herself in at the bar right next to me and was calling after Kai, "A schnapps for Erich!" Kai put his hand to his ear. She pointed down behind the bar, "*Erich!*" Kai nodded his awareness of the situation while screwing the cap back onto a bottle of mineral water. Again, I couldn't think of a damned thing to say to her.

She looked down at the old man like a mother checking on her child, then up to catch me staring at her. Another faint smile. Then, for some reason, I looked at my watch, pointed at the frail old gentleman sitting there waiting for his drink and asked, "Does he dance?"

She laughed, "I don't know, you'll have to ask him." I was trying to think of a follow up line before Kai brought over the drink when she asked, "Where do you come from?" I told her I was American, from New York City. I was disappointed when she answered only with a distracted "Ah," as if to say, "*Oh, so that's it.*"

Kai brought over a glass of schnapps, gave me a quick wink of approval for having made contact, then continued working the bar without waiting for payment. She knelt down beside the man and said something in his ear while pressing the shot-glass gently into his slightly trembling hand. Then she took her glass of sekt from the table and stood next to me, looking down at him with concern until he managed to take a sip, feel around for the table with his free hand and set the glass down on it. When he had accomplished that she turned her attention back to me. I jumped at the opportunity to ask her name. I wanted a name to connect with the face. The music was so loud that I wasn't sure I'd heard it right. "What?" I asked. "Traudi?"

"*Trrraoudee,*" she repeated, trilling the *R* precisely.

I knew it as a short form for several old German names that I had always associated with the Alps. "And what kind of Traudi are you?"

She smiled and said, "My name is Ehrentraud."

I thought it a shame that such a pretty face would have such an ungainly name attached to it. I introduced myself, also needing to repeat my name over the music. "And why are you here in Berlin?" she asked. "Are you on holiday?"

"I live in West Berlin. I came here tonight to visit my friend Kai, the bartender."

When I asked what she did for a living, she tried speaking in English, translating her profession literally from the German, *Krankenschwester.* "I am . . . I am a . . . sick sister?"

"You're a nurse," I said. "The English word is nurse."

An embarrassed smile. "Russian. Russian I can speak well, not very much English."

When she asked me what I did for a living, I suddenly felt the need to make myself important, telling her that I had a company that imported high technology products from America for large computer systems. I suppose it was technically true. Not that it seemed to matter. She arched her eyebrows somewhat and gave a blank nod. To divert the conversation back to her I asked, "You work in a hospital, I guess?"

"Yes, I work in the Charité. You know the Charité? . . . No? Oh, it is a very good one; the most famous in the whole republic. I am very lucky to be there."

Traudi spoke carefully and thoughtfully, with a very slight lisp that I found sympathetic.

There was a long silence. She looked over at her distressed friend who, with her head now on the shoulder of the guy sitting next to her, seemed to be in a better mood. I thought Traudi would excuse herself and go back to them, but when they both looked up at her, she asked if either of them spoke English. Her two friends shook their heads, simultaneously answering, "Russian."

But I wasn't interested in the others. Ignoring them I turned the conversation back to her, "Are you from Berlin originally?"

"Yes, I grew up in Köpenik, but now I live in the Prenzlauer Berg district. And you? I can't imagine living so far from home. Don't you get homesick?"

"It's not so bad. I get to go back two or three times a year."

"Really? So often?"

"It's really not very far. It takes about as long as going from Berlin to Munich by train."

"For me America seems very far away," she said.

I worried that maybe I'd said something in bad taste. Traudi stood there in pensive silence, her lips pursed ever so slightly. She seemed to have a habit of doing that. And when she did, I could almost see a thousand thoughts floating around inside her head, all at the same time.

The dance floor was relatively empty with most people standing along the walls. During the last couple of tunes, I noticed the DJ carefully studying the room. When he had calculated the right moment, he introduced a Monty Python song, *Always Look on the Bright Side of Life*. A general roar of approval filled the room as a herd of people converged on the dance floor. Traudi looked down at the old man, knelt next to him and said something in his ear. He nodded and patted her hand on his shoulder. She then stood up, looked me in the eyes and said, "I would like to dance with you."

I normally wasn't much for that kind of thing, but this would be the only time I'd ever see her, and since here dancing meant jumping up and down pressed tightly together with your partner (and everyone else in the place for that matter), I agreed.

She pulled me by the hand and managed to weave us into the center of the dance floor where it smelled like sweat and cheap perfume. There was hardly room to move. The dancing throng had joined in a sing-along of the repeats of "Always Look on the bright side of life," whistling at the appropriate moments. I watched Traudi swaying to the music with her eyes closed, moving her lips slightly to some of the words. I was being pushed and shoved whole time, but she somehow managed to remain untouched by the crowd. We stayed for another number, and another. She seemed lost in this chaos, opening her eyes only between songs and absently looking around while moving her hand through her hair. The DJ introduced a song called *Alt Wie Ein Baum*, which I'd never heard. Traudi became alert, dancing energetically with her hands on my hips. "Do you know the Puhdys?" she yelled at me, smiling and obviously enjoying herself. "They are an East German band!"

I eventually looked at my watch. It was a quarter past eleven. I had to start thinking about leaving. We moved back to the bar. Traudi immediately knelt down and spoke with the old man. Evidently, he was ready to go. She helped him out of his chair and escorted him as far as the partition. Kai came over, smiling from behind the bar. I asked how much I owed for the drinks. "*Ach,* no money," he said. "Next time come on a Saturday. There is always live jazz on Saturday night; very good mood here." I thanked him for the souvenirs and we shook hands. Maybe it was because of the female contact I had just made, but Kai seemed to have no doubt that he'd be seeing me again soon.

Traudi came back to the bar as I was putting on my coat. "You are leaving?" she asked. I told her it was time for me to go; that I had to leave East Berlin by midnight. I detected a moment of indecision as she looked over at her friends. "You don't have time for another drink?"

It was a tempting offer. Again I checked my watch. It hadn't gotten any earlier. I could imagine that anyone who got back to the checkpoint after the deadline would be subject to a large hard currency fine and a lot of hassle. "I wish I could, but I really have to leave now."

Traudi took a pen from the pocket of her coat and wrote her name and address on a beer coaster. "Perhaps you will send me a postcard from New York sometime." I asked if she had a telephone number. She laughed as if I'd said something funny, shook my hand and went back to her friends.

I gave a last wave at Kai and made my way across the dance floor where sweaty bodies pushed and shoved me in every direction but the one I wanted to go in. I had my feet stomped on, was poked in the ribs by elbows and slapped in the jaw by a dank forearm before finally being expulsed into the street.

With just thirty-five minutes to get back to Checkpoint Charlie, I ran up to the corner and made for the dark silhouetted dome of the Berlin cathedral, then jogged down deserted, dimly lit streets. A guard leisurely strolling around in front of the border area saw me running toward him and waved me in with lazy, looping motions of his hand. All the years of café lifestyle I'd been living in Germany had taken their toll on my constitution. I reached Checkpoint Charlie breathing heavily and with my heart pounding hard. At the border, the steel gates across the Friedrichstrasse had been shut. Only the pedestrian exit was still open. The amusement park was closed for the night, its personnel waiting for the last of the stragglers to get out.

At the American control house in West Berlin I paused to catch my breath, filling my lungs with cool air and just then realizing that I was still clutching the manila envelope Kai had given me.

I walked down to the Kochstrasse U-Bahn entrance. An elderly couple walked up the steps out of the station. They simply walked by, not paying me the slightest attention. Although I felt they should have. I had the peculiar sensation of having just fallen back into my usual surroundings after a trip to another dimension with an envelope full of strange car ads the only proof of my excursion. It could have been an episode straight out of *The Twilight Zone*.

The Very Essence of Her Soul

THE NEXT DAY, I was supposed to meet Kati for the last time before she flew to Turkey with Hanno and Anja. But that morning she called and cancelled. I really didn't care. If Hanno was springing for a three-week family holiday, then he should have his wife all to himself.

The weather outside was typical Berlin miserable: dank and gray and certain to rain again and again throughout the day. I sat at my desk looking at the address written in Traudi's hand, toying with the idea of paying her a visit. What would be a good time? Kai told me the East Berlin clubs were open until 1 a.m. at the latest. Even if she stayed until the bitter end last night, she'd surely be up and around by noon. What if she didn't go home alone? Two o'clock might be a better idea.

Just for the hell of it, I took out my West German map of Berlin, which showed both the West and East. Feeling as if I were preparing for a journey deep into a faraway land, I looked for her address. Only after I found Traudi's street did realization set in that she lived just across town.

I decided to go out for a walk, leaving my apartment with the nebulous intention of heading somewhere in the direction of Checkpoint Charlie and the Café Adler. It was about noon when I took a "Bernd alert," looking through my peephole before running out the door and down the stairs. I now wanted to see the guy about as much as I'd like to see a big red sore develop on my lip. By the time I'd gotten the U-Bahn over at the Mehringdamm station, I had already made up my mind to stay on the train and go into East Berlin, this time via the Friedrichstrasse checkpoint.

The last stop in West Berlin was Kochstrasse. The train then rolled into East Berlin, slowing as it passed through two stations permanently out of service before reaching the Friedrichstrasse Bahnhof. The stations in between were dim, yet clearly to be seen were the silhouettes of border guards carrying assault rifles standing ghost-like on the platforms as the train rolled slowly by.

The border control was at the end of the U-Bahn platform under the Friedrichstrasse Station. The usual routine: face checks, visa fee and the mandatory twenty-five-mark exchange. I found my way out to the street where the first thing I noticed was a small memorial plaque: "*Shortly before the end of the criminal Hitler war, two young German soldiers were hanged on this spot by inhuman SS bandits.*"

I wandered up Unter den Linden, unable to decide whether visiting Traudi was a good idea or not. Giving me her address didn't necessarily mean she had any desire to see me again. The only thing it meant for sure was that I should send her a postcard sometime. Maybe her grandfather collected postage stamps. Suppose I got there and she wasn't alone? What if I barged in on Traudi and her boyfriend having a late breakfast together in the bathtub?

A thick, damp mist had accumulated in the air. When I reached Alexanderplatz, I checked the route to Traudi's apartment that I had drawn on my map, then folded it up and stuffed into my back pocket. I paused again, taking stock of the situation, thinking over the probability and results of different scenarios in my head, finally persuading myself that she most likely just wouldn't be at home. Anything else would mean a few awkward moments, nothing more. It wasn't as if I could accidentally run into her on the street sometime. The East German government was, after all, spending a large part of its gross national product on making sure that could never happen.

I walked up the Prenzlauer Allee, a broad street lined by old, nondescript apartment houses with streetcars occasionally rumbling up and down the middle of the avenue. My plan was just to find the address and worry about actually knocking on the door when the time came.

The mist in the air began to coagulate; it wasn't long before the first cold drops of drizzle were landing on me. I bowed my head and walked quickly. According to the map I should reach a major intersection, the Dimitroffstrasse, and turn left. I walked at a good pace in the cold, increasing drizzle as it flew directly down the broad avenue and struck me on the head. Eventually, I turned into a side street to try and gain a respite from the rain.

I had landed in a dark, foreboding district. Row after row of old, dilapidated apartment houses with ornate turn-of-the-century facades, like those in Kreuzberg on my side of the Wall, but smashed and broken; buildings still pitted by Second World War shrapnel and decayed by more than forty years of weather. Familiar, yet strangely unfamiliar. I was walking through the Berlin I'd seen in photographs taken immediately following the German surrender in 1945; one of those areas still relatively intact. The rubble had been cleared from the streets but the buildings obviously hadn't been renovated since then. I continued over the glistening granite slabs of the old sidewalks. The whole district was like this—one dark, deserted cobblestoned street leading into another. The blurred and shattered exteriors lining them conspired with the weather to obliterate any insinuation of color. Many of the old wooden apartment house doors leading in from the street were half open, exposing dreary back courts beyond the shadows of drab entrance halls. Only the occasional lighted window and a few Trabants parked on the side of the roads convinced me that the entire area hadn't been abandoned long ago. My American-bred instinct began sounding the alarm; kept telling me that I had wandered into a dangerous slum and should quickly retreat. Yet my years of living in Germany had taught me that that grim reality wasn't an inevitable fact of life. Then I wondered if maybe this was a place the East German authorities preferred that foreigners didn't see. But if that were the case, I'd definitely never have been allowed to stray this far. Nevertheless, that thought led me to try and be as inconspicuous as possible. I would try my best to find the way by memory and not draw attention to myself by pulling out a tourist map. If I managed to find the address, fine. If not, maybe it was just as well.

The sky darkened. The acid rain falling from the sky mixed with the dust on the street to form bubbling ooze. Many of the buildings still bore the weathered, hand-painted signs of old Berlin over vacant store-front facades and cellar shops: fruits and vegetables, dairy products, a hair salon, a shop for coffee and tea. All the evacuated remnants of an expropriated middle class slowly fading away unnoticed.

Ultimately, I did reach the Dimitroff, another broad thoroughfare with streetcars. I crossed it and continued up the Dunckerstrasse, keeping my head down and walking briskly against the incessant and increasingly cold drizzle. Each glance upward revealed only that same depressing blur of dark tones and glistening smashed masonry. I soon crossed an S-Bahn overpass and had landed myself on Traudi's street. As luck or fate would have it, her apartment house was right there on the corner.

The building, like the rest of the district, had fallen victim to vicious neglect. The broken plaster facade exposed brickwork and the rusted steel supports underneath. The wooden door creaked loudly on its hinges, echoing through the foyer as I pushed it open and switched on the light: a single bulb suspended from the ceiling by a long wire. Walls painted in an aged institutional green were coated with a greasy film that caught and held dirt and flakes of soot like flypaper. Elegant reliefs of seed-sowing goddesses protruding from under a heavy cover of dust looked like ancient artifacts found in a windswept desert. On the wall near the staircase, over a row of dented mailboxes, I managed to make out Traudi's family name from behind the filthy glass of the tenant register. Just beyond it, the door to the back courtyard was wide open, exposing a desolate space bordered by towering, war-ravaged walls. The clammy, crooked silhouette of a single bare tree stood in the center. Even here, in this depressing and pitiable corner where I was sure the sun could never penetrate to the ground, battle had raged. Stored against a wall to the right, what I first thought was a bobsled turned out to be an old, rusting motorcycle sidecar.

I climbed the first flight of stairs while combing the water out of my hair, realizing then just how soaked I was.

There were four apartments on each floor. The lack of telephones had led residents to hang note pads and pencils next to their doorbells. Up on the second floor, the door to the center apartment was open a few inches. A small brass nameplate identified the resident as *Hubertus Schmid*. I couldn't resist my first peek inside an East German dwelling. Through another half-open door at the end of a short front hall I could see a slice of living room: a stocky old man with thick white hair wearing a frayed pullover was sitting in an upholstered chair, holding a plate up at his chin and gnawing on a stick of salami while watching television. This guy had a telephone. It was on a small table next to his chair. He glanced toward the door to catch me looking at him and froze. I was startled by the suddenness with which he locked his gaze on me. "Oh, sorry," I coughed, and ran up the next flight of stairs.

Traudi had the center apartment directly above. I put my ear to the door. From inside I could hear the faint sound of water running and the gentle clatter of dishes being stacked. A few moments later it went quiet. I got the willies when I noticed Schmid silently watching me from the shadows of the staircase. I gave a couple of timid knocks. The door opened instantly. Traudi gave a very startled *"Uhh!"* It was as if we had collided physically in the street. She stood in the doorway staring at me with a vacant expression, either pure surprise or simple displeasure, I couldn't tell. Maybe she didn't remember me at all. I cleared my throat and spoke in English, hoping to jar her memory, "I was in the neighborhood and thought you might have a cup of coffee for me." She was dressed in blue overalls, a T-shirt, and had her hair tucked under a blue kerchief, immediately reminding me of the statue of the young woman worker I'd seen in front of the East Berlin city hall.

"Oh . . . hallo," she said reaching out to shake my hand. It gradually came back to her. "Ja, of course . . . Last night."

As Traudi stood away from the door I noticed she was carrying a large tin bucket that was filled with soot and ashes. She invited me in and her face relaxed. "You are soaked through," she said with an amused smile, pushing the door closed behind her.

Then Schmid's voice bellowed up from the staircase, "Fräulein Franzke! May I speak with you a moment?"

Traudi looked as if she was being pulled in two directions at once before sending me into the living room, saying she'd be right back.

The wooden floorboards in the rectangular living room had been sanded but not yet coated with anything. The room itself had obviously just been painted; it was bright white. It was also furnished in a strange mix of styles. There were a couple of pieces of old, dark, heavy German furniture, including a writing desk with a chair that looked like a small throne by the window at the far end of the room. To the right of them was a door to another room, and between it and the entrance from the hall, against the right wall, a "fabulous fifties" sofa complete with worn corduroy cushions and a kidney-shaped coffee table before it. In the left corner of the living room, by the entrance from the foyer, was a large coal heating oven faced in ocher-colored tiles with a wicker chair next to it. I took off my wet coat and sat there with it folded on my lap.

Staring at the big makeshift bookshelves, which ran almost entirely along the left side of the room, I wondered what her neighbor was saying about me. Probably that she'd just let some kind of dubious character into her home and they should call the *Volkspolizei* right away. I sat back in the creaking wicker and tried driving the chill from my spine with the warmth of the oven. It gave off a pleasant odor, like burning incense, reminding me of something familiar that I couldn't quite place.

A few of minutes later, Traudi returned with her bucket filled with bricks of coal and put it down next to my chair. She then made a hasty exit, pulling the door to the living room closed behind her. I heard the ringing sound of metal as a pot was taken from the stove, the running water that filled it, the striking of a match, and the igniting of a gas flame. The proximity of the sounds, as well as the shifting shadows projected on the doorway at the far end of the living room told me that the kitchen was directly behind the wall to the right. Her footsteps faded away a bit to another area then came back. She reappeared through the doorway at my end of the room with a towel and a coat hanger. Traudi handed me the towel and took the coat from my lap, hanging it on the side of the coal oven so it would dry out. She did all this quickly and efficiently without saying a word or even looking at me.

I rubbed the towel over my wet head a couple of times, sensing that she was being polite but distant as she sat down on the sofa with her hands folded on her lap. The smile I had seen when I entered the apartment was clearly gone.

"I hope I'm not disturbing you."

"Well . . . no. Actually, I was just on my way down to the cellar to get some coal. When I opened the door you were standing there."

There was a silent void that had to be filled. "This oven is great. I wouldn't mind having one in my apartment," I said cheerfully.

I might have detected a sneer. "I guess you are all used to central heating in the West." Intentionally or not, she said it in a way that made me feel like a pampered child.

The atmosphere between us was clearly fragile, perhaps already damaged beyond repair. I thought it must have had something to do with the man downstairs, so I decided to confront the problem head on. "I couldn't resist a look in your neighbor's apartment. The door was open and I'd never—"

"What?" She apparently didn't know what I was talking about.

"The old man downstairs . . . Schmid? His door was open. He caught me peeking into his apartment."

"No, *really?*" That seemed to amuse her.

"I saw him chewing on a salami. He eats like a rodent, did you know that?"

That amused her even more. Under a giggle she mumbled something about water boiling and went into the kitchen through the door at the far end of the room. I walked over to the desk by the window. On it were two small black-and-white photographs in a silver double frame. One was an old photo of a young couple. From their faces I knew at once that they were her parents. Her mother was probably in her early twenties, her father noticeably older. In the other photo, Traudi must have been about thirteen years old. She was standing with her father, who looked much older than in the first photo, and a teenage boy who, judging by his face, was probably her brother.

I picked up the photos and stuck my head into the kitchen where it seemed ten degrees cooler than the living room. "Are they your parents?" The kitchen was a small room with a shower stall and water heater in one corner and a small balcony that overlooked the street. The walls were covered in faded, old, green wallpaper with thin black, yellow and red lines that ran from top to bottom in strange twisting and curving patterns.

"Ja, my parents and my brother, Sascha," she said as she brought a pot of coffee into the living room and set it down on the table in front of the sofa.

"He has a Russian name."

"Yes, and I have a very German one." Traudi took the photos from me, smiling and shaking her head slightly as though fondly recalling the antics of children. "I think my parents were trying single-handed reconciliation between East and West," she said, placing the photos back on the desk.

"Are they all in Berlin?"

"No," she said as she sat down on the sofa. "My parents are dead. My brother is in the West. I'm sorry I don't have any sugar. Do you take milk?"

"Yes, please. . . How did he get out?"

"*Get out?*" she repeated, as if I'd used some strange phraseology she had never considered before. It took a moment before she answered. "The normal way . . . He applied to go and eventually he went."

There was an evasiveness in her response. This was something Traudi obviously didn't want to discuss. She sat there pouring coffee, never looking at me while she spoke. At that moment she became a solitary figure. Maybe it was just the old furniture, but the room seemed to be a repository of things from past lives. Now she was the only one left to act as curator after all the others had deserted her. The protectiveness I felt for her last night suddenly returned. I wanted to be encouraging about the prospect of a reunion with her brother and decided to sing that hopeful tune—Kai's version. "Well, changes will come. The old men who run this place can't live forever."

But no, that was a mistake. Where she seemed evasive before, she now seemed sullen, staring down at her lap, running the palms of her hands slowly over her thighs. I felt I was quickly squandering any capital I may have earned with my comments about her neighbor's eating habits and needed to change the subject fast. There was another small, framed photo on top of a stack of books on the shelves opposite the sofa: Traudi standing in Red Square in Moscow along with another woman; the obligatory snapshot in front of the onion-shaped spires of St. Basil's. I pounced on the chance to ask her about it. "You've been to the Soviet Union?"

"Yes, I have been three times in Moscow. I have a friend there. She is an old grade-school pen-pal. Do you know Moscow?"

"I've been there twice."

That surprised her. Traudi's mood brightened somewhat as she boasted about Russian hospitality. I moved the throne chair from the desk to the coffee table and sat down. She asked what other Soviet cities I had visited. I rattled them off: Leningrad, Tashkent, Tbilisi, Yerevan, Baku—Traudi was envious. They were all places she would like to visit one day, she said.

We spent a good deal of time talking about where we had each been on holidays. Unlike Kai, Traudi had never been to the West. She spent most of her vacation time in East Germany, but had traveled a bit around the East Bloc. She spoke highly of Hungary and had visited Dracula's castle in Transylvania with an *FDJ* group when she was fifteen. But I was never able to raise the conversation above polite small talk. There was this constantly perceptible distance sitting between us. Not hostile. I could only describe it as distrust. I had the feeling she wanted to ask, *"Just why are you here?"*

It continued that way for nearly an hour; polite conversation with long, silent intervals that lasted until I finally asked a question or made a comment. Feeling dejected, I had already resigned myself to leaving and never seeing her again when I heard something striking the window. It was hailing outside. I watched the tiny white pellets bouncing off the windowpane and thought that, unlike the rain, most of them would bounce off me during the long walk back to the Friedrichstrasse.

"Well, I should go," I said, standing up. "It was nice seeing you again. Thank you for the coffee."

Traudi stared at me for a moment before asking, "Where do you need to go?"

"To the Friedrichstrasse Station."

Perhaps my disappointment at the whole effort was so apparent that it made her feel guilty. Traudi said that she had to go to work and, if I didn't mind waiting while she took a quick shower, she could drop me off on the way. I agreed and she disappeared into the kitchen and closed the door.

While she showered I took a look at the books on her shelves. There were well-fingered and coffee-stained editions of *Das Kapital*, the *Communist Manifesto*, and Lenin's *What Is to Be Done?* There were old volumes by Marx on German history and the worker's movement; by Lenin on German history and the worker's movement; by Stalin on German history and the worker's movement; by Lenin *and* Stalin on German history and the worker's movement. Penned in one of them was the inscription, *Happy birthday wishes and many more years of joyous work for the good of our society. Your friend and comrade,*

Rudolf. There were stacks of booklets yellowed by age; reports of Communist Party conferences held in the 1950s from countries around Europe. Among some Agatha Christie novels and nursing manuals, I pulled out an eleventh-grade history textbook. It contained a table of important events from 1830 to 1970. Listed among such events as the rise to power of Napoleon III, the Russian revolution and the two World Wars was the formation of the "terror organization Ku-Klux-Klan." The New Deal was described as an effort to keep American workers and farmers from taking "massive revolutionary action" while keeping the capitalist system intact, and noted among the major events of the year 1961 was the death of somebody named William Z. Forster, listed as the Chairman of the Communist Party, U.S.A. Not a word was written about the building of the Berlin Wall.

Traudi's shower was indeed a quick one; the water must have run for all of twenty seconds. When she reappeared dressed in fresh clothes, I mentioned something about that being fast. She told me the water, like the room, was heated by coal, and that she hadn't had time fire up the boiler, which generally took about an hour. I suppose my visit had been an imposition in the end.

Traudi was running late. Her hair was still wet as we rushed out the door. I expressed concern that she might catch cold. She patted herself on the head, "It is not made of sugar," she said in English. On our way downstairs, I happened to notice that Schmid's door was still open. That led me to the comfortable assumption that he didn't have anything bad to say about me after all.

Outside, the icy precipitation had ended as suddenly as it had begun. Traudi gave a groan of exasperation as soon as we reached the street. She had forgotten something upstairs. She motioned to a Trabant parked on a muddy center island directly across from her apartment and ran back inside. I walked over to the car, filled with joy at the prospect of a ride in her *Trabi*. It was dull blue, a color described as *ocean blue* in one of the brochures Kai had given me. The chrome bumpers gave the model away as a *deLuxe Limousine*. I rapped my knuckle against the fender. It sounded as hollow as a drum because it wasn't made of metal, but of something called *Duroplast*. And I knew what that meant: *Bad times for rust*.

Traudi returned a couple of minutes later with her nurse's uniform and white shoes packed in a plastic bag. She got in the car, threw the bag on the seat next to her and opened the passenger-side door. Quickly fiddling with the stick shift on the steering column, she turned the key in the ignition even before I had gotten in. I took the plastic bag off the passenger seat, noticing that it was printed with the emblem of the German-Soviet Friendship Society, and put it on the floor between my legs. I then watched her face fill with hope and encouragement at each of several attempts to start the engine. The car gave one agonized whine after another, each a little more despairing, until the battery was nearly dead. Then, just as all seemed lost, it sprang to life with a roar. We backed out into a cloud of blue exhaust that stung my nostrils, and skidded off over the slippery street. Halfway down the block I was getting a feel for the car's extremely hard ride when it just died. Another attempt at starting the engine produced only a grinding sound and a grunt of frustration from Traudi. In her haste to get moving, she hadn't adjusted the choke properly. Nevertheless, even after that was done, the car threatened to stall out at each of the next few intersections unless given plenty of gas, which in turn surrounded us in clouds of exhaust. Traudi apologized, saying that although the fifteen-year-old car wasn't in the best of repair, it had belonged to her father and she could never bring herself to sell it as long as there was an ounce of life still left in it.

And that was all she had to say. For the entire ride to the station, she sat silent and deep in thought. I almost felt the need to remind her that I was along so she wouldn't forget to drop me off. When we reached the Friedrichstrasse she pulled over to the curb near the Hotel Unter den Linden. I unlatched the seat belt and, feeling somewhat disappointed and foolish for my visit, thanked her for giving me a lift. Traudi looked at me with a blank expression for a moment, then asked if I would be interested in seeing East Berlin sometime. "I could give you a tour if you like." Not only that, but she actually called me by my name for the first time. The whole time I was with her, I was sure she had forgotten it.

"Yes, I'd like that a lot," I said.

"And when?"

"Whenever you want. I have plenty of time."

"How would it be on Tuesday? That is a free day for me. If you come early we can have breakfast first. On Tuesday mornings there is usually yogurt at the Schönhauser Allee dairy shop. If I manage to get up early enough before they sell out we can have yogurt with breakfast. Nine o'clock, is that all right?" I told her it would be perfect and got out of the car. She sped away the instant the door slammed shut.

On Tuesday morning, forsaking any thought of work, I took the U-Bahn to the Friedrichstrasse Station. From there I decided to try a new route; I went through the border control, changed money, and then upstairs to the S-Bahn elevated railway. The S-Bahn station at Friedrichstrasse was an unnatural break in what should have been a continuous ride through the city center. It was the last stop for trains coming from West Berlin, where passengers went downstairs and through the border checkpoint before going upstairs to another platform for trains going east. I took the train to Ostkreuz where I transferred for another to the Prenzlauer Allee, just a short walk from Traudi's apartment. While waiting for my transfer, I watched a workman lazily removing graffiti from a stairway wall that read simply, *Glasnost!*, eventually leaving a large swirling smudge in its place. The task was apparently more important to his employers than it was to him.

That bit of theater was the only advantage of taking this route for, as it turned out, it took just as long as walking. Nevertheless, I arrived on time and ascended the old staircase to see Schmid's door was again open a couple of inches. This time I resisted the urge to look inside.

I rang the bell and heard some hectic last second moving around, then quick steps over the hard wood floor. Traudi opened the door. A smile swept over her face when she saw me. She had put on makeup and red lipstick. The kidney-shaped table in the living room was laid with plenty of food, including the yogurt she had promised and a lit candle in the center. I immediately sensed a change in her attitude toward me. The distance bordering on suspicion that characterized our meeting on Saturday was gone. And, although I thought her invitation came reluctantly, she not only seemed happy to see me, but also showed just enough nervous self-consciousness to make me think she had been looking forward to it. She even gave me a quick tour of her apartment, which she didn't offer to do last time. The only room I hadn't seen was the bedroom beyond the kitchen. It had a small coal oven to the left of the entrance and, against the wall to the right, a large Art Deco wardrobe that looked like it had been battered by too many moves. On the floor next to the wardrobe was a big boxy television set that faced her bed against the opposite wall under a window. Between the kitchen and bedroom there was a tiny closet with a toilet inside.

During breakfast I asked Traudi about her job as a nurse. She said that although it was hard work, often with a lot of overtime and night and weekend shifts, she thought it was the most rewarding profession imaginable. She told me that working in the intensive care station was one of the things that gave real meaning and sense of purpose to her life; a service that genuinely helped her community in ways she could see every day. Hearing her talk that way about her work turned me envious. Traudi was quite happy with what was considered to be a good salary of about nine-hundred marks a month. I enjoyed noting that I paid almost that amount in West marks every month for rent, a statistic that astounded her. She paid forty-eight marks and fifty pfenning for her apartment, which was just a little smaller than mine. I mentioned something about the

blinding whiteness of her walls. She said she'd been struggling
to renovate the apartment since moving in two years ago. "The
kitchen is next," she said. "That wallpaper in there—it is
horrible, I hate it. But when I have time, there is no will. When
the will is there, I have no time, just like with the floor here."

After a short pause she asked me about my job. "Do you
like your work?"

"It's empty, stupid nonsense."

"What? Oh no, Richard, it is very important what you
do." Her reaction held intonations of a mother trying to
encourage a child. And at that point I couldn't remember exactly
what it was that I told her I did.

"Doesn't matter," I said. "At least I can live well from it."

Traudi hesitantly asked how much I earned. I told her it
varied from one month to another, but that I averaged about a
hundred-thousand a year, another number that shocked her.
"What?! . . . One-hundred-thousand! *West* marks?"

"Well—no," I said. "I'm paid in dollars."

"You are paid one-hundred-thousand American dollars?
Then what you do is very important, I think. Very important and
very difficult, also."

I didn't care to waste time discussing the matter further
and changed the subject.

After breakfast Traudi asked if there was anything
special I wanted to see in "our capital." I told her that I'd leave
myself entirely in her hands, fully expecting a tour of the city
center around Unter den Linden. I'd already decided to act as
though I was seeing it all for the first time.

In the Trabi I saw a replay of all the hopeful,
encouraging expressions that filled her face whenever she tried
starting the car. Expressions I'd never tire of watching. It whined
and spit and kicked and gave every conceivable protest before
springing to life. Traudi gave me the grand tour that day. She
had made the decision to show me her city and, in doing so, to
expose the very essence of her soul.

We drove to the Husemannstrasse, an old working-class
street that had been restored to its turn-of-the-century state.

Traudi showed me how the typical Berlin apartment building of that period was arranged according to class, with professionals getting the best apartments on the lower floors, then came *Kleinbeamter* such as teachers, skilled workers and ordinary blue-collar laborers on the very top floors or in the back court. The poorest, she said, were often put in the basement. She told me how much she enjoyed walking around the older areas of the city, looking at the weathered signs over the vacant shops and trying to imagine what a particular Berlin neighborhood was like before everything was destroyed. I was given a lecture on the number of small factories and even dairies in the back courtyards of the city's residential districts at the turn of the century, and about the miserable living conditions in the slum areas. When Traudi spoke about these things, she did so deliberately and thoughtfully, with brightness in her eyes and in her smile that told me she was in love with the city of Berlin. I kept waiting for questions about the city on my side of the Wall, but they never came. Traudi eventually suggested having a drink in the Palast der Republik. I found the idea of having a drink in the East German parliament building intriguing.

From a grand staircase we entered the open space of the atrium from which hundreds of clear glass bulbs were suspended from the high ceiling by vertical and horizontal chrome rods. (When I later told Kai that I had visited the Palast, he condescendingly referred to it as "Honecker's lamp shop.") Traudi proudly told me that workers from every district in the country had labored on this building; that it was completed in less than a thousand days without putting any strain on the national housing program, and that it was designed not only as the seat of parliament and for government receptions, but also as a central gathering place for the nation. A Palast of the people. I sat in one of the big, red leather chairs and listened to all the facts and figures about the large concert auditorium for five-thousand people; how many restaurants and cafés were in the place; about the bowling lanes, the discotheque, and the five-thousand hooks in the main coat check room, as if it all constituted one of the world's seven wonders. We strolled along the carpeted walkways overlooking the central atrium, which on each level were lined with large oil paintings glorifying communism. Traudi's favorite was entitled, *When Communists Dream*. I noticed that the glasses, plates and even the thick cotton towels in the men's room were all embossed with the luxuriously ornate, scripted initials *PdR*, appropriate for either a commercial hotel chain or the palace at Versailles.

We each drank a glass of sekt at the ring bar overlooking the Marx-Engels-Forum. The large bronze figures at its center stood with their backs toward us, as if insulted by the pretentious result of what they had started. Traudi silently gazed out over the area, smiling to herself. She seemed perfectly at ease with the world in this temple to a fantasy. The building was clearly a source of gratification, as if just breathing the air within its walls was somehow proof that, despite everything, it could all be worthwhile. She told me that in the 1970s, when she was a teenager in the FDJ and the Marx-Engels-Forum was still a rubble-strewn lot, she would take part in young-communist torchlight assemblies there. "We would chant about fatherland and international solidarity," she said, smiling with amusement, "and, afterwards, there would always be rock-and-roll bands and beer to reward us for doing it."

I asked what was next one the tour. Traudi said there was something she wanted to show me. "It is something everyone should see," she said somberly, adding to the mystery by saying, "Remember, this morning you said that you would put yourself in my hands."

On the way, we drove along a wide boulevard lined on both sides by grandiose apartment buildings in the Stalinist style, similar to the Soviet embassy on the Unter den Linden. It continued block after block, probably for more than a mile.

"Do not worry," Traudi said in English. "You are still in Berlin, not Moscow. Here I like it *fairy* much," she added before reverting back to German. "With these monumental buildings and all the shops, you really get the feeling that you are somewhere. And if that is Moscow and not Berlin, well, I like Moscow, too."

She told me it all was all designed as the first truly socialist avenue in Germany; a boulevard free of the class structure she'd shown me earlier that morning in the traditional Berlin apartment buildings. Here, a professor would live right next door to an ordinary worker. The avenue was to be a sign that the horrible living conditions of the proletariat that had existed before were gone for good. She said that it was here, in 1950, that her parents had met. That, back then, before the area had been rebuilt, people would come and clear the streets of rubble from the War. They did this backbreaking labor, she insisted, not because they were forced to, but out of an inner-conviction. I couldn't help showing my skepticism with a half-suppressed grin. That only caused Traudi to emphasize the point, "You have to remember that back then, in the early 1950s, the GDR was like a new world in creation," she said. "People knew that a better life wasn't going to come easily and were prepared to give a lot for it. They would come here in the evening, after a whole day at work, and look through the rubble of the War, brick by brick, to see what could be used again. They were all convinced that centuries of oppression were over for good. The feeling was that now the world belongs to us—this age belongs to us!"

Some people may have thought that way, but I knew the refugee statistics of that time. East Germans were pouring into West Berlin by the thousands, more and more of them every year. It was the reason the Wall eventually had to be built. And I wasn't totally ignorant about the history of this avenue, either. I knew it was here, during construction of these very buildings, that the famous 1953 worker uprising against the East German government began. It was brutally put down by Soviet tanks on June 17th of that year, a date that was now a commemorative national holiday in West Germany. I wondered how Traudi would react if I confronted her with that fact.

Traudi slowed the car and mentioned with some pride that the facades of the apartment buildings were tiled in porcelain. I pretended to be impressed, but could clearly see that much of the exteriors were broken with large sections of the porcelain frontages missing, exposing the bricks underneath. The stonework on the lower floors was badly stained by the acidic air, which had eaten away at the concrete, exposing the rusted steel rods inside. She was right about it being like Moscow, though—right down to the glum people I saw waiting on a long, winding line outside a state shop called, *Everything from Fish.*

I decided to ask her straight out about the insurrection. "Wasn't this the place where the worker revolt began?"

"You mean the action instigated by agents from West Berlin in 1953? Yes, that was here."

"Do you really believe that the West was responsible for that?"

"No," she said with a laugh, but then added thoughtfully, "I think it was just an instance where the government was not being honest with the people."

I decided to leave it at that. I certainly had no desire to argue with her or start a debate over history. As far as I was concerned, she had every right to believe whatever she wanted. It was none of my business and did no one any harm.

We arrived at our destination, which from the street looked like a densely wooded park. Traudi parked the car in front of a large stone arch with hammers and sickles cut into it. The inscription at the top read, *"Eternal Glory to the Heroes Who Fell for the Freedom and Independence of the Socialist Homeland."*

We walked through the arch and came upon a statue of a grieving woman. "Mother Russia," Traudi said.

Off in the distance, two huge triangles of red granite rose like flags from the ground while bronze sculptures of soldiers knelt in sorrow and reverence before them. In the mist beyond, a giant statue of a Red Army soldier, crushing a swastika under his boot while holding a sword and carrying a child towered above the naked trees. Traudi spoke in a quiet, reverent voice when she told me that the stone for the monument came from Hitler's chancellery, and that the remains of thousands of Russian soldiers were interred here. The granite flags were inscribed with the words, "*Eternal Glory for the Fighters of the Soviet Army Who Gave Their Lives in the Battle for the Liberation of Humanity from Fascist Bondage.*" Between the flags and the statue in the distance was a tree-lined mall. Stone reliefs depicting scenes of war and suffering were placed along both sides, each one engraved with a quote from Stalin. We walked to the monument's base. Inside the pedestal, a circular wall was covered in a mosaic depicting the different ethnic peoples of the Soviet Union laying a memorial wreath. The floor before it was strewn with freshly cut flowers. The word "glory" written in German and Russian was everywhere. It was the most bombastic thing I'd ever seen.

"I'm glad you brought me here. I've never seen anything like this."

"It has recently been made public that twenty-six million Soviet people were killed in the Second World War. Can you imagine?" she said with a sigh of resignation and lament. "*Twenty-six million* . . . all slaughtered by Germans in the name of Germany."

Twenty-six million. It was a number so mind-boggling it made even Stalin's cynical line—that a single death was a tragedy, but a million deaths a statistic—seem quaint. And I could have cited another fact: that just as many Soviets had probably been murdered by Stalin himself. But it didn't seem appropriate. For some reason Traudi was too moved by guilt. For a moment I thought I'd actually detected tears welling in her eyes, a suspicion confirmed when she quickly wiped them away while mumbling something about a terrible history following us all.

I stood beside Traudi at some of the stone reliefs while she read the accompanying inscriptions to me. She clearly wanted to be sure I understood them. I didn't even bother trying to figure out why. At each one I watched her face as she carefully mouthed hyperbole about the heroic Red Army defenders of Moscow, Odessa and Sevastopol; about valor and iron discipline, and absolute victory over bestial ideology. I stared at her as she read, knowing I was making her self-conscious, all the time thinking how much I'd like to kiss the mouth reciting phrases attributed to the tyrant Stalin's twisted, paranoid brain. I was barely listening as she stumbled through some nonsense about a "victorious banner" and "the great Lenin's might," when in the middle of a sentence, she looked at me with an expression full of uncertainty. Before I knew what had happened, I'd kissed her gently on the lips. Her reaction came in advance of my even considering the consequences of what I'd done. That smile. "*Ooooh*, such a one you are!" she said in loud English, putting her arms around my waist.

We left the monument walking leisurely arm-in-arm past a couple of East German guards who shot a disapproving glance our way. By the time we reached the car I'd had enough history and was itching to have some fun with her. "You know, Traudi, I have never been to the top of the Television Tower."

"You haven't? . . . *Really?* Then we absolutely must go there right now!"

We got there to find a long line of tourists at the base of the Tower. We stood at the end. I asked if the people around us were speaking Russian. Traudi listened for a moment and determined they were Bulgarian. The line moved into a large circular room with forward-cantilevered walls clad from floor to ceiling in vertical spars. Here it reeked powerfully of that East German bad-drain smell. I stood behind Traudi, observing it all with my arms wrapped around her shoulders. The long lines of people, the mounting anticipation of the elevator ride to the top, the 1960s architecture; it all transported me back to the New York World's Fair I visited as a child. This could have been the entrance to *Futurama*. For some reason, while standing there in line with all those Bulgarians, it occurred to me that the world I was promised back then should already have already come to pass. It was 1989; a quarter century after the fair had opened. The future was here. By now we should all be eating seaweed grown on farms on the ocean floor, or extra-sized tomatoes harvested by colonists inside domes on the moon. Hunger and poverty should have already met their end, conquered by the ingenuity and resourcefulness of decent human beings working for American corporations. I remembered the pavilion where we were all given radioactive dimes in blue plastic holders with the fair's eminently sane logo, *Peace through Understanding,* printed on it as proof of all the wonders future would hold. I was suddenly astounded to realize how much I had taken it all to heart as a child. How the fair's optimism always remained with me somewhere in my consciousness and became part of me. Only then, at that very moment, did I finally know that *that* world was a total fabrication. Someone else's illusion, the sole purpose of which was to astound, entertain, and advertise to a ticket-buying public. It was a place I'd never get to see no matter how long I lived.

Traudi and I were eventually herded into a small elevator with a group of short, gold-toothed people who had obviously missed a series of Saturday-night baths. Squeezed in tightly we listened to the operator mutter statistics about the height of the tower and the speed the elevator was traveling as a gauge next to him measured our ascent. I kept craning my neck trying to see our progress. The smell of all those unwashed bodies was hard to take.

When we reached the observation platform the doors opened and everyone fell out into a large, circular space wrapped by windows with Berlin spread out below. Although it was hazy we could see as far as the Tiergarten in the West with the Wall winding its way through the city. I pointed out to Traudi where I lived in Kreuzberg among the mass of buildings. She seemed genuinely astounded by the proximity, "Huh! *That's* where you live? It's really not far away, is it?" We looked for Traudi's apartment, she pointed in the direction of the district where she grew up, to the factory where her father had worked, and the hospital where she was now employed. The Charité was large, modern cube just east of the Wall; it was a building I'd noticed every time I'd visited the area around the Brandenburg Gate, or when I rode the elevated section of the U-Bahn to and from the West Berlin city center.

We looked at every possible landmark within sight, East and West, before going upstairs to the revolving café.

Standing there searching for a vacant table gave me a slightly queasy sensation for a few moments. According to the elevator operator, the café was supposed to make one revolution per hour but seemed to be moving much faster.

We found a table and sat next to each other. It wasn't long before we were laughing at the waiters and waitresses as they took orders, went to the kitchen or bar, then had to run around, trays in hand, looking for guests sitting at tables that had moved away. We ordered cream puffs known as *Berliner Windbags* and coffee. I timed the café's revolution to find that it was moving twice as fast as it was supposed to. Then I noticed that the tables were bolted to the floor and wondered whether that was a safety precaution. We joked about the possibility of the café spinning fast enough for cake, food and plates to fly off the tables and about the danger knives and forks would pose during such an event. Traudi was laughing, hugging me and pressing her hip against mine as we tried outdoing each other with contrived images of the panic that might breakout among the people around us if the café began spinning out of control and they lost everything from hair pieces to the gold fillings in their teeth while desperately clawing at the tables anchored to the floor, and I was very much enjoying being with her.

Before we left, Traudi insisted on buying me a souvenir in the gift shop. I picked out a key ring attached to a brass tag engraved with a rendering of Television Tower. Back in the car she asked if I had to go back to the West. I told her I was allowed to stay until midnight. When she asked if I'd like to go back to her apartment for some homemade *Solyanka*, I eagerly agreed without knowing or caring what it was.

Not long after pulling away, Traudi took a concerned glance at the odometer on the dashboard and quickly calculated that she needed to fill up the gas tank. There was no gas gauge. She drove to a gas station on the Prenzlauer Allee. I sat there observing the car on the other side of the gas pump. It was a *Wartburg*, the other automobile produced by the East Germans.

Larger and more expensive, it was surely meant for the more affluent proletarian. The Wartburg was somewhat boxy in shape but, nevertheless, could pass for a real car. I began daydreaming about exporting them to the U.S.A.; they could probably be had for hard currency lunch money. A slogan even popped into my head: "At last, German engineering *everyone* can afford." Then I noticed Traudi had opened the hood of the Trabant so I got out to see if there was a problem with the car. She was standing there watching the attendant leaning under the hood as he pumped gas into the tank, which was situated right over the hot engine.

"You know, Traudi, I like this car. All western cars look the same, but this has a character all its own." My remark pleased her. She smiled happily as she paid the man, then gave me a hug and a peck on the cheek. It really wasn't a lie. The dumb-looking car took on a quality I could only describe as disarmingly honest. No amount of advertising could make the little contraption be anything it wasn't.

In her apartment Traudi took my coat. I sat on the sofa across from the old books. She came and sat next to me. I asked her about the dusty volumes on the shelves. She told me that they had belonged to her parents. I made the observation that, judging by their reading material, one could assume that they were "redder than Lenin." Traudi saw nothing amusing in that. She looked me earnestly in the eyes and said, "Oh, they were. Both of them. What do you think about that?"

What could I say? Sorry they pissed away their lives like that? So I kissed her instead of answering. She fell back on the sofa, wrapped her arms around me and gently, tenderly pressed me down on her body. Deeper and deeper. I felt I could melt into her. Suddenly, she pushed me away. Again that expression—at once blank and earnest. The thousand thoughts were back, swirling around inside her head. She brushed the hair away from my forehead with her hand and surprised me by asking flatly, "Are you going to sleep with me sometime?"

"*What?*"

"Are you going to sleep with me sometime?"

I recited a couple of stupid lines, first about not putting off till tomorrow what could be done today, which got no reaction, then about idle hands being the devil's workshop. Still, Traudi didn't respond. She just kept staring, running her hand over my head as though she hadn't heard me, always thinking, thinking, until she finally got up and led me into the bedroom.

When I saw her I was convinced that she didn't realize how beautiful she was. Her touch conveyed an aching for intimacy too long denied. After all those grinding romps with Kati I'd almost forgotten that sex could be such a warm, gentle experience. Afterward she'd lie there staring at me and her thoughts would return. They would stay with her as long as I'd let them; until I brought her back by saying something. That first time it was a question that had promptly moved from the back to the front of my mind. About birth control. She looked at the ceiling, smiling, innocently twirling her hair around her finger and said, "Do you not want a family?"

"Well . . . not right now. Not tonight."

Traudi said I need not worry. I fell on my back trying not to show my relief while contemplating the implications of having a child on the other side of the Berlin Wall. What an odd situation that would be. I asked about her family. I was most interested in her brother, Sascha, and the details about how and why he immigrated to the West. But that was something Traudi obviously still felt uncomfortable talking about. She quickly but reluctantly told me that there was a time when Sascha grew more and more unhappy with his life in the GDR and finally applied to leave, which he got permission to do in 1979. She no longer had contact with him and had no idea where he was.

Of her mother, who died when Traudi was eight years old, there were only scant recollections of a time when she was not ill; vague memories of a young teacher and idealistic Communist Party activist who had lost her entire family to the Buchenwald concentration camp. Memories reinforced through the years by stories her father would tell about someone who had devoted her life to the cause with absolute faith in the chance to build a new and better world after the War. Her father, she said, had been arrested by the Nazis for communist activities in 1934 when he was seventeen years old and working as an apprentice printer for one of the left-wing newspapers in Berlin. He was sentenced to three years in the penitentiary Brandenburg-Görden where one of his fellow inmates was Erich Honecker. Two years after his release he was again arrested and, as a second-time offender, was sent to the Sachsenhausen concentration camp. (There were enough horror stories about that incarceration to fill a separate book.) Toward the end of the war, the Nazis conscripted surviving camp inmates into penal battalions, using them as cannon fodder in a futile effort to halt the collapse of the eastern front before the advancing Red Army. Like many others, Traudi's father surrendered at the earliest possible moment to the Soviets who, despite his political ideology, treated him like any other prisoner of war. After the penitentiary, the concentration camp and the war came another four and a half years in Soviet prison camps before he was allowed to return to a devastated Berlin in 1949. For her father the reasons for the entire calamity were clear. Traudi would recite them to me—long rants involving indictments of capital, property and a military cast. Her father returned to Germany more convinced than ever that communism offered the only way to prevent a recurrence of it all. Or perhaps that's putting it too mildly. From what Traudi told me, I could imagine that, as far as her father was concerned, Nazism was the innate condition of anyone who hadn't declared himself absolutely committed to the communist cause.

In the mid-1950s Traudi's father spent a year studying in Moscow. After returning he held various posts in the Party, the longest and last was that of Party Secretary at the light bulb factory "Rosa Luxemburg." That her father could have gone much further in a political career but chose not to was a source pride for Traudi. He could have certainly become a member of the Central Committee or Politburo, she said, but he felt that it was most important for the Party to be close to the workers, and that's where he chose to stay throughout his career.

Whenever Traudi or her brother asked their father about his years spent as a prisoner in the Soviet Union, he wouldn't answer. "It wasn't a nice time" was all he'd say about it. Yet he never tired of telling his children about the atrocities the Germans had committed against the Soviet people. Shocking stories of a Nazi-occupied Soviet Union, where the starving were hanged if they were caught baking bread; where women and children were locked inside churches and burned to death, and emaciated civilians forced to dig their own mass graves, then kneel in them before being shot like rabid animals. Her father also seemed to regurgitate numbskull phrases like *"All that we are we owe to the Party,"* or *"To learn from the Soviet people means learning victory."* I guess they came with the territory for someone like him, and I never let on how foolish I thought they were. I wouldn't dare. Traudi talked about her father as though he were a heroic pillar supporting all that was good in the world. Even the stupid slogans he would sometimes recite were obviously seen as an indication of courage and incorruptibility on the part of someone she loved very much. Her behavior at the Soviet memorial now made perfect sense. In a world where hope, guilt and hate can be passed like genetic material from one generation to the next, Traudi was dominant in the first two. She was a vessel stubbornly carrying a spark that had once held promise for millions of people.

Despite all that, I loved watching her smile as if recalling a first love when she talked about her childhood. How, when she was very young, she would lie in bed and fall asleep to the political discussions of her parents in the kitchen, or the Bertolt Brecht songs coming from the record player in the family's living room. She would listen in the dark to her father telling her brother that communism was mankind's greatest hope. That it would one day deliver a world free of selfishness, greed and hate where everyone contributed according to their abilities and took according to their needs.

I would watch her many more times, this daughter of revolutionaries—left alone with her inheritance of memories and books filled with yellowing pages of worn ideology; with her

old mismatched furniture and absurd little car. I would be with
her often in the coming months—the hours spent together in
bed before or after the films at the International or the Kosmos;
the Babylon or the Colosseum. The concerts in the clubs—the
Sophien on Saturday nights with Kai tending bar and Traudi
making sure the little old blind man always got his drink; the
occasional evenings in other places: the Haus der Jungen
Talente, the Franzclub, or the concerts in the jazz cellar in the
Treptow district. I'd spend hours watching her stare at the
ceiling over her bed, twirling her hair, struggling to make pieces
of romantic beliefs inherited from another age fit into
unpleasant realities. With the Berlin Wall, a grudging
concession that, "*Yes, of course people should be allowed to leave
if they are not happy here.*" Then a wide-eyed and innocent
assertion, "*But if everyone leaves, how will the changes ever
happen? How will things ever become what they ought to be? How
will we ever reach the point where people will want to stay? Maybe
there must be this moment of pain before things get better.*" With
the country's hapless economic system, "*Here, everyone has the
power to make their community better overnight, just by doing
their job well. When most people are not employed by private
companies, but by community institutions, it is only logical that
working people will automatically make a better community. It's
perfectly natural, isn't it? And isn't that a wonderful idea? . . .
Isn't that such a wonderful idea?*"

"But it doesn't seem to be working very well, does it?"
I'd say.

"*But it will work one day. It will only be a matter of time
because it is in everyone's self-interest that it works. Sooner or
later people will see that.*"

There were times when, lying there with her in bed, the
world was reduced to such simplicity that I could believe she
was the only sane person on an insane planet. Then, there would
be that inevitable mad dash in the Trabi to get me back to
Checkpoint Charlie or the Friedrichstrasse Station before the
midnight deadline.

That first night I took the U-Bahn back home. Traudi dropped me off and asked carefully in English, "When see we us again?" Days and times were quickly discussed, a meeting set for later that same week. I left her and heard the car sputter and roar behind me. A look back revealed only a heavy cloud of oily-blue exhaust hanging in the air under the streetlights.

The obstinate and needlessly thorough passport and face checks were performed in a large aluminum and glass structure next to the Friedrichstrasse Station commonly referred to as the *Tränenpalast*—the Palace of Tears—because it was the backdrop for so many tearful partings. That night there weren't any. I was one of the few people making the crossing. The police loitering about far outnumbered the people making the trip back. From West Berlin a yellow train arrived at the station. I entered the car alone and stood, observing the seven or eight others, all seated. They read books, early editions of the morning newspaper or sat looking bored by their own thoughts. The train rolled slowly, carefully on its way, through the two closed stations where the murky platforms were patrolled by the shadowy figures of border guards with Kalashnikov assault weapons slung over their shoulders. Then out again, into West Berlin. To the Kochstrasse station where people entered and exited the train. They came and went with their thoughts and their packages; joking with friends or arm-in-arm with lovers. As if this was any train in any city. They went about their business as though unaware of the world through which we had just journeyed; as if oblivious of the city that existed parallel to their own. The train continued under West Berlin at its normal speed. There were two more stations to my stop. I walked up the stairs and onto the familiar street. Passed the Laundromat where I washed my clothes, the taxi stand where I sometimes caught a cab, and the shops where I bought the things I needed to live. I crossed the intersection. The traffic sounds were those I had always known. I could again see the Television Tower at Alexanderplatz, *over there,* pale and distant. Its strobe lights blinked their defiance as they always did. Only her scent told me it was not a dream.

I Don't Think He Exists, But I Believe in Him

A COUPLE OF WEEKS LATER, I went downstairs to see if there was any mail in my box only to receive a sudden slap in the face in the form of an unsigned postcard with a single sentence written on the back, "Sunny greetings from Turkey." **Kati!** That bundle of goose bump-covered libido had, with amazing speed, made the transformation from reality to a theoretical concept to be thought about and considered. Now she was about to return. When? I tried to remember the date. She told it to me a hundred times. What was it? How long does it take for a postcard to arrive from Turkey? It was no use. I shoved the card back in my mailbox, as if that would make her disappear altogether, and went out for a mélange.

The inevitable occurred a few days later when Kati stopped by my apartment bearing a gift: a small bowl made of olive wood. She immediately sensed a change in my attitude toward her. Questioning followed. I was evasive at first. That meant there was someone else. "Who is she?" I finally confessed. "Where does she live?" I told her East Berlin. Kati let out a huge laugh. "For a minute I afraid it was over," she said. I asked her if maybe it shouldn't be. "Why? What does she have to do with anything?" I stood silent. Kati's reasoning was all her own, yet I couldn't argue with her. My excursions to the East always had a dream-like quality about them once I was back home. Events that took place on the other side of the Wall were totally distinct and independent from anything that happened on my side. They were separated by concrete and guarded by a history and ideology that had split the world for forty-five years. And look at Kati. She had a husband and child, after all. I even knew who they were. I had been to their home. I could meet them by chance on the street at any time. And that didn't stop her, did it? In the end it didn't stop either of us.

After that my schedule became more crowded. Looking back, the days of the week seem to have been split between West and East. The Goddamned Job got consigned to a couple of hours each morning and soon was just another part of the daily routine, like taking a shower or using the toilet; to be thought about pretty much only while the act itself was taking place. The clocks were pushed ahead an hour and the short Berlin days grew longer overnight. Even the abominable weather became more and more bearable with the approaching summer.

Checkpoint Charlie was my preferred crossing point when I'd go to meet Traudi. Not because it was more convenient—it wasn't; but because I liked stopping at the Café Adler before going across. I crossed the checkpoint so frequently that I began recognizing the border guards. They in turn processed me quickly. One glance at my face and *BANG*, my passport was stamped, the visa filled out. At times I thought I even detected a stern nod of recognition from some of them.

The 1st of May. A Monday. International Labor Day. A holiday on both sides of the Wall. It was the first time I'd been in Berlin for this event. Since moving here from Münster, my plan had been to watch (from a safe distance) the annual May Day battle between left-wing *Chaoten* and the West Berlin police in Kreuzberg. For three years I'd watched the scene on the evening news. Senseless anger and hate. Young figures clad in black, hiding their identity behind neckerchiefs tied around their faces. Shops attacked, cars set afire, stones thrown at riot police, always people injured. It happened every year, yet nobody seemed to know exactly why. Those who instigated it would tell you that it happened in the name of an ideology. Yet no one ever articulated what that ideology was. Simply because there was no ideology behind it. Just inexplicable rage. But all it took to change my long-standing plan was an invitation from Traudi to spend the day with her at celebrations in East Berlin.

Normally she didn't mind working on holidays, she said, but this time she could have the day off and hoped to spend it with me.

It was there that I got my first look at the East German leadership as they stood together on a platform on the Karl-Marx-Allee next to the Kino International. Behind us a large banner with the words *"Workers of the World unite!"* hung from an apartment block. Other facades were decorated with the red banner of the working class and the East German flag next to big celebratory signs that read, *"DDR 40."* We arrived in time to hear the last few minutes of an opening speech by Harry Tisch, leader of the East German labor union and member of the Politburo. Even before we got close enough for Traudi to recognize who was speaking, we heard his voice echoing over loudspeakers, praising the Party and the country's workers; referring to construction projects in the capital and the progress of the national housing program as proof of ideological success. Traudi told me with pride that it was the Party's goal to make sure that, by end of 1990, everyone in Berlin who needed an apartment could have one.

We watched a parade of school children, young communists, worker brigades and combat militia of the working class. There were smiling faces in the crowd as fathers held young children up high so they could see it all. The old men on the platform who ran the country waved, smiled and accepted accolades cordially. Erich Honecker, looking like a kindly old grandfather, enthusiastically shook his clenched fist in the air, giving the communist salute to the people streaming along in the parade. The defense minister, his white uniform full of decorations, waved to the crowd with a small bouquet of red carnations. Floats from factories rolled by that boasted production and export statistics, and success in fulfilling the five-year plan. It was a huge, nationally televised affair staged, no doubt, by the Party's best advance people. Yet there was something seductive about it all. An invitation to join in the extended family. Do your share, expect little, and your problems would be few. They would take care of you; make sure you felt as though you were an important part of society. Everyone was needed; there was not a single person to spare in pursuit of lofty goals. I saw the quiet enthusiasm in Traudi's clear blue eyes as she stood on her toes, stretching to see the parade. Her smile was as sincere and genuine as a young girl's as we watched marchers carrying signs with slogans like, "*Everything for the Good of the People!*" She was able to lose herself in this spectacle. It was the world the way she always dreamt it would be. It was impossible for me not to be affected by it.

Once during the parade, we took a break and walked up to the Alexanderplatz where there were bands playing and stands with food and drink. Traudi ran into a couple of acquaintances she used to work with and I was introduced as a friend from the West. "Has he seen *the parade*," one asked derisively, making it clear that it was thought of as an establishment taboo.

Traudi answered with a laugh. "Of course he's seen it," she said, moving me quickly along. Around others she seemed to keep her convictions about politics and ideology to herself, the way an adolescent might try to keep unfashionable religious beliefs unknown to peers. Yet I envied her for them; for her willingness to believe in them despite all. And on that day, I also found myself standing there on the Karl-Marx-Allee with clenched fist in the air, cheering the Young Pioneers, visitors from Third World revolutionary movements and the East Berlin fire department. Even pretending to believe filled a gaping void in me. So, in the middle of it all, when she suggested we celebrate the fortieth anniversary of the GDR together in October, I told her I'd be there no matter what.

Later that evening she lay silently next to me in bed with her head on my shoulder. I was staring at the two light bulbs inside the large eye-shaped aluminum street lamp that was suspended directly above her bedroom window when she asked, "Why are there so many homeless people in America?" She surprised me by saying that she had seen a report about the problem on West German television. "I saw your President Reagan. He said that people live on the street because they want to live that way. How can that be true? I always thought the

Americans were a very proud and generous people. A place to live is a basic part of human dignity. Why do the people stand for the situation as it is?"

At that moment I regretted that the Wall wasn't high enough to keep that garbage out. A generation of American leaders that began with the selfless idealism of the New Frontier was not only ending with an abject surrender, but seemed to be spitefully enjoying it. I racked my brain, trying to think up some politically "scientific" answer to give her, but in the end had to submit to the simple truth. "I don't know," I said.

"Huh . . . strange," she replied. "I mean, next to America, the GDR is really a tiny and a poor country, and here no one must live in the street." Still strapped for an answer I didn't respond. Traudi lapsed back into silence. That was the end of that discussion.

That night, on our way back to Checkpoint Charlie, she was eager to show me something. She drove down the Leipziger Strasse, just past the intersection where she usually dropped me off, and parked the car. Traudi hurried me by the arm across the street to the *Haus der Ministerien*. I knew the history of this building from my books on Berlin. It had been erected by the Nazis and served as Hermann Göring's *Luftwaffe* headquarters. Now in the service of the East German government, they had altered it by placing a long mural along one side. This wasn't artwork like the comic book characters I'd seen in the murals at Alexanderplatz, but faces with depth of conviction and strength of purpose. A euphoric view of the New World in creation.

"Isn't it wonderful, Richard?"

I stood before it, taking it all in. I noticed a German flag in the far corner—black red and gold bars without the East German hammer and compass emblem. I asked Traudi if she knew when the mural was made. Of course she did. It was done in 1952. The date was right there on one of the tiles. I couldn't help but think that a year later, the people depicted here would revolt against the government created in their name and be gunned down by Soviet tanks. Right here, in front of this very building, in front of this very mural, Traudi's dream world died before she was even born.

One particularly pleasant day in May, I was sitting outside at the Café Adler before going across Checkpoint Charlie. It was the first time that year they had set up tables on the sidewalk outside the café. In the sun it was warm and the sky was blue; birds were singing and tourists were beginning to make themselves noticeable in large numbers all over the city, especially here at the Wall. I sat there reading the newspaper, drinking coffee and thought, *what freedom this is*. I was like the birds that flew across the border at will, or the rabbits that grazed undisturbed in the middle of the No Man's Land. In demand in two worlds and able to move as I pleased between them. In the *Herald Tribune* I read about the latest events at home; about the vice president who couldn't help humiliating himself in public; the rants of the obese grandmaster of talk radio who'll be dissembling, inciting and hypnotizing his audience with hate for his own personal gain until the day they finally shovel him into the ground; I got the latest on that ridiculous junior senator from my home state who, like a mob boss, always seemed to be under criminal investigation but never did any time. I read about them and knew their stories. To the others sitting around me they were all but unknown. But I knew them. I read yet another filler article about the latest incident of a new phenomenon called "drive-by shooting," and it was all just a lot of hopelessly bad theater to me. I'd been liberated. I folded up the paper and again thought, *what freedom this is*. This was how I should have lived from the moment I'd first set foot in Germany. At the table next to mine, I couldn't help overhearing two men in business suits each order a *Checkpoint Salad*. They lapsed into a discussion about a development that I couldn't help but register despite my busy schedule over the past few weeks. The new reform government in Hungary had begun tearing down sections of the Iron Curtain along its border with Austria. An amazing event. One of so many these days. The two men began debating what it meant for Germany. One, obviously trying to be provocative, said it was proof that the Berlin Wall would come down in our lifetime. The other man responded by saying what everyone always said—that nothing would happen until Honecker was dead. And although he was rumored to be ill with cancer, dictators like him can last almost forever, the man said, citing Tito and Franco as examples. Even then, he guessed, changes would come more slowly than the optimists liked to believe. But on that sunny day, the truth was that no one knew what it meant. Neither they, nor I, or anyone else would have ever suspected that what the Hungarians were doing would send the two worlds colliding before the year was out.

But before the crash came, I moved between East and West Berlin. And each time I returned from *over there*, I saw West Berlin in a different light. I recognized like never before the incredible wealth that surrounded us. What a gilded cage we all lived in. It reminded me more and more of Münster. The only reason it was any more interesting was its preposterous circumstance. The isolation. The Wall. I divided my time, as much as possible, between Kati and Traudi. The boys at the Troika seldom saw me. I'd pop in every once in a while when I had nothing else to do and didn't feel like sitting at home. And all through those months I never once even considered inviting any of my western friends to come to East Berlin with me. I had no desire to hear disparaging comments about it from anyone. Besides, it belonged to me and I didn't want to share it with them.

Just days after the Hungarians began opening their border, local "elections" were held in the GDR. Kai once explained the procedure for casting a "vote" in East Germany: each voter was given an official ballot with one name on it, which they then promptly deposited in the ballot box. In order to vote *against* the candidate, one had to go into a booth and cross out the name—a conspicuous act of dissent that would be noted by the poll watchers. And according to Kai, the name had to be crossed out in ballpoint pen to be valid, yet the booths were supplied only with pencils. Voting was mandatory. Not participating was considered an act of opposition to the state that could come back to haunt you at any time. Kai said he would take part in the "fraud" because he wasn't in the mood for more problems with the authorities. And just then his parents were approaching sixty-five, the age when they would be permitted to travel back and forth to the West. "*Mensch, Kai! You have to vote or they won't give us passports,*" they fretted. "Besides," Kai told me with undaunted certitude, "the changes that are coming won't come by elections."

I accompanied Traudi to the polling station in a school near her apartment. She participated willingly, she said, to "show support for the *Sozialismus*." Inside, there was a single piece of campaign paraphernalia: a poster urging people to elect the candidates of the *National Front*—as if there was any alternative. A portrait of Erich Honecker hung on the wall behind the ballot box as a collection of mostly older people went through the motions, exchanging their registration cards for ballots and depositing them in the box. A single voting booth stood empty in the far corner of the large room, ignored by everyone. Three poll watchers sat behind the ballot box—a skinny old man with thick eyeglasses wearing a flannel shirt buttoned up to his neck who was flanked by two fat women with stern faces. Barely a word was uttered by anyone in the room. I found the atmosphere stifling. Standing there waiting for Traudi, I kept eyeing the booth in the corner and had intended to check whether there was a pen or pencil inside. But for some reason I couldn't summon up the courage to simply walk over and look.

As usual in that "election," the communists gave themselves 98.95 percent of the vote. I couldn't understand why they didn't vary the election results from time to time, just as a change of pace. Sometimes they could give themselves 76.9 percent and sometimes 85.1 percent. Maybe they could even go as low as 69 percent and use that as a call for a sham renewal. Despite all that, the world around us began to change. The first free elections in seventy years were held in the Soviet Union and

Solidarity shared power with the communists in Poland. In China, a massive pro-democracy demonstration in Tiananmen Square was brutally put down in an exhibition of barbaric, ugly repression that shocked the world. The East Germans used that tragedy to intimidate their own population; to show what can happen in their country if the established order was ever threatened. For weeks after the massacre, there were daily reports from China on GDR television recounting the bloody aftermath of "restoring order."

In the middle of June, Gorbachev was received with jubilation in the Federal Republic. Not only do West German politicians openly envy his popularity, but an old brand of German vodka with the same name had begun a big advertising campaign to try and profit from the coincidence. Unfortunately, Berlin was not on Gorbachev's agenda. My disappointment was real. Something inside me wanted to see him; to get at least a glimpse of the man responsible igniting so much hope and change in the world.

Yet, despite all that was happening around us, Gorbi's changes didn't seem to extend to Berlin. During his visit to the West, he made a cryptic remark about the Wall that pretty much echoed what Erich Honecker had said earlier in the year; that it would disappear when the conditions that created it disappeared.

My relationship with Traudi deepened quickly. I was intrigued by this twenty-seven-year-old nurse. Her life, so different from mine, held an exotic attraction. I enjoyed listening to her happy memories of young summers spent at holiday camps on the Baltic coast that were operated by the factories her father had worked at. The same way I enjoyed being shown the small black-and-white photographs she kept in a box in that old bedroom wardrobe; pictures of Traudi during her days as a Young Pioneer, or proudly standing on a school stage during her *Jugendweihe,* a ceremony that was sort of a socialist Confirmation. In her uniforms she looked just like the fresh-faced, smiling young socialist ideal in the mural she showed me and in 1950s propaganda posters I'd seen in books. A childhood driven by political slogans and duty to the cause without the pleasant diversion of *Etch-A-Sketch* or *Slinky*. She amused me with the story of her first awkward sexual experience with a young Russian *Komsomolist* who had been in Berlin for the National Youth Festival in 1979. They were alone in her father's house while he conducted a Party meeting at the plant, certain that his daughter was in the best of hands while in the company of such a fine young man.

In the same bedroom wardrobe where she kept the old photographs was another small box. In it were a handful of medals that Traudi had been awarded at the various hospitals she had worked at; military-style decorations imprinted with slogans like *"The Socialist Way of Life demands the Socialist Way of Work."* Her Communist Party member stickpin was also in that box. I never once saw her wear it. Traudi paid her dues every month and went to the required Party meetings every few weeks at the hospital. Yet, when I asked her what took place at those meetings, she'd shrug her shoulders and say apathetically that they discussed ways of making things work better on the job or sometimes just talked about current events. It wasn't unusual that they would just go and see a Russian film. It all had to do with a point system in which worker brigades competed against each other for an end of year bonus, and that didn't interest her. For Traudi, the Party was little more than a formality. It was the ideology and the ideals it was supposed to represent that she was addicted to.

There were times when I saw that I was as exotic for her as she was for me. Traudi once told me that she had never been very interested in America until we met. "But now I am very interested in all that is happening there," she said. "And when I see a picture of New York—*Ohoooo*, det'z dee hometown of you!"

She often asked me what it was like in the United States. I generally painted a rosy picture of a melting pot where lots of different people were out to have a good time, busy pursuing happiness free of official intrusions. It was a vision I had picked up from Hanno while listening to him talk about the innocent American influence in West Berlin in the 1950s, when people would flock to hear Louis Armstrong and dance crazy dances to swing and early rock-and-roll among the ruins of the city, certain that good times would soon be returning. Yet Traudi had to know how slanted my portrayals were. She had already seen some of the evidence. That big black-and-white *Luxomat* television in her bedroom was perfectly capable of receiving West German programming, which was rich with frank documentaries about the U.S.A. and its social problems. But she didn't seem to care. In fact, I think she liked the illusion I had created because it was mine. A fairy tale created just for her. And since she would never have an opportunity to see the reality anyway, it didn't really matter whether it was pure fantasy or not. I once got carried away and said that maybe we could visit New York together sometime. She lay, staring at the ceiling, twirling her hair and quietly said, "That would *really* be something. But it will never happen."

Yet, for all that, my relationship with Traudi was a paradox that was difficult to explain. So often I left her behind the steel doors and concrete walls. The hour would come when she would drive me back to the checkpoint. We would sit in the car with the motor sputtering; she would look at me with sad eyes, stroke my cheek, and I would want her to come with me. Back to my apartment. To sleep with her in my bed and walk with her through the streets of Kreuzberg or along the Ku'damm in the other Berlin she lived right next to but had never seen. But all that would evaporate soon after I got home. While I always looked forward to seeing her again, the separation was all too real. And I often wondered if Kati was serving as some kind of strange safety valve to be turned on as a distraction; to pull me back into the real world in which I had to live. Or maybe Kati and I were using each other to mock and ridicule all that we were helpless to change. Nevertheless, Traudi became more and more affectionate. At the beginning of the relationship I asked her if she had ever secretly daydreamed about going over the

Wall; about defeating the system. She insisted then that she never had, staunchly adding that she never thought about the Wall much at all. But by mid-summer she confessed without my asking, saying that she would so much like to see where I lived. She even told me that when she was an adolescent, she used to daydream about living in West Berlin. When I asked why, she grinned bashfully and said it was because she wanted to be pretty and be interesting.

"And how was living in the West Berlin supposed to make you prettier and more interesting than you already were?"

She shook her head as though it was something I could never really understand. "My father once took me to the top of the Television Tower at night," she said. "I was fascinated by the view of the West. Everyone up there was fascinated by it. It was so full of light; like a galaxy full of stars. East Berlin was dark, but the West glowed. I couldn't believe that normal people— people like us—were living there. You had to be special to live in a place like that."

Traudi had a love affair with the Russian language and read all the great Russian writers in Cyrillic. When we watched Russian films with German subtitles she always enjoyed pointing out a bad translation. German, she once told me, was a language for petty bureaucrats and their mindless *Ordnung*. But Russian, she insisted, was the language of torn hearts and of love. She began telling me things during tender moments; phrases in Russian that she was too embarrassed to translate but I somehow understood, nevertheless. When her English improved, which it did rapidly, she would repeat them in English, as if anything was easier than her native German. She also realized that, for all practical purposes, the relationship was not real. I suspected that it was the reason she shared her feelings about her ideology so freely with me.

During the spring and summer, I gave purpose to my being in Germany by convincing myself that I was forming a rare and intimate relationship with East German society. Doing so rid me

194 | Michael Califra

of that awful feeling that I'd been wasting away my life. I acquired impressions of the oddities across the border in the other Berlin, many of which remain stamped in my consciousness; vignettes of individual moments in time before the full picture was known. It took a while before I realized that those men riding around on bicycles, covered in soot and carrying crudely-made brooms were not all off to costume parties or to rehearse a Dickens play, but were real-life chimney sweeps. Traudi found my ignorance of that kind of thing engaging. "The simplest things are so strange to you!" she'd say with a good-natured laugh and a motherly stroke of my cheek. On that occasion she took my hand, running to the chimney sweep about to mount his bicycle. "It brings much good luck if we touch him," she said. The chimney sweep took it all in stride as Traudi made sure I got a good amount of soot on my fingers "The more soot the more luck!" she insisted.

Kai, on the other hand, was the absolute realist; the one whom I could always count on for the naked truth. As we stumbled our way through the pitch-dark back courtyard leading to his apartment he'd curse the government for keeping those hundreds of lights burning all night long in the Palast der Republik. When I mentioned that Traudi's father had been the Party Secretary at the light bulb plant, he reacted with the same kind of pained horror he showed when I first mentioned Karl-Eduard von Schnitzler, making it abundantly clear what should be thought of the position and anyone who held it.

One afternoon, Traudi was preparing lunch while I looked over the old books in her living room. Even though her father had scribbled his name inside all the front covers, I thought some of them might have been rare editions and worth good money in West Berlin. I tried convincing her to let me take a couple back with me and have them appraised, but she refused. That day I also rummaged through a stack of old records in Traudi's bedroom and came across a couple of albums by a rugged-looking American from Colorado named Dean Reed. It seems Reed went over the Wall in the opposite direction and became a famous recording and film star in East

Germany. On my side of the border he was an absolute unknown. I asked Traudi if she liked him. With a shy smile she admitted that she was in love with him as a teenager, as most of her girlfriends were. I got her to play one of his records. Among melodramatic renditions of the standards *I Did It My Way* and *Guantanamera* was his own composition entitled *Things I have Seen,* which described the injustices of capitalism with lyrics so awkwardly written, the assumption seemed to have been that no one with more than a broken knowledge of English would ever hear them.

I enjoyed accompanying Traudi as she went about her everyday errands; spending time with people standing cow-like in line at the small *Konsum* state supermarket across the street from her apartment for rationed goods like honey and marmalade, or to the local *Rewatex* state laundry on the Kollwitzstrasse where she got runs removed from her stockings by a man with a strange electric needle. I became accustomed to odd East German brand names like *Pulax, Regulax* and *Prax* on products I saw in the shops and around Traudi's apartment, all of them packaged in raw paper with graphic design that was laughably unsophisticated. Yet, like the Trabant, the lack of pretense in these things struck me as virtuous, and like the car, I began associating them with Traudi. Though there were times when the lack of marketing savvy had unintended results, as with a brand of cigars called *Sprachlos*—"Speechless"—which came across more like a gruesome health warning than superlative praise. Other times the virtue could rub you raw, literally, as with the toilet paper produced by the *VEB United Cellulose and Paper Factory, Works No. 3.*

I constantly offered to bring things over from West Berlin for Traudi, or to buy them for her at Intershops, where a wide variety of western products could be had by people with West marks. But, aside from the wax for her living room floor, she was stubborn about never seeing the need. Although, on a couple of occasions, I got an idea of what a tremendous advantage it was to live in East Berlin over other parts of the GDR. Traudi had an aunt who lived near the city of Halle. She was her father's half-sister and Traudi's only living relative besides her brother. One weekend Traudi planned to visit her and, at the *Konsum* supermarket across the street, she was able to pick up not just two or three, but *five* big cucumbers. Traudi said they'd cause a sensation, not only for her aunt, but for the neighbors who would inevitably ask what goodies she brought from Berlin.

At one point in June, her aunt was visiting. Just as she was about to leave, Traudi brought out a large package with about twenty rolls of *Works No. 3* toilet paper for her to take back home, causing the old woman to joyously remark, "Oh, in Berlin you live just like in the West!"

But even in East Berlin, the general shortage of goods led to sense of camaraderie. I was always impressed by the way people, who really had nothing to do with one another socially, would go out of their way to spread the news about when and where sought-after goods were available. The breathless, joyful way in which any one of the neighbors in Traudi's apartment building would make the rounds, knocking on doors with news of tomatoes or apples and sometimes bananas for sale at this *Konsum* or that *HO* state shop.

There was a solidarity in East German society that impressed me and, for the first time, communism began to take on a meaning that went beyond ideological and Cold War rhetoric. The lack of telephones led people to frequent and spontaneous visits to one another in a way that I'd find unthinkable in the West for fear of being considered a pain in the ass. Kai was almost never alone. When he was at home there seemed to be a constant parade of people stopping by to borrow or return something; or to ask for or offer help with one thing or another. He in turn was often underway; a visit to one friend or another, and there was never any aversion to just bringing me along. When he did, tense, distrustful moments with strangers usually gave way to derogatory and sarcastic remarks about the country they were living in.

Traudi had few friends, not surprising considering she worked constantly. Angele, the distraught woman whom she was with the night I first met her at the club, was probably her closest. I got to her apartment several times only to find Angele crying on Traudi's shoulder about her many personal problems; so many that Traudi couldn't even begin to explain them when I asked her about them a couple of times. Not that I cared. I didn't really know Angele and had no desire to waste the limited time I had with Traudi talking about someone else's problems. I was glad that she seemed to feel the same way.

On a couple of occasions, men in pursuit from the hospital stopped by, each with a small bunch of carnations in hand; smiling faces that immediately turned to disappointment when they saw me there. They stayed for a cup of coffee, making awkward shoptalk for an hour, then left. A couple of young mothers who lived in the building would sometimes just show up with their babies and, without the slightest inhibition, ask if Traudi could watch them for a couple of hours while they tended to errands. If I arrived to find her sitting with a baby in the wicker chair by the coal oven, I knew I might as well disappear for a while. Traudi would sit with the child sleeping against her chest, rubbing her cheek gently against its head as though nothing else mattered or existed in the world.

One summer afternoon, I was scheduled to meet Traudi on the Alexanderplatz. That day I decided to enter East Berlin a couple of hours early and visit with Kai who, unfortunately, was not at home. We never made arrangements to meet in advance; it was always hit or miss. I left a note on his door announcing that I had been there, then walked to the Alexanderplatz where I sat on the edge of the *Fountain of International Friendship*. At the other end of the square a scuffle was in progress. I immediately knew what it was about from West German television reports. Once a week, always on the same day and at the same time, a handful of dissidents came here and, standing shoulder to shoulder, quickly unfurled homemade banners that protested the official fraud in the last election. I watched and was fascinated by how much the reality resembled the TV screen images. Instantly, plainclothes policemen, who seemed to have materialized out of thin air, surrounded the demonstrators. They grabbed their banners even before they were completely unfolded, manhandled the protesters and took them away. People crisscrossing the square looked down at their feet and sped their pace, not wanting to get involved. It was over in no time at all, and the Alexanderplatz looked as it did before. I walked over to a café on the other side of the square, past the spot where an act of courageous patriotism had just taken place. It was there that I had my short encounter with Ines.

Ines was a woman in her mid-twenties. She was dressed totally in black with very short hair dyed black as coal (the uniform of the Berlin demimonde on both sides of the Wall). Her complexion was fair and perfect but her hands were as dirty as a young child's with fingers badly stained from smoking. Even though most other tables were empty, she asked if she could sit with me. Before I could answer, she sat down, began rummaging through her backpack, pulled out a pack of cigarettes and slammed it down on the table. That Ines was angry was obvious. The deep drags she took after lighting up visibly calmed her. She ordered a glass of wine, which she drank down quickly before mumbling bitterly to herself. She eventually told me her story.

Ines was a singer/songwriter who'd spent eighteen months in prison for performing two songs in a youth club that were judged to have seditious lyrics. Since her release three months earlier, she had been put under constant pressure by the Stasi to deliver information about friends who were considered enemies of the state. Her bad mood was due to the fact that earlier that afternoon, immediately after leaving the Centrum department store, she had been approached by two members of the Stasi and hauled in for questioning. For more than two hours, Ines had been bullied and threatened with everything from losing admission to a music college, which she had just received, to being permanently exiled from Berlin and even barred from the pub where she often met friends in the evening. With all the targeted spot ID checks by the police, she insisted, such control over an individual was entirely possible. She told me that right there, in the basement of the dismal gray office building next to the café, there were video screens from which the Stasi were surveilling the entire Alexanderplatz. She had seen it herself just fifteen minutes earlier. I asked Ines straight out if she wanted to leave the GDR. "One way or another I will have to," she said. "I don't know how I will, but this *constant* attempt to try and control you—and it just goes on and on and on. I know I'm going to wake up one day and say, I just can't do it anymore. Little by little they . . . they *rob* you of your existence."

After three glasses of wine, Ines stood up, slung her backpack over her shoulder, asked sweetly, "You can pay for me, can't you?" and walked away.

Until that afternoon, Kai had been the only person I'd met who'd had an encounter with the Stasi. But the more I asked about it, the more I came to realize that the Volkspoliezei and Stasi combined to form a phenomenon much like the scourge of crime in New York. Everyone, it seemed, had their own unpleasant experience or knew someone with a horror story to tell. I heard of a man confined to a wheelchair who was being visited by his brother from West Berlin. When the visiting brother suffered a heart attack and died suddenly, it took the Stasi less than an hour before they began badgering the grief-stricken man in the wheelchair, demanding that he give them his brother's West German passport. Evidently, they were concerned that a family resemblance might allow the crippled man to leave the country with it.

More than once I heard that the ashes of a young man shot trying to flee to the West were sent to his mother in the mail, packed in newspaper. She had been threatened with confinement to a mental institution if she discussed the incident with anyone.

One day I walked by the Kollwitzpark and saw Traudi's friend, Angele, playing with a young child. I wound up spending forty-five minutes listening to her tell me about how her husband had been expelled to the West eight months earlier. She hadn't heard a word form him since and was sure they were not delivering his letters to her. Three years prior, he'd been very involved in the environmental movement, which was considered subversive by the authorities, and was arrested for passing "slander" about East Germany to western reporters. After his release, nothing much happened; he had even been allowed to return to his job as a streetcar driver. But the Stasi seemed to lie in wait until a child had been born and the couple assigned a large apartment in a desirable part of the city before taking action. They showed up at their door with the news that he was being expelled within twenty-four hours. I couldn't take my eyes off Angele's face as she told me all this with her child in her arms. Her voice shook with anger and her eyes welled with the furious tears of permanent unrest. I thought I'd never seen a face so full of malice in all my life when she said, "They treat people like they own them. What the hell gives them the right?! Who do they think they are?!" Just when it seemed she might break down, she was able to pull herself together. A spell seemed to have been broken when she asked if I was on my way to meet Traudi. She told me how lucky she was to have Traudi as a friend; someone whom she could turn to when all the frustration and anger came crashing down on her.

One after another I heard these things; stories of people banned from their professions, isolated, torn from their children, harassed to the point of absolute despair, imprisoned or forcibly expelled from the country. Vengeful, spiteful behavior on the part of the authorities that bordered on masochistic. Yet, there were also those who ridiculed the idea that the Stasi were everywhere, as though the stories that made the rounds went so far that they could no longer be believed.

Kai believed them. "Assume they are true," he said adamantly. "All of them."

Traudi seemed to deflate when I told her that I'd met Angele and knew her story. But other than to say that she felt awful for her, it was clear that she didn't want to talk about it. When I occasionally told her about the other stories I'd heard, she would just go about her business in the apartment as if trying to avoid listening. And other than to despondently mumble, "Yes, I know. It is terrible," she would never comment on any of it. It was all something she had no control over and it was obvious that she would rather not have to think about it.

One Saturday night, we were about to depart the Sophienclub after a concert. Traudi followed as I pushed my way to the bar in order to give Kai the customary hardy handshake and thanks for all the free drinks. He pointed out a woman standing with a group of friends. "See that woman there?" he said. "She is PM-12. It is stamped in her identity card. That means she is considered politically unreliable and not allowed to leave the country, not even just to Poland." Kai told me told me the woman had been targeted by the Stasi because she had once joined a group advocating the abolition of mandatory military service. "She is having a party next week. Why not come?" he said, adding in English, "Dare will be many interesting peoples dare." I assumed he meant people who were against the regime.

"Are you sure you can just bring me along?"

"*Ach*," he said with a dismissive wave of his hand. "Of course. It is no problem."

We arranged to meet at his apartment where another friend would pick us up and drive us to the party. Traudi didn't like the idea. We got into the Trabi and she sat staring silently at the steering wheel. I asked her what was wrong. "I think you should not go there," she said softly.

"Go where?"

"To this party."

"Why not?"

She hesitated a moment, then turned to me and confessed, "If they think you are mixing with dissidents they won't let you come back again."

To hear Traudi refer to the East German regime as "they" was somewhat strange. It wasn't just a rare admission of the reality of things, but a declaration of betrayed ideals that saddened me. I gave in, promising I wouldn't go. But by that time I was hungry for possible experiences to talk about in the future and had no fear whatsoever that "they" might keep me out.

. . .

The party was in a ground floor apartment not far from that stretch of the Berlin Wall that divided the Friedrichshain district in the East from Kreuzberg just across the Spree River in the West. We arrived to find about twenty people crammed into the living room. They were talking in small groups, nibbling on cheese and drinking beer or wine. The woman from the Sophienclub spotted Kai and came over. Her name was Sieglinde but everyone called her "Siggi." Kai gave her a bottle of sekt that he'd lifted from the club and introduced me as a friend from America. It was nice to have me, Siggi said before making the observation that she had seen me somewhere before—yes, at the club where Kai worked and always with that pretty blonde woman. "We are so very international tonight," she said, mentioning that there was a woman from Czechoslovakia somewhere in the room.

I'm not sure what I expected, but I found the party disappointing at first. This was a normal gathering of friends that could have taken place in West Berlin, or anywhere else for that matter. Kai fell into conversation with acquaintances about clubs and upcoming concerts. I hung around with a bottle of beer in one hand and a wedge of cheese in the other, eavesdropping on conversations, listening for the code words, trying to decipher anything that sounded like angry accusations of abuse by "die Firma," as the Stasi was known. For a brief time I joined in a discussion between a couple of people who were complaining about how inefficient it was to have the copy machine at their office bought from and maintained by a company from West Berlin. The arrangement made using the copier so expensive that it was kept under lock and key while official permission from a manager had to be gotten for each page to be copied.

When Siggi found me sitting alone in a corner chair, she took pity on me and knelt at my side for some small talk. "Your friend has deserted you?" she asked. I seized the opportunity to ask about her political problems. She was indeed "PM-12" and not only forbidden to leave the country, but required to report to the police once a month. It was a kind of lifetime parole. Being labeled "PM-12" meant that you were especially open to any and all harassment by the authorities. Siggi told me about her efforts to oppose military conscription, and about the afternoon she was arrested at work. How she spent more than two years in a cell with only two small glass blocks for a window. During that time, she was permitted to write only one single-page letter per week to one family member. The contents of the letters were severely restricted; she was not allowed to give information about prison conditions, her legal case, or even mention the names of anyone but the person to whom the letter was addressed. Siggi seemed unable to stop herself from telling me about the damp cold of the prison, the constant headaches caused by poor ventilation, the hunger, the endless humiliation heaped on inmates by guards, and the false stories told to her by the state prosecutor about how friends and family on the outside were incriminating her. Her husband, fearing for his professional position, eventually left her. She lost her job as a textile engineer because of her imprisonment and was offered only a couple of menial jobs, thereafter. She took the most agreeable, washing dishes in a people's plant cafeteria, which she was never allowed to quit. *Arbeitsplatzbindung*, they called it. Lose that job for any reason and they'd see to it that you never worked anywhere ever again. In telling me all of this, Siggi was amazingly matter-of-fact. It was only when she spoke about the isolation in prison that she became visibly bitter. Siggi had a daughter who was three years old at the time she was arrested. "They would never tell me what happened to my daughter," she said. "I had left her at the daycare center that morning, and they deliberately would not tell me what they had done with her, and for that I will never forgive them. *Never!* In this country, if you have children, you are immediately open to coercion by the state or any asshole who might be out to get you," she said. "You have no idea how easy it is to have your children taken away from you in this country. No idea."

I checked my watch and was glad to see that it was getting late. Her ordeal was beginning to weigh on something inside me. I stood up, telling her I had to find Kai so he could drive me back to Checkpoint Charlie.

"It's a shame you cannot stay with us a little longer," Siggi said.

I agreed and thanked her for her hospitality. Another guest who had overheard us said, "You can come back tonight if you like. Just go to the West for fifteen or twenty minutes and come back again."

I explained the official rule: that I had to wait until 7 a.m. before I'd be allowed back. He dismissed that statement with an impatient shake of his head. "If you just pay another twenty-five mark exchange they will let you back in. You know the Buffet at the Freidrichstrasse Station? Go there and you will see it is filled with people who dropped off friends from the West and are waiting for them to come back again. Try it, it won't be a problem."

I told him I just might do that, though I had no desire to return that night. But it was an interesting option and I was a bit angry with myself for not knowing about it sooner. The people who ran this place would gladly kidnap the head off Lenin's corpse for some hard currency, and there were so many nights I would have liked to have spent with Traudi in their entirety.

At that moment there was loud pounding on the apartment door accompanied by the shout, "*Volkspolizei!*" For a split second I thought it was somebody's idea of a bad joke, but no one around me was laughing. The whole room had gone dead silent. Window shades were pulled back to reveal the street filled with flashing blue lights. The door opened and five or six uniformed policemen filed in demanding to see identity cards from everyone. It wasn't long before the angry shouting started, then pushing and shoving with people knocking over lamps and falling onto chairs or against walls. That sent even more policemen streaming into the already overcrowded room. Two actually came in through the windows from the street. One of them was overweight, had gotten stuck, and had to be pulled in by two others. People who resisted or couldn't produce their identity cards were forcibly led away. What should I do? I was thinking about slithering up the hall and hiding out in the bathroom when I heard Siggi yelling at a policeman *"When will this stop? You bastards! When will it ever stop?!"* She was standing at the entrance to the bedroom clutching a young girl in her arms who must have been asleep back there all evening. The child quietly sucked her thumb with her head against her mother's chest and tears running down her cheeks. The policeman kept insisting on seeing an "authorization" for the party. "This assembly is taking place in a border area," he kept saying.

A policeman tapped me on the shoulder and asked for my identity card. I gave him my passport. He flipped through the pages before handing it to another policeman who had appeared at his side. The second policeman disappeared with it while the one next to me quickly adjusted his cap and started writing in a small, shiny black book with the routine calm of an officer filling out a parking violation. Through the window I could see the officer looking at my passport with a flashlight while talking on the phone in his police car. Meanwhile, the confrontation between Siggi and the police was being mediated by one of the other guests who was reassuring her while calmly asking the *Vopo*, "Since when is this considered a border area? It never was one before."

The policeman reappeared with my passport and, without a word, gave it back to the officer still writing in his book. He looked up and said, "You do not have much time if you are to get back to the Zimmerstrasse border crossing by midnight. How did you get here?"

"A friend drove me."

"Is this person still here?" I scanned the room, which looked like it had been ransacked. It was quiet except for Siggi huddled on the floor in the corner, sobbing and clinging to her daughter. Four or five policemen stood over her with one of her friends kneeling beside her. Everyone else was gone. The officer said that he would arrange for a ride if I had no way to get back to the checkpoint. Outside, I found Kai and his friend waiting in the car just where we had parked it. They drove me back to

Checkpoint Charlie. There was a tense silence in the car, as if we were criminals who'd just experienced a harrowing escape from the law. I thought about the officer knowing that I had come through at Checkpoint Charlie that night, what he referred to as the "Zimmerstrasse crossing," and not via the Friedrichstrasse Station. I asked if anything serious would happen to Siggi. "*Nein*," they replied together, as if trying to reassure themselves as well as me. "Nothing will happen," Kai said. "It is nothing too serious. They just try to intimidate, nothing more. The people who didn't have identity cards with them will be released tonight or early tomorrow at the latest." But a moment later there came an unaccustomed burst of frustration from Kai. "*Faack it,*" he said, banging his fist on his knee. "*Faack it!*"

On my side of the Wall, on the way back to the apartment, Siggi's desperate cries kept replaying in my head. Although there was nothing I could have done to change any of it, I had the nagging feeling of having run out, of just abandoning that poor woman. I kept thinking of the phrase that Ines used—*they rob you of your existence.* I didn't feel like going home so I stopped at the Troika where I told Ulrich and Klaus that I had just been to a party in East Berlin, presenting what happened as a lark. They both reacted with an amused detachment, especially when I told them about the fat *Vopo* getting himself stuck in the window. Ulrich sat back in his chair with a content smirk and said, "I hope you don't have your heart set on ever going back there, Richard. There's no way they're going to let you back in again."

That stunned me. I asked Klaus if that was true. He just shrugged his shoulders. He didn't know. He never knew anything.

It was more than a week before I was to meet Traudi again. When the time came, I went to Checkpoint Charlie and slid my passport to the border guard under the thick slab of glass with a good deal of apprehension. It was immediately clear that something was wrong. The usual rhythm wasn't there. The guard was studying the passport when he should have been filling out the visa; still flipping through pages when he should have stamping. Finally, he looked up and said, "Very soon you will need a new passport. This one is almost full." I let out a sigh of relief as he buzzed me in.

But Traudi was working an extra heavy schedule. We had planned to meet three or four times, but when I showed up at her apartment, I'd find a note on her door saying she had to work unexpectedly. I began to think she was avoiding me. Maybe she found out that I had gone to the party with Kai after all and was disgusted by my selfishness. I took each note back with me, studying each one in the U-Bahn on my way home. From the handwriting I was sure that they had been written in haste and I could imagine her scribbling them as she rushed out the door. It would be nearly three weeks before I saw her again. She left a note telling me to meet her at the wine bar in the French church on the Platz der Akademie.

On that evening, from the steps of the church turned restaurant, I saw the blue Trabant race up the street, twenty minutes late. Traudi had come straight from the Charité. The long hours of work had visibly taken their toll. She was worn out. Her face was drawn and there were bags under her eyes, her usually perfect complexion blotched with stress. We each ordered a glass of wine on the terrace. Traudi said that she didn't have much time; that in two hours she would have to work another shift. She said that there was a severe shortage of nurses on her station; that three from her brigade alone had gone to Hungary on holiday and never came back. Her appearance worried me; she didn't look well. I told her she should get some rest. She brushed it side, said she was fine.

"You look ill," I insisted.

"I spend a lot of time around people who are ill," she snapped back, stamping out a cigarette butt in the ashtray. "I guess some of it rubbed off."

Not only wasn't I accustomed to that kind of irritation in her voice, but I had never seen her smoking so fervently, and never so early in the evening. The only time Traudi ever smoked was late at night during a concert in a club, and even then only one or two that she'd manage to sponge off somebody.

We sat in depressed silence watching the late August sunset over Berlin. The western sky beyond the Wall, fiery red, had ignited many facades east of the old square in glowing shades of yellow and orange. Traudi lit up another cigarette. The shadows on the ground below had grown long and the realization set in that this was one of the last summer days. Soon the gray would be returning. I asked when I would see her again. She couldn't say. We discussed the dilemma. How would I get word? She suggested that she send me a postcard. I didn't trust the East German mail. "Then you will have to come back again and again. It will be expensive for you." I told her I didn't care about the money. We decided on once a week. She told me to drink her wine. One glass of wine and she would fall asleep, she said, swapping glasses.

I watched Traudi staring down at the empty glass in front of her, deep in thought. Something seemed to be gnawing at her from inside. It was as if the empty wine glass were a crystal ball in which she had just seen the world coming to an end, leaving her struggling for the right way to break the news to me. She blew a long plume of smoke out of the corner of her mouth. Her tired face looked as if the very essence of life was slowly being drawn from it when she asked if I believed in God. I was unprepared for the question. "I suppose it depends how badly I think I need one at any given moment," I said. She turned her gaze back to the glass in front of her. "And you?" I asked. "As a rose-colored communist? You're not allowed to believe, are you?"

Traudi thought for a moment then forced a smile; a smile born of what she thought was a clever answer. It was a shadow of the one I had known. "I don't think he exists," she said. "But I believe in him."

Nothing Would Be What It Was Before

THOSE NURSES AT THE CHARITÉ are my first recollection of a situation that seemed to explode in the news later that same night. Of the 175 countries in the world, the East Germans were allowed to travel to just seven. Hungary was probably their most popular tourist destination, and for months, word had been spreading across the GDR that East Germans had been crossing the now perforated Iron Curtain into Austria while Hungarian border guards looked the other way. With summer drawing to a close, tent refugee camps had sprung up in Hungary that were soon swelling with thousands of East Germans hoping to emigrate to the West. A tense diplomatic standoff developed between the two Germanies with the new Hungarian government caught in the middle of it all. Obligated by treaty with the East Germans to repatriate any of their citizens trying to flee, they also couldn't afford antagonizing the West Germans who happened to be their largest creditors. And while officially passing it off as a German-German problem, the Hungarians were making a major effort at trying to mediate a solution. East and West German television each began broadcasting nightly news reports from Hungary. The West Germans interviewed East Germans fed up with life inside East Germany while the East Germans depicted the whole thing as a giant conspiracy by West German news organizations waging a "media war" against the GDR by spreading concocted stories about the hard lives of a discontented populace.

. . .

The day after I met Traudi at the French church, I took the U-Bahn out to lush, green Dahlem and had pages added to my passport at the U.S. embassy. Although describing it as "full" was somewhat of an exaggeration, border guards had mentioned it several times now with increasing annoyance and I felt it could no longer be put off.

The sprawling embassy complex sat nestled among trees, almost hidden from view except for the towering antenna mast with its four-dish array shooting up into the sky. American cars drove along the roads and U.S. troops walked the Clayallee, to and from the Truman shopping plaza, dressed in camouflage uniforms.

Inside the embassy, I walked through a metal detector then upstairs where I slid my passport under a slab of anti-terror glass to a woman with a matronly face who spoke English with only the slightest German accent. I told her I needed to have pages added. She flipped through the book, looking at all the green and blue-colored GDR stamps on just about every page, then eyed me suspiciously over her reading glasses, "Yes, I see that."

I watched as she attached a long accordion strip of new pages to my passport with the help of Elmer's glue-all and a hot iron. She disappeared for five minutes while it dried and I sat back in my chair, staring at President Bush smiling genially from his official portrait on the wall. The passport was ready in no time. The woman slid it back to me while holding an official form up to the glass in front of my face. "We don't have you registered," she said.

"Why do I have to register?" I asked, somewhat offended.

"You don't have to," she said defensively. "It's up to you. But we advise all U.S. citizens living abroad to do so."

I surrendered at once when I heard it wasn't mandatory, quickly filling out the form.

A week or so later, I retrieved a note from Traudi's door. The situation at the hospital had stabilized to the point where she knew when she'd have a free evening. She wrote a date and time for the next week when she would be at home. Instead of going straight back to West Berlin, I stopped by Kai's where I was again confronted with the flight of the discontented East Germans. Kai was just about to leave his apartment with his skinny colleague from the club. A friend had given them the keys to his apartment and permission to take his stereo and whatever else they wanted. Hoping to become part of the assault on the Hungarian-Austrian border, he preferred letting his friends take his possessions to having them confiscated by the state, which was what would happen when the Stasi realized he'd gone. If things didn't work out as planned, he wouldn't need those things anyway. Everyone was familiar with §213 of the East German legal code dealing with *Republikflucht*—"fleeing the Republic"—a crime that carried a two to five-year prison sentence.

We drove to the Kastanienallee. There, in a war-ravaged second back courtyard, we parked the van. Within fifteen minutes, Kai and his friend had nearly emptied the place with the quiet precision of professional thieves. I waited downstairs, casually organizing everything in the back of the van while they went up for more. With the last load they both jumped up front and quickly drove off discussing the fact that nobody had seen them. "So what if they had?" I said. "You had permission to take these things."

They both laughed. How could anyone be so naive? Only then was I told that, according to the law, we were all accomplices. "If he gave us the keys to his apartment and told us to take whatever we wanted, then we must have known what he was going to do, right?"

One afternoon, I returned to my apartment after lunch. I pushed the button for the arthritic elevator, listening to the dull electric hum as it descended. When the doors folded open, Geoffrey was inside.

"Oh, there you are, Richard," he said calmly. "I've been waiting for you."

"In the elevator?"

"Up and down like a whore's drawers for the last thirty minutes . . . Why, do you normally take the stairs?"

One day I'll be visiting you in an asylum, I thought to myself. "So . . . what's going on?" I asked cautiously. Visits from Geoffrey were rare. They meant one of three things: either he wanted to treat me to dinner, borrow money, or he'd been evicted from his room and wanted to "crash" at my place for a while.

"I'm afraid I've gotten myself into a bit of a sticky jam, old man."

As usual, Geoffrey's predicament had to do with money. He had sold a painting to an American soldier who'd given him an unusually large one-thousand mark down payment. Now, having second thoughts, the soldier cancelled the contract and wanted to return the painting and get his deposit back, which he had every right to do within ten days. The problem was that Geoffrey had spent the deposit.

"How the hell did you blow a thousand marks in less than a week?" I asked, unlocking my apartment door.

"Well . . . I've actually *paid* my rent," he said cheerfully, as if I'd have no choice but to be pleased. That's when Geoffrey said he needed a favor; that the whole dilemma was a misunderstanding instigated by an encyclopedia salesman—an old enemy of his.

"The old boy must have been put off when the sergeant didn't buy his books and took it out on my painting. He told him it was rubbish painted in the Philippines from a picture postcard! Can you imagine such libel?"

"So what? It's true, isn't it?"

"Well—*really.*" Geoffrey seemed genuinely hurt and offended. "You know, Richard, I expect that kind of talk from Ulli, but I'd always imagined we were friends."

I apologized.

"Besides, I stopped working for *that* gallery six months ago. This fellow's just had his confidence shaken, that's all. He's new to the art world, you see. Just needs a little reassurance that he's made a sound investment."

That reassurance was to be provided by me in the form of a visit. In a scheme that must have come from a bad television sitcom, I was supposed to go to the soldier's home posing as an art dealer, and in the process of trying to sell him a painting, lavish praise all over the one he'd bought from Geoffrey.

"Look, Geoffrey, I'm willing to help you anyway I can, but I won't help you rip-off some poor guy."

"Then could you possibly lend me a thousand marks until the end of October?"

The next evening, I cancelled a date with Kati and was again on my way out to Dahlem. Geoffrey picked me up in his station wagon, its rear stacked with oil paintings and frames. During the drive he was in a pensive mood. The air in the car was a stale mixture of cigarette smoke and sticky oil paint. The ashtray under the dashboard was piled with a pyramid of butts and ashes that sprinkled to the floor whenever we hit a bump in the road or turned a corner. Wipers swept the windshield intermittently, even though the sky was perfectly clear. I kept waiting for him to turn them off, but he just sat there not noticing. It bothered me. Having my evening hijacked had ruined my mood to begin with. Not only was I about to take part in an idiotic conspiracy to commit fraud, which I wanted nothing to do with, but I had to keep brushing cigarette ashes off my left pant leg. And there was that crazy breathing. Whenever Geoffrey drove a car, he'd mindlessly start drawing air through his mouth and holding it in his lungs a few seconds before pushing it out his nostrils so that he sounded like an engine letting off steam. Finally, I found myself flinching irritably with each pass of the windshield wipers and asked scornfully if he saw it raining outside. Geoffrey switched them off without comment, picked up a dusty cassette and shoved it into the tape player, which then blared with the tune, *"Don't Touch Me There!"* A couple of minutes later, Geoffrey turned it off and spoke. "Wait until you meet this chap," he said cheerfully, trying to convince me that it was all going to be such a *marvelously* fun prank. "He's the oldest sergeant in the Army, and a double dipper at that! Used to work as a policeman in Carolina or Florida or one of those places. Retired with pension at age forty and joined the military. In a few years he'll retire again, have two pensions and, *hopefully,* a priceless masterpiece by Henke," he said, snorting a laugh.

I thought about the last time I had accompanied Geoffrey on the job. It was an excursion into the British Sector. A visit to a client. Geoffrey passed me off as his apprentice. Prospects looked bad from the start when a young girl came to the door, saw Geoffrey's face and sounded the alarm, "**Mummy!**" then skipped away singing, "Mummy says we're not buying anything from you ever again." Yet, despite the initial stiff skepticism at his mere presence, an hour and a half later he'd left behind one of his Alpine landscapes, collecting a five-hundred mark down payment on a nearly two-thousand-mark sale. I watched, astounded, as Geoffrey worked the couple, wearing them down with promises of painless monetary gain while showing one painting after another until, at last, there was a slip; that slightest acknowledgement of interest from the wife, "Oh, that *is* a pretty one, isn't it?" Geoffrey set it aside in full view of the woman and moved on to others with ever more glowing boasts of increasing value and responsible investment in the future, while almost reluctantly admitting that the frail mortality of the artists made each painting "more sound than an insurance policy." Then, proof that he finally had them hooked: "May I see that one again in a frame?" asked the wife.

"You left that one aside intentionally, didn't you?" joked the husband.

"It *is* my job to tempt you," answered Geoffrey with modest good humor.

Before we left, the couple expressed concern that perhaps the painting they'd bought previously was hanging too close to the heat. By some strange metamorphosis, Geoffrey was no longer just an ordinary door-to-door salesman, but an expert collector and restorer. He perused the painting as if scrutinizing an invaluable old masterpiece, searching every brush stroke for some hint of damage before assuring them it was "doing just fine."

We drove down the Clayallee, past the U.S. embassy and into one of the side streets. Just as we turned the corner, someone in a black van driving in the opposite direction honked his horn and hatefully bellowed, "Biggs, you're dead meat!"

"Friend of yours?" I gloated.

Geoffrey scornfully raised an eyebrow but didn't respond.

Sergeant and Mrs. Broyhill lived in one of the garden apartments common for allied troops in West Berlin. We parked half a block away under the cover of twilight. I knocked on the door. Broyhill delivered a friendly, "Yes sir, how can I help ya?" when he saw me standing there. He was in his early fifties, tall and slim but with a developing paunch hanging over the waistband of his jogging suit. I introduced myself with a false name, telling him that I was from such and such an art gallery while handing him a rival's brochure that Geoffrey had gotten hold of.

"Once a year we take the collection on the road so people can have a look," I said, just as Geoffrey had instructed me to.

Broyhill took the brochure, barely glancing at it and asked, "You in the art business? I've got something here I'd like your professional opinion about."

Without even trying I was invited into his home. The television was loud with the canned laugh track to an American comedy series on AFN. Broyhill turned down the sound but left the TV on. My assumption, that I had caught him just as he was about to go for a jog, was dispelled when I saw that he was wearing slippers. He introduced me to his wife, a short, pleasant woman who sagged everywhere and had a neck like leather. They asked me to sit down; the wife asked if I wanted anything to drink or eat. In fact, they were both so cordial that I started feeling guilty about it all. Geoffrey's painting was hanging on a wall over the sofa between a smaller painting of two praying hands and some kind of army commendation in a frame. They'd bought a bird's-eye view of Neuschwanstein castle sitting atop an alpine mountain under a flaming red sky that looked, more or less, like a skillfully done paint-by-numbers scene. I walked over and observed it from several angles. "Well, what do you think?" Broyhill asked eagerly. "It is beautiful, after all. Beautiful colors too, aren't they? And the frame—you know it was *included* in the price? The frame alone costs a bundle, I bet." It was as if he was trying to sell the picture to himself all over again. I could only imagine what had Geoffrey told him, but he obviously wanted to believe it.

"It is a Henke," I said with authority. "It's brilliant."

"Hear that, Irma?!" Broyhill shouted in a voice that fully expected exoneration from fault.

Mrs. Broyhill was in the kitchen pouring me a glass of Coke from one of those enormous plastic bottles only available in the States. "Could you tell us what it's worth?" she asked.

I let a mouth full of air pass slowly through my lips. "Hard to say. Henke is recognized as *the* Alpine landscape master."

"Well, what's your most educated guess?" asked Broyhill hesitantly as his wife brought me my drink.

I was torn. I wanted to tell them that if they were uncomfortable with it, they should just return it. I fingered the glass of Coke nervously, stepping backwards, studying the painting and buying time until I'd backed up against the dinette set. I apologized and was straightening out the chair when I spotted the kitchen garbage pail where an empty carton of *Mrs. Paul's Fish Sticks* rested next to a big empty jar of *Marshmallow Fluff.* Then I saw a box of *Lucky Charms* breakfast candy on the kitchen counter top. "Wow, where did you get this?" I asked pointing at the garbage.

At first Broyhill wasn't sure what I was talking about, "Get what?" Then he realized, "You mean the food? At the Truman Plaza."

"Are you telling me the military ships all this stuff over from the States? Why don't they just buy food here?"

"It's not the same," he said. "Take the Coke here. You can tell American Coke from German Coke in a minute. It just doesn't taste the same. I can't drink that German stuff. Must be the water."

The thought of United States military transports crisscrossing the Seven Seas with cargo holds filled with fish sticks and Marshmallow Fluff started me fuming. Those infamous six-hundred-dollar air force toilet seats were nothing compared to this! And Broyhill; he had immediately made himself the object of my scorn by confessing that the finer points of sugar water manufactured by the ton in a giant factory could be so important to him that he thought it worth larding the taxpayer with the cost of shipping it four-thousand miles.

There was a knock at the door. It was Ted, the neighbor from upstairs dressed in his military camouflage carrying a shoebox under his arm. He wanted to borrow some packaging tape.

"You shippin' that back home?" Broyhill asked.

"Yep, sure am," said Ted.

I got a momentary shock when Ted slowly pulled a handgun out of the box, which was filled with popcorn. For a split second, I thought about dropping everything and running out the door. A filler article in tomorrow's *Herald Tribune* popped into my head about Ted, the nice quiet guy upstairs who assassinated the army's oldest sergeant, his wife, and a door-to-door oil painting salesman who just happened to find himself in the wrong place at the wrong time. The questions that would leave my next of kin were mind-boggling.

"Isn't that a beauty? I'm gonna enjoy this baby," Ted bragged as he worked the gun back into the popcorn, indicating that his only interest was sending the thing back to the United States in a shoebox. "Oh, by the way, Irma, thanks for the kidneys. They were delicious. I ate the whole pot in one night."

"My pleasure, Ted. It's always nice to cook for someone who enjoys eating like you do."

"Excuse me," I interrupted. "Is that allowed? . . . Just to send a *gun* through the mail like that?"

Ted smiled slyly and shrugged his shoulders.

Broyhill, not at all disturbed by the idea, retrieved a roll of tape from the kitchen drawer, thoughtfully picking at its end before turning it over to Ted. "This fella's just giving us an appraisal," he said, pointing to the painting on the wall.

"Well, what's the verdict?" Ted asked with amused interest.

Neither Ted nor Broyhill had any idea that they'd awoken emotions in me that I hadn't felt in months. That I was assigning their faces to a gallery populated by those who were somehow responsible for cheating me; for arming Ulrich with all his knives and making sure they were good and sharp. I asked Broyhill how much he paid for the painting. He hesitantly confessed, "Thirty-one hundred marks."

"*Three-thousand!*" I shouted before pulling myself together. Congratulating Geoffrey in my mind, I told them that if they really wanted their money back they should call me. "I'd be more than happy to take it off your hands for that price," I said, scribbling a phone number on Geoffrey's brochure. In my angry haste I had written down my actual telephone number and had to change the last two digits, tracing over them several times with the pen. "And if I were you," I told Ted on the way out, "I'd buy myself one of those real fast—if you ever get the chance. Henke. That's the name to remember."

I pushed the aluminum screen door closed behind me, listening to Broyhill confidently give Ted another reason he should by a Henke: "His liver is fulla cirrhosis and he's got syphilis that's reached his brain. The second he drops dead this painting's worth three times what I paid for it."

Back in the car, I explained to Geoffrey exactly what had happened. He was convinced that Broyhill would keep the painting and said that he'd stop by Ted's next week with "the last Henke on earth. More likely two of them." Then he asked if he could treat me to dinner.

"I thought you had no money."

"I have a lot more than I did twenty minutes ago— *Bombay Palast?*" When dining out with Geoffrey, one had no choice but to go spicy.

We both ordered the same dish, Vindaloo, probably the hottest thing on the menu. As always, Geoffrey added to the order, "Be sure to tell the chef to use three sticks, will you?"

The turbaned waiter grinned guilefully, bowed slightly and went to the kitchen.

"Was that necessary? It's usually hot enough when it's just mild."

"It's better this way, I promise you," he said.

Geoffrey sat silent until the food arrived when he amused himself by asking, "Gonna *dig in?*" It was like eating raw flame. Soon, Geoffrey's face was covered with an oily film and the back of my neck was soaking wet. We sat there, eating, sweating and not saying very much. From the moment he'd picked me up that evening it was clear that Geoffrey had something on his mind. During dinner, he would take a mouth full of food, put down his fork, sit back in his chair and stare off into space. At one point he came out of his trance long enough to tell me a joke; one of those barroom witticisms drawn from current events that everyone seems to know immediately:

"Margaret Thatcher, Helmut Kohl, Mikhail Gorbachev and Erich Honecker are all together at a summit meeting. Without warning, Thatcher rips open her blouse, bares her breasts and says, 'Here are two British pounds!' Gorbachev tears open his shirt, throws forth a hairy chest and says, 'This is the Russian bear!' Helmut Kohl then drops his pants, bends-over and shouts, 'This is the divided Germany!' By this time, old Honecker is totally confused, ja? He's totally confused. Finally, he sees the whole thing as a conspiracy to get him to open up in the spirit of Glasnost. He becomes obstinate, unzips his fly, pulls out his piece-of-pork and declares, 'Here is the border post of the GDR. It will never go up again!' "

We both had a good laugh at that. "Marvelous, isn't it?" Geoffrey asked, wiping the sweat from his brow with his napkin, "Just fabulous, I think." Then he lapsed back into another pensive trance. I had to ask a couple of times if something was bothering him before he came out with it. When he did, I was finally and absolutely convinced that I'd never understand his thought processes. That very morning, Geoffrey had plucked away his first gray pubic hair. "It's the kind of thing that gets one thinking," he said soberly, as if accidental early detection had saved him from a death sentence. He then told me the story about the evening his very old grandfather passed away. Geoffrey was nine at the time. The family used to keep the grandfather in a kind of highchair in a corner of the dining room at mealtime. "We were eating. Gramps was sitting in the corner in his chair. I happened to look at him and he barked at me, 'What about *Burma*?!' Then he dropped his head into his porridge. Dead."

Geoffrey stared glassy-eyed from across the table. You might have thought he'd just gotten the shocking news of the old man's passing. Finally, he forced a smile, "Put everyone off their supper, as you might well imagine." But a moment later he slipped back into his melancholy and said, "Makes one think, though, doesn't it? About the importance of family. Do you ever think about dying alone, old man?"

I never thought I'd hear him talk that way. Geoffrey lived life on a tightrope without a net. Falling off one side put him in at the hands of taxmen; the other landed him out on the street. Avoiding both and playing his numbers game were usually all that concerned him.

"Thinking about settling down, Geoffrey? I always got the impression you're perfectly happy with your life the way it is."

"I can't say I have anything to complain about, really," he said. "Although, if I have to be honest, my world isn't quite all the glitz and glamour it might seem to be from the outside."

I involuntarily let out a loud yelp of laughter that made me choke on my food. My eyes watered as I grabbed my glass and took a drink. Geoffrey gave me a thoughtful look. "You've caught yourself a cold, haven't you?" he said, offering me a tissue. Now realizing he was serious, I took one, blew my nose and wiped the grin from my face.

"Sometimes I wonder if, at heart, I don't really have a fundamentally domestic nature," he continued. "More and more, when I'm lying in bed at night, I get this strange feeling . . . As if nothing really exists at all. Like I really don't exist. It's frightening sometimes. Difficult to explain, really. Hard as I try, I can't figure out what all this is supposed to accomplish. Sometimes I wonder if offspring might help. But then, the thought of being around them day after day, and dealing with the mother on top of it, day-in and day-out." Geoffrey grimaced. "Still," he pondered, staring at the cruet stand on the table. "Something's missing. Something's not at all right. I wish I could put my finger on it." He shook off another trance, "Terribly muddling, the whole thing."

Geoffrey's reflective mood dictated that we would be having a few drinks after dinner. We drove to the Troika. As we were making our way along the bar, a shout came from the back of the room, *"Gruss an Hochwürden!"*—"Greetings to His Eminence!"—followed by uproarious laughter. As a result of Knut's bragging, the phrase was well known as the one he yelled out whenever he reached a sexual climax. Sure enough, we got to the back and found Christoph, Ulrich, Klaus and Torsten sitting together with Knut, dressed in his usual sport jacket, poly-blend shirt and tie. He'd arrived in Berlin early that afternoon. Knut had visited Christoph a couple of times before so he was already known at the Troika; his presence was even considered a rare treat. This visit, though, had completely slipped my mind. As it was originally planned, I was to have met him at the station and he was going to spend a couple of nights sleeping on my sofa. I apologized for having forgotten. "Don't worry about it," Knut said. "There's a free bed at Christoph's place. Cliadhna is out of town."

Although she hardly knew him, Cliadhna couldn't stand the sight of Knut. I expressed surprise that she would allow him to stick his head in her room, never mind sleep in her bed.

"Are you kidding?" Christoph said happily. His mood was always good with Knut around. "Do you really think she's going to know about it? I overheard her on the phone with that boyfriend of hers. She said she'd be away all week. Besides, after Knut picked the lock he detected the devil in her room and promised to exorcise it before he leaves. She'll never know how lucky she's been that Brother Heino came to town!"

Everyone laughed. Drinks were delivered. Knut stood up and lifted his glass in another toast to His Eminence. "*Gruss an Hochwürden!*" the table shouted back.

The rest of the evening is sketchy. I know that we all piled into Geoffrey's car and drove to another bar, then another. In the car, there were a few bars of the Heino fanfare from Christoph, which failed to ignite a chorus. I remember some nervous remarks from Ulrich about Geoffrey's drunken driving. Then there was Geoffrey's insistence that we all drink *Underberg,* which eventually led to a table somewhere being covered by a forest of those tiny bottles wrapped in brown paper. At one point, an intoxicated Geoffrey was leaning over a moaning Torsten, urging him to "go downstairs and stick your finger down your throat. You'll feel better, I promise you." I remember, very late in the evening, Knut displaying some of that aggressive behavior I'd seen a few times while we were living in Münster. Sitting among the rest us, who were by then so drunk that we were slumped in our chairs with the posture of overcooked noodles, he would down his Schnapps, slam the empty glass on the table and angrily shout "*Scheisse!*" with a restless, disdainful sneer on his face. As though he couldn't stand another minute stranded on this earth, or stuck in this life. I remember Knut pushing Geoffrey around a little, pretending just to have a little fun, and Geoffrey so drunk he almost didn't notice what was going on. Only when the shoving became slapping would Geoffrey give a delayed reaction, mumbling with a vague indignation, "Now, there is no need to be rude."

The next morning, I was woken by loud banging sounds. From the floor I could see Christoph asleep on his bed, still fully dressed. I was in his room, lying face down on the fat hardcover dictionary I was using as a pillow with my head raging and aching in every stiff joint. The noises were coming from the kitchen directly across the hall; cabinet doors being slammed shut accompanied by someone swearing loudly and irritably to himself about how disgusting something was. A minute later, he slammed the apartment door behind him and ran down the stairs. I sat up and immediately knew I was going to be sick. I rushed into the bathroom and fell to my knees in front of the toilet, gagging and heaving. When the spasms ended, I sat there on the floor and looked at my watch: it was five past nine. At five o'clock that afternoon I was supposed to meet Traudi at her apartment. I had the rest of the day to get healed and was sure I'd need every single second of it. Ten minutes later I gathered the confidence to pick myself up, walk over to the sink and wash my face with cold water. Outside in the hallway, I was caught by a powerful stench that almost made me sick again. Back in Christoph's room I put on my pants and asked, "Hey, what's that smell? . . . Do you smell that?" But he was in a state of profound unconsciousness. I tied my shoes and went back into the hallway. Cliadhna's door at the end of the hall was shut tight. As much as I wanted to get home, something told me to check on Knut before leaving. The further down the hallway I went, the more powerful the odor became. There was an indescribable foulness to it. I covered my nose with my handkerchief. The door to the room next to Cliadhna's was wide open. The bed was unmade; things had been thrown around. Whoever occupied it apparently left in a hurry. It must have been the roommate I heard swearing to himself. I grabbed the doorknob to Cliadhna's room. It took a moment before I mustered the courage to throw the door open. When I did, the sun immediately cracked through the morning cloud and bright light poured into the room through the window across from the bed, luring me to behold the scene. Knut was sleeping peacefully on his side in dingy underwear with his back toward me among a couple of large, stuffed animals. Not until I was standing over him did I see that he had vomited in his sleep. Afraid he might asphyxiate himself in it, I tried waking him, shouting his name while nudging him. Finally, I had to jab him violently in the ribs a couple of times before he groaned and rolled over onto his back. I hurried out of the room, wrote a note for Christoph telling him to check on our friend, and left.

Outside, I noticed Geoffrey's station wagon parked on the sidewalk across the street, blocking a driveway. Several people were standing around it and an old woman was knocking on the driver's side window with the crook of her umbrella. I walked over slowly, trying not to agitate my stomach, and took a look inside. Through the fogged glass yet more evidence of last night's excesses: Geoffrey insensible, curled up in the fetal position on the back seat. A woman in a floral-print house dress was leaning out the window of her ground-floor apartment, dryly asking again and again if she should call the police. Behind her the television was on. I recognized the face in front of the microphone. It was a face that had become a familiar sight over the past couple of weeks. Hungarian Foreign Minster Horn was making an announcement. I couldn't hear what he was saying. It wasn't necessary. The cutaway scenes of joyous East Germans said it all. They had obviously been given permission leave Hungary for the West.

I pressed my nose against the passenger-side window and took a close look at Geoffrey, watching until I was sure he was still breathing. A stocky man bent over next to me, looked in the car and grumbled, *"Unverschämt!"* I agreed, hailed a passing taxi and went home.

Back in my apartment, I threw myself on my bed and turned on the clock radio. My assumption about the news of the day was quickly confirmed. The West had won the diplomatic tug of war. Speculation had already begun as to how much money the West Germans promised the Hungarian government in return for letting the East Germans go.

I tried to sleep for a few hours, but a pulsating headache made that impossible. Finally, it was time to drag myself to Checkpoint Charlie. When the train reached the Kochstrasse, I couldn't gather the energy to stand up and walk out. I went through the border control at the Freidrichstrasse Station. Maybe it was just my imagination, but I thought I detected a little extra bitterness on the dour face of the border guard sitting in his booth. The East Germans had just been handed a very public defeat. It must have been bitter medicine for the gatekeepers of the socialist paradise to accept that, despite the intense brawl over this issue that surely took place behind the scenes, nothing in the East German diplomatic arsenal could work the wonders that the simple promise of a little hard currency could.

Traudi had worked the 6 a.m. to 2:30 p.m. shift that day, plus two hours of overtime. When I arrived, she was making herself something to eat dressed in a nightshirt that almost reached her knees. Although she was tired, there was again life in her face. I was relieved when I saw it. Relieved to see that she was again the person I knew. We embraced in one of those honest moments that defied the Wall and slighted fifty years of world history. Then I had to sit down.

She asked if I wanted some food but I couldn't think about eating. I went into the bedroom, turned on the television and sat on the floor with my back against the side of bed. Traudi sat on the bed beside me, finishing the last bit of *Stulle* on her plate. She said that she would have Saturday evening off and asked if we were going to see each other. I nodded. She put the plate on the floor and wrapped her arms around my neck, "You are hanging over?"

"That's *hungover*. And yes, I am."

"What did you do last night in West Berlin?" she asked in a tone implying that I'd been a bad boy. I didn't feel like getting into the whole story in all its nauseating detail, so told her only that I spent the evening consoling a friend who was undergoing a personal crisis. When she inquired, I told her all about Geoffrey and his corporal discovery, which amused her no end.

A report about the East Germans in Hungary came on the screen in a news update. East Berlin, which routinely sold its political prisoners to the West, was angrily accusing Bonn of "trafficking in human beings." Traudi breathed a heavy sigh of relief when she saw the pictures. "It is good that they go," she said. I got the impression that she thought the whole episode was now over and done with. She fell back on the bed saying that she could sleep for a week. I reached forward to change the channel. When I leaned back against the bed, Traudi put me into a mild stranglehold with her smooth, fleshy inner thighs and gave me that smile while twirling her hair. We indulged vigorously in one another to the background dialogue of the East German TV series, *You and Your Household Pet.*

I opened my eyes in a dark room bathed mildly in the milky light of the street. The faintly lit clock face at the head of the bed told me that it was 2:15 a.m. I contently thought to myself that there would be four more hours before she goes and pulled her warm body close to mine. Up over the silhouette of her head, I found myself squinting at the two light bulbs glowing in the large eye-shaped aluminum street lamp suspended outside the window. They were familiar. I knew them. They belonged with Traudi. It took a few moments before my heart skipped a beat. They shouldn't be there! I shouldn't be here! *It was a quarter past two and I was still in East Berlin!* "Hey, wake up!" I shouted, shaking her out of a deep sleep. "Look at the time!" She sat up, stunned, sweeping her hand over her head. I jumped out of bed, stumbling around looking for my clothes on the floor. Traudi picked up the clock and held it up to the light of the window. "Why didn't you wake me?" I said, struggling with my pants and accidentally kicking the dinner plate Traudi had left on the floor, sending it sliding across the room.

She got out of bed and turned on the light, "I was sound asleep."

"Look at the television. I didn't turn it off, you must have! Why didn't you wake me?"

"I don't remember turning it off," she said, collecting her thoughts with her hand on her forehead. She switched off the light.

"What are you doing? I can't see!"

"We already missed the deadline," she said calmly, taking me by the hand and pulling me back into bed. "It makes no sense to go back now. We can just as well wait until morning."

She was probably right. And I'd rather not have to approach the border guards and suffer the consequences in the middle of the night. I felt Traudi's hand slowly, reassuringly stroke my cheek until she fell asleep. East Berlin was perfectly still at this hour. Dead quiet. I tossed and turned for what seemed like the entire rest of the night, but must have fallen asleep at some point because I didn't see the sunrise, and when I looked at the clock again it was suddenly after nine.

Traudi was gone. On my way to the kitchen where water was coming to a boil in a pot on the stove, I noticed that the front door was halfway open and could hear her mumbling with Schmid down in the stairway in front of his apartment. Traudi occasionally used his telephone. In the living room, the coffee table was set for breakfast. I sat on the sofa and thought about going back across the border. For the first time after all those months, it was suddenly a threatening prospect. Under normal circumstances the situation would have been bad enough. But now the East German government was smarting from a humiliating defeat at the hands of West German capital that the whole world had witnessed. The state apparatus might respond like a wounded animal; might try to demonstrate they were still in control by making examples of those who showed a blatant disregard for the system. I recalled the ride back from Münster last winter when Christoph and I picked up Kati at the rest stop and there were three people in the car instead of two. Another infraction of the law would not be tolerated again, the border guard said back then. Somewhere there was certainly a record of that. Then there was Siggi's party. They would know that I had been there, too. She had been given solitary confinement for passing petitions around. What kind of sentence could I be looking at? And what the hell would the Americans do for me? Ulrich's cynical line, "*Oh, what a terrible thing, vote for me"* popped into my head. Hard as I tried, I couldn't imagine the Bush administration lifting a finger unless there was a vote to be won from it. All I could imagine were smug assertions that I should have thought about the consequences before I decided to take joyrides behind the Berlin Wall.

Back in the kitchen Traudi greeted me with a happy *"Guten Morgen"* and wrapped her arms around my waist. "Breakfast is almost ready," she said.

How could she think about food at a time like this?

"I just called the hospital. Today I don't have to be there until two o'clock in the afternoon. I'm working my favorite shift, two till ten," she said cheerfully while pouring the pot of boiling water into the sink and quickly taking out a couple of soft-boiled eggs. Why the hell was she in such a good mood? Was it really because the refugee story was finally put aside and she could again immerse herself in her father's stupid daydream about what a wonderful world all this bullshit was going to bring? Evidently she didn't care that I might be about to disappear into the clammy cellar of an East German prison for the next two years! I sat with her on the sofa and watched as she casually buttered a roll, put it on my plate and talked about how she had to make a quick trip to the *Konsum* supermarket but then wanted to go down to the Alexanderplatz with me and look for new shoes.

"Have you lost your mind? I can't spend the day standing in a shoe line. I have to get out of here!"

She found that amusing for some reason. "Are you really so worried about that?" she asked smiling, biting into her *Brötchen.*

"What the hell is it with you? Don't you realize where you are? When are you finally going to wake up? What should I tell them when they ask me where I spent the night? How funny are you going to find it then?"

Her lips pursed ever so slightly as she stared down at the food on her plate. It seemed like years since she'd worn that expression. *"Doch,"* she said quietly. "I know very well where I am." She looked me earnestly in the eyes and said, "You tell them everything they want to know. And, Richard, you mustn't worry."

I didn't touch my food and managed to harass Traudi so much with my impatience that she couldn't finish her breakfast. Desperate to know just what I was in for, I insisted that she drive me straight to the Friedrichstrasse Station. She was quiet all the way back, sensing my anger and frustration. When she let me off, she told me again that there was nothing to worry about, then asked carefully in English, "See we us on Saturday?"

"Yeah, sure," I said dismissively, and jumped out of the car without looking back.

Inside the Tränenpalast, I moved ever closer to the border guard with growing apprehension, wondering just what his reaction would be when he saw the entry date on my visa. Finally, I was standing in front of him in his tiny booth, my way out blocked by a locked door. He took my passport without looking at me and flipped through the pages, glancing at my face only once before making a telephone call that seemed to last no more than one sentence. Then, without any emotion, he said, "You are late. You should have been here yesterday before midnight." He gave my passport to another guard who took me inside the station, up and down stairs, then into a small room where I was to take a seat in front of a desk and wait. The guard pulled the heavy wooden door firmly closed behind him as he left.

There was nothing in the room but a gray steel office desk, the surface of which was empty except for a blotter and heavy, steel table lamp, and a gym locker in one corner next to a small, dirty, enameled sink. In the wall opposite me was a single window. The glass was frosted but the light coming through betrayed the bars outside. My awareness of them pushed me into a state of despair. At that moment I was ready to say or do anything if it would only get me back across the border just one last time. I sat there alone for close to fifteen minutes, legs crossed, filled with a queasy nervousness while listening to the muffled rumble of the trains entering and leaving the station somewhere overhead. Another officer eventually entered the room with a file folder. He sat down at the desk without saying a word and opened it. My passport was inside along with some other papers. He looked them over for a few moments before speaking.

"You realize, of course, that you have violated the terms of your visa," he said, flipping over the pages in the folder. I didn't answer. He asked where I had spent the night. I told him with a friend. He wanted to know the name of that person. I gave it to him. He asked for her address and I gave him that, as I did her occupation and place of employment. And with each confession that was met by nothing particularly ominous or negative there came the increasing feeling that the end was in sight; that I was closer and closer to being set free. He asked me how much East German money I had with me. Just the twenty-five marks I exchanged yesterday. It was confiscated and I signed something. He looked at me and said that I should be careful not to violate GDR law again in the future. That every time I visited East Berlin I was there as a guest and should act accordingly. I told him he was right and apologized for my behavior. Then he stood up and escorted me quickly to the U-Bahn station. When we got to the steps that led down to the platform, he stopped and showed me the way with his hand. "*Bitte*," he said, officially polite.

That was it. Not only was I free to go, but evidently to come back again. I could have waltzed down the stairs, brimming as I was with good feeling and pride in my fellow man for the mercy just shown me. Traudi was right. There was nothing to worry about. It was no big deal. And on the way home I felt ashamed of the way I had acted toward her. It also occurred to me that this was the first time I hadn't spent every possible minute I could have with her. Inexplicably, I deeply regretted it.

Back in my apartment, I was greeted by two messages on my answering machine from Christoph, one panicked the other nasty. He was angry with me for leaving without having had the decency to help clean up after Knut. I was accused of being a "creep" as well as an "egoist." Later that afternoon I received a visit from a Kati who was angry with me for canceling our date two nights before and not calling back. But most unsettling was an envelope from the police I found in my mailbox. A single-page form letter in official civil service German stating that I was under investigation for "violation of §92 of the Alien Code of the Federal Republic of Germany." It went on in standard form to say that I had the opportunity to answer the charges in person. The date, time and place were typed in. This is coming Friday at 11:30 a.m. It wasn't even at my local Polizeirevier. I was to go to a police headquarters in the Moabit section of the city.

I called Wolf and read him the letter. He checked his old law books and found it had to do with illegal residence, which made no sense at all since my resident visa was still valid. Wolf offered his usual calm, sound advice, "Just go there on Friday and see what it's all about."

When Friday came, I went to the police headquarters, which was housed in a complex of turn-of-the-century brick buildings not far from the Wall. Inside, a good deal of renovation work was being done. The person I was supposed to see had been moved to another area. A stocky policeman with a gray beard and ruddy complexion that made him look like a big garden gnome accompanied me to the right place. Along the way, he asked me where I was from. I told him I was American. That started him talking about all the time he had spent in training in Virginia twenty years ago. "*Tja,* some people in this town have their hearts in Moscow," he said. "Mine is in America."

"Very nice, I'm glad," I answered, just wanting to get down to the business at hand.

He brought me to a room where a policeman sitting at his desk looked at my letter, then asked me to wait outside. I sat on a chair out in the corridor thinking how harmless it all looked. It was more like a hallway in a university building than a police station. Officers in their green uniforms leisurely walked from one room to another over polished linoleum floors like college professors with the sound of a typewriter somewhere off in the distance. There were no parades of menacing, handcuffed thugs being led to and from holding cells; no people racing around carrying dossiers swollen with unsolved crimes; no telephones ringing off the hook with new reports of bodies being found or felonies having been committed. There was nothing that I had come to expect as routine in a police station. A few minutes later, an officer walked up the corridor through double steel doors that were marked with a handwritten sign, "No Passage for the Public" and approached me asking my name. He escorted me down the hall to his office and took a seat behind his desk. There was a file folder in front of him with fifteen or twenty pages inside. The policeman put on his eyeglasses and began scanning it.

"I didn't think you were going to show up," he said in English. "You prefer English, I suppose?"

I replied in German that it didn't matter. He said he would continue speaking in English because he wanted to be absolutely certain that I understood him. As he flipped through the pages I realized that the entire file must have been on me.

"Is all that about me?"

He didn't answer that question, nor did he register it. He began making small talk, asking me questions that he had to have already known the answers to: How long had I been living in Germany? "About three years." What I did I do for a living? I told him that I sold computer software. He wanted to know what kind of software I sold. "Mainframe software," I said. He flipped over a few more pages, "Have you ever heard of the Committee for Multilateral Export Controls?"

"Yes," I said, "I know what CoCom is." Anyone who read a newspaper did. Not only was it was a relief to finally realize what this was all about, but it was also hilarious to imagine anything having to do with the Software Company constituting a threat to the Free World. As he scanned more of my file, I couldn't help thinking about the greedy, dope-smoking bunch sitting in their cubicles in that cramped, dirty office in New York: "Hardwick Johnson" and his obscene sales calls; Jerry and his express-mail drug delivery; Steve Metropolis asking customers on the phone if he was "legible." Those people were more of a threat to western civilization than anything the communists could ever come up with. I pictured Bob running out of his office, gagging battling salesmen with his hands. The Goddamned Job! If this guy sitting here in West Berlin with his office hidden behind steel doors and his holy mission to keep the world safe for democracy could only see them all. He'd feel like such an imbecile! I let lose a laugh with a grin on my face. The officer looked at me with an extremely annoyed expression that asked if I felt like going to jail. To show I was taking it all seriously, I told him in no uncertain terms that I was a loyal and patriotic American; that I had never done business with the East Bloc and had no intention of doing business with them. Instead of acknowledging, he asked if I had ever been contacted *by* or had any contact *with* East German or other intelligence agencies. I said no, absolutely not. Although I found the question flattering for some reason. He waited a moment before stunning me by asking, "Do you have a girlfriend in East Berlin?"

"I know a few people in East Berlin," I said.

"Why are you being evasive?"

"I'm not being evasive . . . Yes . . . I suppose I do. As far as it is possible . . . to have a girlfriend there."

"And how long have you known her?"

"Five or six months, why?"

"Have you ever delivered any magnetic tapes—"

"*What?*"

". . . magnetic tapes, user manuals, *or source code* to this person?"

I was flabbergasted. I couldn't do more than stare at him.

"Would you like to have a lawyer?" he asked.

"A lawyer? No, I don't need a lawyer. I've never taken any of those things across the border. Absolutely not! Never!"

He looked at me suspiciously in the eyes for a moment, then took the file and left the room. He returned ten minutes later with a statement for me to sign. I was to read it over carefully and be certain nothing was misrepresented. There weren't any misrepresentations. It was everything I had told him.

I'd barely finished running my signature over the paper before he was jovially showing me out of his office. He walked with me down the corridor as far as the double steel doors. "You seem to be doing well here in Germany," he said. I agreed without knowing exactly what he meant by "doing well." "Remember, the line between friends and accomplices can be a thin one. If I were you, I'd act accordingly. Just cool it. It would be a shame if you were made to leave the country when you obviously like it here so much."

I left the police station convinced that visits to East Berlin were out of the question; that further excursions across the border would automatically subject me to arrest, deportation and who knows what other problems once I got back home. I telephoned Wolf and told him the West Berlin police were concerned that I might give source code to the East Germans. He suggested that maybe I should move back to Münster, and for a day or two thereafter, the fear of making a wrong move that might send me hurling forever out of respectable society actually had me considering it.

As Saturday came and went, I wondered what was going through Traudi's mind when, for the first time since I'd known her, I didn't show up as planned.

Over the next couple of weeks, I watched events develop in the East on television with a growing feeling of frustration and guilt. Frustration at having East Berlin and its people put off limits to me by my own side; guilt at the way I had left Traudi and just disappeared. And hadn't I been just a little cavalier in delivering, not only her name and address, but also her profession to the East German border guard? How could I have done such a thing? I wondered what implications that might have for her. What if she lost her job because of me? That thought slowly gnawed at me as I watched history unfold. Demonstrations inside East Germany became more frequent while a flood of would-be emigrants invaded Czechoslovakia, then Poland—practically the only places on earth they could still go without hard to get visas. They occupied the West German embassy grounds in both countries, hoping a deal would be cut that would also let them emigrate. On his *Black Channel*, von Schnitzler insisted the migration of East Germans had been blown all out of proportion by the western media. What the West Germans claimed to be a mass exodus was, in reality, only 1.15 percent of a population of seventeen million, he said, calling the other ninety-eight percent, citizens who were "true to the GDR." Nevertheless, the East German government became desperate to end the situation. The prospect of celebrating the fortieth anniversary of the founding of the nation on October 7th while humiliating news footage of its citizens frantically fleeing the country was beamed around the world was too much for them to stomach.

One afternoon during all this, I was sitting in the Café Adler with my passport in my pocket and the intention of crossing Checkpoint Charlie into East Berlin. With time, the more I thought about the interview with the West Berlin police, the more absurd it became. After all, they had never actually accused me of anything. There was no way they could have had any evidence that I was involved in anything fishy, simply because I wasn't. They had me sign a farce "confession" in which I confessed to nothing. It was all beyond ridiculous. There was that registration form at the American embassy when I had pages added to my passport. On it I had filled in my profession as "mainframe computer software sales." I remembered the reaction of the woman behind the glass when she saw all the East German stamps in my passport. Maybe they thought I'd get myself into trouble eventually and wanted to intimidate me just enough to prevent that from happening. That obviously didn't explain everything; I had no idea how they found out about my relationship with Traudi, but I didn't care. This was a city where everyone was spying on everyone else. Why should the fact that the West Berlin police were also doing it to foreigners living West Berlin be so surprising? And what did the police officer tell

me? "Just cool it?" More and more I took that to mean cool it—
for a while.

A couple of days earlier, I had enlisted Kati to help me discern whether or not I was being followed; a job she undertook gladly when I told her about my interview with the West Berlin police. She considered it an unforgivable abuse of authority, just as I knew she would. We packed up Anja and traveled the city, always on the lookout for anyone who might possibly resemble a police tail. There were a dozen false alarms. Kati mistook a man we'd seen at a bus stop for someone we saw eating ice cream at the self-service restaurant in the airport. There were the two old women in the toy department at the KaDeWe who she swore were the same two she thought looked suspicious walking around the zoo. Then she was absolutely certain that the man who sat across from us in the U-Bahn was the same guy we had seen in a café an hour earlier. The fact that he was now bald, wore different clothes and had a beard didn't matter. "Look at all that hair in his ears," she whispered while staring unceasingly at him. "Don't tell me he's not the same person. You don't realize who you're dealing with, Richard. They can do anything, but they're so arrogant that they get sloppy sometimes."

By the end of the day it all seemed dumb. Nevertheless, I found myself sitting there in the Café Adler, observing the border with last minute anxiety, looking at the newspaper without reading it, eyeing the people around me, and the American soldier in his hut, leaning back in his chair with his hands clasped behind his head looking bored, and I thought the hell with all of them. I'd go straight to Traudi's apartment. If I didn't find her at home before I had to come back, I'd leave a note apologizing for not showing up last time and ask her to leave a note for me tomorrow if she wanted to see me again.

I paid for my coffee, left the café, and walked slowly, cautiously toward East Berlin, half expecting to suddenly be yanked by the shoulder from behind. It didn't happen. I walked through the Wall and into the customs building. I stood in line behind a couple of people. By the time I got to the window there were two or three others standing behind me. I slid my passport under the thick glass. I knew the guard's face. He gave me that stern nod of recognition and this time, fearing incrimination, I wished he hadn't. The guard worked the passport, then mumbled something as he gave it back to me. Without thinking I automatically slid five marks to him. This time he spoke with a good deal of hostility in his voice, *"Sie sind in der DDR unerwünscht!"* he said, pushing my passport and five marks back at me under the glass slab. All of the sudden I was an "undesirable" in the GDR. I took my passport and money. Without saying a word I quickly withdrew, past the expressionless faces in line behind me, at that moment feeling only embarrassment for my rejection in front of all those strangers.

I retreated to the Café Adler, taking the same seat I had just vacated. The same waitress came over smiling. "Back again?" she asked. I ordered a cognac with a nervous chuckle in my voice that said, yeah, silly me, I'm back again so soon. Then I was hit by it. The new reality. Little explosions went off inside my head as I realized what had just happened. That the door to East Berlin would be closed to me forever. I'd never see Traudi or Kai again. It was a situation as arbitrary as it was permanent. I had no recourse to even try and change it. For the first time I understood what the Berlin Wall was. For the first time I saw how idiotic and callous I had been in my assumptions about it until then. I felt like a member of that army of frivolous foreigners who came here to gawk and giggle. Unfortunately, I had been the one singled out to be put in his place.

Days later, the East German government declared that it would make a "special humanitarian gesture" designed to end the suffering of the innocent children forced by "unscrupulous parents" to camp out on embassy grounds in Prague and Warsaw. Special trains would take the East Germans holed up in Czechoslovakia and Poland to West Germany via the GDR. The East Germans were insistent on that point. Although the trains wouldn't stop in East German territory, they have to pass through so the people inside could be listed as officially expelled, never able to return. I'll never forget the dark, grainy images on the evening news the night the West German foreign minister, standing on the balcony of the embassy in Prague, announced to the crowd that he had secured their passage to the West. Before he had even finished his statement, his amplified voice was drowned out by thousands of wildly cheering people who fell with joy into one another's arms. All those people who had been so viciously slandered in the East German media as "asocial," "traitors" and "criminals" by their government. I wondered if I had met any of them. I wondered if the person whose stereo and other personal belongings I helped load into the van that night was among those now about to start a new life in West Germany; or had he been sent back to the GDR with that special stamp in his identity card that called for the attention of the Stasi? All those faces so joyous and triumphant in the courtyard of the embassy in Prague. All the others in Hungary and Poland. I was certain that Kai wasn't among them. He had already chosen to stay; to make his way in the system as best he could and wait for the changes he was sure were coming. But what about Siggi and her daughter? She was "PM-12" and not allowed to leave the country, but could she have found her way across the border somehow? And what of Ines or Traudi's friend Angele? Given the chance, they would certainly have gone. How many others had kept their intentions secret? As the trains arrived triumphantly in Bavaria, I knelt in front of my television, filled with excited anticipation at the prospect of finding a familiar face in the crowd. But it was impossible. There were just too many people.

At the same time, I did my absolute best not to think about Traudi, because when I did my heart sank in my chest. I couldn't help but wonder what she might have been feeling, sitting alone among the old books and the old promises, watching and wondering what it would all bring. Whenever I caught sight of the Television Tower, its strobe lights took on the characteristics of a distress signal; the tall structure that of a drowning person's hand reaching desperately into the air.

Events accelerated, passing in a kaleidoscope of images—new waves of East Germans in the courtyards of the West German embassies in Prague and Warsaw; in Dresden, a riot by ten-thousand people broke out in the first street battles in the GDR since the 1953 uprising; protesters were also clashing with police in the streets of East Berlin and Leipzig. I watched the news footage; scenes that took place no more than two miles from my apartment, which I was barred from witnessing in person, were delivered into my living room via West German television. Karl-Eduard von Schnitzler used his *Black Channel* to denounce the demonstrators as hooligans paid by the West. The turmoil caused the East Germans to announce that border crossings into East Berlin would be closed during the fortieth anniversary commemorations, giving me a respite from the guilt I'd been feeling for telling Traudi I'd be there with her, "no matter what." Gorbachev, in East Berlin as guest of honor for those celebrations, warned Erich Honecker that "life punishes those who come too late" and that "danger awaits those who fail to adjust to changing times." At the Troika one night soon afterward, I found Ulrich and Christoph casually discussing the likelihood of a violent "Tiananmen Square solution" for dealing with the demonstrations. "If they are going to do it, they'll do it now," Ulrich said, leaning back in his chair, picking the dinner from his teeth. "They just had to get their anniversary celebrations over with and Gorbachev out of the way." Monday night protests in Leipzig had grown to over 100,000, all defiantly chanting, "*We are the people!*" when the Politburo suddenly ousted Erich Honecker. After eighteen years in power he was written out of history with a ten-second segment on the East German evening news thanking him for his years of service. The new leadership talked a lot about the need for dialogue and reform, but the only real change seemed to be the lifting of the ban on the magazine *Sputnik* and the sudden yanking of Karl-Eduard von Schnitzler from the airwaves. After thirty years on the air, his final *Black Channel* broadcast consisted of a bitter five-minute farewell in which he let it be known that he regretted nothing. Citizens' Committees stormed Stasi headquarters as even more people poured into demonstrations in cities all over East Germany. In East Berlin, on November 4th, a million people filled the Alexanderplatz demanding political change. I watched on television as Schabowski, the East Berlin Party leader, talked about moving ahead "with our Soviet friends" and Krenz, the new General Secretary, talked about standing "shoulder to shoulder with Gorbachev." But it was far too late. The Party had no reserves of goodwill available to it. One after another, the leadership was booed into submission. It was the dissidents—the artists and writers—that people wanted to hear. And when the author Christa Wolf uttered the phrase, *"Imagine there is socialism, and no one leaves,"* I found myself hoping that Traudi was there to hear it.

Yet, despite all that was happening, for the first time I literally *felt* West Berlin closing in on me. I found myself daydreaming more and more about getting out; about covertly going over the Wall into East Berlin. It got so bad that I couldn't sleep unless Kati was there to sap my energy or unless I was half drunk. The old joke: *West Berlin, where two million free people live in the same cage,* seemed all too real. What I wouldn't give to get out of this city for a couple of days! On the spur of the moment I threw a few things in a bag and decided to visit Wolf and Ina in Münster. The trip got off to a bad start when I tried starting my car only to find the battery was dead. I hadn't driven anywhere in months. But it reminded me that, after being branded an "undesirable" in the East, I was surely banned from using the transit highway, anyway. So I jumped in a taxi and got to the airport where I paid an obscenely high price for a flight to Frankfurt. From there I caught a train to Münster.

It was really good to see Wolf and Ina again. Their familiar warm smiles and hugs when I showed up unannounced at their door were like finding shelter from a fierce storm. I didn't even mind the discussions with Wolf about business over dinner, or the stories about the stupid habits of the new people working at the office, none of whom I knew. We joked about the fact that the small ad I stumbled across in the *New York Times* four years earlier was having consequences for people living in

Münster whom I'd never even met. We talked about the eruptions in the East really only while watching the evening news. The night I arrived, there were reports about the tense atmosphere between the police and the hundreds of thousands of people at the Monday demonstration in Leipzig; the next night we learned that the East German Prime Minister and his entire cabinet had resigned; the night after that it was the entire Politburo. Watching it all each evening, Wolf would turn to me with a grin and say something indicating a general disbelief, as if he'd just been given the latest cheap sleaze in an on-going soap opera. While the eruptions in the East were topic number one, to the exclusion of everything else that was happening in the world, here it all seemed remarkably distant to me. Especially since Wolf, on the first night of my visit, after telling me about the strange habits of new people in the office, dropped his bombshell: Bob wanted to take the company public. Wolf and I would be among those receiving shares—enough to make us both instantly wealthy. That was all we were inclined to talk about when we played squash together or went for a sauna, just like we used to do when I lived there. Wolf knew next to nothing about how often I'd been visiting East Berlin, and even less about Traudi and Kai. I'd rarely had the chance to tell him. Most of our contact over the past few months had been reduced to him leaving messages on my answering machine with questions about accounts, and me calling him back and leaving messages with our secretary because he was on the phone, or in meetings, or away visiting clients. And the whole time I was there, I hadn't felt the slightest inclination to tell him anything about all that. The way we figured it out, Bob was about to give us an initial sum of more than half-a-million dollars each. After you win the lottery, there's not much of a desire to think about anything else.

It was about seven o'clock in the evening when I got back to my apartment in Berlin. The first thing I did was look over my business files and plan a strategy for calls the next day. I was now motivated to work like never before. About forty-five minutes later, I had barely settled into my rocking chair in front of the TV when the telephone rang. It was Kati wanting to know where I'd been. "Do you know how often I've tried to reach you? How was I supposed to know that they hadn't locked you up?!"

"Lock me up? Why would anyone want to lock me up?"

"Why? Because maybe they think you're passing trade secrets to the East Germans, remember?"

"Oh, yeah. I forgot about that."

"You forgot? Do you know how worried I've been about you?"

That kind of concern coming from Kati never seemed quite convincing, yet it was still nice to hear. So when she demanded remuneration in the form of being taken to dinner and a movie, I agreed, even though I had no desire to go. After an entire afternoon on trains and planes, I wasn't in the mood to do anything but spend a quiet evening at home watching *Cleopatra*, which I knew was going to be broadcast on East German television. But I had to eat anyway, and going out would be far less exhausting than having her come over so early, which is what she would have done otherwise.

We met on the Savignyplatz and ate in a trendy restaurant under the S-Bahn. I found myself talking non-stop about the company going public and the half-a-million in shares, undisturbed by the fact that Kati showed no interest in any of it. We walked down to one of the "shoebox" movie theaters on the Ku'damm and sat through a film. When it was over I waited in the lobby while Kati went to the ladies' room. I stood against a wall, finishing up the last of our popcorn and looking through the doors out onto the street. A parade or something was taking place. People who'd just left the theater were standing around outside on the sidewalk watching and cheering. A popular soccer team had obviously won a game somewhere. That always prompted spontaneous demonstrations by obnoxious fans who packed into cars and drove around yelling, waving team flags and drinking beer, stopping only long enough to urinate or vomit. And it was now after midnight, just the right time for such a display for it always had to be made as annoying as possible. I threw away the popcorn container, walked across the lobby to the entrance and looked out to the street. The Ku'damm was filled with cheering people. I went outside, pushing my way toward the curb. A line of cars was moving slowly by. There was a Trabant. How did that get here? Behind it was another and then a Wartburg. My God, they are all Trabants. Trabis and Wartburgs. What the hell was happening? All around me people were yelling hysterically, "*Herzlich Willkommen! Herzlich Willkommen!*" And the faces in the cars—victorious smiles; tears of joy and disbelief were everywhere. Those people came from East Berlin. The Wall! It was open! I ran back inside and found Kati. "Come here, quick, they've opened the Wall!"

She looked at me like I'd gone crazy, "What? What are you talking about?"

I pulled her by the arm and pushed through the crowd to the curb. Over the shouting, joyous howling and beeping car horns I yelled, "Look! Trabants! The Wall—It's open!" Kati took a deep breath, covering her open mouth with both hands, the way I would imagine her looking if it were possible to shock her with vulgarity.

We both stood there watching the faces in the cars. I couldn't tear my eyes from them. I'd never imagined anything so ecstatic. Almost beyond comprehension. "My God, do you believe that? Look at that!" I shouted, "*Look at that!*"

Kati was dumbfounded; in a stupor I had to shake her out of. "How did this happen?" I heard her asking again and again as I pulled her by the hand down the Ku'damm, past all the smiling people handing flowers to jubilant faces in their dumb little cars. One man stood on a corner giving out plastic cups of sekt he poured from a huge bottle shouting, "Welcome! Welcome!" Everywhere there were eyes filled with tears; everywhere there were dazed, perplexed expressions that were not quite sure it was all really happening.

Kati hurried, bouncing and swaying after me as we made our way down to the Memorial Church. There were tears

244 | Michael Califra

streaming down her cheeks that I don't think she realized were there. I couldn't stop moving. I wanted to see the faces. I wanted to see each and every single one of them. Down by the Wittenbergplatz, a city bus inched along on its route, caught in the historic melee. Its side was plastered with a giant advertisement for *Vodka Gorbatschow,* which ignited the crowd in a spontaneous victory chant, *Gorbi! Gorbi! Gorbi!* We pushed our way through the throngs; past people welcoming strangers with hugs, kisses and flowers; people weeping for joy. Kati couldn't keep up. I often had to stop and wait for her, almost losing her a couple of times of times in the crowd. The entire city was out on the street. Millions of people were on the move. And there was not an angry thought among them. Pure exuberance. Unqualified goodwill. As if humanity had suddenly rid itself of all its hate. Any hopelessness had instantly vanished. All the things that blighted our presence on this earth had evaporated. An overwhelming yet unspoken awareness abounded—that the grotesque hysterics, which ruled so much of the twentieth century, had, at this moment, come to an end.

We walked down to the Brandenburg Gate. I wanted to see it. I had to see it. We got there to find hundreds of people *standing* on the section of the Wall that looped around in front of it. More and more people were being pulled up onto the top. Many of them were soaking wet, having been hosed by East German guards trying to get them down. But the Wall had lost its power to divide. It was now a magnet, drawing people onto it from both sides. We made our way onto the same platform that we stood on earlier in the year, a slow process involving a lot of pushing and waiting. From the top we could see that the other side was filled with intimidated border guards standing around in the weird light of the flood-lit space among ecstatic citizens. The whole point of the guards' professional existence had been instantly removed. The police state's policemen were on the defensive, made so by the size of the crowd before them; by a world suddenly turned upside down.

Kati and I eventually made our way over to the border crossing at Invalidenstrasse. It was sea of elated expressions.

West Berliners had forced themselves well into East German territory as Wartburgs and Trabants inched triumphantly westward engulfed by the cheering throngs. Westerners drumrolled their fists on the roofs of the cars as border guards watched sour faced, like children beaten at a game they'd never even considered losing.

I got separated from Kati. At one point I heard her shouting my name, but I couldn't find her. She was gone. I don't know how long I stood there watching; looking at the faces. People coming through the pedestrian crossing jumped with joy and disbelief when they stepped into the West, triumphantly holding their East German identity cards above their heads. Some, obviously planning to stay, spitefully tore them up in front of border guards or TV cameras and threw the pieces into the air. Still others limped past, simply exhausted by it all. From the arms of his elated mother I heard a young boy ask nervously, "And they *really* won't shoot anymore?"

I walked back to the Brandenburg Gate and on to Checkpoint Charlie. People had begun chiseling away at the Wall, filling the cold, damp night with the sharp sound of steel striking steel accompanied by the powerful muted thud of a lone sledgehammer. Checkpoint Charlie was another sea of people. The Café Adler was still open for the occasion, its windows filled with the silhouettes of patrons standing on chairs looking out. The American control house had just about vanished in the mob. I stood there and watched, losing all sense of time. Before I knew it, the sun had begun to rise with the first hint of a brightening, turquoise sky. The sun rising and setting in the East for the first time, I thought. So proud was I of that line that I guarded it jealously in my brain, mumbling it just once to myself. In my drunken elation, I was convinced that one day I would use it to write about what happened that night.

I started back to the Memorial Church, getting a ride as far as the New National Gallery on a flatbed truck that was filled with people passing around bottles of beer and wine. They sang songs and chanted for Gorbi. The person sitting next to me was an East Berliner, probably my age. He told me he never thought he'd see this moment. "I always thought that I'd have to wait until I was sixty-five years old to see the day I'd be here," he said, fighting tears. "You know, I often used to walk along the Freidrichstrasse and hear the U-Bahn under my feet. I could *feel* it as it went by. I knew there were people riding around down there. Do you know what that's like? . . . To know that you will only be allowed to join them when you're an old man?"

I could only shrug my shoulders.

"It hurts," he said. "It hurts a lot and makes you angry."

"Now it's over. Now you can ride with them."

"Yes," he said smiling, his face red with emotion. "Now it's finally over. Now we can all ride together."

The truck was moving too slowly for me. I wanted to jump off. We shook hands and he pulled me in an embrace. We parted as if we were the best of friends yet I never even learned his name.

By the time I arrived back at the Breitscheidplatz the city was fully engulfed in the light of a new day. I sat by the Memorial Church but couldn't keep still for more than two minutes. I had to keep moving. I should have been dead tired by then, but I wasn't. There were still so many faces to see. I've seen so, so many but I was impatient to see more. I crossed the street and walked down the mobbed Tauentzienstrasse. It was only possible to move if you kept away from the curb and close to the buildings. Then, in the distance, I finally set my eyes on it. A glimpse between bodies. A long, beige gabardine coat. I didn't even have to see it swing open exposing a nurse's uniform to know who it was. I stopped and waited. She gave a big smile when she saw me; I felt myself grinning from ear to ear. Neither of us was surprised to see the other; more outlandish things had already happened that night. Two people accidentally meeting on the street was the least of it all. We embraced and she slid a kiss into me. She tasted like sekt. My first words were uncontrolled; I couldn't stop myself from saying, "I'm sorry, I'm sorry." She didn't seem to hear me. With her head against my shoulder she said something that sounded like, "Isn't it wonderful?" Neither of us really heard what the other had said.

It didn't matter. We walked arm in arm without saying anything. Talking wasn't important. Neither of us could stop moving. Neither of us wanted this to end. Communism had finally brought about the paradise it had been pledging for the last hundred years. This was the world promised to her by Marx, Engels, Lenin and her father. That it didn't come about in the way they had expected didn't matter. What mattered was to experience as much of it as possible before exhaustion took hold.

At the Potsdamer Platz, Traudi pulled me to the graffiti-covered Wall where she reached out and touched it with her finger tips, mumbling almost to herself, "Huh. You had to live with it, too." Here, the scaffold was also packed with people. We pushed our way to the top and saw the view of her city that was familiar to me, but she was seeing for the first time. In the distance, the Television Tower was blinking in celebration. American and British military helicopters hovered overhead, keeping to the western side of the border. I thought it strange that the watchtower was still manned by a guard observing at it all through binoculars. I heard an East German on the platform tell her child, "Look, you see? That's where we live." Traudi heard it, too. She said she see wanted to see my home; she wanted to see where I lived. We walked along the Wall to Checkpoint Charlie, which was still a mass of ecstatic people. One of them was giving out money. I got a ten-mark bill pressed into my hand and Traudi and I both had to laugh. We made our way into the U-Bahn entrance at Kochstrasse. The narrow stairway leading down to the platform was so jammed with smiling faces that it took a good twenty minutes to negotiate. Packed trains arrived, each car filled with happy, watery-eyed easterners arriving for the first time from the Friedrichstrasse Station. We had to let three or four trains go by before we could finally squeeze onto one. In the train there was an announcement over the loud speakers welcoming East Berliners to West Berlin, which caused a deafening eruption of wild cheering.

Back out on the street, we passed a bank with a long line of people waiting outside. Then I remembered that bit of common knowledge. "We have to get your *Begrüssungsgeld!*" Traudi didn't know what I was talking about. I pulled her to the end of the line, telling her that all East Germans who made it to the West were entitled to one-hundred marks "welcome money." She only half believed it. We waited on line for I don't know how long—one hour, two, maybe even longer—we were standing outside time among joyous cries of "*Die Mauer ist weg!,*" watching the perpetual motion of wonder on the street and listening to the symphony of church bells ringing all over the city. Finally, she produced her East German ID card and got a blue one-hundred-mark note put in her hand. "One-hundred West marks . . . crazy," she said shaking her head and smiling as we left the bank. "What shall I do with it?"

"Well, you're always running out of laundry detergent," I said, only half joking. "Maybe you should buy some."

"What!" she said stunned, clutching the crisp new bill as if it was too precious to spend. "Have you gone insane? I can't use *this* to buy laundry detergent!"

I led Traudi down the Gneisenaustrasse. Soon we were standing in front of my apartment building. She looked up at it in awe mumbling, "So *this* is where you live." When I pressed the button for the elevator she rolled her eyes and laughed, as though it was a wild extravagance for there to be an elevator in a building this size. In my apartment she took off her coat and threw it on the sofa, then strolled around the living room giving everything in it a general look over. That was when the strangeness of it all set in. Traudi surrounded by my four walls. Something I never thought I'd get to see. So out of place that it had to be a beautiful dream. She seemed almost spirit-like, floating about with her white clothes and golden hair. My eye was caught by the red light on my answering machine blinking non-stop, signaling a long stream of calls. It was an intrusion I didn't want to deal with so I shut it off and took the telephone of the hook. Traudi had gone into the bedroom where she sat herself down on the bed, kicked off her shoes and reached out for me. Afterward, she lay there running her hand over my head, smiling and giggling, as if we'd just done something scandalously naughty. I asked what it had been like. She immediately knew what I meant. She thought for a moment and covered her eyes with her hand. "It was terrible," she said. One day she'd stopped to watch a candlelight demonstration near the Gethsemane Church when someone shouted, "*The Stasi is here!*" She recalled scrambling inside the doorway of an apartment building; the heavy sound of military boots running en masse; watching from behind the door as the police beat people bloody. One man who was just walking by with his bicycle had gotten caught in it all, beaten unconscious and dragged away. When she went by there again the next day she saw his bicycle on the sidewalk where he had dropped it, surrounded by lit candles. For the first time in her life she was afraid of them, she said. Then she couldn't say any more. I moved her hand away from her face and saw her eyes filled with tears. These weren't tears of joy. They didn't belong here. I changed the subject, asked if she would have to work at some point. She arched her eyebrows as though she was going to cry again and said, "I have today and tomorrow free!" as if that was the most amazing thing about all that had happened. Out the window next to the bed we could see waves of people moving along the Gneisenaustrasse.

"Let's go buy some food," I said. "We can make dinner here tonight." We both jumped out of bed, thankful for an excuse to get back into the crowd. I gave Traudi some clothes and we made our way to the supermarket where we had to wait on line to get in. The East Germans were using their "welcome money" to buy up everything in sight. It was funny to see so many people walking around with their arms full of citrus fruits and bananas. They were acting just as they did at home on the other side of the Wall—the moment something was available, it was snatched up for fear it would be a long time before they'd see it again. Inside the mobbed supermarket nearly all the shelves had already been picked clean. We split up. "Get whatever you can find," I told her. At the back of the store, as if by a miracle, I saw a lone chicken lying on its back in an otherwise empty freezer surrounded by nearly empty shelves and grabbed it. I found Traudi carrying a box of crackers, a big bag of frozen potato croquets, a container of yogurt and a bottle of mineral water. I held up the chicken triumphantly and she gave an elated smile, "a *Broiler!*"

"You think this is enough?"

"Are you kidding?" she said, switching to jubilant English. "To-night weel both be fed-up!"

We carried the groceries around Kruezberg for another hour or so before hunger forced us back home. The chicken and potatoes were in the oven. I turned on the television to see that a big rally had taken place in front of the Schöneberg Rathaus. Chancellor Kohl and Foreign Minister Genscher had broken off a state visit to Poland to be there. Willy Brandt, old and in ill health, was also there and I felt happy for him; that he had lived long enough to see this day. West Berlin's mayor said that today the Germans were the happiest people on earth. I left the TV on and went back to the kitchen were Traudi was preparing the food. There was a knock on the door. "*Naa, neighbor?!*" It was Bernd, shaking my hand warmly. He had invited two women from East Berlin to dinner in his apartment and wanted to know if I'd like to join them. I thanked him, but said I've got company of my own. Bernd seemed honesty disappointed. Would I maybe have a bottle of ketchup he could borrow? Of course I did. I got him the bottle from the kitchen. He said he'd replace it as soon as he could get into a supermarket. I told him not to worry about it. "Let's have breakfast sometime next week," I said as he put the key in his door. Back in the kitchen, Traudi asked, "Your neighbor?"

"Yeah, that was Bernd. He's a great guy, I like him," I said, meaning it sincerely.

Fifteen minutes later there was another knock. I went to the door and was surprised to find Kai standing there with a big grin on his face, "Wery glad to find you at home dis night, sir." I shook his hand, pulling him into the apartment. Traudi stuck her head out of the kitchen and, upon seeing him, yelled out his name with such excitement that it startled us both. Overjoyed that she was not the only one to have survived it all, she ran over and engulfed him in a hug, the intensity of which caught him by surprise, almost knocking him down. Then Traudi reached out for me and the three of us were standing together in my living room embracing and laughing, each with a little embarrassment over the tears in our eyes.

"How did you find me here?" I asked. Kai took a crumpled slip of paper out of his pocket. It was the one I had written my name and address on the first time we met. Just a few months' time that now seemed like years.

Kai stayed for dinner and I listened as he and Traudi traded war stories about what they had seen and experienced in East Berlin over the past weeks—about the anger in the streets; Kai's elderly neighbor who had advised against demonstrating, "If you think things are bad now just wait until the tanks roll," he said; about the rumor that made the rounds that people were going to storm the Wall at the Brandenburg Gate on November 3rd, and I found myself wishing I had been there with them.

Later that evening we walked over to the Troika, which was so crammed with happy people we could only squeeze our way in as far as the middle of the bar where Ulrich and Christoph were standing against the window bank. When Ulrich saw me he raised both fists victoriously in the air. All three members of the Troika were busy behind the bar at the same time, a sight never before seen. Ulrich said that Easterners could drink for free tonight, but in reality nobody's been paying anything. Christoph had obviously forgiven me for the Knut incident. He spoke to me for the first time in weeks, telling me Kati had been here earlier looking for me and that I should call her. Traudi and Kai were received warmly by my two West friends. Ulrich stood on the window bank and, over the heads of the crowd, engaged in some strange sign language with Rolf that eventually produced beer for all of us. "Did you hear the statement from the White House?" he asked me, smiling.

"No, what did it say?"

He shook his head as if I wasn't going to believe what I was about to hear. "They called all this an encouraging step or something like that," he said with a dismissive wave of his hand. "Can you believe it?"

I suppose for the old cold warriors hunched together in the basement of the White House trying to figure out what was going on, releasing that kind of fabulous understatement was thought to be the prudent thing to do. But no one who had witnessed what happened here could have any doubt about what it meant. The West German foreign minister said it best earlier that day, "The world will never be what it was before."

A Sand Castle in the Rain

A EUPHORIC CARNIVAL ATMOSPHERE lasted for days. Traudi stayed
with me in West Berlin until Sunday when, before she had to go
back to work, we stood in the bitter cold with a large jubilant
crowd at Potsdamer Platz, watching the mayors of East and
West Berlin preside over the opening of a new crossing point
through the Wall. That afternoon, I called Kati who had left
several messages on my machine. When she heard my voice she
immediately demanded to know why I left her the night the
Wall fell and had stayed out of contact since.

"First of all, you got lost in the crowd."

"Bullshit!" she snapped. "Where do I stand now?"

Strangely, after all the time I'd spent with Kati, I was
totally unprepared for her being so blunt. "Well . . . everything's
different now," I said.

"Tell me, what could ever be different?!" Her belligerent
tone made me angry. I resented that even the earth-shaking
events of the last couple of days couldn't soften her cynicism.

"What could be different? Just look out your window.
It's a good time to try and make peace with the world, Kati.
Time to finally recognize when it's good and not to keep
screwing it up."

"Richard, what the fuck are you talking about?"

I couldn't believe she could be so oblivious. "Everything
has changed now for everybody," I said. "It's good this way.
What the hell were you thinking, anyway? That the world could
just keep going on as it was forever?"

Kati was clearly disgusted, "Richard, you've got a lot of growing up to do."

I didn't know what else to say. We were talking past each other and I just wanted to get her off the phone. After an uncomfortable silence, Kati gave an angry, "*Alles klar!*" and hung up. I thought it best to just leave it at that.

Traudi came back to West Berlin several times during that early period. But for her, the shine soon wore off the western city. It was too glitzy. Too smooth. Too wasteful. Too full of *things*, none of which she could afford with her east marks. It was also full of her compatriots who were engaged in a kind of turbo-materialism, hoarding anything and everything they could somehow pay for and haul back across the border. At times, West Berlin looked like it was being looted during a power failure. That first weekend after the Wall fell, we witnessed a crowd of East Germans climbing over each other for complimentary packages of coffee and chocolate that were being thrown from the back of a truck as a welcoming promotion for a supermarket chain. It was like a feeding frenzy at the zoo, and oddly humbling to watch. The look on Traudi's face told me what she thought. I wasn't surprised when she later said that West Berlin was a nice place to visit, but she wouldn't want to live there.

One event I was sorry to have missed was Klaus' tearful reunion with his mother. She had indeed gotten a letter from him; therefore knew his address and hurried to Berlin a few days after the Wall fell. She arrived by train one evening and went to his apartment. He, of course, was at the Troika, as he was every night. One of his neighbors knew where he could be found and walked her over. There was a sudden uncontrolled burst of emotion the moment she and Klaus set eyes on each other. The way I heard it from Chistoph, tearful cries of "*Mutti! Mutti!*" and "*Oh, my baby boy!*" produced a rush of applause and cheering from everyone in the place who immediately sensed what it was all about.

I went back to East Berlin later that first week. Border checks had become a simple formality; the "undesirable" list either gone or unchecked. In contrast to the West, the eastern city was now a place of quiet streets and well-stocked shops. For a while, the small *Konsum* state shop across from Traudi's apartment, like others in the district, was full of fruits and vegetables that were rare before. Even oranges and bananas were to be had. Rumor was that these were goods brought in to calm the populace during the days of mass protests. Only now were they getting to market. It was an odd circumstance for a while, shopping for food in East Berlin because of the long lines and empty shelves in the West.

Additional crossing points in the Wall were soon opened, each one a media event with crowds cheering workmen as they cut through and hoisted away slabs of concrete. Streets that had been blocked for nearly thirty years were reconnected; the city's infrastructure gradually sewn back together. Each new border crossing provided additional proof that the change was irreversible. Speculation soon began about whether the Wall should be torn down entirely. After all, it was now a pointless eyesore. That kind of thinking only prompted the new General Secretary, Egon Krenz, to make a bizarre remark about the Wall still being necessary to keep drugs and AIDS out of East Germany.

One night after having had a few beers, I accompanied Christoph, Ulrich and Geoffrey to the Potsdamer Platz. We were all intent on getting ourselves a piece of the Wall. Ulrich had the obnoxious idea of taking a few bananas from the Troika's kitchen to see if he could tempt a border guard into swapping them for his service cap. We arrived to find people chiseling at the Wall from the Brandenburg Gate to Checkpoint Charlie in the cold night, turning the whole area into a surreal outdoor sculpture studio. The air was filled with that steely *chink, chink, chink* sound as people hammered, then stepped back for a moment to thoughtfully consider the progress of their labors while exhaling clouds of frosty breath. *Wallpeckers,* as they were known, had cut big gaps between the concrete slabs, exposing the steel reinforcement rods inside. Young East German border guards had begun patrolling the western side of the Wall, walking along the narrow strip that was officially East German territory. In a halfhearted display of the official displeasure at the Wall's destruction, they tried their best to quietly approach people while they hammered, and quickly confiscate their tools. They rarely caught anyone. If you noticed a patrol coming, you just needed to step back a few feet into West Berlin and the guards would walk past with a playful expression that said, "Next time we'll get you."

Through one of the large gaps in the concrete, Ulrich dangled his bananas at a couple of border guards like monkeys in a cage while they stood expressionless on the other side. Not only were there no takers, but only angry remarks at his efforts from people on our side of the Wall. Border guards, considered the ugly face of the East German regime, and until a week ago maligned as murderers, had suddenly become objects of pity. But where the bananas failed, a West German twenty-mark note was successful as a young soldier covertly pulled his floppy service cap from under his belt and slipped it through a hole in the Wall in exchange for the bill. Ulrich wore it proudly for days.

Near Potsdamer Platz, we rented a hammer and chisel from someone who had several laid out on a blanket on the ground and began hitting away at the Wall in turn. But the Wall was unbelievably hard, causing a juvenile comedy of errors to ensue, with one of us always certain he could do it better than the other, nagging for his turn only to wind up suddenly dropping the tools while cursing injury to fingers and hands. Yet in the end, we each managed to get a chunk complete with graffiti. And that night, while walking along the Wall with our souvenirs, we came across the fat man who had harassed Kati and me at the Brandenburg Gate the previous winter. He was standing behind a group of *Wallpeckers*, telling them that they were vandalizing an internationally recognized border and property of the GDR, and that they had no right to do it. People laughed, snickered, and threw out insulting comments under their breath.

But reality soon caught up with events. Inside of a month, the overcrowding in West Berlin got on everyone's nerves as millions of Easterners from all over the GDR poured relentlessly into the city. Sidewalks were full of those pale, ruddy-faced people from the East German hinterland that one usually saw only at rest stops on the transit highway. Shops were constantly packed with people and quickly sold out; streets choked with smoking Trabants and Wartburgs; transit routes were clogged with traffic, and trains to anywhere West were overcrowded, making it impossible to leave the city without a taking a huge reservoir of patience with you. Even movie theaters, many offering discounted tickets to East Germans, were difficult to get into. Yet, West Berliners dealt with it all as rationally and calmly as possible. I never saw anyone lose their heads. Under bitter grumbling about the way "they" drove or all the goods "they" were snatching up, everyone carried on. Berliners simply learned to deal with it all the same way they learned to live with all the other strange events their bizarre history had brought them.

Opening the border didn't end the problems for the East German government, however. An entire population had found its voice, and despite the firings, resignations and proclamations about cleaning up its act, nothing the East German government did could ever make good for all the years of locking up the population behind concrete walls and barbed wire; for the border guards and their shoot-to-kill orders, or all the coercion and threats the people were forced to endure over the past forty years. An energized citizenry poured into the streets, at first demanding simple dignity, then an end to the communist regime and, finally, reunification with the prosperous West. It wasn't long before the place *over there* dissolved before our eyes like a sandcastle in the rain.

One night, not long after the date for reunification between the two Germanies had been announced, I managed to steer Traudi over to the Troika, which she always referred to wearily as the "*Trinkhalle.*" Not that she particularly liked or disliked the people there. But as with everything in West Berlin, she began to despise what she saw as its conceited indulgence with a greater intensity as the decline of her world became more and more apparent and unstoppable. "Why people would let themselves be shot at for this is beyond me," she once said bitterly.

That night, Kati was at another table. She often turned up at the Troika now. For a while she had taken to sitting with one or another of her many friends and would sometimes stare at me with a frown, which I would greet with a friendly wave. Once or twice she came over to the table and stood there making small talk for a minute or two while her eyes were drawn to Traudi sitting next to me, as though trying to size her up or figure her out. But it wasn't long before Kati had a new guy. Hermann Friedlander was in his early twenties, had come to West Berlin in order to avoid the draft, and went by the ridiculous name "*Pino*." Pino always dressed as the stereotypical South American revolutionary, complete with three-day beard and Che Guevara beret. He'd sit at a table, holding a cigarette between his fingers while his tired eyes looked as though the weight of the entire world's injustice lay solely on his shoulders. Only Pino's sandy blond hair and Swabian accent revealed him as a native. Klaus was no longer a fixture at the Troika. Sometime in early April, when it was clear that the National People's Army was collapsing under the weight of desertions and low morale and there had even been talk of doing away with it altogether, he left for home without saying goodbye, at least not to me. It was an offense for which I easily forgave him when I learned that he left without paying Ulrich the large balance on his loan, a situation that often caused Ulli to rant bitterly about "those lazy *Ossi* ingrates."

Traudi and I sat with Ulrich and Christoph. Despite Klaus absconding with his cash, Ulrich was gleeful as usual these days. He never complained about the overcrowded city or prospect of a costly reunification, which Christoph often did. As far as Ulrich was concerned, everything that had happened since the Wall fell was confirmation of all that he'd ever believed in.

According to Ulli, the Americans had won the Cold War by recklessly engaging in fierce arms buildup, supporting brutal dictators around the world, and nun-killing death squads in Central America, all of which bankrupted them financially and morally. Now the future was clear. Europe was ascendant. The former East Bloc would copy the *German Way* and the entire continent would flourish in a renaissance never before seen, providing an example for the whole world to follow. I actually agreed with him and now told him so openly. Despite all the confusion and uncertainty about unemployment or the cost of absorbing the dilapidated and chemically polluted East, it was impossible not to be optimistic. World orders, institutions, and enemies we had been prepared to live with our entire lives had disappeared, practically overnight. *The People* had shown a basic decency and integrity. To be glib about it all was impossible. After everything that had happened in such a short time, the sky was the limit.

That night, as Traudi and I took seats at the table, Ulrich and Christoph were busy discussing the current controversy over the border with Poland. Germany had given up a large piece of territory to the Poles after World War II. Now, with the Cold War over, some German conservatives were voicing the opinion that Germany should get it back. The East German interim government had already officially reaffirmed the current border. Chancellor Kohl, trying to soothe the far-right wing of his own party before the upcoming elections, had been dragging his feet, saying he could speak for the entire German nation on the issue only after reunification. Christoph told me that Linda would soon be coming over from America to stay a couple of months. "We can all celebrate reunification together," he said. Ulrich, not yet ready to change the subject, shook his head with a big, oily smirk on his red face. "They will sell it to us," he said with a vile drunken laugh, his thick lips the color of liverwurst. "The dirty, stupid Poles will wind up selling us that territory for next to nothing, just wait and see! Germany will be whole again!"

Christoph, now fully incited, interjected with his finger in the air, "Did you know that used to be the most productive farmland in all the Reich before the Poles got it?" he said before adding bitterly, "And now look at it. Those people can't even feed themselves!" Ulrich's laughter grew louder and more savage at that remark. I looked over at Traudi. She was staring at both of them, horrified. After that, whenever I suggested visiting the boys at the *Trinkhalle* she always found an excuse for not coming along.

For weeks prior to reunification, Traudi went about her usual routine, hiding her wounds in silence. She worked as much as ever. We saw films, went to concerts and, on those days she had off, she showed me the environs outside Berlin that had been off-limits to me before. Beautiful areas normally devoid of people. Her favorite places were the lakes at Leuenberg and Tiefensee, where her father would take the family swimming when she was a child and where she still liked to go on warm summer days when she had the time. One day she brought me along. We sat alone on a grassy bank. Traudi had just finished telling me about the time long ago when, from that very spot, she and her brother were finally able to surprise their father while he read his ideology and successfully send him tumbling into the water. Her recollections of the good-natured fracas that followed between the three of them contradicted the image of a stern old man I had in my mind. Then, slowly, those thousand thoughts took over; began swirling around inside Traudi's head. Gazing at the lake and without saying a word, she stood up, casually stripped away her clothes and walked into the cold water, swimming then floating silently on her back. I wasn't invited in, nor did I intrude as I watched her stare at the sky, bathing in the memory of innocent days faraway from present realities. One rainy afternoon, we visited the site of the Sachsenhausen concentration camp where her father had been imprisoned. Traudi bought flowers and laid them at the base of a memorial there. Her mood never varied much from what it was on that solemn afternoon. For weeks she had been displaying the melancholy disposition of a person who had just lost a loved one. It was all perfectly natural, I thought, and was sure it would pass with time.

Then, a few days before reunification on October 3rd, during all the final official acts of a nation extinguishing itself— the last assembly of the East German parliament in the Palast der Rupublik before the building was closed for good; the last military changing-of-the-guard in front of the Neue Wache; the dissolution of the National People's Army, and the ceremonial folding of the East German flag for the very last time—Traudi just disappeared. She was supposed to come by my apartment one afternoon, but didn't show up. I left several notes for her at her apartment, but whenever I went back to retrieve a reply, they were still stuck to her door where I'd left them. The only thing I could imagine was a family emergency, which meant something to do with her elderly aunt. On the morning before reunification, I went by the Charité, entering the building I had so often seen from a distance for the first time. I combed the halls asking nurses if they knew her. The place was so big and there were so many people working there that it took half an hour before I found a nurse who even knew who she was. She said that Traudi had called in sick a few days before. That worried me. If she was ill, then why wasn't she at home?

I went straight back to her apartment and knocked loudly on the door. I stood there listening, but heard nothing. I was wondering what to do next when one of her neighbors came up from the stairway carrying a basket of groceries. I asked if she had seen Traudi. She told me that she saw her leave the apartment early that morning but not since. "Was she all right?" A nonchalant nod indicated nothing unusual. I was relieved but puzzled. Why was she avoiding me? And not just that, I could never imagine Traudi calling in sick at work if she could possibly get there. That was the strangest thing of all. A couple of hours later I found a note from Traudi on her door asking me to meet her at Marx-Engels-Forum at four o'clock.

That's where I finally found her, sitting alone on a bench under a chilly, overcast sky, wrapped in her beige coat with her hands buried between her legs, looking like a lost child. I sat down next to her and asked where she'd been. She shrugged her shoulders, "I've been walking," she said, staring at the now dark Palast der Republik but looking at nothing in particular.

"Walking where? I've been looking all over for you. I even went to the hospital. They told me you were sick."

She just sat there gently rocking with her hands sandwiched between her legs.

"Why didn't you come over the other day? Did something happen?"

Traudi looked down at her lap and reluctantly said, "I can't believe they are throwing it all away."

In an instant it was clear; the moment I had hoped wouldn't come. I gave a resigned sigh, leaning back against the bench and observing the big bronze figures of Karl Marx and Friedrich Engels. Someone had spray-painted the words "WE ARE INNOCENT" at their feet.

"Traudi, nobody is throwing anything away."

"They are," she said, dead serious. "They are throwing it all away. Everything. The work of millions of people . . . millions of people who gave their lives . . . and they are throwing it away for bananas and used Volkswagens."

I had no desire to have this discussion. As far as I was concerned, we all had to live in the Real World now and I saw no reason why she should be resentful of her situation.

"What then?" I asked. "Tell me what it is that they're throwing away."

She didn't answer but I knew what she was thinking. I couldn't have heard it more clearly if she had said it out loud: the *Sozialismus*. "It doesn't work!" I shouted, maybe a little too harshly. She responded by saying that "they" never gave it a fair chance. I could only repeat myself by clearly pronouncing each word, "It. Doesn't. Work."

Traudi shook her head with tears welling up in her eyes. "I'm glad my parents are not here to see all this."

"Try being reasonable," I said. "Take a good look around. Look at what you're getting and tell me what's so terrible about it. Do you see people living in the gutter who have to pull their dinner out of garbage cans? Or people being tormented because of their politics? Believe me, Ehrentraud, I've seen a lot worse and so have you. Count yourself lucky."

So strange was it to hear me call her by her full name that, for a moment, Traudi smiled and laughed. But in an instant, and without a noticeable transition, her laugh dissolved into sobbing as she fell limp with hopeless resignation against my shoulder and cried.

On television in my apartment later that night, after all the discussion, long walks; the prolonged relapses of tears and the reluctant confession that she was fearful of what was to come, we watched a misty-eyed Chancellor Kohl address what would very soon be one nation. "In a few hours' time," he began, "a dream will become reality." He said we should never forget the families torn apart by German division, those who suffered for their political beliefs and those who died at the Wall. He thanked the Americans, British and French for standing by Germany during the Cold War, Hungary for opening its border, and Gorbachev for making it all possible. The Germans, he said, had learned from their history and were now a peaceful and peace-loving people. He assured everyone that the West German economy was in excellent condition and never better prepared for the challenges of reunification, promising, as he had so often over the past few months, a "blooming landscape" in what had been the GDR. He ended by calling Germany "our fatherland" and a united Europe "our future."

Two minutes after Kohl went off the air I got a call from an exuberant Ulrich. He wanted to be sure I'd seen the speech. "Times, they are a changin' " he said. "Be grateful to be alive during all this." I asked him if he and Anne were going to join us for the celebrations the next night. The near dire predictions of the size of the crowd that would be pouring into Berlin for the occasion had convinced them to stay home with a bottle of champagne and watch it all on television. "The ceremony isn't important," he insisted. "The future is important. And the day after tomorrow it will be here!"

The evening of reunification, Christoph and Linda came to Traudi's place. I had to give Christoph directions as if he was coming in from out of town. When they arrived, Traudi took their coats and I was proud of her when she ironically welcomed them to "the capital of the German Democratic Republic." Neither Christoph nor his girlfriend had ever seen an East German apartment. Traudi showed them the coal heating oven and answered questions from Linda about the way the system worked in the East while I showed Christoph her father's old books. Kai arrived with the attractive French music student he'd met recently. He was aglow with the buoyant and alert confidence of someone who was about to achieve a personal triumph. It infected us all. I opened a bottle of champagne that I'd bought earlier that day. We lifted our glasses in a toast to the future, and then sat around talking and drinking. After four bottles of blatantly Bulgarian wine, we'd forgotten all about German reunification and probably would have stayed there in the apartment all night if Kai's date hadn't glanced at her watch and sounded the alarm, "*Ooooohh-lá! Es ist now alreadie zehn-zertie!*"

We started down to the Reichstag, swept along by the flag-waving multitudes toward the Brandenburg Gate. Kai ran into a friend and fell further and further behind as they talked. He and his date eventually disappeared. Unter den Linden was lined on both sides with stands selling food, drink and souvenirs and, by the time we arrived, the disrespectful, dank smell of beer hung heavy over the historic old avenue. We were pressed tightly together in the crowd as it moved through the narrow confines of the Brandenburg Gate. The Berlin Wall had been removed months ago, but I still hadn't grown accustomed to the view of the area without it. On this night it was barely a year since massive opposition from the people had forced Erich Honecker from power. Now the state that he helped to create and had ruled with an iron fist for so long was only minutes from becoming a footnote in the history books.

At the Reichstag, the official ceremony was already well underway with the West German leadership and invited dignitaries assembled on the front steps of the massive stone building. We were able to get surprisingly close and had an excellent view of everything. From the start I was impressed by the subdued, almost reflective mood of the crowd. Aside from a few pockets of wild flag waving and shouts of "*Helmut! Helmut!*" for the West German Chancellor, it seemed as if people had just woken up to the reality of what was happening and realized that maybe it had all gone just a little too fast. But I had no such misgivings. I was about to witness the birth of something new and promising and was proud to be there and to be part of it. At one minute to midnight, after all the speeches, a large black, red and gold German flag began rising over the crowd, climbing up a new flagpole planted for the occasion accompanied by the chiming of bells. I took a step back next to Linda and watched Christoph and Traudi observing it all before the altar of the Reichstag. When the flag had reached the top of the pole the two nations were officially one. As the West German national anthem filled the air, I shook Christoph's hand and congratulated him. Linda did the same to Traudi with a kiss on the cheek. The act of congratulation surprised them both for some reason. Christoph actually asked, "What for?" His girlfriend had to explain it to him, "For being reunified, dummy."

Then fireworks lit up the night sky as brilliant bursts of color exploded high over the Brandenburg Gate, enabling the crowd to put aside any thoughts about what had just taken place, expressing only their veneration at the display with "*oooohs*" and "*aaaahhs.*"

When I woke the next day, Traudi was already sitting up in bed thoughtfully looking out the window. It was our first day in a united Berlin and a reunified Germany; a nation absent from the map since the defeat of Adolf Hitler. I put my hand on her back and gently rubbed her spine. She turned to me and said, "Richard, you were right. I feel so ashamed."

"I was right? About what?"

"The sun rose this morning," she said, "Just as it always has."

Weeks followed. The Earth, unimpressed by the weight of the human tribulation it carried, spun just as it always had, and always would. The sun rose in the morning, set in the evening, we all celebrated the arrival of another new year, and Lech Walesa became president of Poland.

At the end of February, Traudi's old aunt from Halle died after a short illness, leaving her the grim task of spending a week in her home while making burial arrangements and disposing of her possessions, all of which she insisted on carrying out on her own. Yet, once back in Berlin, Traudi seemed able to put it all behind her fairly quickly. A new position, teaching nursing at the Charité, which she had started in January, helped a great deal. The work was arduous, with long hours of preparation to be done at home, but she thoroughly enjoyed it and now had regular working hours. She didn't even seem to mind that the economic policy of "internal devaluation" inflicted on the East meant she earned only sixty percent of what people a few blocks away in West Berlin were earning for the same job. But, eventually, there came short bouts of depression that would last a day or two. She would turn inward, sulk a bit, not talk very much, and then it would be gone as suddenly as it started. Although she never told me, I was sure I knew the cause. It had been nearly eighteen months since the Wall fell and there was still no word from her brother. The extended family of the socialist state had been abruptly yanked from under her and, with time, it had slowly sunk in that her aunt was really gone. I thought it only natural that Traudi's thoughts would turn more and more to him. I had been looking forward to Sascha turning up; one more of those reunification stories that brought a tear to the eye. But not only did Sascha stay away, Traudi never once mentioned him. On a couple of occasions, I suggested we try to locate him. In Germany, where everyone was registered and categorized, I didn't think that would be such a difficult thing to do. But Traudi wouldn't hear of it. Whenever I brought it up she would brush aside the suggestion with a disdainful wave of her hand and a firm "*nein!,*" which left no doubt that if Sascha ever wanted to see her again, he would have to be the one to take the initiative.

Traudi and I traveled a lot together over the next months; weekend trips mostly. She showed me the East, a place that, for the most part, seemed frozen in time with drab-quaint villages, cities still ravaged by war and a dilapidated infrastructure. When we drove west, I could point out the abandoned border checkpoint where I used to spend my time waiting in line with all the other West Berliners. The Soviet tank monument, now painted pink, no longer looked so heroic with its gun turret swung around to the rear, pointing at the ground.

In the summer, we drove through the Alps and on to Italy. It was there that we got wind of a scandal at the Charité; horror stories in the popular German press that told of East German political prisoners having been forced to donate organs, and mentally retarded newborns systematically drowned in hospital basins. It ruined the rest of the holiday. Over the next week, Traudi's mood alternated between those dips into depression and a fuming indignation at what she insisted was a shameless attack by the West, which she said was out to destroy anything that had to do with East Germany. The stories passed quickly, as popular scandals normally do. But I would hear that same angry indignation from Traudi about the West again and again.

I took Traudi to Münster where I introduced her to Wolf and Ina and she spent hours playing with their little girl. We walked around the town, which was prim and perfect and wealthy as ever. I pointed out my old apartment directly across the street from the Latino bar where Christoph and I pissed-away our evenings, and she had to laugh at it all, saying she could never picture me living in such a place.

268 | Michael Califra

One night during of our visit, Wolf, Ina, and their daughter had to spend a previously planned social evening with neighbors down the street; not the kind of thing I felt like doing. The moment they left us sitting in their living room, Traudi became despondent. As usual, she was unwilling to discuss what was bothering her. That night I was able to persuade her to have a drink with me at the *America Latina*, hoping a change of scene and a little alcohol might get her to open up and talk about her brother. Knut happened to be there that night, sitting alone, dressed in his jacket and tie with a glass of beer in front of him. Knut and Traudi had never met. I introduced them and asked Knut what he was doing in Münster. He confirmed my suspicions by saying that he was in town "bestowing greetings upon His Eminence." That brought Traudi to ask what he did for a living. When Knut told her that he was a priest, she suddenly took a keen interest in him, asking questions about his work and religion. A few minutes later a familiar face from years ago called my name. I excused myself and went to the bar.

From there I watched Traudi and Knut. I watched her talk to him, hesitantly at first, then more and more until she was doing all the talking and he was listening with that exaggerated expression of faux concern I knew all too well; a single facial gesture that made a mockery of two-thousand years of religious faith. That man Knut. He had attained his goal. I missed his ordination. In fact, I didn't remember seeing him at all since the day he vomited all over Cliadhna's bed. Nevertheless, his cynical routine was so unrelenting and had gone on for so long now that, not only had it gotten boring, but it had become incredibly annoying. When I saw him write something down on a beer coaster, give it to Traudi, then clasp her hands in his, I impatiently excused myself and went back to join them. I got to the table as Knut said, "Remember, Traudi, the soul is indestructible."

I took my seat. Knut let go of Traudi's hands. She smiled a little uncomfortably, he with a sly grin. Then Knut said he had to catch a train back to Cologne. After he'd gone, I asked Traudi about their conversation. She smiled and said Knut was a good man and she was glad to have met him. When I pressed her further she just said happily, "Oh, what did we talk about? . . . God and the world." I told her irritably that she shouldn't talk about those things with Knut. She laughed, "But why not? He's a priest!" Yet, whatever it was they discussed clearly put her in a much better mood. No longer depressed, she reached under the table, squeezed my thigh and suggested we go to bed early, before the others got home.

At the end of 1991, the effects of the revolutionary convulsions we had witnessed were still running their course. Gorbachev himself had been overtaken by the changes he'd unleashed; he was out of power, the Soviet Union was neither Soviet nor a union, and there were a dozen independent states in its place. A red, white and blue flag flew over the Kremlin and the Russian Federation began lurching toward capitalism and democracy like a drunkard staggering along the side of a busy highway at night, on the edge of disaster every moment.

In Germany, it took no time at all for a general disillusionment with reunification to set in. "Blooming landscape" had become just another slogan to be mimicked with ridicule and Chancellor Kohl had been pelted with eggs on a visit to the eastern provinces where he, not long ago, had been welcomed as a conquering hero. In the once child-fertile East, there was zero population growth and real unemployment had skyrocketed to Great Depression levels in many areas. But the German government taxed and borrowed and was able to prevent a social explosion by providing the new jobless with just enough money for a roof over their heads, a few drinks at the local bar, and video rentals for the VCRs they'd bought when the new West marks that had magically replaced the worthless East marks in their bank accounts made them all feel suddenly so well off. But for many that wasn't enough as disillusionment turned into rage in the form of xenophobic, violent neo-Nazi attacks against foreigners. One after another, hundreds of incidents had taken place, the most notorious while the German neighbors of the victims looked on and cheered. And while intellectuals were hypothesizing about the "end of history"—the notion that humanity would now toss aside all ideologies in favor of tolerant liberal democracy—there was a news report about a young former member of the Communist Party who had just been sentenced to two years in prison for incitement; for standing on a soapbox and preaching that the Holocaust never happened, although he was sure it would have been well deserved if it had. Such incidents always caused what I thought to be an absurdly exaggerated reaction on Traudi's part. She'd turn away from the television and mumble to herself, asking in anguish whether "the peace can hold."

The world in Berlin, however, was in still in order. I was still earning money and in the city itself, despite the official decision taken the previous summer to move the government here from Bonn, and all the colossal building plans that accompanied it, nothing much had changed. One still had to dial the West German country code when calling West Berlin from the East and vice versa. The Wall was gone, the Friedrichstrasse Station now just another stop on the train and the Tränenpalast a discotheque, but West was still West and East still East. For as long as it stood, the Berlin Wall separated a people who said they desperately wanted to come together. Now that it was gone, those same people preferred to remain among themselves. Defeating what had become known as "the Wall in the head" will be a daunting exercise that would probably take a generation. I got a taste of that when I met Kai at a café one afternoon. I arrived to find him sitting irritably across from three well-dressed West German students who were loudly and obnoxiously discussing how wrong it was to have "given so much away to the lazy *Ossis*" with reunification. As soon as Kai saw me enter the café, he jumped out of his seat and hurried me out the door muttering, "Let's go somewhere else. Shit *Wessis* are getting on my nerves."

. . .

"They even conserved the body odors of political prisoners!" Ulrich shouted with a boisterous laugh as he arrived one night at the Troika. "They made them wipe their sweaty armpits with rags or fart on cloths and kept them archived in marked jars in case they ever had to use dogs to sniff them out!" It seemed Ulrich was always finding new reasons to be overjoyed these days, and lately, it was with a good amount of vindication as more and more about the methods of the Stasi became known. The reach of the East German security apparatus was breathtaking. The GDR had developed into the most efficient police state in history. The Stasi kept files on its enemies that were complete down to the smallest, useless details, such as what they ate for breakfast. Over one-hundred miles of these files have been secured; evidence of tentacles that reached into every crevasse of national life. Unpaid informants, so called I.M.s, were everywhere; hundreds of thousands of them. They were even among the well-known dissidents who claimed the moral high ground and made the revolution. For people who were personally untouched by it all, it was all a droll lesson in human nature. And with every new accusation of being an informer for the Stasi that was met by passionately indignant denial until the files were finally produced; with every revelation of yet another life gone to shambles; with each additional well-known figure exposed, one or another of us sitting around the old table at the Troika would laugh and poke fun, certain in the knowledge that *we* would never have been capable of such atrocities.

Soon the archives would be opened to the public. An agency had been created to let the population see the files that were kept on it, and even learn the names of those who fed information to the Stasi. Hundreds of thousands of people had applied for a chance to read them. Betrayers, who would so often turn out to be neighbors and relatives, husbands and wives, would now themselves be betrayed.

. . .

Months passed with what seemed like increasing speed as dull normality continued easing itself into our lives, unnoticed. By early 1992, Christoph had finished his studies and was bitterly complaining about the pressure he was getting from his parents to find a job; Geoffrey was still pushing his oil paintings, but now was frequently on the road mining other parts of Germany, spending weeks at a time away from Berlin; Ulrich was still the proud optimist despite all the dire predictions about Germany's wealth becoming a crushing debt thanks to reunification. As for the violent right-wing extremism that continued raising its ugly head, the unemployment, new homelessness and crime that were on their way to record postwar levels, Ulrich could often be heard savaging the Poles, Russians, Japanese, or any number of other nationalities as somehow being responsible for all of that. Like millions of others, Ulrich refused to believe that his world could never be what it was before. He, Anne and Torsten were still to be found at the Troika, as were Kati and "Pino" on occasion. But by now it was clear that everyone was drifting apart. Being present at the table wasn't the habitual duty it had been for so long. Not so much because we were all moving in different directions, but really only because we'd become bored by one another.

It was during the summer of 1992 that my relationship with Traudi changed. There was a drive through Switzerland that August; a weekend in Zermatt, when we walked atop the snow-covered Klein Matterhorn marveling at the view in the thin air. "Look over there," I said, checking my map. "You can see all the way to France. According to this, that peak over there is the Mount Blanc."

She stood staring in the direction I was pointing, then looked at me through her sunglasses and said, "Richard, I want to have a baby. I've been thinking about it for a long time now and decided that's what I have to do."

The ensuing discussion lasted until we were off the mountain, had had dinner in the village and were in bed. It continued the next morning, over the next day, and all the way back to Berlin. I had plenty of arguments against the idea. For one, I had no intention of doing anything that would trap me in my job. "Software salesman" was a phase that would end at some point. Being forced to stay with it for the rest of my days under the weight of supporting a family was out of the question. "And besides, do you realize what a baby would mean? It would mean we wouldn't have a free moment together for the next fifteen years at least. Is that something you really want? A child would demand all our attention. We would have to provide for it at any price, both emotionally and financially. We'd be spending the next two decades, our best years, raising somebody who's just going to get up one day and walk out the door saying, 'Thanks for everything.' And you know what we'll be then? Old, wrinkled and poor, that's what. And why? What's the point? To put ourselves through all of that, and the result is that there's just another person sitting in a room somewhere—*thinking Lord-knows-what!* Is that something the world really needs? That's something you *have* to do? Whatever happened to the good socialist girl who was satisfied with making the world a better place by just doing her job well?"

My rambling only saddened her. "I have no one," she said. "Richard, there have been times when I've felt alone and afraid; without family or friends. But I've never felt anything like the emptiness I feel now. I just want to have a family of my own. I have no one."

"How can you say you have no one?" I asked, grateful for the chance to feel insulted. "Am I *no one?*"

"You will not want to stay with me," she said. "If you did we would not be having this discussion, would we? You don't have to have anything to do with it if you don't want to. It will be my responsibility alone. I will deal with it."

"Oh, sure. I'll just have to have that hanging over my head for the rest of my life—feeling like the evil bastard for not being there. And if I really don't have to have anything to do with it, what the hell do you even need me for? Why don't you have your baby with someone else?"

That hit her in the chest. Her expression went blank and she looked down at her lap, "I really must tell you that, Richard? If I must explain that to you, then it is all really hopeless."

The plot to this story was all too familiar; I'd seen it a dozen times: the girlfriend gets pregnant, they get married and everything becomes a forced routine that has to be planned around school holidays. The height of hopeless tedium. I was angry with her for wanting that and told her so. When we arrived back in Berlin, I drove her home. When she asked why I wasn't coming upstairs, I told her I felt like being alone. She got out of the car and slammed the door behind her.

The next day Christoph told me he had gotten a job in the city of Aachen starting immediately. When that miserable question, "You gonna help me move?" came, I was only too happy to drive him and his possessions to his new home, even though it meant a journey over the crowded Autobahn all across Germany to the Dutch-Belgian border.

That ride turned out to be an unending hell starting the moment I arrived at Christoph's door. He and Ulrich had packed up the rented van the previous night. What was left for me were twelve hours of bitter complaining that singed my nerves as the radio reported one Autobahn traffic jam after another. It was as though this trip to Aachen was to be the final event of his life; an unjust rendezvous with the electric chair. At the Magdeburg exit, he was being taken from his cell; by the time we reached Braunschweig he'd had his head shaved; approaching Salzgitter he was having the contact butter rubbed on his scalp and was being strapped-in under the jaw, through it all carrying on non-stop about his new job, "Reinsurance! You know what that is? They insure the fucking insurance companies. Can you believe this shit? This is what I spent the last seven years preparing for? Can you imagine a more pointless existence?"

It was near Göttingen, when I made the mistake of innocently asking who insures the reinsurers that he exploded in flames yelling, "They insure each other! It's just a bunch of big companies passing money back and forth! That's the whole point! Don't you fucking understand what I'm about to do? I'm about to go to these people with the next thirty years of my life on a silver plate saying, 'take them, they're yours!' "

"If it's not what you want, then why are you? —"

"I have no choice!" he screamed.

When he eventually tired of complaining about the job, he started moaning about Aachen, quoting something Heinrich Heine wrote about the city in the nineteenth century; something about it being so boring that even the dogs wandered the streets with expressions that said, "*kick me, please.*" And, on top of everything else, Linda was "starting in with that marriage business again." It got to the point where I wasn't even listening. I could see his mouth moving, but I was really only aware of wanting to reach over, open the passenger door, and push him out of the van with my foot.

It was all precisely the wrong prescription for the mood I was in. When we finally reached Aachen at about midnight and found his apartment after driving around for an hour, I helped him unload the van as quickly as possible. He had mercifully little: a desk, a bed, a couple of chairs, a computer and a few boxes of books and magazines. When it was done, Christoph asked me if I felt like going out for a beer. I said, "No thanks," got back in the van and drove away.

It was a couple of days after I returned to Berlin that I saw Traudi again. I went by her apartment one Saturday afternoon to see if she had come to her senses. I suddenly found myself transformed into an old friend; someone she'd known for a long time. So long, in fact, that anything more than friendship was unthinkable. Her attitude was outgoing and open. She smiled a lot as she washed dishes in the kitchen sink, asked about my trip with Christoph and whether I was going to miss my friend now that he was gone. Friendly, interested, and just out of reach. That was the air she maintained. I was the one who had to make suggestions that we do something together. "Oh, ja," she'd say, "that would be nice." We met a couple of times for dinner and a film, each going our separate way afterward. I naturally hoped things would somehow return to what they had been before. When I told her that one night, she dropped the happy demeanor. "I will no longer believe in saving what cannot be saved or try to make work what cannot work," she said. "I won't do that anymore, Richard. I just can't."

Then, a week or so later, there came that strange, almost panicked call from a phone booth in the middle of the day. Even before I heard Traudi's voice, the heavy background hum meant the call was from eastern Berlin. Behind the noise I heard Traudi frantically asking, "What are you doing right now? Can you come over here? I have to talk with you right away!"

"Right now? I was just about to make some business calls. Is it important?"

There was a click and the hum grew louder. I could barely hear her shouting into the phone, "Richard, if it wasn't important would I be calling you like this? If you don't want to come just say so! Don't make silly excuses, I can't stand that!"

"Calm down!" I shouted back. "I'll be there in forty-five minutes."

I was sure it was about the neo-Nazi firebomb attack on the Sachsenhausen concentration camp memorial that had taken place the previous day. When I saw the pictures on the evening news I knew that for Traudi it would be a painful event; an act of unthinkable sacrilege in the place of her father's incarceration. On my way to her apartment, I concocted a lecture about how she shouldn't let these things upset her so much; that it was pointless and unhealthy. But when I saw her it was clear that there was more to it than that. I was startled by the state she was in. She looked as if she hadn't slept in a week. Evidence of her chain-smoking was everywhere; extinguished butts were in ashtrays that were overflowing, in the kitchen sink, in coffee cups and on saucers.

She led me into the living room. I sat on the sofa while she stood nervously in front of me. I asked her why she wasn't at work. Instead of answering, she sat down next to me and said, "Let's go away to America."

"What?" I said with a stunned laugh, "Is *that* what was so important?"

Traudi took hold of my hand. "Yes, let's go away to America, you and me."

"Are you out of your mind?" I said, pulling my hand from hers. "What brought this on all of the sudden?"

"Why shouldn't we do it? There is really nothing keeping us here, is there?"

"You just want to pack up and leave? What about your job? Why do want to just give up your job all of the sudden like this?"

Traudi stood up, composing herself with her hand over her mouth. A moment later she grimly sat down in the wicker chair next to the coal oven and, looking down at her lap, said hesitantly, "I've been fired from the hospital."

"They fired you? . . . Why?"

It took a moment before she could continue, "Richard, I have to tell you . . . There is no one else at all I can . . . They found my name."

I suppose everyone eventually experiences a moment in life when, suddenly, the world around them no longer makes sense. When, from one second to the next, all that they once held as self-evident becomes impossible to understand. When it seems that the very air they breathe and even the gravity that holds them to the ground have been deceitful. This, for me, was that moment. I sat there listening to Traudi tell me that she had been one. An "I.M." An *Inoffizielle Mitarbeiterin*. An informer for the Stasi. For long moments during a confession that alternated between anger and self-pity, I had to stop listening. I had to stop and convince myself that the situation was real; that I was indeed sitting opposite Traudi and she was the one telling me all this. That she had delivered information on students, fellow nurses, doctors, and even patients lying in their sickbeds. That she had to sign a document last year when she started teaching, swearing that she'd never had any contact with the MfS—the Ministry for State Security. An eventual bureaucratic check exposed her name registered in the files and led to her dismissal. She had been told that she might now face legal prosecution in a court of law from people who'd suffered as a result of what she'd done. By the time Traudi finished telling me all this she was sitting there rubbing her forehead with her finger tips and squinting as if she was in a good deal of physical pain.

It took a while before I could speak. "How could you have done such a thing? To ruin people's lives . . . For what? . . . Why?" I looked down at the floor under my feet and said something I wasn't even conscious of until it was too late, "No wonder your brother wants nothing to do with you."

I looked up to see Traudi staring at me in horrified disbelief. "You bastard!" she yelled, "You bastard! What the hell do you know about it?!" Raging with tears streaming down her face she jumped up, grabbed one of her father's old books and threw it against the wall over the wicker chair she'd been sitting in. "God damn you! God damn all of you!" she cried as she ran out of the living room and into her bedroom, slamming the door closed behind her. I sat there listening to the muffled sobs coming from the other end of the apartment, "God damn all of you! I just wanted to be a nurse!"

I lifted myself up off the sofa feeling as if a six-pound stone was sitting in the pit of my stomach and walked over to the book on the floor by the coal oven. The force of the impact against the wall had separated the pages from the spine. The old paper was so brittle that some of it had crumbled to dust. I pushed it all back together as best I could and put it back on the shelf before I left.

I walked aimlessly that afternoon, with my brain spinning, unable to control the thoughts flying around inside my head. The interview with the West Berlin police when they asked me straight out if I had delivered any computer material to Traudi was the most prominent thought. The moment the Wall fell, the incident became an unimportant, distant memory. But now it was back. Soon, other thoughts were working their way into my skull, each one more damning than the last: the faces of the border guards and their stern nod of recognition; my being let off so easily after spending the night in East Berlin, with Traudi so confident that there would be no serious consequences. I was standing on a street corner waiting for a red light to change when a thought popped into my head that made my heart skip a beat: the party I went to with Kai! Siggi clutching her daughter as if the world were coming to an end. Traudi made me promise not to go. Could she have been responsible for the police showing up? Surely her informing went beyond the Charité. How many other horror stories could she have been connected to? Then, a recollection that almost knocked me off my feet: all those hours Angele spent crying on her "good friend" Traudi's shoulder; all the harassment culminating with her husband being expelled to the West! The expressions on Traudi's face the first night I'd set eyes on her at the club. I could suddenly remember every gesture, every uncomfortable arch of her eyebrows, each slight grimace as she sat there listening to Angele talk. They were now etched in my mind indelibly, and became as incriminating as a fingerprint at a crime scene.

The smallest details began uncontrollably falling into place, filling in the blanks of a puzzle I didn't know existed and I couldn't quite comprehend. Who was this person I thought I knew so well? From one moment to the next she was a stranger; someone capable of monstrous acts. I looked around. Everywhere there was deceit. Everywhere there was treachery. I had never even imagined this magnitude of betrayal.

A couple of weeks passed with all this gnawing away at me each minute of every day. I finally had to confront her face to face. I needed to know exactly what had transpired and why. I went to her apartment and knocked on the door. She wasn't at home. I stopped by three or four times that day but she was never there. Finally, in my frustration, I banged and kicked her door so hard that her neighbor came out of her apartment, looked at me in complete bewilderment and said, "Don't you know? She's gone. Traudi moved away."

"She moved? Where?"

"Somewhere in the West. Very suddenly, about a week ago."

"She moved to West Berlin?"

"No, somewhere in West Germany," she said, neither of us noticing that we were speaking in obsolete jargon. "I didn't catch the name of the town; she left so suddenly. I can't believe you didn't know."

I gave her my phone number. She promised to let me know if Traudi contacted her. But that very same evening, before I'd even had time to plan my next move, I got a call from Knut. Traudi was in Münster of all places. He had gotten her a room there through the Catholic Student Congregation placement service. Knut spoke in an extremely annoyed whisper when he told me that, "She's been calling here at two and three in the morning."

"Why, what's happening?"

"I'm not allowed to tell you," he said. "Those are the rules." He went on to remind me that he no longer lived alone, and the two elderly priests he shared the house with didn't appreciate the telephone ringing in the middle of the night. "The boys like their peace and quiet," he whispered. "And it doesn't exactly look good for me at this point in my career to be getting phone calls at all hours from distraught female voices." He gave me Traudi's telephone number and demanded that I call her. "Tell her to give me a break," he said. "If she wants to save her soul, tell her to do it during regular business hours!"

"That's very big of you, Knut," I said with disgust.

"At least *I'm* true to my own self," he whispered defiantly before hanging up.

I called her immediately. She didn't answer. I tried again and again. Eventually did she did pick up, waiting a few moments before cautiously uttering the word, "*Ja?*" Her voice was so deep that it was hard to recognize. She wanted to know how I'd gotten her phone number, hesitatingly asking if I had "talked to Father Heino."

"I spoke to Knut," I said, wanting to keep the conversation rational. My tone automatically turned indignant, "Why did you leave? How could you just go without telling me?"

"I had to leave," she said. "I tried to tell you that but you wouldn't hear it. I don't expect you to understand, but there was nothing else I could do. People are going to see files. People are going to know who did what and not care about circumstances, and maybe they shouldn't. If there was some way I could change it all I'd give anything to do that, but I can't. I'm the one who has to live with what I've done and I'm not going to explain myself to anyone else, and certainly not to you. You are not the one who is going to be violated over and over again by countless vindictive eyes."

Her tone turned bitter when she spoke about not explaining herself to me. My off-the-cuff comment about her brother was evidently something for which I'd never be forgiven. Traudi spoke with such a lack of will that night that it scared me. She attributed it all to being run down with the flu. I didn't confront her then or during any of our other talks the way I had planned to. I telephoned her just about every night over the next couple of weeks. I tried to get her to call Wolf and Ina; I didn't think it was good for her to be isolated in a place where she didn't know anyone. But she absolutely refused and made me promise not to tell them she was there. The only reason she moved to Münster in the first place was that Knut had been able to arrange an apartment so quickly.

During our talks her mood swung like a pendulum, always in motion. At high points there was a veiled allusion to someone who might have been a boyfriend, then (to my secret relief) no mention of him again. On another occasion she was excited about the prospect of working in a hospital; her landlord happened to be a retired doctor who said he could get her a job. Then that was forgotten, as was a plan to teach a course in Russian at the evening university. Through all this I was careful never to accuse her of anything. I was determined just to be there and wait for answers to come in their own time. Finally, her attitude toward me began to soften. I could sense the same intimate nostalgia that I had developed during our conversations as she, from time to time, briefly lapsed into reminiscing. One night, during one of her low phases, she said that she wanted to see me.

. . .

Traudi's apartment was in southern section of the city, not far
from the Ludgeriplatz. The closest parking space I could find
was five blocks away. When I got to the Goebenstrasse, I noticed
the Trabant parked at the curb. It looked completely out of
place here; laughable in a way. It highlighted the fact that
reunification hadn't meant a thing for the residents of this place.
The inconvenience of a slightly larger tax bill perhaps, but
nothing more. Life went on here just as it always had. No
upheavals or rude awakenings. No shattered lives.

From her tired smile it seemed that Traudi was relieved
if not happy to see me. Yet her remote and distant behavior
reminded me of the first time I showed up at her apartment in
East Berlin. When I entered, she stepped back to another corner
of the room as if she didn't trust me. The apartment was an attic
studio, typical for students, sparsely furnished with a bed, short
sofa and desk. It was paneled in blonde wood and there was just
one small window at the far end of the room. A good deal of
space was rendered useless by the slant of the roof. At the near
end, there was a kitchen counter with a sink and a hot plate. The
small bathroom was crammed with a shower stall and a toilet.
Most of the apartment was taken up by the moving boxes on the
floor, many of which were still unopened. We had to constantly
step over them to get around. Her clothes were strewn all over
the place, and the kitchen sink was crowded with dirty dishes.
Plates with half-eaten sandwiches had been left on the sofa and
on the floor by the bed. Cigarette butts were everywhere, in
whatever could be used as a receptacle. I never pictured Traudi
living in that kind of confusion. The little room in its disorder
reeked of distress; of agitation and fearful thoughts.

Over the next couple of days, we moved cautiously
around each other. I was reluctant to say anything that would
rile her and she seemed content just to have my familiar face in
the apartment while she moved from the bed to the sofa and
back again, chain smoking. We slept together in her bed but
never touched; quite a feat considering how narrow it was. I
asked how she had managed the move. She paid an unnamed

person with a van to do it. The things she left behind, including all her old books, were in storage in another unnamed friend's basement in the Köpenik district where she'd grown up.

I spent time cleaning up the place, bought groceries and went to the laundromat. I eventually ran into the old doctor-landlord who lived on the ground floor with his wife. The first time I met him he was somewhat annoyed, immediately wanting to know if I was now living there, too, saying that the apartment was too small for two people. When I told him I was just visiting his mood changed. I don't know why, but he seemed sympathetic to my presence in a way that suggested that he thought it was a good idea for Traudi not to be alone.

On the third or fourth night, Traudi and I were lying in bed, the atmosphere still as frigid as it was the moment I first entered the apartment. The room was so pitch-black at night that the only thing visible was the glowing end of her cigarette as it moved from her mouth to the ashtray resting on her stomach and back again. Lying there, shielded by darkness, I decided I had nothing to lose by asking a few questions. I knew that I couldn't stand being there much longer under those circumstances, anyway. I was surprised when she answered them as easily and as calmly as she did. "Don't ask me how it all started," she said wearily between drags on her cigarette. "Don't ask me because I don't know myself anymore."

"How long had it been going on?"

"I don't know. Maybe ten years," she said, casually exhaling smoke.

"Ten years?" I was stunned. "And you don't know how or why it started? I can't believe that."

"But it's the truth."

"That's not good enough. I can't believe you spent a decade writing about people's private lives for the Stasi without knowing why you were doing it."

"Maybe not, but that's all I can say about it. And I never *wrote* anything. It was all recorded."

"What difference does that make?" She didn't answer. "What the hell kind of information could you have possibly delivered over all that time? It's not like you had much of a social life. You never had a lot of friends that I could see. What could you possibly have told them about people?"

"You always hear things from people who aren't even aware that they are saying them. It was mostly nothing that wasn't already well known—who was connected to the church, to peace groups, environmental groups, that kind of stuff. Anything, really."

Her nonchalant tone angered me, "Anything really? You destroyed people's lives with *anything really*, and don't even know why? Didn't it ever occur to you that what you were doing was fundamentally and morally wrong?"

"I knew it was wrong," she said quietly.

"Then . . . *why?* Did they pay you?

That caused a quick burst of rage in her. She kicked me under the covers and told me not to be insulting.

"Well . . . did they force you to do it?"

It took few moments until she said, "I wish I could tell you, but I don't know how it all happened. That's the truth."

I couldn't believe she'd spill such a lame answer. It was offensive to listen to such garbage. "And what about me?" I had to ask. "I never told you, but I was interviewed by the West Berlin police. They had the strange idea that I might be giving you software code."

I heard Traudi exhale a long plume of smoke. "Did I ever once ask you for anything? Did we ever once talk about any of that? If I mentioned you at all it was just so they would continue to let you come over. How the West Berlin police found out anything is beyond me. One side was just as bad as the other."

I didn't want to talk about it any further. I detected clear intonations of self-righteousness in that last statement and could imagine that, given a few more minutes, she'd start blaming others for the things she had done. I rolled over and tried sleeping but felt myself getting more and more angry. She asked if I was still awake. I said that I was. "What are you thinking?"

"You did what you wanted to do," I said with contempt. "But you had no right making other people your unwitting accomplices in it all."

"What do you mean? . . . What accomplices?"

"What do I mean? How about me and Kai for starters. Remember that party he invited me to? The one given by that woman at the club that you didn't want me to go to? I was there when the police turned up. Or did you know that already? Do you know what hell that poor woman had been put through? Did you know she lived in constant fear of losing her daughter? And why? That's what I would like to know. That's what I want *you* to tell me."

I was desperate to hear her proclaim her innocence, or at least ignorance of the whole thing. Even a twisted assertion that she thought it had to be done for some reason would have been something. Like an indulgent parent I was ready and willing at that point to consider any excuse. But she didn't say a word. Nothing. No response. Finally, without hiding my disgust, I said that I wouldn't even ask about her friend Angele. "I don't even want to know about that," I said. Five minutes later, Traudi stamped out the cigarette in the ashtray on her stomach, went into the bathroom, carefully pushing the door closed as if she didn't want to disturb me, and cried her quiet, aching sobs.

I may have slept for an hour or two that night. When I woke, Traudi was curled up on the sofa, smoking and staring into space with eyes that were red and swollen. That was the position she seemed to hold for the next week. She ventured down to the corner only two or three times for cartons of cigarettes. She never seemed to sleep or eat. She smoked, stared into space, and hardly said a word unless I forced her to speak. Orange blotches developed on her face and the bags under her eyes became puffier. Eventually, she began trembling slightly as she brought the cigarettes to her lips. She had turned into the most joyless person I'd ever known. A soul never at peace. I could now see her as an old woman, a vision unimaginable until then. I constantly tried getting her out of the apartment by inviting her to go for walks with me, which I took every day. But she refused. Those walks around the neighborhood quickly became the high point of my days there. The atmosphere in the apartment had become suffocating. Between Traudi's mood and the stagnant air, it became impossible for me to sit in that room. I'd wake up, hang around all morning out of a sense of obligation and pity, then between noon and one o'clock, I'd work up the courage to leave her alone and go out. With every act of stepping out of the apartment came a feeling of relief, like being released from a forced confinement.

On one of those afternoons the sun poked through the clouds, the temperature moderated and the sky turned blue. Although it was early December, spring suddenly seemed in the air. I stayed out well after the sun went down that evening, mixing with the holiday crowds in the city. The day had lifted my spirits to such an extent that I couldn't imagine it not having the same effect on Traudi. I called her from a telephone booth planning to tell her to meet me in town and we'd go eat dinner somewhere. I called two or three times, but she didn't answer. Yet with each try, the ringing telephone filled me with a kind of surging confidence. She had gone out! This was the beginning of a return to normal.

I decided to go back and wait for her, thinking that when she came through the door, probably carrying a bag of groceries, I'd invite her out, maybe even to a movie, and she'd gladly accept.

I ran back to the apartment and jogged up the stairs to her room only to find her sitting in the same spot on the sofa, still in her nightshirt and sucking on another one of those goddamned cigarettes. "Why the hell didn't you answer the telephone? I've been trying to call you!"

Traudi stared glassy-eyed into space, shrugging her shoulders while exhaling a cloud of smoke. I don't know what came over me. Before I knew it I was attacking one of the unopened boxes on the floor, tearing off the packing tape and dumping out what was inside. That brought her out of her stupor, "What are you doing? Stop that!"

I ignored her, and the more she protested, the further I went, tearing open the next box and turning it upside down. "If this is where you want to live then you'll do it like a normal human being," I said, moving to the next carton. She shouted for me to stop, started hitting me in the back then kicking me. I wanted her to tell me to leave; to just get the fuck out and never come back. But she didn't. I sat down on the bed and watched her wiping tears from her cheeks while she slowly repacked what I had dumped on the floor. "Let's get out of here," I said, "even if it's just for half an hour. I can't stand watching you sit in this place another minute."

"I can't do it anymore," she murmured, hardly able to get the words out. "You go, Richard, please. I can't."

No Man's Land

I WALKED AROUND TOWN. I ate something somewhere, had a cup of coffee and a beer at another place, then drank another beer somewhere else. I guess it was around midnight when I wandered over to the Latina, well past what used to be known as "VIP time" when I was a regular there.

The bar was, as always, packed with people, the large room filled with warm cigarette exhaust. The usual crowd were all still there; all the "VIPs" huddled together at the bar, sitting on the same bar stools I'd left them sitting on nearly four years ago, in addition to the half-dozen other faces that constantly decorated the place like portraits on a wall, but whose names I'd long since forgotten. There were those preliminary, surprised greetings; that habitual small talk and questions about what brought me back to town. I gave that one-word answer that immediately satisfied all curiosity, "business," and ordered a beer. Before long, someone was calling my name from across the room. I looked up and saw Fritz waving with Willy standing at his side. I moved over, cutting my way through the thick, polluted air.

Fritz was a big bear of a man with a dark beard and glasses who spoke English with only the slightest German accent. Willy was a tall, lanky black American whose quick tongue and New York slang made me feel at home, instantly lightening my mood.

"I was hoping you'd show up here," Fritz said, one huge hand shaking mine, the other holding a beer glass. "I saw you the other day. I called your name but you were off in another world. You walked right in front of me, almost stepped on my feet and didn't notice a thing."

"Yeah, man. You been seen but not heard," said Willy. "Good to seein' ya again. What brings ya back to town?"

I again recited the magic word that satisfied everyone. "Well, you turned up at just the right moment," Fritz said. "How would you like to go flying tomorrow? I wanted to ask you the other day, but you were off in a cloud of your own."

Fritz owned a private plane and was always flying around Germany on business. What kind of business I've never been sure of. Something to do with real estate, I think. Years ago I had taken a couple short hops with him over the border to the Netherlands and thought it was tremendous fun. Plans for other trips always fell through for various reasons. I jumped at the chance to get away from Münster, even for a few hours, and asked where we were going. "Back to where you came from— Berlin. There in the morning, returning here in the early evening."

That was an extra bonus. I could take care of a few things like pay my rent, which was now very late, and return any calls on my answering machine. "One of my clients has an important meeting there tomorrow," Fritz continued, "so I told him I'd take him. I'll pass you off as my copilot. This way I won't have to sit next to him making small talk for an hour-and-a-half each way."

"You can tell he really likes his *Kunden*," retorted Willy as he returned his empty beer glass to the bar and zippered up his baseball jacket. Even when speaking his native language, Willy liked injecting a German word into every sentence, usually with the same inflection he would use when speaking Black English. I asked him if he was sure he didn't want to take the trip instead. "Nah," he said. "I ain't flyin' around in that thing. I'll tell ya what, though. I will put on my chauffeur's cap and drive you two over to the Flug-*platz*. How 'bout that, Fritzi my man? You can show your clients that you like travelin' mit *Stiiil!* Then Willy took his leave with a slap on the back and a big, "Have a good trip, *mine Herren!*"

Fritz answered with a yawn and a quick shake of the head as he counted his money and gave it to Mario behind the bar. He suddenly looked tired. "What time are we leaving tomorrow?" I asked.

"Can you be at Greven at eight o'clock?"

"Sure," I said. "No problem." But the look on my face must have given me away.

"Well, eight-fifteen would be okay, too. In any case, I have to be there at eight. You remember hangar four, where we were that time?"

I did, and he was gone.

It was now about one o'clock in the morning. I began figuring out the schedule in my head. To be at the airport in Greven by eight-fifteen meant waking up by seven o'clock; half an hour for a shower, shave and maybe a quick breakfast if the last of the milk hadn't gone sour, then drive, hoping the morning traffic hadn't drastically increased in the years since I'd been away. But the thought of walking out on Traudi so early in the morning pained me. At that point I regretted accepting the invitation. I paid my tab and hurried back to her apartment in a taxi.

She was sitting up in bed in the dark when I got back. When I switched on the light she didn't seem to notice. There was no sudden flinch; no sign of discomfort at having to adjust to the brightness. She was as white as alabaster, her eyes were red and puffy and her face drawn as it had been for more than a week. She acted as if I wasn't there. Everything I had dumped out on the floor was now back in boxes. One of the things I noticed earlier was her alarm clock. I walked carefully over to one of the boxes and gently rummaged through it. "I need the alarm clock," I said, trying to sound as passive and non-threatening as possible. I waited for her to ask why I needed it, but she didn't. I had to volunteer the reason. "I'm going back to Berlin in the morning."

Then came the first reaction since I entered the room. She looked down at her lap, stating with flat resignation, "You are leaving."

"Just for the day," I said. I told her about my friend Fritz and his airplane and being able to pay my rent, which was now late, and all the rest. As I was telling her, the whole thing seemed like a farce; a made-up excuse for getting out. She just repeated herself quietly, as if she didn't believe a word of it, "You are leaving."

I insisted that I'd be back tomorrow evening, then set the alarm and went to bed. A minute later Traudi got up and went into the bathroom. I lay there listening, but didn't hear anything. Not a sound. I watched the thin sliver of light under the door but could detect no movement. I watched and listened until I finally fell asleep.

Sometime during the night, I felt her slide under the sheets and, thereafter, was wide-awake and frustrated by a maddening desire to touch her, eventually probing the possibilities with seemingly unconscious contact of limbs until she easily, and without any comment at all, responded. It occurred to me during the act that she might be trying to get herself pregnant. But I didn't care. Not if it meant returning to normal. At that moment I was even looking forward to seeing her belly swollen with part of me.

At seven o'clock the alarm rang out with a vengeance, just as I had set it to do the night before. Reaching to shut it off, I saw that the room was still dark; something I had failed to reckon with when I accepted Fritz's invitation last night. That started me toying with the idea of staying right where I was; simply rolling over and lapsing back into my blissful coma. Just as I was about to fall over the edge into that vast emptiness, I reached over for Traudi. She wasn't there. I sat up and heard that lifeless voice, "It is time to wake up." It came from the sofa, from somewhere behind the end of a glowing cigarette floating in the dark. I heard an extended exhale of smoke being pumped into the air before feeling it in my nostrils. I tried coaxing her back into bed, thinking that if I ever happened to see Fritz again I'd just tell him that my car wouldn't start or something like that. But Traudi wouldn't have it. "No, you must go now. Your friend is waiting for you."

Aggravated that nothing had changed, I jumped out of bed and took a shower. I was getting into my clothes when I heard her say, "They took everything I have ever had, you know that?" I switched on the light. She was sweaty and alert, looking as though she had just broken a delirious fever. "And you know what? I never sat in judgment of anyone. Everyone knew what was possible. So why am I any more to blame for it than anyone else is?" Not in the mood for a debate, or even to try and make sense of what she said, I sat down next to her and asked if she was ready to go home. A skeptical grin swept across her face when she asked if I was going to take her there. "Tomorrow," I said. She wanted me to promise. I did. Her grin broke out into a motherly smile as she squeezed my hand and told me to go, that my friend was waiting for me.

I was on the road somewhat later than planned. Avoiding the Autobahn, I stuck to the Landstrasse, driving past the farms that make up the Münsterland. The sun rose rapidly; the day was cool and overcast but not windy and it didn't seem like rain. I thought about the logistics of the move back to Berlin. Tomorrow I'd rent a van. We could leave both our cars in Münster and retrieve them on another visit, or she could follow in one of them. We should probably just abandon the Trabi, it had certainly seen better days. But I couldn't imagine her going along with that idea and decided not to mention it. We'd have to move into my apartment since she had given hers up, but that shouldn't be a problem. Although I was going to miss her old place with its coal heating and drafty floorboards and found it hard to believe that I'd never get to spend another night there. Then I started to wonder what Traudi thought I meant by "home." I worried that maybe I had promised to take her back to a place that no longer existed.

By the time I got to the airfield it was almost eight-thirty. My thoughts were consumed with the move and what might come in its aftermath. I parked the car and ran over to the terminal entrance where Fritz was already standing outside. "Sorry I'm late."

"That's all right, my client's not here yet."

I started thinking that, if Traudi did get pregnant, we would have to find a bigger apartment. Maybe we should just go to America after all. A new, young president with an ambitious agenda had been elected and was preparing to take office. And, although I knew all too well that the ritualistic sense of renewal now gripping the country would last all of about thirty seconds after inauguration day, I felt somewhat disappointed for not being part of it all. Besides that, Germany was still reeling from the latest in a long series of horrifying neo-Nazi skinhead attacks against foreigners. A family had recently been destroyed; a mother and her children burned to death in the village of Mölln because they weren't German. Fleeting moments, but they made it easy for me to think along the lines I wanted to think. I was now convinced that I had to get Traudi out of Germany, at least for a while.

"Did you stay much longer last night?" I heard Fritz ask.

"Stay much longer? . . . Where?"

"At the Latina."

"I left right after you," I said. But Fritz kept staring at me, waiting for me to say more. "We're flying into Tempelhof, I guess?"

"No, Berlin-Schönefeld in the East. The landing fees are a lot cheaper there."

We stood around awkwardly for a minute or two. Realizing that I was no longer in the mood for this pointless joyride, I was just about to ask Fritz whether he'd mind if I bailed out when we spotted someone walking over from the parking lot. Fritz cut the air with a big wave. The man waved back then broke into a trot. When he reached the curb he apologized for being late. "It doesn't matter at all, Herr Grohmegma," Fritz said, smiling broadly and shaking the man's hand. He introduced me as his copilot saying, "I never like to fly alone when I'm flying passengers."

The man seemed to accept my role without hesitation. He shook my hand while introducing himself. Grohmegma was probably in his mid-forties, rather big, well over six-feet tall and big-boned with short dark hair and a perfect set of short, stubby teeth, like those of an ape. He carried a briefcase and a fat roll of blueprints in a clear plastic tube under his arm, which I offered to carry for him. He gave it to me noting that I was American. My accent always gave that away.

The three of us walked straight through the terminal building and out the other side onto the tarmac. Fritz's plane was just a few yards away—the same twin- engine propeller plane I'd flown in before. It sat six people: four in the back in pairs facing each other and two seats in the cockpit. Fritz opened the passenger hatch in the middle of the left side of the plane and helped Grohmegma into his seat, adjusting the three-point safety belt. I was standing near the nose on the right side of the cockpit where there was another, smaller hatch over the wing. From my previous flights with Fritz I knew I had to wait for him to enter the cockpit first before I could climb in. I was thinking about the situation with Traudi while absentmindedly looking through the window at Fritz leaning over Grohmegma, buckling him in. Grohmegma was looking back at me, standing around with my hands in my pockets, probably looking totally absorbed in nothing. He must have thought that there was something a copilot should be doing about now: looking over charts, checking the wings, kicking the tires; something other than standing around with his hands in his pockets and a blank expression on his face. But I couldn't bring myself to start a sham inspection of the plane. The thought would have made me feel stupid even if I cared about making this trip, which by now I didn't.

Fritz secured the passenger hatch then walked around the rear of the plane and over to me. "Ready to go?" he asked cheerfully. Before I could answer, he had opened the hatch, pulled his bulk up on the wing and had swung himself into the cockpit and over to his seat.

I passed Grohmegma his tube, then tried a similar maneuver, but wound up falling clumsily into the deep seat with my right foot hanging out the hatch. I had to pull it in with both my hands. As I buckled myself in, Fritz reached over, pulled the hatch closed and secured its two latches like a father getting ready to take his child for a drive. My ineptitude was becoming somewhat embarrassing. I put on the headphones, which let Fritz and me talk to each other over the loud engine noise, avoiding the urge to look over my shoulder at our passenger in the back.

Fritz started up one engine, then the other, and the plane rolled toward the runway. While taxiing, the pilot put a navigational chart and a thick binder on my lap. It was opened to a page titled "*Schönefeld*" which showed various landing approaches and procedures for the airport. With all this complicated-looking stuff in front of me, I dared take a glance over my shoulder at our passenger in the back. He had his briefcase open on his lap and was shuffling through some papers.

We reached the end of the runway. Fritz throttled-up the engines and the plane bolted forward. Within moments we were in the air, flying up through a layer of low cloud. When we reached our cruising altitude of 9,000 feet, it was sunny with blue sky all around. Below, however, was a continuous blanket of gray cloud. It was impossible to see the ground at all. We flew for about an hour without saying a word. It was clear that Fritz wasn't in a talking mood. I suppose that's why he'd asked me to come along in the first place. He sat there with his hands folded on a clipboard on his lap, occasionally entering numbers he received from the ground into the autopilot. I guessed he was tired from last night.

I sat there listening to the chatter of the ground controllers. The same voice was guiding large passenger jets as well as small private planes. Before long, my eyes were getting heavy. I hadn't gotten a decent night's sleep in weeks and last night was no exception. I was feeling so tired that I had trouble focusing on the instruments. The lack of conversation and the continuous low drone of the engines weren't helping matters. And now that it seemed life might finally be returning to something resembling normal, it was a pleasure to just switch off my brain for a while and float here above the clouds. I turned my head so that neither of the others could see my face and closed my eyes. I started drifting off, caught myself, but a minute later did it again. Catching myself a second time, I gave my head a quick shake, determined to stay awake. The thought of Grohmegma, sitting in the back, watching as the copilot slumped against the cockpit hatch, sound asleep, while a stack of important-looking navigational aids slipped from his limp hands into a messy pile on the floor was incentive enough. That scene, I thought, might cause trouble for Fritz. The guy there in the back was, after all, a business associate of his.

I looked over at the pilot. He was still sitting with his hands folded on his lap, staring intently at his instruments. Finally, I asked "How much longer?"

"Oh, only about fifteen minutes," he said.

Soon we were in contact with the control tower at Schönefeld and had started our decent. We broke through the clouds and the sprawling city below came into full view. It seemed to reach to the horizon in every direction. We flew in from the northwest. Below, the Reichstag, Unter den Linden and the Brandenburg Gate were all visible, as was the long, vacant scar of the No Man's Land winding its way through the city center. The runway at the airport came into sight. Fritz, correcting against gusts of wind, set us gently down upon it. The "Follow Me" van was waiting at the appointed exit from the runway. The entire airport seemed to have become a subsidiary of *Lufthansa*. Their planes were everywhere—at the gates, taxiing to the runways, lined up waiting for takeoff. At the edge of the field I noticed a few of the old Soviet-made *Interflug* fleet sitting idle and empty. The East German national airline had flown into oblivion along with the state it had once served. Its planes, like so many functionaries of the old regime, were still awaiting an uncertain future in the new Germany.

Inside the terminal building, a man and woman were waiting. The man knew Grohmegma and introduced him to the woman who was his secretary. Then we all introduced ourselves to each other in stiff German style, with a handshake and a quick recital of our last names. It was agreed that we would all meet back at the airport at five-thirty, and they left.

I followed Fritz into an adjacent room where he paid a landing fee of about 100 marks and filed his flight plan for the return trip, all of which took about fifteen minutes. It was about ten-thirty when we were headed into the city.

After breakfast at a café in Kreuzberg, Fritz said he wanted to look up a woman he knew. I took that to mean we should each go our own way for the rest of the day, which is what I'd planned to do, anyway. When the check came, Fritz was slow in reaching for his wallet. I paid for the food. Outside on the street we each went in opposite directions.

In my apartment I checked my answering machine. There were a couple of calls from Christoph and Wolf. I telephoned Wolf and told him I'd been in Aachen visiting Christoph. I decided to leave Christoph for another time. I caught up on some work, went to the bank and paid my rent, then went to the *KaDeWe* where I bought a big box of Belgian chocolates for Traudi in the specialty foods department. With a couple of hours to kill, I thought it would be fun to visit the Café Adler. I couldn't remember when I'd been there the last time.

I took up my old post at the window and ordered a cognac and coffee, just like I used to do. Sitting there, I examined the Friedrichstrasse for some evidence of the spot where the American control house once stood. I had to take a long, hard look at the pavement before I could see where the liquid tar had been poured, joining the new asphalt to the old. Like a minor wound to the skin, any trace had all but disappeared. The Berlin Wall museum across the street had expanded, but according to the newspapers was now having serious funding problems and its future was by no means secure. On what had been the *other side*, the low brick barrier and a lookout tower were still there, but nothing more of the border remained. The customs buildings were long gone and the ground they once stood upon was now serving as a parking lot where a Turkish family was doing a brisk business selling remnants of the East German state as souvenirs from the trunk of an old Mercedes. Three years after the fact, it was just as hard to imagine that the Wall had ever existed as it was to believe that it had fallen. There were plans to build here—three or four new buildings in a complex to be known as the *American Business Center*. That the history of this place would probably one day be assigned to a small plaque on the side of one of those buildings depressed me for some reason, and that thought made me want to get on with my life all the more.

I needed to get back to the airport. I left the café and walked across the ground where the notorious border once stood and over to the U-Bahn entrance; one of the stations that, in the old days, was closed and haunted by those shadowy figures in dim light. Now it was back in service, its platform brightly lighted and its walls painted institutional green.

When I reemerged from the U-Bahn I saw that it had rained, just as it had been threatening to since we landed. The air was wet with cool mist and the dark pavement brightly reflected the headlights of the rush-hour traffic.

The waiting area in the terminal building was empty except for an attendant. I took a seat and started thinking about how I'd play the ride back, deciding that unless I got a clear signal that I was to keep up the act, I would just sit back and enjoy the ride, maybe even take a nap.

Five minutes later, Fritz walked in. "We're the first ones here, good," he said, taking the seat next to mine. Almost immediately, the man who had met us here this morning with his secretary, Kortmann was his name, entered with a big bald man in a long, brown wool coat. Again there were handshakes and quick last name introductions. The bald man kept his coat buttoned up to his thick neck and sat with his hands buried deep in his pockets.

"Well, how did it go, gentlemen?" Fritz asked.

"It couldn't have gone better. Everything is set and all the paperwork is going to be finalized early next week."

The grinning bald man nodded in agreement.

"Excellent, that's just excellent," Fritz said. He seemed so pleased that I couldn't help wondering if he'd had a stake in the deal, whatever it was.

I asked if they were architects. Kortmann said they were West German developers cashing in on unification; part of a consortium that had succeeded in acquiring a huge chunk of land just outside Berlin on which they planned to build what he described as immense retail outlets that looked "like aircraft hangars surrounded by acres of asphalt parking lots." His descriptions of the project didn't bother him or the others in the least; in fact, they were all cynically amused by them.

"And you?" he asked. "You come from America, I hear. Are you in Germany checking out our crowded air corridors?"

I didn't know what to say. Was he serious, or did Grohmegma tell him that he'd flown over with a friend of Fritz's who liked to play airline pilot? Fritz jumped in, "The air traffic can be quite bad in the States as well, especially around places like Chicago. Isn't that so, Richard?"

I agreed. Obviously, I was still his copilot.

"Ah, here comes Rüdiger," announced the bald man, speaking for the first time. The top of his head was perspiring. Grohmegma walked triumphantly into the terminal wearing a broad grin while holding up a bottle of wine and two glasses. "It looks like there is going to be a little celebration on the way back," Kortmann said.

The men were all in a very good mood. I watched them smiling, laughing and shaking Grohmegma's hand. Grohmegma said something about neglected socialist woodlands finally being put to good capitalist use. Everyone laughed. I noticed that he had picked up a bottle of the new *Beaujolais Primeur*, making me realize that yet another year had come and gone. The bald man said that he had to be going, wished everyone well and walked toward the exit, one hand in the pocket of his coat, the other wiping the top of his great dome with a handkerchief. It was now clear that Kortmann was coming back with us.

The terminal attendant unlocked the door that led to the tarmac. We all piled in the van parked just outside and took the fifteen-second ride to the plane with the two businessmen talking rapidly to each other about the day's events. When we arrived, Fritz interrupted them, suggesting that they put their briefcases in the luggage compartment in the nose section. Fritz took off his parka and stuffed that in, too. Then he opened the passenger hatch and helped Grohmegma and Kortmann into their seats. They sat next to each other facing the rear of the plane. It was dark and getting cold. I could see the pilot's breath as he walked over to the cockpit, shivering without his coat. He opened the hatch over the wing and quickly got in. I followed, pulling the hatch shut and pushing down the first latch near my knee until it reached the "Closed" position. The second latch over my head turned with a snap, which I didn't expect. As I put on my headphones, I took a glance to the rear where Kortmann was supervising Grohmegma as he worked the wine bottle with the corkscrew on a Swiss Army knife.

Fritz started the engines. The windscreen was so fogged that it was almost impossible to see through. I was surprised when he started moving toward the runway without wiping it clean or waiting for it to defog. To me, the view outside was a confused maze of blue and green lights reflecting off the wet tarmac in the darkness. Our two passengers, now into their first glass of wine, were oblivious.

I heard the control tower tell Fritz where to enter the runway. We rolled slowly along with the pilot squinting through the filthy windscreen, trying to find the correct entrance. I mentioned something about the airport being deserted compared to this morning. That broke his concentration. "What?" he asked, turning his head toward me. In that moment, the plane swerved slightly to the right and the propeller on the right wing struck one of the lights along the taxiway, shattering it with a loud **POP**. Kortmann turned his head to the front. I lifted the headset from my ear to hear him. "Hey, are you two celebrating as well? You should be flying!" I gave an uneasy smile. Fritz reacted with a forced laugh.

The pilot was still having trouble finding the right approach to the runway. We pulled into the next entrance. The dimly lit sign on the ground would have been difficult to see even if the windscreen had been clear. Fritz rolled closer until we were almost on top of it. "Shit," he said calmly, "this is the wrong one." He radioed the tower and asked how much runway was left from this approach. The reply was instantaneous. "That's plenty," Fritz said, and got permission to enter the runway there.

The pilot throttled up the engines. The plane raced down the runway and into the air. During our ascent, I felt a cold draft on my face coming from an open vent as I watched Schönefeld recede into the night. Suddenly, I heard Fritz through the headset, *"You didn't close the door!"* I thought he was joking until he reached over me and grabbed the top of the hatch, yanking on it a couple of times. The plane took a sharp dip. Fritz recovered quickly. I heard him lecture himself, "Okay, first fly the airplane, take care of the problems later."

"What are you talking about? Of course I closed the door."

I looked up at the latch. It was turned to the "LOCK" position, just where I had set it before takeoff. "Look, it's locked," I said, trying to convince him that I'd done nothing wrong. Then, right before my eyes, the latch snapped to the "OPEN" position and immediately back again to "LOCK." The wind was playing with it. Somehow, it didn't catch properly when I closed it. The noise level inside the plane was unusually loud. "It's pretty noisy in here," I said.

"Yeah, and it's gonna get worse when we reach cruising altitude."

Fritz took a concerned look to the back where our two passengers were carrying on their conversation and drinking their wine, unaware that anything was wrong.

I looked up above my head. Although it was dark, I could see that the top of the hatch was slightly ajar. I saw what seemed to be a black rubber seal between the door and the plane and a cold stream of air was flowing through. Trying to squeeze it closed was no good; the air pressure against it was just too strong.

We continued climbing. Fritz was concentrating on getting to our prescribed cruising altitude of 8,600 feet so he could put the plane on autopilot. At about 7,000 feet I lifted the headphones from my ears. The noise had gotten much louder. It was now at an uncomfortable level. Grohmegma and Kortmann were still conversing and drinking as if nothing unusual was happening. Again, I looked up above my head. The force of the air had separated the hatch from the plane a bit more. I could now see that the black strip wasn't a seal at all. It was the cold, dark night outside and it was streaming in over my head.

We reached 8,600 feet. Fritz was right, the noise had gotten much worse. The separation between the top of the hatch and the plane had opened up even more. It was now at least an inch wide. I looked over at the pilot. He had just entered some numbers into the console and was sitting in his customary position with his hands folded on a clipboard in his lap. He gave me a worried look before glancing to the back and again at me, shrugging his shoulders and asking calmly, "What can we do?"

I was beginning to fill with dread. What if the wind should rip the whole thing off? The plane would probably become uncontrollable. It would be the end! I lifted the headphones from my ears. The noise in the cabin was at an ear-splitting level. I wondered how the two in the back could stand it. But they didn't seem to care. They sat there, drinking and carrying on a conversation by screaming into each other's ears. Fritz again looked to the back, then at me with the same concerned expression, asking, this time with resignation, "What can we do?"

We were flying through a thick layer of cloud. Outside there was only the glow from the light on the end of the wing, which disappeared periodically in the dense mist. Eventually I began seeing white streamers flowing horizontally past it. It was snowing outside! Icy needles began striking my face as they flew in through the opening above my head. The cabin was dark except for the eerie red-orange glow of the instruments. I became convinced that this flight would never reach Münster. I knew the scenario; I saw it just about every other week on the evening news. A small plane crashes into the ground shortly after takeoff in bad weather. The camera pans over the twisted bits of wreckage. The only parts recognizable are usually the tail and one of the landing gear sticking up out of the mud. "Rescue" workers always carried the bodies away in blue bags. The investigation always came to the same conclusion: pilot error. Of course it was pilot error, I thought bitterly while staring over at Fritz. The pilot didn't check the hatch before takeoff, did he? I looked up above my head, blinking and turning away from the cold, sharp needles hitting me in the face. I couldn't help but notice how frail the plane was. How thin the barriers that separated us from the unthinkable. How could we possibly make it all the way back? The unimaginable was stalking us just beyond these flimsy walls. It was gleefully running its fingers through my hair!

Outwardly I remained calm. Panic would have been just one more embarrassment. Fritz was sitting there rubbing his hands slowly together. He was visibly cold. "I should have kept my jacket on," he said.

"What's the temperature?"

He took a penlight from a pocket next to his seat and aimed it at the windscreen where there was a thermometer imbedded in the glass. "It's minus twenty-five degrees Celsius," he said.

It couldn't have been much warmer inside. Ice-cold air was pouring into the cabin and snow had accumulated on the panel over my head. Fritz looked at our passengers, took off his headset and leaned to the rear, shouting something at them over the loud noise. I wondered if he were merely explaining that there was a "problem" with the door, or was telling them that "he," meaning I, didn't close it properly. Whichever version it was, it didn't seem to matter to them. Fritz put his headphones back on. "They say they're fine," he said, shrugging his shoulders in disbelief. I tried removing my headset but couldn't stand the noise for more than a few seconds. It was deafening; like being locked inside a small, concrete room with a pounding jackhammer. I had to wonder if our passengers were going to suffer any permanent ear damage should we be lucky enough to survive the flight. I looked back at them. They were drinking and screaming at each other with obvious money signs in their eyes, but despite the incredible noise and severe cold, seemed perfectly fine. Fritz must have been suffering. He sat there in his thin V-neck pullover rubbing his hands slowly together. He kept checking the temperature with his penlight, as if he couldn't believe what he was seeing.

When we finally reached Hannover the weather cleared and I became more optimistic. We were halfway home and I was beginning to think we would probably survive the trip after all. When I saw the city lights below, I hoped that Fritz would make a landing at the Hannover airport so we could close the hatch properly. But he never even mentioned it. I couldn't understand why; he was turning blue with cold. Maybe it would have cost him money he didn't want to spend, or maybe he didn't want to risk inconveniencing our passengers any more than we already had. Whatever the reason, the last forty minutes were long ones. Freezing air never ceased pouring into the cabin while the two in the back continued being oblivious to it all.

After what seemed like an eternity, we started our decent. I could feel the wind above my head getting warmer. The landing strip at Greven came into view and Fritz set us down upon it. We taxied off the runway and over to the same hangar we had started from this morning.

When the propellers stopped turning, I opened the one properly closed latch that saved us and got out, frozen to the bone. Fritz followed, walking stiffly over to the passenger hatch where he dutifully helped Grohmegma and Kortmann out of the plane. I stayed near the nose, hoping that they would simply wave goodbye and leave, but they all started walking toward me. I remembered the luggage. Fritz opened the compartment, pulled out his parka and quickly put it on before handing the other two their bags. I was standing right behind them all and felt the need to say something. For some reason I wanted to know where I stood.

"Quite a ride, eh?" was my pathetic attempt to provoke a response.

Fritz sneered as he firmly closed the luggage compartment door. There was no reaction at all from the other two. It was as if they hadn't heard me. Then I realized—they probably hadn't. Kortmann turned around with a grin on his face, shook my hand and shouted in a hoarse voice, "Auf wiedersehen!" His ears must have been ringing like the Cologne cathedral on Easter Sunday.

Grohmegma looked at me, also smiling, and shouted, "Next time remember to close the door!"

"I thought you might enjoy the fresh air!" I shouted back.

He gave me a confused look before walking toward the terminal building behind Kortmann.

Fritz was busy inspecting the propeller that stuck the taxi light at Schönefeld. It had a tiny knick in it. "Is it bad?" I asked.

"No, it's nothing serious," he said. All the same, he didn't look pleased.

I was frozen stiff and wanted to leave, but thought it would be bad form to just walk away. I waited there shivering for ten or fifteen minutes until Fritz finished getting his plane in order, considering it a penance for the sin I'd committed. Finally, we started back to the terminal building. While Fritz didn't seem at all happy, I had the feeling the he was more angry with himself than with me. "Sorry about the door," I said.

"That's all right, it wasn't your fault."

Absolution! I said goodbye. Fritz went to the men's room.

I got in my car. The chocolates I bought were as hard as a rock. Frozen solid. Sitting there, reviewing the whole thing in my head, I had to laugh. A few moments later I was laughing so hard that I had trouble putting the key into the ignition. Does life get any more absurd than that? What craziness! What a story! I couldn't wait to tell Traudi about it.

I got lucky with a parking space and ran upstairs to her apartment. The room was dark. I switched on the light. She wasn't there. I took a look in the bathroom, then went and sat on the bed, wondering where she might have gone. It was about eight o'clock.

306 | Michael Califra

Maybe she'd stepped out for some air or something to eat. I looked over the room. Something wasn't right. Things had been moved around. A path to the doorway had been cleared of moving boxes, as if something large had been taken out into the staircase. I didn't have a good feeling but couldn't say exactly why. The room seemed too serene. Too vacant. I scanned the surface of the rumpled, unmade bed. When I noticed what I was sitting on, I nearly jumped out of my skin. The latex surgical glove might as well have been a poisonous snake for the effect it had on me. I ran out of the room, down the stairs and out into the street with my heart pounding. I sat on the fender of a parked car, looking up at the dark sky with the blood pulsing in my brain, telling myself over and over that it couldn't be true. That she had just stepped out for a while and would come back soon. I went to a bar across the street and sat over a beer for an hour, then to another place where there were a lot of people and loud music and did the same thing. There was no way I'd go back before eleven o'clock. No way I'd go back to that apartment until enough time had lapsed and I was sure she'd be there again.

In the crowded bar I was able to pump myself up with encouraging thoughts. Of course she would move things around, we were leaving tomorrow. And Traudi was a nurse after all. She had spent years working in hospitals. It was perfectly natural that something like a latex glove would find its way into her personal belongings. In her hectic move from Berlin she probably hadn't taken much care about what she packed and what she didn't. In her state of mind at the time, speed was of the essence. At about ten o'clock I couldn't stand it any longer and ran back to the apartment. I took a deep breath, put the key in the lock and threw open the door. The apartment was still empty; the box of chocolates still on the bed where I'd left it. I didn't know what to do or what to think. I didn't want to go back inside and told myself that I should have waited until at least eleven o'clock like I'd planned to; that it was still early. But when the old doctor who lived down stairs emerged slowly from the stairway with his dispirited eyes locked on me, it became painfully clear that any hopeful thoughts were nothing more than an illusion. Later, when

I asked about a grave, I got the breath knocked out of me when a voice said that she'd been cremated, like the rest of the family.

That was a dream I had during one of the three nights I'd spent in the penetrating emptiness of that little room after getting back from the airport. I slowly catalogued the very few things she had taken with her as I realized, one by one, that they were missing from among the boxes and cigarette butts. At midnight on the third night, I admitted to myself that waiting was pointless. I popped the last chocolate into my mouth from the box I'd brought back from Berlin, got out of bed, got dressed, packed my things, and walked across town to Wolf's apartment. He answered the door in his pajamas. I tried to quell his astonishment at seeing me by making the comment that he and Christoph were the only adults I knew who wore them. There was a small fuss when the little Katrin woke up and Ina took her back into the bedroom. Knowing better than to try and make sense of my surprise late-night visit, she told Wolf and me that she'd see us in the morning.

I sat on the sofa in the living room. Wolf got a couple of bottles of beer and two glasses from the kitchen. "Was it really so boring?" he asked with an all-knowing grin as he poured a bottle for me. For Wolf it was clear: another last-minute party and nowhere to stay. Until that very moment I had planned on finally telling him everything that had been happening. But it wasn't until I was sitting alone with him that I realized it was impossible, at least for now. Something about the whole situation made me feel so asinine that I couldn't begin discussing it with anyone, even Wolf. And having offered his own instant reason for my showing up unannounced at that hour sealed my decision to keep it all to myself. I asked him about business. That pretty much ended the need for me to make further conversation. Bob's plan to take the company public, like so many of his projects, had been abandoned almost as soon as it was mentioned. But that didn't matter anymore. I sat relieved, listening to Wolf's stories about salesmen, new products Bob told him were on the way, and all the revenue they would bring. Like all truly optimistic people, Wolf had a way about him that was genuinely contagious, no matter what the topic. A couple of hours later, he brought me a pillow and blanket for the sofa.

I left for Berlin the next afternoon. Walking back to my car, I saw the blue Trabant still parked at the curb. Weather-beaten and broken, it looked as forlorn as a shivering puppy. On the Autobahn, I was swept along by the cascading certainty that there would be either a letter from Traudi in my mailbox or a message from her on my answering machine when I got home. But there was neither. And over the days and weeks that followed, with the letter that never came and with every flashing light on my answering machine signaling calls from people other than Traudi, the numbing mix of emotions inside me began to settle and consolidate into anger. I'd been betrayed yet again. What a coward she turned out to be. Commit the crimes and leave others to deal with the mess when you're gone. How German of her! It ate away at me just as it did before she'd left for Münster. And now, by disappearing, she made sure that I'd never get any relief.

Eventually it consumed me. There was never a moment when it was absent. With all this churning inside me all the time, the slightest inconveniences took on monumental, almost conspiratorial proportions. I couldn't bring myself to stand in line anywhere for more than five minutes; not at the bank, not at the post office, not anywhere. I had no intention of discussing it with anyone I knew in West Berlin, and as a consequence, they bored the hell out of me more than ever. I couldn't stand the sight of the Troika, my apartment, or even the street I lived in. I found the people who lived in my building and their petty problems nauseating and hated going to bed at night knowing that they were sleeping all around me. I even had words with Bernd. We never did have breakfast together, but that never stopped him from asking me to, even if it was less frequent now. But he finally asked one time too many. I stunned him by telling him to leave me alone and called him an "ass-faced creep."

A couple of weeks later, yet another new year—1993. I sat in the corner of a packed barroom and watched a crowd of people ringing it in. When the big moment came, I was sufficiently numb with drink; able to distract myself by scrutinizing the way the rising hot air played with the colorful streamers that festooned the ceiling.

Not long after the New Year there was a letter from the police in my mailbox. The driver license business that Bernd warned me about so long ago had finally caught up with me. I wasn't surprised. At the same Polizeirevier on the Kruppstrasse where I was told that there could be a fine line between friends and accomplices, I was made to pay a fine of two-thousand marks and told I could not to drive again until I acquired a German license. In order to spite Bernd I tried to see the bright side; to convince myself that he'd done me a favor. I thought that taking a course in a driving school would be good for me; provide me with a goal to occupy myself. I registered in a course and bought the book. Looking through the sample multiple-choice questions on the way home, I came upon one that made me angry: "*You have just dirtied the roadway with your car. What do you do?*" How the hell can anyone dirty a roadway with a fucking car? What the hell is wrong with these people? I threw the book away before I'd even reached my apartment. The next day I got my deposit back and a week later sold my car, getting less for it than I'd had to pay in fines.

One day in February I was walking along the Otto-Grotewohl-Strasse. That was all I seemed able to do. Walk. Keep moving. The avenue consisted of East German prefab housing not far from the Potsdamer Platz. I noticed that many of the apartments seemed to be vacant, with no curtains or lighting fixtures visible from the street. I asked around, found out who was responsible for renting them, arranged to see one the next day and, there on the spot, took a studio in one of them. It was a rash, spontaneous decision I undertook as a kind of rancorous distraction. But it was also a declaration of defiance that, not only was I moving to the East, but the apartment was just a block away from the socialist mural Traudi had so proudly showed me on that 1st of May. I even took a certain *Schadenfraude* in the fact that the Haus der Ministierien itself, in the service of yet another German government, was now home to the *Treuhand*, the hated agency responsible for selling off East German state assets, throwing tens of thousands of people out of work in the process.

But my new home also resulted in forced isolation. I didn't realize until I moved in that the apartment had no telephone. There was a jack in the wall all right, but it was of the East German variety. I had to apply with the Telekom to have it changed to the West German standard—a request that, in the end, took them nearly seven months to fulfill. Each of my attempts to accelerate the process was met with the same official arrogance that I was convinced had built the gas chambers. It took no time at all before I just quit trying. From the time I moved in, I couldn't work and couldn't have cared less. The Goddamned Job was just one more stifling pile of crap I wanted out of my life, anyway.

For all practical purposes the move put me in a different city. Christoph was gone and Kai was now the only person in Berlin whom I considered a friend. I never went by the Troika and never heard from any of the people there. Out of sight, out of mind. I told Kai that Traudi had gotten a job in another city and that pretty much ended the story for him. It was, in any case, a time when many old personal relationships seemed to be drifting apart.

There would be moments when my anger would wane; keeping it up constantly was physically demanding. There had to be breaks now and then. During one of them, I went to the local authorities to see if there was a forwarding address for Traudi. There wasn't. She was still registered at her old address in the Wichertstrasse, and the anger returned. There were other short lulls. Sometimes morbid thoughts took over my mind and clung to me like rot, never leaving me in peace. I'd think about the state she'd been in while she was in Münster and about that dream with the latex glove. Could she have actually done herself in somewhere? I'd ask myself how she might have done it. With pills? A bottle of vodka in the bathtub? What thoughts might have been swirling around her brain as the blood stopped pulsing? Could she have been thinking of me? Of course not. If she had given me the slightest consideration she wouldn't have left the way she did. But then bitter reason would take over. She would never go to such an extreme. What she had done was appalling enough, but it wasn't anything unusual. By now it was well known that the Stasi had been everywhere in the GDR. The society was infested with informers. Some estimated that one person out of five was somehow caught in the web, and there was a long list of prominent people keeping Traudi company.

There were a couple of fleeting, absentminded moments. Moments when, out of the corner of my eye, I would register a blonde female on the street or in the U-Bahn with a long, beige gabardine coat and, for a split second, think it was Traudi. Then came a series of realistic dreams—she would call out my name from a dark entranceway, or approach me in a crosswalk as calmly as she did on the night the Wall fell, and explain that her disappearance was an elaborate scheme to remove herself from the threat of prosecution. But, inevitably, I'd wake up to the stark finality and brutal disappointment of never seeing her again. I'd think of the last patronizing smile she gave me before telling me to go, that my friend was waiting. She knew then that I'd come back and she'd be gone. She decided she could simply start over; remake her world without having to own up to anyone, including herself. Create a happy new existence that I was judged unfit to be part of. And that, more than anything else, is what would give me no peace. And what led me over the next few months to turn myself over to the smoke-filled bars of eastern Berlin with the other losers of reunification to keep me company. Like them, I had developed a resentment of the trendy West German tourists who visited the East's new "in" spots, marveling at the decayed state of what was around them. I inhabited the places where the late nights and dizzying effects of alcohol numbed the frustration and often led to a nameless woman's bed, the memory of whom would dissipate as quickly as the smoke in the bars.

Yet the morning after one of those encounters stands out. I awoke and noticed a thick ream of paper on the floor under the nightstand next to me—hundreds of photocopied pages from the *Ministry for State Security of the GDR*. A Stasi file. It was the first time I'd seen one. The first time I'd felt the weight of one in my hands. I sat up in bed and began scanning the pages, turning them over one at a time, reading intimate details of the life of the stranger still asleep next to me. She was eleven years older than I, born in Potsdam, and had been labeled by the Stasi with the code name *Spatz* — "sparrow." She was a midwife by profession, had been married and divorced twice and had a nineteen-year-old daughter named Astrid. When she was a child, her mother had forbidden her to take part in the communist youth organizations—the Young Pioneers and the FDJ—raising her in strict accordance with her Protestant religious faith. The file was complete with clandestine photos of her entering and leaving her home, shopping, waiting for a streetcar. There was a map with a detailed description of how to get to her home (always coldly referred to as the "*residential object*") by car or by public transit. It was noted that she lived so many meters or blocks from a supermarket, a library and a cinema. There were hand-drawn charts depicting a circle of friends orbiting around her name, showing how close she'd been to each of them, as well as photocopies of letters she had written to various people and even the envelopes they were sent in. It went on and on and on.

The woman whose life was so meticulously described in the pages on my lap woke up. She reached over me to a pack of cigarettes and a lighter on the nightstand. The last thing she did in the evening was the first thing she did in the morning. "You're reading my file," she stated, full of early grogginess before lighting up and blowing a fatigued plume of smoke up at the ceiling. I asked what she had done to warrant such scrutiny. "It looks like you were public enemy number one."

"What did I do?" She thought silently for a few moments. "The answer to that is nothing. Nothing that would make any sense to you, anyway. Maybe I said the wrong thing to the wrong person at some point; either you were with them or you were against them. If someone went to them and said you were against them, that's the very least you could expect," she said motioning with her chin to the pile of paper on my lap. She took another drag on her cigarette and shook her head thoughtfully, almost in disbelief. "So much of what's in there is absolute garbage. That bit about my being raised in a religion is absolutely false. My mother was against all sorts of religion, including the state's. There are people in those photographs described as close friends whom I don't ever remember meeting. And all those other pictures—they even photographed my daughter playing in the sandbox at the playground. What could have been the point? The first time I saw it all I found myself laughing and crying at the same time. So much of it is so . . . farfetched. So little of it had anything to do with the reality of my life. It was just in someone's interest to report the things they did; who knows why. But it was all written down, filed away and accepted as the truth, no questions asked."

When I asked if she knew who did the informing, she shrugged her shoulders. The names of informants were blacked out in the files. One had to apply to see a separate catalogue to discover who they were, an extra step designed to give a person time to prepare emotionally for what might turn out to be a severe shock. *Spatz* said she simply had no interest in any of it anymore.

That attitude was impossible for me to accept. But her weariness with the whole subject showed itself in her increasingly disinterested reactions to my escalating obstinacy on that point. How dare she not want to know! She had to want to know. They all had to want to find out who betrayed them because it might have been the same person who betrayed me. Somewhere there had to be justice of one sort or another. "Haven't you people learned anything?" I lectured. "Not finding out just legitimizes all the shit that you and everybody else had to endure in that fucking place!"

A simmering dispute was prevented from coming to a full boil when she asked, not too subtly, if maybe I didn't feel like going home. I was sent out the door with the defensive, angry assertion that at least in the GDR, unlike here and now, she was never unemployed.

When I later told Kai about it, he shook his head and said angrily, "I would want to know. And if I ever get to see my file, I'm going to find out!"

I was glad to hear him say that. As far as I was concerned, it was a duty as much as a right.

Berlin, like all large cities, is really a collection of many small towns. Eventually, in one place or another, you see familiar faces unexpectedly and, after an initial moment of recognition, must quickly determine whether to make or avoid contact. It was during one such encounter that I was able to betray the informer.

On the street outside a grocery store I spotted Traudi's friend, Angele. I immediately initiated conversation. She knew that Traudi had moved away but didn't know where, and had assumed we had gone together. I began mentioning facts about our mutual friend that grabbed her interest. Her eyes, which I so clearly remembered welling with tears of permanent unrest, at first winced with disbelief, which gave way to rage as more became known.

We met several times after that, trading stories and information, detailing an indisputable record of treachery and creating an obsession on the part of the victim and her husband to locate the offender, which they somehow managed to do in less than two months.

Traudi was living in Amsterdam, working as a shift manager in a fast-food chicken restaurant. That alone seemed punishment enough to dispel the vengeful feelings on the part of the couple who had found her. Some whose lives were still intact preferred leaving the past in the past. But I couldn't. I went to Amsterdam planning simply to show up at her place of employment and see what she had to say for herself.

The fast food restaurant Traudi worked in was on the Damrak, not far from the Central Station. I had to go there several times over the course of a couple of days before I saw her. One night, I stood outside, peering through the window from behind a poster bearing the bizarre face of the food chain's founder; a trademark becoming known around the globe. The place was crowded. Traudi came out of a back office to help up front. I didn't recognize her at first. It wasn't just that her hair under the paper cap was much shorter, or that she was dressed in that demeaning red and white-striped shirt with a plastic name tag pinned to her chest. There was something in Traudi's face that appeared sad and superficial; all consumed by mundane routine. I watched her mechanical motions as a group of eight or ten rowdy Dutch adolescents formed a loud mob at the counter. They were all dressed in the garb of the American ghetto that they'd seen in too many Hollywood films: pants so enormous the crotch hung at the knees, baseball caps worn backwards, basketball sneakers—all authentic right down to the appropriate corporate trademarks. I'd been planning, when this moment came, to just walk up to the register, order some of those "crispy strips," whatever the hell they were, and wait for her reaction. But I couldn't bring myself to do it. Any emotion in me was so ambiguous, so vague at that point, that it merely dispersed whenever I tried to grab hold of it. The longer I stood watching her, the more I found myself asking, *"Just why am I here?"*

The next afternoon I was back in Berlin drinking coffee in the Café Kisch. I sat looking at the bust of Lenin in the courtyard of the Russian embassy across the street. Recently, they had put a wooden crate over him and erected a big Christmas tree in front. With the holidays over, he was uncrated again. They can't seem to decide what to do with him. It was a bit like Traudi's image in my mind. All the details of her life: that obscure sense of loneliness and isolation I'd so often associated with her; the fact that she never had any children, although it was now obvious to me that she would have loved to long before she'd said so; all those things that I'd willingly overlooked I now attributed to the secrets she was living with. It was as if Traudi was the product of abusive family behavior that she then heaped on everyone else she knew. Who was the perpetrator and who was the victim in all this? Hard as I tried, I couldn't figure it out. The line between them was too fluid.

Walking home I was over taken by a calmness that I hadn't known in what seemed like years. I stood on the corner, staring at that hulking Haus der Ministerien. Instead of going upstairs to my apartment I walked over to the mural. It was the first time I had taken a close look at it since the night Traudi had shown it to me. Since moving to the Grotewohlstrasse, I hadn't had the courage to more than glance at the building from a distance. When I finally saw the mural again I was amazed at how empty the faces seemed. How false and spiritless. As hollow as a broken promise. Not at all the way I had kept them in my memory all that time.

A couple of days later I went back to Traudi's apartment. I saw it for the first time since the day I learned she'd moved away. The building was covered from top to bottom in scaffolding. Like many others in the district, it was getting a long-overdue facelift. Sometime in the not too distant future, all the unpleasantness of the past will be plastered over and painted pleasant colors with just enough of it enshrined here and there to be respectable. Inside, her name was still listed on the tenant register. From the bottom of the staircase I could hear loud noises echoing from somewhere above—the banging of hammers and the creaking of dried wooden planks being pulled until they snapped. Upstairs I noticed that the small, brass nameplate had been removed from Schmid's door. On the floor above, the door to Traudi's apartment was closed but the doorknob and lock had been removed. I pushed it open. Everything inside had been pulled out. The walls had been knocked down, the coal ovens were gone, and even the floorboards had been pulled up. It was one vast space except for the bedroom. I walked over to the windows in what had been her kitchen and, in my mind, replayed images of the life that had been lived here in the days before everything changed so suddenly. Busy construction noises faded away as I remembered all those hours listening to daydreams about what the future would bring while she stared at the ceiling over her bed. I saw her face before me, twirling her hair slowly around her finger, and thought about all that had happened since. I knew then that her facial expressions weren't manifestations of hope but confessions of fear. I remembered the sobbing last words I heard her speak in this apartment, "I wanted to be a nurse." It occurred to me that I didn't even have a photograph of her. A construction worker appeared at the door carrying a big white bucket and asked abruptly, "What are you doing in here?" I automatically asked if he knew when the apartment was going to be available. When I said that, a sensation of loss opened up inside me and I felt the sorrow rolling down my face.

That was almost a year ago. Since then I've been hanging around, putting this to paper as best I could in my struggle against time's effect on memory, and not doing much of anything else. Just sitting passively and watching. I watched as East Berlin was invaded by Chinese food, döner kebab and pizza joints. I've seen the city fraying under the economic burden of its reunification, with more and more tattered, hopeless people left behind to beg on the streets and sleep in the S-Bahn. I've watched as police armed with automatic weapons had to be posted twenty-four hours a day around Jewish institutions to ward off neo-Nazi skinhead attacks. I've experienced a resurgence of East German pride; that longing for an own identity that seems to grow with every passing year is accompanied by the defiant conviction that "not everything in the GDR was bad."

Periodically, the media report on what are referred to as "Wall trials" as former border guards are being sentenced to years in prison for having shot people trying to flee to the West. But convicting the people at the top who gave the orders is more difficult. Many were judged too old and infirm to be held accountable and Erich Honecker was eventually able to flee to Chile. Yet the fate of those whose injustices sparked a revolution not so very long ago no longer interest people busy trying to make ends meet. "The big fish always get away," they say with a tired wave of the hand, as if it's all an inevitable fact of life they can't waste time talking about.

Over the past few months I've also witnessed the end of an era marked by the steady withdrawal of all foreign troops from the city. The endless series of military parades and commemorations by the U.S., Russians, British and French made it seem as if they really didn't want to leave. But now they're gone and Berlin is a normal city again. In that time, too, I've found some of Traudi's old books for sale at the Berlin flea markets, complete with her father's name scribbled inside the front covers. I've also managed to confirm my belated suspicion that Schmid was indeed the person who had been responsible for recruiting her. When I discovered that he worked for the Interior Ministry, I began remembering the way she used to act around him; how she always seemed a little nervous when we happened to meet him. I remembered that on the ground floor of her apartment building, there was this depressing little bar where we would often see Schmid sitting at night whenever we went back upstairs. Traudi would always hurry past with her head down in an obvious attempt not to be noticed by him. I even asked her about him once. She told me that Schmid had been a good friend of her father's, and that after his sudden death from a stroke, he had done a lot to help her, including getting her the apartment she was living in. Traudi also mentioned that Schmid was the *Verwalter des Hausbuches*—the "House Book Administrator." I'd never heard the term before. When I asked her what it meant, she stumbled all over herself with an awkward explanation, finally telling me to forget it, that it wasn't so important. A week or so later, I asked Kai about it. He told me that the House Book Administrator was a designated person in an apartment building with whom residents were to register any overnight guests and visits from foreigners. But in a city like Berlin, with so many people constantly coming and going, Kai said, it was really a useless task. And when I asked him if he knew who the House Book Administrator was in his building, and he laughed and said, "Right now it's me," it really didn't seem worth talking about. For whatever it might be worth, I know that Schmid now drives a taxi to make ends meet. I also know that Traudi's name has surfaced in the Stasi files again and again in ways that made her subjects laugh and cry at the same time.

I briefly considered applying to see if the Stasi kept a file on me. I found it hard to believe I could actually have one, but I've read that over two million westerners, many of whom were frequent visitors to East Berlin, were catalogued there. I imagined sitting with the folder in front of me, wondering if I really cared enough about what might be inside to open it, and decided I didn't. Things have settled into their own comfortable pattern in my mind and I see no point in stirring up the muck yet again. And when I recently read a quote from a prominent East German dissident who described the files as a place where there is "only blackness, foul smells and filth piled upon filth," I know I've made the right decision. Besides, I have no intention of waiting around for the privilege. Very soon I will be leaving Berlin for good. The change in the city has begun to accelerate over the past few months, impinging on my memories. It started slowly with street names being arbitrarily changed and old monuments to out of fashion heroes being removed or left to vandals. I suppose all shrines to glorious causes inevitably become dilapidated, graffiti-covered memorials in time. Much of Berlin has also become one big construction site, and in the mad rush to rebuild, the new city center seems doomed to be an absolutely soulless place when it's all done. But that doesn't seem to bother anyone now. Government officials are desperate to demolish anything that was built by the old East German regime, as though tearing down buildings will instantly wipe away unwanted history. And I, for some strange reason, have no desire to see the wrecking ball slam into the Palast der Republik, which is at the top of their list.

The few things I'm taking back with me have already been sent home. Tonight I'll be going out for a farewell dinner with Kai, although I already know I'll be seeing him next summer in New York. With single-minded determination he managed to secure enough private funds to open his own café; a small place named for a huge East German power generating facility that always symbolized hope and progress in his youth. I often sat there over the last year, among the artifacts of the GDR that decorate the walls, and talked with my friend about the past. Kai's business success has shattered the anti-western sentiment that had been brewing in him when no bank would help him get started. Yet, despite that success, he's been somewhat lackadaisical lately. "Things were more exciting in the old days," he told me recently. "At least there was always something to believe in. Now it's all the same—just buying and selling. I never thought it would all be reduced to that."

Tomorrow I plan to take a final walk around the Brandenburg Gate and up the Linden at daybreak, the only time the air in this city is remotely breathable. In the evening I'll climb aboard a train bound for Aachen and go visit Christoph and his wife, Linda. Since I've had my phone in the Grotewohlstrasse apartment, he's called me daily from work. At first he kept repeating the refrain that his job was just a new form of slavery, "They pay you just enough to be comfortable but never enough to stop working!" I also listened to daily rants about his boss, a Bavarian named Hueber. Although I'd never once met the man, I know of his preference for petroleum-colored suits and of the nervous twitch in his right shoulder. I also know that his job description seems to consist solely of making Christoph's life miserable. Every day I heard the words, "How did I ever get myself into this?" Then his wife became pregnant, and the job wasn't so bad anymore; calculating reinsurance premiums was suddenly "very interesting work."

While I'm in Aachen I might even get to see Knut. According to Christoph, he has become totally invested in his obligations and duties and has turned uncompromisingly zealous in his religious convictions. He even has a new theme song that he keeps singing: *"What shall it profit a man if he should gain the whole world and lose his own soul?"* After that I'll go up to spend a few days with Wolf and Ina in Münster. I'm looking forward to spending time in the big house they've just bought before I finally fly off, over the horizon and into the unknown of the rest of my life with a Television Tower key chain in my pocket and a head full of memories. One of those memories is named Kati. A few days ago, a spate of nostalgia caused me to walk by her apartment building. The nameplate next to the intercom that used to read *"Hanno & Katarina Weber"* was covered by a piece of masking tape. The name *"Hanno Weber"* had been penned on it in ballpoint so definitely that it seemed to end in a subliminal exclamation point. I couldn't help but think it was written in a moment of liberation. I take it all to mean she's moved out. It's a shame, for more than the obvious reasons. Although we experienced an exciting moment in history together, I've managed to completely lose contact with her. If she should ever happen to read this she should know that it was unintentional, and that if she is ever in my part of the world, she should look me up. I've come to realize that she was right about a lot more than I was willing to give her credit for at the time.

Made in the USA
Columbia, SC
06 May 2018